Jemima Montgomery Freifrau von Tautphoeus

At Odds

Jemima Montgomery Freifrau von Tautphoeus

At Odds

ISBN/EAN: 9783337039547

Printed in Europe, USA, Canada, Australia, Japan

Cover: Foto ©Andreas Hilbeck / pixelio.de

More available books at **www.hansebooks.com**

THIS WAY UP.   P. 151

BY THE

BARONESS TAUTPHŒUS (née MONTGOMERY),

AUTHOR OF "THE INITIALS," "CYRILLA," AND "QUITS!"

LONDON:

RICHARD BENTLEY AND SON,

Publishers in Ordinary to Her Majesty,

1873.

AT ODDS;

A Novel.

By THE BARONESS TAUTPHOEUS,

AUTHOR OF "THE INITIALS," "QUITS," ETC.

LONDON:

RICHARD BENTLEY AND SON,

Publishers in Ordinary to Her Majesty.

NEW BURLINGTON STREET.

1873.

CONTENTS.

—o—

AT ODDS.

INTRODUCTION.

AT the commencement of my residence in Bavaria, few things surprised me more than the vivid recollection of the war at the beginning of this century possessed by all old, and many scarcely elderly people. Names that for me belonged to history were mentioned familiarly, and many a hearty laugh indulged in, at the expense of very celebrated personages.

My mother-in-law was inexhaustible in her stories of the Teutonic Order—of the French when quartered in her neighbourhood, where they made themselves at home in the old castle at Dinkelsbühl, in which she then resided—of her husband driving off at midnight with papers of importance—of the raising of floors and removal of ceilings for the purpose of concealing plate, etc.—but I cannot say that even her best-remembered squabbles with Caulaincourt about the loan of forks and spoons for his dinner parties, and his wonderfully polite assurances that nothing lent by her should ever find a place in his or any of his followers' portmanteaus, interested me much, until a friend of her youth came to spend the winter with us in the

1

country, where the reminiscences ceased to be mere anecdotes, and lengthened into wide-branching stories, that at
length attracted my attention and excited my interest so
effectually, that I felt as if I too had known the persons,
and seen the places, so often and graphically described.

A more intelligent and amusingly talkative person than
this friend of my mother-in-law, I have seldom met—a
German Scheherezade, who never allowed day or lamp
light to interrupt her discourse until she had completed
her story; and if the motives of the actions recorded by
her strongly resembled, or were precisely the same, as those
which actuate the world around us now, the violent political
convulsions and desperate military struggles of those times
exercised not unfrequently their influence on families, and
even individuals, in a manner that threw a gleam of ro-
mance on many a commonplace event, or gave rise to
connections or estrangements that would be more than
improbabilities in the present day.

It was when walking through the old town of Ulm for
the first time a few years since, that I became fully aware
of the deep impression made on me by these recitals. I
actually felt as if 1 had been there before, and were well
acquainted with the narrow streets and ancient houses—as
if I had stood before the cathedral half a century ago—had
walked on the ramparts—watched the Austrian soldiers
working at the entrenchments that were to spare them a
capitulation to Napoleon; and at length I could almost
imagine I saw Marshal Mack and his brilliant staff galloping past, while from one of the windows of a certain corner
house, well known from description, I could fancy the face
of my cheerful old friend as it may have appeared at that
time, with its profusion of auburn curls, bright brown eyes,
well-formed mouth, and teeth that were faultless even at
seventy years of age! I saw her lean out of the window

to look after the young men with whom she was to dance in the evening; and where from that same window, not long afterwards, she watched with not a little anxiety the entrance of the French into the town! The reputation of the latter at that time was not good, and no sooner had her father ascertained that he was to be favoured with the company of some officers, than she and her sister were ordered to retreat to the cellar, where their beds were made, and they were provided with lamps and provisions by their maid, who constantly recommended patience, and daily assured them that the French officers had awful whiskers and beards! Either a weariness of such imprisonment, curiosity, or (as my friend assured me with heightened colour, even after the lapse of half a century) a desire to move about and make herself useful, induced her one day, when she knew her father, and supposed the strangers, to be absent, to assist in carrying bread from the cellar to the kitchen. Scarcely, however, had she appeared above ground, than, encountering a bearded face with a pair of coal-black eyes intensely expressive of amazement and amusement, she dropped her loaves, and retreated precipitately to her prison. This officer, it seems, expostulated effectually with her father on his want of confidence in French "*honneur*," and so forth, for she and her sister were released that evening, and not only restored to the light of day, but their company required (not requested) to a ball given by the officers who remained in Ulm under the command of General Labassée, where they danced in the same public room and to the same music as with the Austrians but a short time previously;—that many of the ladies were unable to speak French, and scarcely any of the gentlemen a word of German, in no way interfered with the general hilarity.

I should not have mentioned this lady nor my late

mother-in-law, had it not been from a wish to prove to my readers that if I write of a period that now belongs to history, my information (of how some—I trust not altogether uninteresting—personages lived and loved at the commencement of this century) has at least been obtained from contemporaries whose pleasantest recollections were of those times, notwithstanding the anxieties, losses, and perils to which they were then so continually exposed.

While assuring my readers that in the following pages no poetical liberties have been taken with history, I avail myself of the opportunity of adding, in the words of Montaigne, " *Je n'enseigne pas, je raconte.*"

CHAPTER I.

THE HOUSE OF THE WALDERINGS.

AT the end of the long Bavarian plain that extends south-eastward from Munich towards the frontier of Austria there is a very extensive and beautiful lake called Chiemsee, and in its neighbourhood, for miles around, a number of others of smaller, and even very small, dimensions, that more than probably some centuries ago formed with it one vast sheet of water. These unknown, unnoticed, and sometimes nameless lakes are frequently bounded by gently-rising slopes or hills, many have wooded promontories stretching far into the water, but almost all are more or less disfigured and contracted by the flags, bulrushes, and other marsh plants, that grow along the margin of the water in wild luxuriance.

At the commencement of this century the family of Waldering were in possession of a thick-walled, small-windowed, high-roofed castle on an island in one of these lakes. The proper denomination of the building would have been "house," had not the weather-beaten walls of bound-masonry, descending into the water, and a draw-bridge inspired respect, and made it, though towerless, deserving of the name of castle. And, in fact, Westenried, or the West Marsh, had been a fortress, and considered nearly impregnable in its time—that is, before the dis-covery of gunpowder; for, were the drawbridge raised, there was no communication with the mainland, the only means of approach being a long lightly-constructed causeway, if one may so call the planks laid on piles driven into the marsh, and easily removed in case of need, while the water beneath the drawbridge and surrounding the island was of very considerable depth.

The castle formed three sides of a quadrangle, open towards the island, which had been converted into a garden and orchard. That the offices occupied one side of the court, and that the stable was opposite the hall-door, seemed a matter-of-course to all its possessors—at least, no effort had ever been made to place them elsewhere, and, in fact, they corresponded well with the more useful than ornamental garden and orchard, in the former of which but a small portion of ground had been reserved for flowers, and the latter was a mere meadow where apple, plum, and pear trees had grown to a good old age, without any particular care having been devoted to their cultivation.

The pedigree of the Walderings, in the approved form of a tree, was hung up framed and glazed in the flagged corridor leading into the chief apartments; and if it did not, like that of a well-known Hungarian nobleman, commence with Adam reclining gracefully in a shady part of the Garden of Eden, the warrior from whose broad chest the wide-spreading family tree seemed to rise might be supposed a near relative of Hermann the Cherusker—at least, if one might judge by the primitive shape of his weapons and the savage nudity of his person. There were family pictures, too, serving effectually to conceal the unpapered walls of the corridor and larger rooms; many with gilt backgrounds, brilliant colouring, and the Chinese disdain of perspective that proved almost beyond a doubt their antiquity. Had a catalogue of the numerous portraits been made, the words 'painter unknown' would have been of more than usual occurrence; but then in the corner of each picture the name and rank of the original, with his or her coat-of-arms, gave them a value in the opinion of most of the Walderings far surpassing the name of an artist, even had the man been Albert Durer himself.

The second floor of the castle contained a tolerably large suite of apartments, usually reserved for the widow of the last possessor,—a sort of jointure lodging, seldom, however, used by them, for Westenried was considered a very dull place,—so dull that even the rest of the building was only occasionally visited by the Count in possession when he came to shoot or fish or look over accounts with his steward; but the latter, a pensioned officer and personal friend of the family, resided there constantly in a few rooms over the arched way that led from the drawbridge into the court.

Mr. Pallersberg might have had what he would himself have called better quarters, had he been disposed to occupy them; but both he and his wife considered it particularly desirable to have a view of the high road that had been made along the margin of the lake, and windows whence they could watch the progress of loaded waggons in summer and sledges in winter, packed alike with salt, for the conveyance of which the road had been made. The village and its church were also visible at no great distance, and the inn where the waggoners passed the night so favourably situated that the well-known figures of the priest, the schoolmaster, and the woodranger, could be recognized as they sat under the trees before the house in summer, or made their presence evident in winter by the illumination of the window of the small room reserved for them or any chance traveller of distinction.

The architecture of this inn denoted the vicinity of the highlands. The low shingle roof stretched far over the small square windows; the wooden balcony, bronzed by age, extended the whole length of the gable; and above it a fresco painting represented St. Florian in the act of pouring a bucket of water on a house which, by stretch of the imagination, might be supposed a miniature picture of the inn itself, with red and sulphur-coloured flames issuing from every window, while beneath it, in the form of a scroll the usual words, " Oh, holy Saint Florian, save my house —burn others down !" in all its unchristian selfishness, was considered a preservative against the danger of conflagration.

Late in the afternoon, at the close of the year 1800, several persons holding official situations in the nearest town and all the peasants of the neighbourhood were assembled at the inn ; the latter in groups before the door, talking anxiously and eagerly of the battle of Hohenlinden, where Count Waldering (from whose funeral they had just returned) had lost his life a few days previously.

Some village politicians had just begun to discuss the possibility of the French army crossing the river Inn, and passing through their part of the country, when their attention was attracted by the appearance of a Bavarian officer, who rode quickly up to them, and was instantly recognized as the nephew of the late, and eldest son of the present, possessor of Westenried. The hostler, who, at first supposing him a stranger, had rushed out to take charge of the horse, and even, from force of habit, laid his hand on the bridle, no sooner looked up to the rider's face, than he drew back and raised his cap, while the peasants, following his example, fixed at the same time their eyes on the young man with looks of intense inquiry.

" Is Mr. Pallersberg here ?" he asked quickly.

" He is within," answered the hostler, " and just now thanking the gentlemen for their attendance at the funeral."

" Tell him I wish to speak to him."

The peasants crowded round the officer, and, though

no one singly ventured to address him, a confused murmur of questions reached his ears. "The French likely to cross the Inn ?—Road lie this way ?—Danger for us ?"

"I hope not—I trust not," replied the young man, biting his lip. "Some Wurtembergers and Austrians may march through the village to-morrow perhaps."

These words produced a very remarkable consternation, when it is taken into consideration that the arrival of friends, not foes, had been announced; but though Westenried had hitherto escaped the visitation of marching armies, the inhabitants had suffered enough from war contributions, and heard enough of the misery caused elsewhere, not to feel easily and seriously alarmed.

Through an open window the ill news reached the peasants within the house, and so great were the panic and eagerness to leave the inn, that Mr. Pallersberg found his progress to the door greatly impeded, notwithstanding the respectful efforts of the gesticulating villagers to make way for him.

Every trace of colour had fled from his ruddy, weather-beaten face, making the hard brown lines that furrowed it unusually perceptible; his lips were parted, his eyes distended, and long before he reached the door he seemed vainly to gasp for breath and utterance.

"Your son is safe, Mr. Pallersberg," said the officer, in answer to the mute inquiry; "not even wounded in this unfortunate affair. You will see him to-morrow on his way into Austria. As far as I have been able to ascertain," he added, "we alone in this neighbourhood are mourners."

Mr. Pallersberg drew a long breath, and, laying his hand on the mane of the jaded horse, that with outstretched neck had begun a slow walk towards the castle, he observed, "Your uncle died, as he always hoped he would, Count Sigmund, a soldier's death on a field of battle, and I trust

he fell without knowing that his life was a useless sacrifice."

"You must apply to your son for particulars, Pallersberg, for our Bavarian chasseurs were in front, and I was
among the first who got into action; the Austrian cavalry
must have been engaged much later, as they were in the
rear."

"And in such a place," murmured Pallersberg; "on a
road—in a wood!"

"You don't imagine we had a choice?" said Sigmund.
"Moreau was supposed to be retreating, and never was an
army taken more by surprise than ours when we encountered
the French. The most desperate efforts were made to get
into the open field, but all in vain; the advance of artillery
and cavalry served no other purpose than to block up the
road and make matters worse; the sudden attack, the
darkness of the wood, the snowstorm, all combined to put
the troops into constantly increasing disorder. The Austrian cavalry were, I hear, greatly cut up, especially my
uncle's regiment, and it is said the Archduke himself has
been wounded."

"And what has become of your aunt's nephew, the
young Irishman who was here with your uncle during the
truce, and left us to enter the army under his auspices?"

"Killed, most probably," answered Sigmund, carelessly;
"they say he was a reckless sort of fellow, always putting
himself into danger, even when it was not necessary. The
loss is not great, however, as there are half-a-dozen brothers
of his still in Ireland, though I doubt any of them wishing
to enter the Austrian service now that my uncle's death
has deprived them of such powerful interest."

"I fear," observed Mr. Pallersberg, "I fear this will
be a great additional grief to your aunt."

"No doubt, but it will prevent her from bringing any

more of her English and Irish relations to us. My uncle travelled to Vienna last year in the depth of winter to get this O'More appointed to his regiment, and felt greater interest for him than for any of his own family."

"Because he had it in his power to be useful to him," replied Mr. Pallersberg; "and, after all, the young man belonged to the family, being nephew by marriage to your uncle, and consequently first cousin to his only child."

"Hilda's cousins are not my cousins as yet," said Sigmund; and then, after a pause, he asked when his father and brother had arrived at Westenried.

"Yesterday evening."

"With the—the—?"

"With the corpse of your uncle, which was frozen as hard as marble."

"Well, well," said Sigmund, "regrets are useless; his fate may be mine to-morrow or the day after, and with less chance of being buried with my forefathers. War blunts the feelings, as, perhaps, you know from experience, Mr. Pallersberg."

"It may be so," he answered gravely, "with respect to misfortunes on a great scale, but not for the loss of personal friends." .

"My uncle's death will not affect you personally, Pallersberg, as I take it for granted that you will remain at Westenried, but the loss to your son is, I fear, irreparable; my uncle was a powerful friend for him, both as his commanding officer and in consequence of his influence at head-quarters."

"I did not mean that, Count Sigmund——," began Mr. Pallersberg, with heightened colour.

"But it would be very odd if you did not think of it," rejoined Sigmund, "for ideas of this kind force themselves

on such occasions into the mind of the most disinterested
of human beings!"

This speech, carelessly uttered, gave serious offence,
unnoticed, however, by the young officer as he passed
under the arched way, and entered the court of the castle.
When he alighted and strode with head erect into the
flagged hall, Pallersberg looked after him, while thinking
it was very evident that Sigmund was resigned to a loss
that had changed his position in the world so advan-
tageously.

Murmuring something about "want of a sense of decorum," Pallersberg ascended the narrow staircase leading
to his apartments, and there expatiated to his wife in no
measured terms on the heartlessness of the future heir of
Westenried. Alas for human nature! The words that
had given him such umbrage were but the expression of
the thought that had actually passed through his mind on
hearing of Count Waldering's death, and his wife, who
now nodded a sorrowful assent to all he said, had frequently and without reserve deplored the change in their
son's prospects; but then *they* were not, as she justly
observed, the late count's relations—they were merely—
friends.

CHAPTER II.

THE FAMILY.

SIGMUND WALDERING sought and found his father in the
room that had been used by his late uncle for transacting
business, nor was he in the least surprised to see him
seated at a writing-table, covered with papers, and so en-

grossed by the examination of them that the entrance of Sigmund was for a short time altogether unnoticed.

As a rule, that had been for some generations without exception, the eldest son in the Waldering family had been a soldier, the others lawyers or foresters, according to choice; and as want of intellect was not common among them, they had generally been prosperous, and advanced to high rank in their respective professions. Sigmund's father was a Director of the Court of Appeals, and from the time of his elevation to that position, had been by his family, friends, and acquaintance called " The Director." Either his gastronomic tastes or the sedentary habits incident to his profession had impaired the symmetry of his figure, or rather given it an unusual degree of corpulence ; but his head was still handsome, with its well-formed features, intelligent eyes, and still thick hair, just enough powdered to conceal the grey tufts in the vicinity of his temples. He had been long a widower, and altogether indisposed to accept any of the rational matches offered to his consideration by his various female acquaintances, who, invariably supposing objections on the part of his sons to be the cause of his refusals, continued with untiring perseverance their matrimonial speculations. Separated almost constantly by the intranquil state of Europe from his brother, who had early entered the army of the then Emperor of Germany, and greatly disappointed by his having married the widow of an Irish officer in the Austrian service, just when his advanced time of life had encouraged reasonable hopes that he would remain unmarried, and make Sigmund his heir,—his death had, nevertheless, both shocked and grieved the Director. Having, however, fulfilled his duty of seeking his brother's remains on the battle-field of Hohenlinden, and having buried them with as much pomp as circumstances would

permit, he rejoiced without a qualm of conscience in the
thought that his brother's only child was a daughter, and
set about the examination of his inheritance with all the
ardour of a man of business.

Scarcely any interruption but that of his son's arrival
would have been welcome to him just then. Sigmund,
however, had so recently escaped death, their position in
the world was so suddenly changed, and their interest
henceforward so completely identified, that they met with
unusual emotion; and after an interchange of a few hasty
questions and answers concerning the movement of the
army, it may be taken as a tribute to the real or supposed
goodness of the Director's heart, that his son gravely deplored their recent loss, and said not one word about the
uselessness of regrets or the effects of war upon the
feelings.

" Yes, Sigmund, this a severe affliction, and if so to us,
what must it be to my brother's widow ? "

" I suppose she is inconsolable," replied Sigmund,
" though of course my uncle has provided well both for
her and my cousin Hilda."

" Her own fortune was very considerable, you know,
Sigmund ; and she allowed it to be employed in paying off
the mortgages that encumbered Westenried. This is
secured to her, and a will has been found leaving everything at your uncle's disposal to her and Hilda. One
cannot blame him for taking care of them ! "

" Of course not ; but her claims on the estate are
rather alarming, if she demand immediate restitution of
her fortune."

" She will not do so, if you declare your intention of
fulfilling the engagement made last year with your uncle
concerning Hilda."

" Time enough to talk of that some years hence,"

answered Sigmund; "it would be absurd my engaging myself formally to such a mere child!"

"Yet something of the kind will be necessary," suggested his father; "otherwise, I fear your aunt will persevere in the plan of returning to England or Ireland as soon as the state of public affairs will permit her."

"Who has put this idea into her head?" asked Sigmund, almost angrily.

"Her daughter by her first husband, who, you must have heard, came back to her a couple of months ago during the truce. She has been educated in Ireland, greatly dislikes Germany, and openly expresses her desire to return to the uncle and aunt with whom she has passed almost all her life."

"But," said Sigmund, "I understood this daughter was scarcely of an age to have influence on such an occasion."

"It seems she has. My sister-in-law explained that your uncle's dislike to, or rather jealousy of, this daughter was the cause of her being entrusted while still an infant to the care of an aunt who was married and lived in Ireland; that now but just returned to her after an absence of twelve years, she was unwilling to make their union unpleasant by a compulsory and no longer necessary residence in a land that was disagreeable to her. When I took this into consideration, and remembered that my sister-in-law had numerous relations both in England and Ireland, I confess I was completely at a loss to discover anything that could be urged as an inducement to her to prolong her stay here."

"All this may be true," replied Sigmund; "but how, in the name of all the saints, are we to raise such a sum of money in times like these?"

"That is precisely what has been the subject of my

thoughts for the last half-hour," said his father; "and I can discover no other plan than that you should profess your desire to fulfil your late uncle's wishes by entering into an engagement with your cousin Hilda, and declare at the same time your wish that she should not leave Germany. This, I think, will suffice; for it is more than probable that the daughter your aunt has had with her constantly is dearer to her than the one who so unreservedly proclaims her preference for other relations."

"I cannot say that I like binding myself in this way," said Sigmund.

"Remember," continued his father, "that Hilda will inherit a considerable fortune from her mother; your uncle alone has left her enough to satisfy a reasonable man; and, besides this, she has expectations from her grand-aunt in Ulm that, if fulfilled, will make her far more wealthy than any of our family have ever yet been."

"I don't say that I will not marry her when she grows up," said Sigmund; "but don't you perceive that she being now but a child of twelve years old, will be at liberty to refuse the fulfilment of the engagement some years hence, while I am bound to await her decision? Under such circumstances, you can hardly expect me to consent to a betrothal."

"Then," retorted his father, "you have no right to interfere with your aunt's arrangements, and she will assuredly go with both daughters to England, while we may prepare to fell the woods here as the only means of raising such a large sum of money in times like these. This is, however, your affair, not mine; for, having no intention of ever living at Westenried, I give you full power to fell and sell every stick on the property."

"She cannot travel to England now, even if she wished it," observed Sigmund, in a voice of extreme agitation.

"Nor need you come to a decision until there is either a peace or a truce that will admit of her leaving us," answered his father, rising from the table, pushing aside the papers on it, and walking deliberately out of the room to end a conversation that was so evidently verging towards one of those ebullitions of temper to which Sigmund not unfrequently yielded.

More displeased than obliged by his father's forbearance, Sigmund strode up and down the room, with firmly-folded arms, until a slight movement of the door leading into another apartment, and a soft voice demanding permission to enter, attracted his attention.

"Come in!" he cried harshly, and a very young girl availed herself of the gruff permission, who, at any other time and under any other circumstances, would not have failed, notwithstanding her extreme youth, to attract him in no slight degree; but the dark-blue eyes and delicate loveliness of Doris O'More's face and figure were just then ineffectual to dispel the scowl that lowered on Sigmund's countenance, when it occurred to him that in her he saw the person whose longing for a more cheerful home than Westenried was about to cause him so much embarrassment.

She had spoken French, but, supposing that the language of "the enemy" had given umbrage, now began, with some difficulty, to make inquiries in German about her "cousin Frank," who must have been with Count Waldering at the battle of Hohenlinden.

"How should I know anything about your cousin?" he asked, sternly.

"I thought, perhaps, that as he was with your uncle, and as you were able to send a messenger from Hohenlinden to Munich to announce *his* death, you might have obtained some information at the same time concerning Frank."

2

" I made no inquiries about him," said Sigmund.

" You were able to give Mr. Pallersberg the assurance that his son lives," continued Doris, " and it is for this reason I apply to you: they were together—in the same troop ; you spoke to one—you may have seen the other."

" I did *not* see him," said Sigmund, beginning to feel a very unamiable satisfaction in watching the varying colour and increasing agitation of the young girl.

" If," she began, with trembling lips, " if—he—had—fallen—would they have brought him here for burial ? "

" Certainly not. What right has he to be buried at Westenried ? "

The rudeness of this speech seemed to strike her : she had mistaken his short answers for a desire to spare her feelings ; but now suddenly perceiving that ill-will or anger could alone prompt such harshness, she caught at the shadow of consolation, and, trusting that one so hard-hearted was not likely to conceal any painful intelligence, her hopes revived, and she turned away, murmuring, " As you have not heard of his death, we may hope to see him again."

" Your chance is not great," said Sigmund ; " for your cousin was last seen with my uncle completely surrounded by the enemy, and, if not killed, he is certainly missing, as he was not with his regiment when I spoke to Pallersberg after the battle."

" And what will be his fate, if missing ? "

" Years of imprisonment in France," answered Sigmund, as he walked across the room, and only stopped for a moment to look back at the poor girl, who had covered her face with her hands in the vain endeavour to hide her grief from so unsympathizing an observer.

CHAPTER III.

FRIENDS.

SIGMUND WALDERING left Westenried the next morning to join his regiment; his father's departure for Munich followed a few hours later. About noon the widow and her daughters had removed to the second floor, while a single room on the first gave evidence of still being inhabited, not only by the open jalousies of a couple of windows, but also by the not unfrequent appearance of a youthful head and figure that, careless of cold, leaned out to feed and watch the flights of the inhabitants of an adjacent dovecot, or follow with interest the various occupations of the busy pecking fowl that with permission had taken up their residence in the offices for the winter, two or three small openings having been considerately made in the wall for their convenient ingress and egress. Geese were there stretching their necks and flapping their wings with horrid screams, indicative of dissatisfaction that the frozen lake no longer afforded them their accustomed recreation. Waddling ducks consoled themselves by gobbling up everything eatable that came in their way; a turkey-cock strutted about unnoticed by a pair of magnificent peacocks perched on the icicled iron railing of the fountain; some pet rabbits scampered, and a tame raven hopped about the court; so when we add that a couple of cats gracefully boxed each other's ears when an opportunity offered, and dogs were ready to bark at any unusual sound, it is to be hoped that some good-natured readers will not altogether despise the Director's youngest son, Emmeran, for braving the hard frost of a December day, in order to contemplate such ordinary sights; the more so, as, although of a decidedly meditative disposition, he probably just then made no moral reflections on, or playful comparisons between, the animals before him and persons of his acquaintance. If one might judge by the expression of his countenance, the pompous turkey, aristocratic peacocks, gluttonous ducks, the quarrels of the cats, the snarling of dogs for the possession of a bone long bleached and marrowless, afforded him amusement in exact proportion to the noise and commotion caused, and, as far as lay in his power, he increased the propensity to strife by frequently flinging bread among the combatants.

The cold was, however, intense; and ever and anon a retreat into the room became necessary, where, with the latest work of Jean Paul in his hand, and student cap still on his head, he walked up and down, reading and meditating alternately.

Emmeran Waldering was a tall, delicate-looking young man, without any pretension to good looks, but gentleman-like, and of not altogether uninteresting appearance in his black velvet elaborately-braided Teutonic coat, open shirt-collar, tight pantaloons, and boots, or rather buskins of soft black leather that could be drawn over the knee at pleasure. The smart little blue and silver *cerevis* cap was planted so jauntily on his head, that it seemed more intended to keep his long fair hair in order than for any other purpose. The length of his pipe would have satisfied a Turk, and there were blue and white tassels pendant from it that might have served as terminations to bell-ropes, with the addition of the blue and white ribbon that he wore across his breast. His position in the world to a German eye was as plain as if he were habited in a military uniform. He was a student of the corps "Bavaria," and to a nice observer the fact that this badge ribbon had three stripes—that is, "white, blue, white,"—sufficed to indicate him as a person of importance in his corps—one to be consulted in cases of "scandal," which means in English, "rows," and the duels that generally followed such events.

Before Emmeran had acknowledged to himself that solitude was becoming irksome, Mr. Pallersberg appeared at the door, and informed him that the first detachment of Austrians having reached the village he was going there to see his son, adding, that if Emmeran had nothing better to do he might as well accompany him. A request had been made for forage, which he believed it would be necessary to attend to.

"Of course, of course," cried Emmeran, "and bread and wine, and—and—in short, whatever we have to give."

"In fact," said Pallersberg, "we may as well be generous, for what we do not give them may be taken by the enemy before long."

"Do you mean that the French are following ? "

"I fear," he answered, "there is but little chance that they will not do so."

"Indeed ! then let us destroy our causeway and raise the drawbridge."

"Of what use," said Mr. Pallersberg, "when the lake is frozen as it has not been these ten years, and the ice so strong that they can walk into the orchard and court at pleasure ? "

"This frost is a confounded nuisance," said Emmeran, "and I was foolish enough this morning to rejoice in the prospect of skating. What are we to do ? "

"We must conceal the plate and other valuables in the panelled ceiling of the dining-room, where a place was made for such things in times even wilder than these."

"And you really think that such precautions are necessary ? "

Pallersberg shrugged his shoulders. " Let us not lead even our enemies into temptation," he said. " Should we have time, I propose removing wine and linen to the little Chapel-island in the middle of the lake : they will scarcely have time to rummage the vaults of the church-ruin there. It is the habit of the French to make war support war, and they will assuredly help themselves to whatever they want. And now I believe I must beg of you to walk on quickly, as my son has but one hour to remain in the village, and my wife is waiting on the bridge intending to accompany us, and is taking with her provisions that will make her very welcome not only to him but also his comrades." He turned round before leaving the court, and, looking up to one of the windows, raised his hat.

" A pretty girl that Mademoiselle O'More," said Emmeran, following the direction of his eyes and raising his cap, although the young lady's arrival at Westenried had been so recent that he had not yet had an opportunity of becoming personally acquainted with her; " a very pretty girl ! "

" Yes, poor child ! " answered Pallersberg; " and she is just now in despair about her cousin, who has been missing since the battle of Hohenlinden. She wanted to go with me to the village to make inquiries in person, but her mother very properly would not consent, and I consoled her by a promise to send a messenger in case my son should be able to give any further information concerning him. She knows nothing of such scenes excepting from books or newspapers, and expects a list of the killed and wounded three or four days after the engagement."

As Emmeran and Mr. Pallersberg disappeared beneath the archway, Doris slowly left the window and returned to the drawing-room, where her mother was seated at a small work-table cutting up bits of muslin and crape, in the vain endeavour to make herself something resembling that hideous and essentially English head-gear—a widow's cap. Her eyes bore traces of long-continued weeping, but the swelled eyelids, though red, were tearless, and there was a look of resolute self-control, not only in the small features of her still interesting face, but even in her figure, and the manner in which she pursued her occupation. Stooping towards her youngest daughter Hilda, who sat on a foot-stool beside her, she whispered a few words, probably a request to be left alone with Doris, for the young girl instantly rose, kissed her mother's cheek, and went out of the room without speaking.

"Doris," observed the Countess Waldering after a pause, "I regret much being obliged to refuse this first request that you have made, but the village when occupied by troops on the march is no fit place for you, and Mr. Pallersberg will get from his son all the information that can be obtained about Frank."

Doris walked to one of the windows without replying, and appeared to gaze on the half-frozen lake and trees white with frost, while large tears fell slowly from her eyes.

" Could I have foreseen," continued her mother, " had I even thought of the possibility of what has occurred, I should never have desired. your coming abroad ; but a peace seemed so certain, that it was natural I should take advantage of your being able to travel here with our friends the Beauchamps. You can understand my wish to see you again, and regain or obtain your affection, Doris ? "

" Yes, mamma, but it is a useless effort if you expect me ever to like you as well, or half as well, as my aunt, who has been, indeed, a mother to me ! "

" Never mind what I expect, Doris. Let me hope that in time, without any diminution of your regard for your aunt, you will give me also a place in your heart."

" I don't at all—dislike you—" began Doris.

" That will do for a beginning," said her mother, with a faint smile.

" But," continued Doris, turning completely towards her, " but I could almost do so when I remember that *your* letters were the cause of dear Frank's leaving his country, and being now either a prisoner or dead; perhaps lying still unburied on the snow at Hohenlinden, a disfigured frozen corpse like Count Waldering's ! "

Fresh tears started to her eyes at the picture her imagination had conjured up, and she glanced indignantly at her apparently unmoved mother.

" Thank Heaven ! " she continued, " Feargus was less dazzled than Frank by your description of the glories of the Irish Brigade, and the manner in which our national names were respected on the Continent ! Poor Frank's head was completely filled with the idea of becoming Field Marshal, or Grand Croix of the Theresian Order, a Count of the Roman Empire, or I know not what all, like the O'Reillys, O'Connors, O'Donnels, and all the rest of them !"

" In times such as these," said her mother, " his chances were as good as those of any of his predecessors, and the letter that so displeased you, Doris, was written at the urgent request of your uncle."

" My uncle ?"

" Yes, he wrote telling me of the embarrassed state of his affairs, and the difficulty of providing for seven sons more inclined to live at Garvagh in gentlemanlike idleness, than to pursue the studies necessary for the professions they had chosen. He even asked me to use my influence with your step-father to obtain admission in the Austrian army for both Frank and Feargus, and was thankful that my letter had induced one at least to leave home, and make an effort to become independent."

" And now ?" asked Doris, " what will he say now ?"

" I know not," answered her mother, " but I have resolved not to write until I have some certain information to give him."

At this moment the sound of hasty steps on the flagged floor of the corridor attracted their attention : it was that of booted, spurred feet, and in breathless anxiety they awaited the approach of the expected messenger from the village, simultaneously answering the hurried knock which scarcely preceded the entrance of a young man in the uniform of an Austrian dragoon. He seized the extended hand of the Count Waldering and pressed it repeatedly to his lips, while incoherently uttering some words of condolence, made more than intelligible by his extreme agitation.

" I thank you sincerely, Captain Pallersberg, for this attention," she said in a low voice ; " it is most kind, for from you alone I can hope to hear all that occurred at Hohenlinden."

" And unfortunately," he answered, " unfortunately I have but a few minutes at my disposal ; we march in half an hour."

" Then tell me only of the fate of that poor boy, who, perhaps, has escaped death, as you did not see him fall."

" No ; but he was with Count Waldering and in imminent danger when I last saw him, so gallant and so fearless that we can only console ourselves with the hope that he has been overpowered by numbers and taken prisoner. I mentioned this to Sigmund Waldering, but, as he was not personally acquainted with your nephew, he may have forgotten to speak of him."

" Not exactly," said the countess ; " for he told my daughter, when she asked him, that Frank was either killed or a prisoner ; but we hoped that since then you might have obtained some further information."

" None on that subject," he answered sorrowfully, " but more on another than you will like to hear. The French are not only following us, but their right wing having crossed the Inn at Neubayern, there is little doubt of their being here directly. My father agrees with me in thinking it better for you and your daughters to remove to the vaults under the ruin on the Chapel-island. The chances of a thaw are too slight to admit of a thought of refusing entrance to the castle, but the water round the Chapel-island is not likely to be frozen at present; some arrangements can be made for your reception there, and the discomfort, though great, will not last long."

" That is of little importance," she said ; " and if there are others who wish to take refuge in these vaults, I must request your father not to reserve them for me alone."

" The villagers," he answered, " propose sending most of the women and all the children out of the neighbourhood, and intend to drive their cattle into the woods. Whatever cannot be removed or hid must be sacrificed, and they are tolerably resigned, though they have been obliged to supply our troops with rations and forage. I trust that this first may also be the last time that the chances of war will bring the plague of marching armies, whether friends or foes, to this hitherto so fortunate place."

The sound of trumpets caused him to cease speaking.

" I know what that means," said the countess, " and shall not attempt to detain you. I wish I could—perhaps I can be of use. You mentioned, in a letter to your father, that you were badly mounted. Count Waldering left one of his horses here for me that is quite at your service, and you shall be put into immediate possession."

The young man made a faint attempt to decline the welcome present, to which no attention was paid; but when they reached the court and the well-known charger of his late colonel was led from the stable, he stooped down on pretence of assisting the groom to fasten the bridle, in order to hide his emotion.

" I have given you a good master, old fellow !" said the countess, caressing the horse's head as he bent it towards her and stamped his forefoot impatiently on the pavement. " I wish I could add a talisman to save you and your rider from the fate of him who left me on this spot but a few weeks ago! If warm wishes for your safety and fervent prayers for the speedy termination of this war be of avail, Captain Pallersberg, I can promise both. Farewell and speed well !" she added, as once more the sound of trumpets from the village reached them ; and the young officer, after a vain effort to express his thanks, vaulted into the saddle and dashed, almost in full career, over the drawbridge and up the hill beyond.

" He rides well," said Doris, musingly, "and was perhaps kind to Frank. I—believe—I could like him, though he *is* a German !"

CHAPTER IV.

FOES.

THE court of Westenried, during the remainder of the afternoon, was a scene of turmoil and confusion ; the peasants' wives brought every portable object of value there, and could with difficulty be made to understand the impossibility of attempting a defence of the castle. They entreated permission to put some of their effects in the cellars, and, notwithstanding Mr. Pallersberg's assurance that they were by no means safe there, packed every place unoccupied with beds and boxes.

The Countess Waldering brought some order among the despairing women when she proposed their sending money, trinkets, and whatever else they had time to remove, to the Chapel-island, and a superstitious feeling of security took possession of them all when they found themselves preceded to the flat-bottomed boats by the priest carrying the silver vessels of the church. These boats, the hollowed trunks of trees, were shoved along the ice as far as it reached, then launched on the water, and before long the little Chapel-island became for the time being visibly inhabited, the bright colour of the women's dresses gleaming in the sunshine beneath the leafless trees, and contrasting strongly with the grey walls of the ruin and snow-covered ground.

"This will never do!" cried Pallersberg, impatiently; "these women will spend the whole afternoon putting their goods in order, instead of returning here and giving us time to make some arrangement for you and your daughters' comfort before the French arrive."

"We shall not want much for so short a time," answered the countess, "and we are well provided with fur and warm clothes, so that with a basket of provisions we shall do very well. I have left the keys in the wardrobes, as I do not wish them to be broken open in the idea that they contain things likely to be useful. What I possess of real value is in this trunk, and we are ready to emigrate the moment the boats return."

"Mr. Pallersberg," said Doris, coming from the stable, where she had been looking round her anxiously, "what have they done with Brian Boru?"

She had given this not very appropriate name to a young Hungarian horse, her mother's first present to her after their meeting.

"*Bronboor* has been turned into the marsh," he answered, smilingly; " and I am much mistaken if he allow himself to be easily caught. I wish I were as sure of finding all our live stock safe after our unwelcome visitors have left us as of seeing him, with disordered mane and mud-encrusted legs, on the margin of the lake."

" And my pony ? " cried Hilda; " where is he ? "

" The pony," said Emmeran, joining them, " is safe; his diminutive proportions will prove his best protection. And now, Hilda, ask your sister if she will acknowledge our relationship, and permit me to call her ' cousin ' ? "

" Are you, in fact, my cousin ? " asked Doris.

" Do not examine this relationship too accurately, Doris," interposed her mother; " remember that I consider Emmeran *my* nephew ? "

" He is, however, only a cousin by marriage, not a real *cousin-german*," said Doris.

" No, I am only a *German cousin*," he replied, laughing, as he bowed over her reluctantly-extended hand, and lightly touched it with his lips.

Before Doris had recovered from her surprise at what appeared to her a foreign and very theatrical mode of commencing an acquaintance, Madame Pallersberg came towards them directing the carriage of baskets filled with clothes, among which Emmeran, to his no small astonishment, observed various articles of his own apparel, the appearance of which was justified by the explanation, " that there was no time for long consultations; clothes were just the things of all others likely to be carried off by the French republicans, who were notoriously in want of them —especially trousers ! "

Just then observing a wounded Austrian officer and some soldiers carried into the court, she hurried towards them, followed by Doris and her mother, while Pallersberg, first shouted vainly to the loiterers on the Chapel-island,

and then with Emmeran's assistance commenced drawing
the trunks, baskets, and bags across the ice to the water's
edge.

The sun was already perceptibly disappearing behind
the wooded hills, and shining red with expanding disk
through the frosty evening fog ; an orange-tinted sky was
reflected dimly in the still unfrozen part of the lake, and a
coloured brilliancy pervaded the crystals of ice that began
to form a crust on every tree, pine needle, and still visible
shrub. Before long Pallersberg found the same process
commencing on the long hairs of his moustache, and was
raising his hand to remove what he considered more
attractive on plants than human hair, when he heard a
distant *ranz des vaches* blown through a cow-horn, the long,
low, peculiarly inharmonious sound of which seemed to
startle in a peculiar manner every hearer. It was, in fact,
the signal from a neighbouring hill that the French were
in sight, and one of the boats instantly left the Chapel-
island, into the other the peasants crowded in a disorderly
manner, while Doris, Hilda, and their mother ran through
the orchard, and sprang upon the ice, followed by servants
carrying camp-stools, a table, and some bedding.

" I knew they would dawdle about the vaults until the
last moment," muttered Pallersberg. "March! off with
you!" he cried impatiently to the terrified peasants, as
they tumbled over each other in their endeavours to leave
the boat; and then he added, as he assisted the countess
into it, "The gardener and his son will remain on the
island with you, and well armed, though I do not think
there is the slightest chance of your being disturbed or
alarmed there."

" Nor do I feel any anxiety on that account," she
answered; "for though the lateness of the hour may
induce the enemy to pass the night in the village and its

environs, it is not probable that any one at this time of year will have any inclination for a cold bath ; and as we shall have both boats on the island, no one can reach us otherwise than by swimming."

" Just what my son said when he proposed your going there: for my own part, I only thought of the vaults as a place of safety for our wine and linen. Adieu, madame. I wish it were this time to-morrow, and I stood here to release you from imprisonment."

The Chapel-island was in the middle of the broadest part of the lake, and was, and is still, covered with beech-trees of unknown age, chiefly preserved for their leaves, which, in forest districts, are considered a good substitute for straw. Through the denuded branches some undefined masses of ivy-covered walls were visible, and in the midst of them the ruin of a chapel evidently of later date, but roofless, and the long narrow windows retaining their form alone where the carved stone frames had resisted the dilapidations incident to constant exposure to the weather.

In the interior of this ruin a sort of shed had been erected to shelter the trap-door entrance to the vaults that had formerly been concealed by the altar. These vaults were, of course, said to be haunted, and many a courageous man in the neighbourhood would have declined passing a few hours of the night alone in them. Nevertheless, no vestige of human bones had been found there within the memory of man, and both extent and architecture were calculated rather to lead to the supposition that they had been the cellars, perhaps also the prison, of the stronghold that had stood on the island in the tenth century, and which had been built so as completely to command the Roman road, still easily traceable through the wood on the opposite shore, in appearance a long, straight, green avenue

—masses of stone on which grass but not trees could flourish.

If Doris had felt any dismay on descending the steps conducting to these vaults, it was quickly overcome; for the resemblance to the hold of a ship occurred to her the moment she reached the ground and looked round the space but dimly lighted by a lantern which the gardener carried before her mother. Boxes, trunks, and parcels were heaped in a not altogether disorderly manner around the place below the entrance, while the adjoining cellars, though furnished with grated openings for the admission of air, had been left unused, the rows of bins being supposed to have originally served as receptacles for coffins.

Though Doris was not more afraid of ghosts and goblins than other young people, perhaps even less so, she never boasted of her courage, and openly expressed her dislike to hearing "little noises" at night, or having "queer dreams;" yet being blessed, *or* the contrary, with a vivid imagination, the long narrow niches had made a disagreeable impression on her also, and she perceived with satisfaction that her mother moved on to the more open space immediately beneath the church—a crypt-like place, with its low closely-vaulted ceiling supported by two rows of short, thick, rough stone pillars. Against the dark walls, bright-coloured bedding was heaped; for most of the peasant women had made an effort to save at least their best bed from the enemy. On these Hilda made a few childish bounds, stumbling afterwards over the linen and Sunday clothes that lay beside them, and finally seated herself on the ground in order to examine at her leisure the numerous crucifixes and prayer-books reverently placed together by the peasants. Doris, when called upon to look at them, observed that the care taken of them showed much religious feeling; but, in point of fact, they would have been in no danger whatever, and might as well have been left in the houses.

"I'm not so sure of that, miss," said the gardener; "for since the French have left off being Christians, they would as willingly light a fire with them as with chips!"

"I only meant they would not take them away with them," replied Doris.

"It is one of the misfortunes of war," observed her mother, "that more things are wantonly destroyed than used from necessity; and this not only by enemies, but also by friends, and not unfrequently even by soldiers moving about in their own country during war time."

"But, mamma, I wonder the officers don't interfere on such occasions."

"So they do, my dear, but it is impossible for them to be everywhere, and little time is necessary for much mischief."

"I am sure," cried Doris, "that English troops would never take anything from poor villagers without paying for it—no, not even if they were enemies!"

"And I am afraid, Doris, that men so much resemble each other, that all civilized nations are much on a par in war. This morning the Austrian troops slaughtered several oxen, but gave the proprietors written acknowledgments, which will entitle them to compensation from government: that the French will take whatever they want from their enemies, and without acknowledgment, is a matter of course."

"The poor villagers!" said Doris, "how I pity them, and how I hate the French—all—all—from the First Consul in his cocked hat to our émigrée governess, Madame Fredon,—and from her to the smallest drummer now marching past the lake."

"A wide range for hatred, Doris! but it is not very intense, perhaps, and subject to exceptions."

3

"Only one exception, mamma, and that no longer one."

"Probably the young French legitimist recommended to your uncle's good offices by the Abbé Edgeworth?"

"Yes, mamma, we could not help liking Henri d'Esterre when he was living with us at Garvagh, but now that he has gone back to France and turned republican, we quite detest him, and made a law among ourselves never to name him."

"And how many other Frenchmen and women have you known, Doris, for that also should be taken into consideration?"

Doris was silent, and her mother continued, "I can easily imagine your feeling some dislike to a governess whose duty it was to compel you to speak a language you young people thought it patriotic not to learn; she may also have made herself personally disagreeable: but of two, to like one is a strong testimony in favour of our enemies, at least as far as your actual experience reaches."

"I acknowledge that as usual you have the best of the argument, mamma," said Doris with ill-concealed annoyance; "my *aunt* thought me capable of forming an opinion, but it is evident you consider me childish, and perhaps even more frivolous than I really am."

"I think you have very strong prejudices, Doris, and an unreasonable aversion to everything foreign or unlike what you have been accustomed to at Garvagh."

"My hatred of the French a prejudice?"

"As far as it concerns individuals, yes."

"And my dislike to Germany and the Germans?"

"Also prejudice, because you as yet know nothing of either; but to prove I do not think you so childish as you suppose, let me tell you that your openly expressed antipathy to every thing and person here has given me great pain and caused me much embarrassment. I trust, however, as I am about to return to Ireland on your account, you will be satisfied with the sacrifice."

"Sacrifice, mamma? Is it possible you do not rejoice to leave such an uncivilized country and this wild uncultivated place?"

Her mother shook her head.

"Not long to see my darling uncle, who speaks of you with such affection? Is it possible that you can dislike or be indifferent to him?"

"Quite the contrary," said her mother.

"And my aunt? your own sister?"

"I am sincerely attached to her, and owe her a debt of gratitude for her care of you that I shall never be able to pay."

"And then all our other relations and friends?"

"They have forgotten me, Doris, for so long and complete a separation is death to most friendships, and when I left Ireland I never intended to return."

"Yet had my father lived——" began Doris, and then stopped suddenly on observing that her mother turned towards her with a look of piercing inquiry.

Here the gardener entered to exchange the lantern for a lamp, and as he placed the latter on the table, observed, "The enemy is on the way to the village, and my son thinks there are horses and soldiers in the court of the castle,—at least something moving and shining can be seen through the trees. I shouldn't wonder if most of the generals and colonels were billeted on us, and they will no doubt make free with all my winter vegetables."

"Take care, Doris," said her mother on perceiving her following the gardener towards the stone steps; "take care you do not attract attention."

"Not the least danger, mamma, if I cover myself with a white cloth and represent a ghost—what a place this would be to burn salt with spirits of wine, and make people look like corpses! Oh, forgive me, I ought not to have reminded you——I—I really seem doomed since I came to Germany never to say or do anything right. You must send me back to Ireland, mamma, the first opportunity, and —forget me altogether!"

Throwing a white quilt over her head and shoulders, and letting it fall around her, Doris left the vault with rapid steps, her mother's thoughtful eyes following the movements of her slight figure as long as it remained in sight.

" Will you let her leave us, mamma?" asked Hilda.

" Yes, my dear child; as I cannot make her like us or our country, she shall return to Ireland the first opportunity that offers, and you will be once more my only hope and treasure."

CHAPTER V.

REMINISCENCES.

THE glow of sunset was over, and the frosty air had become colder, when Doris, with the gardener's assistance, mounted a heap of stones, and began to peer through one of the window-frames of the ruin. Lights glimmered from all the houses in the village that were in sight, and an inauspicious illumination of most of the apartments in the castle had already commenced. Candles and lanterns, *ignis fatuus* like, seemed to hover about the stables, throwing gleams of light on shining objects that most probably were pyramids of arms, while dark moving masses might still be distinguished on the road, and confused sounds of horses' hoofs, rattling wheels, drums, bugles, and human voices reached her sufficiently distinctly to cause the first feeling of personal anxiety she had as yet experienced.

"Do you really think there is no danger of their coming to the island?" she asked the old man who stood beside her. "I have read of the French crossing rivers on pontoon boats that they carry about with them."

"Very likely, miss, when they knew what it was for; but, after a hard day's march, few of them will think it worth while to look towards an island like this, without a house upon it."

"Very true," said Doris; "it was absurd my supposing such a thing at all likely to happen; but this is the first time I have ever been near marching armies, and I cannot help feeling a little uneasy."

"You may go to bed, and sleep as sound as a dormouse," he answered good-humouredly; "Mr. Pallersberg has told us not to give alarm by firing gun or pistol except in the last extremity, though we may slash about us with the old swords and sabres if any one attempt a landing."

"I am very sorry it is so cold for you and your son—" began Doris.

"Michael doesn't mind it, miss; he was often out shooting with the count in colder weather, and will be on the look-out until daybreak, when, as that is about the time I am generally up and busy, I can take his place."

"And then," said Doris, "I shall come here again. It is getting so dark now one can only see the lighted windows, and the water around us that looks as black as ink. You must promise to waken me when your turn comes to mount guard," she added, as they descended to the vaults; "I shall be so glad to see those hateful French marching off."

Doris found Hilda already stretched on a mattress fast asleep. A similar bed had been prepared for Doris, who immediately took possession of it, saying, as she lay down, that, having satisfied herself that they were in no danger, she intended to sleep soundly until morning.

"I hope you may," said her mother, reseating herself at the table so as to shade Doris from the light, while leaning forward she bent over one of the prayer-books rescued so nxiously from the dreaded impiety of the republicans,— a Latin missal belonging to the schoolmaster, which opened, as it were, of itself at the Requiem. This was not pleasant reading, and may perhaps have been one of the reasons that caused the face of the reader to grow paler and paler. Before long, however, her thoughts evidently wandered to other, though scarcely more cheerful, subjects; for her eyes slowly left the page of the book and settled on the ring of bright light thrown by the shaded lamp on the table, and rested there with the absent, almost sightless, gaze of Reverie. Was it the Requiem or her daughter's heedless words half-an-hour previously that recalled so vividly the image of her late husband's frozen corpse? Most probably the latter; for after a harrowing recollection of all that had occurred during the last few days, a flash of memory brought before her a lofty dining-room, with lights extinguished, and on a table in the centre a dish with salt in spirits of wine burning bluely.

Intervening time was forgotten, and she was passing a Christmas in Ireland with her only sister, who had been many years married to Mr. O'More of Garvagh. Half-a-dozen wild boys were there, who with busy hands stirred the salt until the very portraits on the walls seemed turned to corpses; while the younger ones, not satisfied with their already frightfully cadaverous appearance, made the most hideous grimaces, turning to her as if for encouragement and approval. Beside her stood her sister's brother-in-law, a captain in the Austrian army, at home on leave; and well she remembered that then and there he had first alarmed her with vehement professions of love and a proposal to share his roving life in a foreign country. Never had she seen a face so disfigured by anger as his on hearing her refusal; never had she heard such violent and voluble reproaches as his for having received his attentions more willingly than those of others; her excuse that with him, as a sort of connection, she had felt unrestrained, being listened to with scorn and derision.

From that time she had avoided and feared Captain O'More, and greatly rejoiced when he left home before the expiration of his leave of absence, ostensibly to join his regiment in Germany. Such was, however, by no means his intention. He returned secretly to the neighbourhood, concealed himself in a peasant's house for some time, and found at last an opportunity, late one evening when she was walking alone in the demesne, to carry her off by force, and with the assistance of some lawless friends he kept her prisoner until she consented to become his wife.

Such daring acts of violence to women were by no means uncommon in Ireland at that period, or even much later, and they were judged by the public with a leniency that now seems incomprehensible. The relations on both sides endeavoured on this occasion to give a flagrant case of abduction the name of elopement, and little more was known than that the handsome Austrian dragoon had carried off an English heiress who had left Ireland with the openly-expressed determination never to return there.

The hard trial of living with a man she could not love, and whose violence she had learnt to fear, was of short duration. Some months after their marriage he lost his life in a duel, and a year later she became the wife of Count Waldering. Thenceforward the only drawback to her happiness was her husband's jealous dislike to her infant

child Doris, which not even the birth of his own daughter
Hilda could mitigate; and at length she had been obliged
to send her with her own maid to Ireland, and eventually
resigned her altogether to the care of her sister.

It is a dangerous experiment on the part of any mother
this confiding the education of a daughter to others, and for
this reason, probably, boarding-schools are now seldom
resorted to in England, excepting in cases of absolute
necessity. Had Doris been at one, she might have felt a
sort of satisfaction in the hope of obtaining freedom from
restraint by the change; but having left unwillingly a
happy home and idolizing relations, she met her mother
almost as a stranger, and soon made it evident that a
careful education had formed her mind and manners in an
unusual degree for her age.

Doris's proud reserve towards her step-father during
the short time they had been together her mother easily
excused, when she remembered that her daughter was
aware of his having been the cause of her banishment.
She was even prepared for some estrangement from herself, but not for such complete alienation as she had latterly
perceived; and Doris's request to be sent back to her uncle
and desire to be forgotten had wounded her mother's
feelings in a peculiarly painful manner. Accustomed to be
loved, the supposition that she could not easily acquire the
affection of her daughter had never even been taken into
consideration, and she now, with the sensitiveness peculiar
to women at her time of life, began to doubt the continuance of her power of pleasing, and unhesitatingly resolved
not to accompany but to send Doris back to the home she
loved so much as soon as an eligible opportunity could be
found.

This resolution and the preceding recollections caused
the already tearful eyes to overflow in a burst of intense,

but fugitive and vehemently suppressed grief, which had scarcely subsided when, raising the lamp from the table, and shading it carefully with her hand, so that no ray of light might disturb the sleepers, she placed it behind one of the stone pillars and turned towards the steps, up which in complete darkness she slowly groped her way, until she felt the freezing night air on her burning forehead, snow beneath her feet, and saw a sky full of stars above her.

CHAPTER VI.

A MAIDEN ON GUARD.

DORIS was wakened in a very unceremonious manner at daybreak the next morning by the gardener, who shook her shoulder while informing her that the enemy were already up and on the move. She roused herself with difficulty from her profound healthful sleep, seemed more inclined to consider the gardener her enemy than the French just then, and looked towards the mattress that had been arranged for her mother as if half willing to be refused permission to leave her place of rest.

" Oh, she's been up all night," said the old man; " one sees that she's been a soldier's wife, and used to this sort of life—had wine ready for my son at midnight, and is making breakfast for us all now with a lamp, as we dare not light a fire."

And at the foot of the steps Doris found her mother, who merely looked up for a moment and nodded a " good morning."

Doris stopped. She was not accustomed to be treated

carelessly, and though she received demonstrations of affection as a matter of course, and had hitherto returned her mother's negligently enough, she did not like the change, and began to consider what could be the cause of it.

To her credit be it said, a good many reasons occurred to her, and she approached her mother diffidently while saying, "I hear you have been up all night—why did you not waken me and let me keep you company?"

"Because I was very glad to see you free from all anxiety, and able to sleep so soundly."

"There was not much to be feared, mamma, or you would not have allowed Janet to remain at the castle."

"Very well reasoned, Doris, and it is too late for anxiety now, as the French are preparing to leave us as quickly as they can; an hour or two hence we may hope to hear the unmelodious signal with the cow-horn, that will, no doubt, be as welcome to you as to me."

"Yes," said Doris, "I should rather like to be in my room, and able to dress comfortably."

Her mother raised the flame of the lamp, and appeared wholly occupied with her coffee-pot.

"Mamma, why did not you say 'good-night' yesterday evening, and why have you not wished me 'good morning' as——as usual?"

A bright smile passed like a gleam of sunshine over her mother's countenance as she bent forward, and, lightly kissing her on each cheek, whispered "This is 'good night' and this 'good morning' as usual, Doris."

Satisfied with this evasion of an answer that could scarcely have been satisfactory, and relieved not to hear reproaches she feared she had deserved, Doris began to skip up the cellar-steps, trailing after her the long quilt, which she gladly drew round her as a shawl on reaching the piercingly-cold air above. It was less dark than when she had last stood on the same spot, for a gleam of light was slowly spreading over the eastern sky that began to render indistinct the expiring watchfires, and glimmering candles still seen red and rayless through the mist.

Silently Doris gazed on the wintry landscape, while daylight spread dimly over it, the gardener occasionally stopping beside her, but perceptibly prolonging his excursions towards the entrance to the vaults, from which a strong odour of coffee began to emanate. At length having seated himself on the first step, whence a view of the interior was scarcely possible, he continued to descend in the same manner, resting when midway his elbows on his knees, and contemplating with a wide smile of satisfaction the preparations going on beneath.

Meantime the increasing light showed Doris a greater expanse of frozen water; she began even to see parts of the shore, some chimneys of the castle, and the outline of a window or two, when her attention was attracted by a loud noise from the shore, and immediately afterwards she saw a number of soldiers rush upon the ice, who began to run tumultuously in the direction of the Chapel-island. They were evidently in pursuit of a young man, who, in his shirt-sleeves, with wildly-flying hair, had the advance of a few steps, or rather springs. He dashed forward with a recklessness that proved his flight had been attempted in desperation, and, fortunately for him, many of the soldiers following, getting unawares on slides industriously made at leisure-hours by the village children, lost their balance, fell over each other, and, accoutred and packed as they were for a march, with difficulty and much loss of time only regained their feet when their assistance was no longer required by the two who had still contrived successfully to follow the fugitive. These did not at first appear to gain upon him perceptibly, but one soldier being considerably in advance of the other, the young man stopped suddenly, as if to recover breath. The moment, however, his pursuer came within arm's length he knocked him down with a single unexpected blow, that seemed to stun him effectually for some time. The race that succeeded was more equal: the other pursuer was light, youthful, and probably an officer, as he was without a knapsack, and had during the short time gained ground considerably. He advanced gesticulating, and Doris could hear his shouts and orders to surrender as they almost together approached the water's edge. Interest, anxiety, and a feeling of utter helplessness, kept her motionless and silent, while the young men suddenly faced each other, one armed, the other with even his shirt torn from his shoulders in the scuffle that had preceded his escape. He seemed to feel his disadvantages keenly, clenched his hands, and advanced towards his antagonist, who was in the act of drawing his sword from the scabbard: before, however, he had time to do so, he was seized round the waist and dragged struggling forward towards the thin ice, that soon began to crack in all directions, and almost immediately yielded to their weight, one long loud crash accompanying the fall of both into the water, where the danger of getting beneath the ice seemed suddenly to terminate their animosity. The advantage was now clearly on the side of the fugitive, who, unencumbered with arms and lightly clothed, stretched out powerfully into the water, leaving the other to seek a place where he could regain footing on the surface of the ice, and which he at length found on the spot whence the boats had been shoved off the previous day.

The soldier who had first been put *hors de combat* rose slowly and came to the aid of his officer; then, after having assisted him to mount on the ice, he raised his musket and deliberately aimed and fired at the head of the bold swimmer, who, to Doris's horror and dismay, sank instantly beneath the water. She started up, clenched her hands furiously towards the soldiers who were now return· ing at full speed to the castle, and, while calling her mother and the gardener, ran down the slope to the water's edge, where, apparently entangled in the overhanging branches of a beech tree, she saw the drooping figure of the young man whose desperate effort for freedom she had watched with such intense interest. That he was not dead was evident, for he panted, or rather gasped, loudly, apparently unable to make the slight exertion necessary to land.

"Are you wounded?" asked Doris, compassionately. "You shall have assistance directly."

The swimmer raised his head, shook back the long black hair that had concealed his features, and Doris saw the laughing, handsome face of her cousin, Frank O'More!

Their mutual exclamations of delight soon brought her mother to her side, and Frank favoured them alternately with his dripping caresses as inconsiderately as a young Newfoundland dog, the exploits of which in diving and swimming he had recently so successfully imitated.

CHAPTER VII.

THE CAPITAL O.

When Mr. Pallersberg, a few hours later, gave the expected signal, and walked across the ice to receive the boat that almost immediately left the Chapel-island, he was not a little surprised to perceive an additional person in it—still more so when, on a nearer approach, it became evident that the said personage had taken the liberty of dressing himself in the suit of snuff-brown cloth that he was himself in the habit of reserving for Sundays and holidays; but no sooner had the wearer sprung on the ice than he shouted out a welcome, and altogether declined listening to the excuses or explanations offered by Frank, who had not ventured to supply himself from Count Emmeran's wardrobe, with whom he was as yet unacquainted.

Emmeran, without waiting for an introduction, assured him that he should be happy to share with him all that had been so fortunately rescued from the enemy; everything of the kind in the castle and village having been carried off in a perfectly unceremonious manner.

"Did I not tell you so?" cried Madame Pallersberg, almost triumphantly turning round, though in the midst of a despairing enumeration of the mischief perpetrated in the neighbourhood. "Did I not tell you how it would be? and did not you laugh and jest about 'sans-culottes' and clothes-baskets until the French were in the very court of the castle?"

"I confess with shame that this is true," answered Emmeran, "and I now receive my small wardrobe as a sort of present from you; for most assuredly, if my 'culottes' had not been sent by you to the Chapel-island they would now be on the march to Braunau."

"It is astonishing," observed Mr. Pallersberg, "the mischief these soldiers contrived to do in a quiet way in one night, and it would have been far worse if we had not had time to drive out the cattle. They were furious when they perceived how much had been put out of their reach; in fact, so much was concealed and otherwise disposed of, that the greater number of them had to move on. Those, however, who remained effectually plundered the village and ransacked the castle."

"I rather expected," said the countess, "that the officers would have quartered themselves in our apartments."

"Well, so they did, and made themselves quite at home there, too."

"At home!" exclaimed his wife, who had only heard the last words. "Do you call it making themselves at home the killing of every living thing about the place? Didn't I see one of these same officers, a middle-aged man, too—probably married and the father of a family—chasing the fowls about the court with a drawn sword, while a younger one, who was more alert, beheaded the peacocks before my very face!"

"Beheaded our peacocks!" cried Hilda. "Oh, who would think of beheading a peacock!"

"They beheaded, plucked, and roasted them," continued Madame Pallersberg; "and as to the geese, I saw them springing headless round the fountain. It was a horrible sight, and—and they slaughtered our pigs, and——"

"Well, well," said her husband, "be satisfied that no human beings lost their lives. As to the geese, I expected nothing else, and would have sent them to the water, if I had not feared it might have attracted attention to the lake and the Chapel-island, which is their favourite place of resort. I won't say that I would not have made free with a goose myself had it come in my way when marching through an enemy's land, so let us put all to rights, and say no more about the matter."

"Very easy for you men to talk so," she replied; "but I should like to know what we are to say to the poor women who put their beds into our cellars?"

"There is nothing to be said. I told them they could not choose a worse place."

" And what has happened to the beds?" asked Hilda.

" They were pitched out of the bins with bayonets," he answered; "rents made in them, and consequently all the feathers were strewed on the ground, which had been previously turned into mud by spilled beer and wine."

" Oh, mamma!" cried Hilda, "Doris was right—the French are dreadful men. I dare say they have killed my rabbits and white pigeons!"

She was right. Of all the animals that four-and-twenty hours previously had afforded Emmeran Waldering so much amusement, the dogs and tame raven alone remained —the former sniffing about the damp straw that was littered profusely in the court; the latter gravely pensive, perched on a water-spout.

Doris was a good deal disgusted to find that the flagged entrance-hall and adjoining store-rooms had been converted into stables, and that careless feet had conveyed wisps of dirty hay far up the stone staircase.

The Waldering pedigree seemed to have given umbrage to some furious Republican, for not only was the glass smashed to atoms, but the parchment cut up with a sword or bayonet—want of time having evidently alone prevented the completion of its destruction.

" We must have this thing patched up some way or other before Sigmund sees it," observed Emmeran, laughing rather irreverently.

" Its restoration," replied Mr. Pallersberg, gravely, "shall be the occupation of my winter evenings."

" And," continued Emmeran, " while you are about it, couldn't you just give the old fellow at the foot of our tree a drapery, or sheepskin, or something to make him look less savage?"

" Dare not take such a liberty without the Director's

permission," said Mr. Pallersberg, beginning to pick the pieces of broken glass from the frame.

The countess, followed by Doris, Hilda, and Frank, were in the meantime ascending the stairs to the second story ; and Emmeran, after a moment's hesitation, followed them, entering the sitting-room unheeded, and looking with some curiosity round him, and through the open door of an adjoining bedroom, where an eager conversation had commenced with Doris's old English maid, who had insisted on remaining with the wardrobes under her care.

"After all, ma'am," said the latter, "we have no reason to complain, for the General that slept here was civil, and told me I might lock the presses and keep the keys ; and the young man they called the Edgekong spoke a little English, and asked a great many questions after he saw the little ivory picture."

" Doris's picture ? the miniature ? "

"Yes, ma'am ; he found it on the table, beside the harp, and asked me if Miss Doris did not sing Irish songs, and if we had all forgotten him, though he had been so long at Garvagh, and would remember us as long as he lived. It was the beard and the whiskers that had changed him, Miss Doris, but he does not look so much amiss after all for a republican and a sans-culottes."

" Louis d'Esterre ! " exclaimed Doris ; " it is odd enough his being here."

"Nothing more probable," said Frank ; "he is, of course, with Moreau, who is related to him some way or other."

" Then I must say, Frank, I wonder you did not apply to him when you were taken prisoner."

" For what purpose ? I knew he would have required my parole, and I had firmly resolved to make my escape the first opportunity that presented itself."

" Oh! I did not think of that," said Doris.

Just then her mother went to the door of the room to speak to Mr. Pallersberg, who had come to consult her about the wounded Austrian and French soldiers left in the castle, to die or recover, as the case might be. She turned back for a moment to say she was going to visit them, and should afterwards go to the village—" Did Doris wish to accompany her? "

" No, thank you, mamma; I know so very little German, and shall be so perfectly useless, that I believe it will be quite as well if I remain quietly here with Frank."

" May I go with you? " asked Hilda.

Her mother held out her hand with a smile; and no sooner was the door closed, than, perfectly indifferent, or rather altogether oblivious of the presence of Emmeran Waldering, Doris and Frank drew a couple of arm-chairs towards the great green stove, that, with its Gothic orna- ments, and niches containing statuettes of saints, occupied the greater part of one side of the room; then placed their feet on footstools, close to the warmed tiles, and became absorbed in a conversation, that commenced by Frank asking Doris if she had learned at last to like her mother?

" Well, I believe I have; certainly better than I ever expected, for you see she is very good and sensible, and remarkably ladylike; but though I am sure she is very fond of me, I can see that she thinks me full of faults; and, some way or other, I never can do or say anything right, which is discouraging, when I remember how differently I was judged at Garvagh."

" We certainly did consider you altogether faultless there," said Frank; "and so you are, Doris, you may take my word for it."

" Yet mamma more than gave me to understand that

she considers I have been somewhat spoiled, though she acknowledges it was hardly to be wondered at when one takes into consideration that I was the only girl in the house, and had seven cousins to obey my commands."

" Well, if we liked to obey you, I suppose there was no great harm done. I cannot imagine what my aunt would wish changed, for you certainly are as near perfection as can well be imagined."

" I am not quite sure of that, Frank ; mamma has not said, but she has made feel sometimes as if I were selfish— in short, an egotist."

" That you are not ; she does not yet know how kind and affectionate you can be when you like people."

" Oh! she is not satisfied with that sort of goodness which is common to all well-disposed persons, but expects me to judge every one leniently, and to be kind to people I don't care about in the least."

" Now, I must say, Doris, that is quite absurd."

" You would not think so, Frank, if you heard her speak on the subject. I don't mean all that about the beam in one's own eye, which you know is in the Sermon on the Mount, and quite true, of course ; but she says, for instance, we should never condemn any one, even when they do wrong, without considering the measure of temptation to which they have been exposed, and that in most cases it is difficult to form an opinion of the extent of culpability."

" It must be rather dull, talking of such things," observed Frank, balancing his chair on the hind legs.

" No, I like it," said Doris ; " I like talking in this way well enough, but I don't like putting it into practice. I judge of people just as I find them ; I like some, and I hate others."

" So do I," said Frank.

" For instance, I hate the French," continued Doris.

" And I also," he chimed in.

" And since I have been here I am beginning to hate the Germans," she added.

" No, you must not hate them," said Frank, " for I'm a German now—or at least an Austrian."

" I don't know any Austrians," said Doris, " but I have taken an antipathy to some Bavarians."

" Not old Pallersberg, I hope," said Frank, " for I think him a capital fellow."

" And what do you think of his wife ? " asked Doris.

" Well, I declare I don't know ; a good sort of woman, rather."

" Exactly ; but because she is good in a small way to the people about here, mamma expects me to overlook, or not perceive, her horrible Swabian brogue and unrefined manners."

" People in this country don't care a straw about brogues," observed Frank. " Count Waldering and Captain Pallersberg thought it a famous thing that we had had that infernal old French governess at Garvagh to teach us her lingo, but they could not at all understand the advantage of my having been educated in England, or your having an English maid to improve your accent."

" And do you know," said Doris, " mamma calls all such things prejudices ; I think she only observes what— not how—people speak. Then fancy her expecting me incessantly to admire the woods and lakes about here, without considering that there is not a gravelled road in the one where it is possible to ride or drive, or a boat on the other that is better than the float over the ferry near Garvagh."

" I have no objection to the woods here," said Frank ;

"they are on a grand scale—something above our planta-
tions, you must allow."

"I should prefer a beech-tree walk or shrubbery, such
as we had at Garvagh," said Doris, thoughtfully; "or the
long avenues, where even the bog parts were made beautiful by flowering rhododendrons and single fir-trees, with
branches sweeping the heath. I am not so insensible to
beauty of that kind as mamma supposes, but I like grounds
kept in order, and well-mowed lawns, and a garden with
glass-houses, and a gardener who knows his business; and
oh, Frank! I now have learned to value such a house as
Garvagh—so quiet and so comfortable! I long for the
carpets and curtains, and the thousand luxuries there, and
especially the library, with its pleasant places for reading,
where one could sit undisturbed, even with a house full of
visitors."

"Yes," said Frank, thoughtfully, "that library is a
pleasant, cheerful room,—I often think of it; but the
visitors were too numerous, Doris; my father was terribly
embarrassed in his affairs lately."

"So mamma told me yesterday," she answered.

"And," he continued, "and that was the chief reason
why I left home, and why we must hope that Feargus will
soon be here too. I wonder what he is about just now,
Doris?"

"Probably coursing in the bogs or out shooting," she
suggested.

"Out shooting," he repeated, musingly; "and then he
will come home and scamper up the stairs when he hears
the dressing-bell has rung, and——"

"There is no dressing-bell here," interposed Doris;
"no one ever thinks of dressing for dinner here as we used
to do, excepting perhaps when there is company; but I
believe no one ever comes here; I do not imagine we have

any neighbours at all, for the people in the town are nobodies ! ''

" Doris, can you fancy you see the drawing-room as they come into it one after the other ? ''

" Oh, yes ! '' she answered, her face lighting up at the recollection; " I think I see my aunt sitting on one of the sofas beside the fireplace, my uncle standing before the fire, and Henry, and John, and George, and Feargus, and most probably some of the Lavilles, and Lady Mary Sullivan, and the dear old Conroys. Frank, I count the days now until I can return to Garvagh. Had my stepfather lived there would have been no chance for me, but now mamma has promised to return as soon as we have peace, or even a truce.''

" Promised to return to Ireland ! '' he exclaimed—" to Garvagh ? ''

" Yes, but she talks of it as a sacrifice made to me, a wonderful effort of affection which I cannot, I confess, appreciate very highly.''

" There you are wrong, Doris, for it is and must be an effort on her part, though you do not understand why, because you have been kept in ignorance of the events that preceded her expatriation or emigration, whichever you choose to call it. She did not leave Garvagh willingly, but will undoubtedly return there most unwillingly, and I will tell you the reason.'' Here he lowered his voice to a sort of emphatic whisper, and, with the fluency of speech peculiar to his country, told Doris the mournful story of her mother's first marriage.

Emmeran, who did not understand a word of English, had nevertheless found watching the speakers sufficiently interesting to induce him to remain a silent and motionless observer near one of the windows ; and when Doris began to listen with evident painfully intense interest to her cousin's eloquent recital of events that had occurred before her birth, but yet so nearly concerning her, he taxed his imagination to the utmost in surmises respecting the subject of discourse.

"Frank, I ought to have heard this sooner," she observed reproachfully, when he had concluded and seemed to expect her to speak. "Had you told me this before we came here, I should have felt and acted quite differently towards my mother, whose only fault seems to me now, the having forgiven my father his altogether unpardonable crime!"

"Oh, come, Doris, don't take the matter so very seriously; all stratagems are fair in love and war, you know, and there was not a shadow of a hope for your father excepting in this desperate expedient, for I have heard that my aunt had a score of adorers, and more offers of wedding-rings than she had fingers on her hands to place them on."

"No excuse," said Doris, shaking her head.

"Don't say so, dear; for if we had remained at Garvagh, and you had ever thought of marrying Henry, I won't answer for myself that I——"

"Frank!"

"Well, there is no use in talking about such things; my aunt was not the first in our family whose marriage was compulsory."

"I hope she may be the last," said Doris, gravely.

"So do I, for it must be a damned disagreeable ——"

"Now, Frank," cried Doris, impatiently, "I have told you several times that people here don't swear; it is very wrong, and very unpleasant to hear."

"Yes, dear, you certainly have reminded me often enough that people here don't swear in drawing-rooms; that people here don't drink after dinner, as in Ireland, and so on; all very praiseworthy and proper, no doubt;

but for a person who professes to be disgusted with every-thing German, as you do, I don't see why the devil——"

" Frank ! "

" Well, why the deuce——"

" That means just the same thing."

" Speak plainly, Doris, and confess that you have the old prejudice against everything Irish."

" No, Frank, quite the contrary ; but it is only since I came abroad that I have learned to appreciate Ireland as I ought."

" Precisely what has happened to me," said Frank ; " I no longer wish to be taken for an Englishman, and have written to Henry to beg he will never again think of leaving off the 'O' before his name : we ought to value it as the French do their ' *de*,' and the Germans their ' *von* ; ' in short, as a proof that we are descended from——"

" From 'decent people,' " interposed Doris, laughing ; " unfortunately, however, no one knows anything about that here."

·" But most people, I suppose, know that ' O ' is a peculiar prefix to Irish names ? "

" Perhaps they do, perhaps not," she answered. " I remember the time I should have preferred a name without an ' O '—an English name of three or four syllables ; and it is only very, very lately that I have learned to like being an Irishwoman."

" And I," said Frank, " to boast of being an Irishman, and to value our ' O ' as a sort of stamp of my country ; for as the rhyme says,—

> * By Mac and O
> You'll surely know
>   True Irishmen alway ;
> But if they lack
> Both O and Mac,
>   No Irishmen are they ! ' "

CHAPTER VIII.

NEUTRAL GROUND.

EMMERAN WALDERING had left the room unperceived, and the short winter day was drawing to a close before Frank and Doris began to feel hungry and to wonder when dinner would be ready.

"We must not be impatient to-day," observed Doris, "for most probably there is no sort of provision in the house, and we shall have to wait until a messenger can procure supplies from the town."

"If," suggested Frank, "if our enemies have not created a famine there also. But suppose we go and inquire about the wounded ; there may be some Austrians among them ; and as I suspect my aunt is one of those women who will make no sort of difference between a wounded friend or foe, we had better undertake to look after our own people—that is, the Austrians, you know."

In the meantime, Doris's mother had gone to the village, and with dismay seen the devastation caused there by four-and-twenty hours' campaigning : horses had been seized and carried off, all the cattle that had voluntarily returned in the evening to their homesteads had been slaughtered, every kind of provision consumed, and an incalculable quantity wantonly destroyed, while the houses were crowded with soldiers whose wounds had been sufficiently slight to enable them to continue the march from Hohenlinden, but who now lay prostrated by fever brought on by fatigue and inclement weather.

The villagers were wonderfully resigned ; they seemed to feel the uselessness of complaints, were even thankful for what had been retrieved and that no one had been made houseless, and they set about putting their dwellings into order without delay. The want of bread had been severely felt until Mr. Pallersberg produced the flour he had concealed in the island; and when it became evident that the inhabitants of the castle were in no respect better off than the poorest among them for the time being, the people ceased altogether to murmur, and were as attentive as circumstances permitted to the unfortunate invalids left to their care.

Doris met her mother returning home; she looked fatigued and dejected, and, without speaking, gave her daughter a note that had been left for her at the village inn. It was from Mr. d'Esterre, requesting her good offices for a friend and comrade compelled by dangerous wounds to remain at Westenried.

"Cannot we have this poor man brought to the castle, mamma? it would be so much more convenient."

"He cannot be moved, Doris—he is dying."

"You have seen him?"

"Yes, and promised to return, as no one can understand or speak to him."

"Have you any objection to my going on to the inn?"

"None whatever. But this young officer is frightfully wounded in his face, Doris, and I do not know whether or not you can bear seeing anything of that kind."

Doris looked alarmed.

"You had better not go," continued her mother; "his jaw is completely shattered, and the wound of so dangerous a nature that he made extraordinary efforts to reach the next town in order to put himself under the care of a surgeon; but at last he found it impossible any longer to bear the motion of a carriage, and remained here, most probably to die a few hours hence."

" We can send for the surgeon, can we not ? " asked Doris.

" I doubt his being able to come, for there are, of course, more wounded left in the town than here ; however, your friend Mr. d'Esterre said he would endeavour to send some one, and got the address of a surgeon from the innkeeper."

" If I thought I could be of any use,——" began Doris.

" I believe," suggested her mother, " this unfortunate young man would be thankful for a look of sympathy if accompanied by a few words spoken in his native language, giving him the assurance that he was not altogether friendless."

" Then I will go," said Doris, resolutely.

" Do so, dear girl, and you may depend on my coming to release you as soon as I possibly can."

But when her mother joined her an hour afterwards she found Doris by no means so useless as she had supposed. The surgeon had arrived, but immediately pronounced the case utterly hopeless, and without a moment's hesitation both mother and daughter resolved to remain with the young foreigner during the night that proved the last of his life. His death, which took place soon after daybreak, was the first that Doris had ever witnessed, and made a deep and painful impression. As she gazed shudderingly on the corpse, more disfigured with wounds than even Count Waldering's had been, she exclaimed, " Oh ! mamma, war is much more dreadful in reality than any one can at all imagine from description ! "

Her mother assented, and seemed inclined to hurry her departure from a scene that now agitated her to no purpose.

" I did not think it possible," continued Doris, looking back into the room with tearful eyes,—" I did not think it possible that I could feel so much commiseration for a stranger and a foreigner, especially a Frenchman; but it was terribly afflicting to see this poor young man die in such torture, far away from all his friends and relations."

"And his fate is that of thousands, Doris."

"Then I trust we shall soon have peace, mamma, on any terms; for, indeed, it would be better to give the French everything they desire than continue sacrificing life in this way."

"Unfortunately," replied her mother, "the more this French Consul gets the more he requires, so that while he lives I am inclined to think no peace will be of long continuance. But now, Doris, we must return to the castle, where there are so many invalids that it almost deserves the name of hospital. I fear, however, what you have seen this night will make you unwilling to enter a sick-room again for some time."

"No, mamma, I will go where you go, and at least try to be useful."

"Where the sacrifice of time and personal comfort is chiefly required, Doris, people in our position can always, if they wish it, find opportunities of being useful: at all events, you have convinced me during the past night that you would not require a long noviciate to fit you for the order of the Sisters of Charity."

"Do you, indeed, think so, mamma?" asked Doris, exceedingly pleased at the unexpected praise; "then I will assist you and Madame Pallersberg to take care of the wounded soldiers now at the castle."

"More than the half of them are French, Doris?"

"Yes, mamma; but I now understand what you said about hospital-wards being completely neutral ground."

CHAPTER IX.

THE FAMILY COMPACT.

SOME months subsequent to the events related in the fore-going chapters, the peace of Luneville was concluded between the First Consul Napoleon Bonaparte and the then Emperor of Germany. An inauspicious peace, in which, resigning the territory on the left bank of the Rhine and leaving the so-despoiled princes to seek indemnification among themselves, a disunion was caused that finally led to the dissolution of the German Empire. Emissaries were sent to Paris to remonstrate or protest against the spoliation, and Napoleon seized the opportunity of making judicious concessions in order to turn some of his bitterest enemies into friends and allies. It was on this occasion that the first separate treaty of peace was made between Bavaria and France, and consequently the political opinions of Count Sigmund Waldering, when he returned to Westenried in the autumn of the following year, were very different from those entertained by him immediately after the battle of Hohenlinden. He came this time to accept and thank the Countess Waldering for the proposal lately made by her to remain in Bavaria and await his convenience for the liquidation of her claims on the estate; he had also to inform her that the opportunity she desired for the return of her daughter to Ireland had been found, as a family with whom she could travel in perfect security would pass through Munich in the course of the ensuing week.

"Thank you! I am, however, happy to say my daughter's wish to remain with me has induced her to give up all idea of returning to Ireland for the present."

"Then I presume it is your intention to reside chiefly in Munich?"

"By no means. I may go there occasionally, on account of Hilda; but Doris already possesses most of the accomplishments which would have made a residence in a town desirable for their acquirement."

"Knowing that you consult her wishes on most occasions," he observed, smiling a little ironically, "I may, I suppose, take it for granted that she is quite satisfied with this arrangement?"

"Perfectly. She is becoming attached to me and her sister, and beginning to feel at home here. Mr. Pallersberg is giving her lessons in German; she accompanies him on the harp or pianoforte when he wishes to play the violin; and then she rides, and is fond of boating and gardening, and all sorts of country occupations."

"For a year or two this may answer; but afterwards?" he asked.

"In times like these it is better not to make plans for the future," she answered. "I am satisfied that my daughter not only voluntarily proposed remaining here, but was more shocked at the idea of a separation than I had at all expected."

At this moment the sound of a harp from the adjoining room so completely attracted his attention that he remained perfectly silent for some time, listening in astonishment to music that might have been supposed to proceed from the dexterous fingers of a first-rate artist.

This instrument—then so much esteemed in Ireland—had been preferred to all others by Doris, and even as a child she had played with a strength and skill that had given her a sort of celebrity. At fifteen, she might have competed with most public performers; and if her mother at times felt inclined to regret the many hours that must

have been daily devoted to the acquisition of this accomplishment, she certainly found it difficult, if not impossible,
to do so on occasions like the present.

During the first pause Sigmund rose, opened the door
of communication, and poured forth a flood of eulogium,
mixed with professions of surprise and admiration, that
were heard by the youthful performer with a composure
verging so manifestly on indifference, that he stopped short
in the midst of a request that his " fair cousin " would continue to delight him with her enchanting national music.

" National music ! " repeated Doris ; " would you not
rather hear the Austrian ' God preserve the Emperor ' ? or
—no—the ' Marseillaise ' will suit you better now ; " and
with a mischievous energy, that might have been mistaken
for enthusiasm by a French auditor, she made the room
ring with the ill-famed melody.

Had Doris looked a whit less pretty and graceful while
enacting this piece of saucy censure, Sigmund, though a
complete man of the world, might have in some way shown
his displeasure ; but war of any kind with pretty faces was
not his habit, so he observed, good-humouredly, " I never
expected to hear the ' Marseillaise ' with pleasure, but you
have convinced me that it is very inspiriting."

" So much the better," said Doris, " for you will soon
have to march to it."

" Not so, mademoiselle ; peace is signed with Napoleon,
and I am most willing to arrange the preliminaries of something similar with you."

Doris shook her head very resolutely, and scarcely
seemed to touch the strings of the harp while producing a
succession of sweeping minor chords.

" I am sorry," began Sigmund, " very sorry, that
I alarmed you so unnecessarily about your cousin the first
time we met ; " and then added, on perceiving that his

regrets obtained little credence, "the bearer of ill news seldom makes a favourable impression, and I fear I shall require long to efface that evening from your memory."

"Just—exactly—as long as I live!" replied Doris.

"You are not serious?"

"Perfectly."

"Am I to consider this a declaration of hatred?" he asked, smiling.

"Consider it what you please," she answered, carelessly, while beginning to cover her harp with its brown leather case.

"I shall make you forget, or at least forgive, this offence before long," he said, following her as she walked across the room towards the sofa where her mother was seated.

"I hope you may," she answered quietly; "for it is much pleasanter liking than disliking people one cannot altogether avoid seeing."

His answer to this speech was a perfectly hearty laugh, so thoroughly was he amused at the complete and unexpected *sang froid* of the young foreigner. He had been surprised that she had not blushed at least a little when he had approached her, still more so that she had evinced no embarrassment at his warmly-expressed admiration of her musical talents, accompanied by looks which he had intended should convey the idea even to her youthful mind that he admired herself quite as much as her music; but he had yet to learn that Doris was so accustomed to the society of men, and considered their attentions so much a matter of course, that she attached no sort of importance to words or looks that would have put a German girl of the same age into a flutter of embarrassment and agitation.

The person who best understood the little scene just enacted was Doris's mother, and she was more amused than surprised to see her daughter retire to the most

distant window, and become completely engrossed in torturing a piece of muslin in the then most fashionable
manner.

Sigmund turned to Hilda, and hoped she would explain
to her sister that he was not often so impatient and unamiable as on the unlucky evening they had first met.

"I have told her so," she replied, "but she will not believe me; she says you are proud and heartless."

"Well," he said, with affected earnestness, "I must
hope that time will enable me to prove the contrary; for it
would be very unpleasant if she were not to learn to like
me before I become her brother-in-law."

This allusion to his marriage with Hilda was heard by
the very youthful *fiancée* with childish indifference. No
efforts on the part of her mother had been able to prevent
Count Waldering, during his lifetime, from speaking openly
and frequently of this family compact, nor had Sigmund
himself thought it necessary to use any reserve on the subject either during the infancy of his cousin or now, after
having assured his aunt, in a formal letter, that he was
willing, when Hilda had attained her sixteenth year, to
fulfil the engagement made with his uncle concerning their
marriage.

The countess looked up hastily, and drew Hilda towards
her, while she observed, "I hoped to have had an opportunity of speaking to you alone concerning your last letter,
Sigmund: for I believe it would be better both for you and
Hilda if this engagement were cancelled. Four years hence
you may wish for freedom; Hilda is now scarcely twelve
years old, and at that age cannot possibly decide on so
important a project."

No one knows the exact value of things or persons until
the chance of their loss had become possible or probable.
Sigmund Waldering had first felt well-disposed towards

5

Hilda because she had not been of a sex to deprive him of an inheritance he had almost learned to consider his by right; and secondly, because she was an extremely pretty and engaging child: nevertheless, a year previously, on finding himself actually heir-apparent, he had risen so much in his own estimation that necessity more than inclination had induced him to continue and latterly to renew his engagement. The disposition on the part of his aunt to release him had the immediate effect of fully convincing him of the advantages of a union with Hilda, and he therefore hastened to answer:

"I cannot agree with you, my dear aunt; for besides being in a manner bound by a solemn promise to my late uncle, I really have become so accustomed to this engagement that I cannot feel free unless made so by Hilda herself."

"A few years hence——" began his aunt.

"No," he said turning to Hilda; "child as she is, she can decide, at least, as to the continuance of our engagement. Tell me, Hilda, will you not be my *fiancée?*"

"I thought I must be," she answered, smiling; "but indeed, mamma, I have no objection to be engaged to Sigmund, though I don't at all wish to marry him!"

"You see," said her mother, "it is absolutely absurd your talking to her in this way at present."

"By no means," replied Sigmund, laughing; "I think we are in a fair way to understand each other. Now come here, Hilda; you have no objection—that is, you rather like being engaged? Is it not so?"

"Yes."

"And who made you like it, dear?"

"Grandmamma and Mina Pallersberg."

"Probably, when you were in Munich the year before last?"

"Yes; grandmamma said it was a great advantage my not having to lose my name, and that all I should inherit from my aunt in Ulm would remain in the family; and Mina said——" she paused.

"What did Mina say?"

"That she could imagine nothing more delightful than being engaged—especially to you."

"Indeed!" and Sigmund coloured very perceptibly, perhaps in the consciousness of having taken some pains to gain the heart of his grandmother's youthful *protégée* and companion.

"Doris thinks quite the contrary," continued Hilda.

"So your sister gave her opinion also? I am curious to hear it."

"She does not at all wish to be engaged," replied Hilda, "especially not to you, for she thinks you quite odious."

Sigmund laughed. "This," he said, "is a case of strong prejudice, which, however, I do not despair of being able to overcome. We only require time to become better acquainted; and now," he added, turning to his aunt, "may I hope for your permission to ride with Hilda and her sister while I remain here?"

"Of course; but remember Hilda must not attempt to leap fences, or race in the meadow with Doris."

"I did not imagine that young ladies ever thought of such things," he observed, glancing towards the window where Doris was sitting.

"I don't suppose they do here," said Doris, "because your horses can seldom be induced to take a leap."

"You must allow me to prove the contrary," he said, rising.

"By all means. Let us try the broad drains in the marsh-meadow to day—now."

Sigmund left the room, accompanied by Hilda, jumping

joyously, and Doris was following, when her mother called her back.

"Doris, your sister is not to go into the meadow with you."

"No, mamma."

"And—and—do not speak to her any more about this engagement to Sigmund; the less she is reminded of it the better."

"Yes, mamma; I suppose you fear I might prejudice her against him; but I assure you I don't intend to hate or like people until I know them, in future. You shall see me put into practice all you have said on that subject."

"And yet," said her mother smiling, "it is scarcely half-an-hour since you told Sigmund pretty plainly that you disliked him!"

"Yes, mamma; that slipped out some way or other, because, you see, he certainly did make a most unpleasant impression on me that first time I saw him; and even when he was just now laughing and speaking so gently to Hilda, I could perfectly recall his scowl, and harsh, rude manner, while answering so very unkindly my inquiries about Frank."

"At that time, Doris, he thought you the cause of my resolution to return to Ireland, which would have inconvenienced him greatly; and to-day, when he made a sort of effort to conciliate you, he had heard from me that you had consented to remain here—an arrangement that he naturally supposes calculated to make me less than ever likely to press the refunding of my fortune; and I believe this impression will be the cause of most of his attentions to you in future."

"Now, mamma, just tell me one thing; you do not like him, do you?"

"I scarcely know him, Doris."

"Then why did you not insist on breaking off this engagement?"

"Because Hilda's father wished it, and made the promise to Sigmund years ago."

"And so poor dear Hilda *must* marry him?"

"Not for some years, at all events."

"And if she then tell him that she hates him?"

"She is not likely to have any cause for hatred, Doris, though it is very probable she may not be greatly attached to him."

"But in that case, mamma, you will not allow her to marry him?"

"I shall let her do precisely what she pleases; her father's promise to Sigmund will prevent me from interfering."

"Well, mamma, I at least will remain with you, for I have resolved never to be what is called 'in love' with any one."

"A very wise resolution, Doris, and I should like you, half-a-dozen years hence, to give me the assurance that you have kept it."

"You, of course, mamma, hate all men?"

"No, my dear; why should I?"

"That dreadful marriage with my father."

"Don't you think you had better put on your habit, Doris?"

"Yes, mamma, directly; only one word—you must allow that, if my father was lawless and violent, Hilda's was vindictive and selfish. It was quite horrible his making you send me away, and hating me so unreasonably."

"He endeavoured to like you when you returned to me, Doris, and who then hated unreasonably?"

"Mamma, I never *could* have liked him."

" You said the same of me, Doris, a year ago—and now ? "

" And now I love you better than any one in the world, and will never leave you again."

" Until you find some one you like as well, or, perhaps, a little better," suggested her mother.

" Mamma, I hope you have some reliance on me, and do not think such a thing possible ? "

" Possible, probable, desirable, even, some years hence ; and now don't talk any more about what you do not understand, and, above all things, learn never to keep people waiting for you."

" No one objected to wait for me at Garvagh."

" Perhaps not; but you are not again likely to have seven humble servants under the name of cousins ! "

" Sigmund calls himself one, and I shall put him to the proof, if you have no objection, mamma ? "

" None whatever; he is not likely to allow you to be troublesome."

This permission gave infinite satisfaction to Doris, and she tried the patience of her German cousin, and future brother-in-law, in every possible way. Strange to say, her wilfulness amused him ; and, while on all occasions requiring the most absolute obedience from Hilda, he yielded, without an attempt at resistance, to a tyranny that openly defied his power of endurance.

CHAPTER X.

SPARRING.

THREE years passed over in quiet monotony, only interrupted by a few months spent in Munich, for educational purposes, and the same in Innsbruck, while re-letting some houses there that had been purchased by Doris's father, and were now the property of her mother.

The Director regularly passed six weeks every summer at Westenried, while Sigmund and Emmeran paid flying visits at all seasons, and found themselves from year to year more at home with their aunt and cousins.

In the autumn of 1804, the whole family assembled to celebrate Hilda's sixteenth birthday. Cousins german and German cousins learned to live together in perfect amity, and nothing disturbed the serenity of their intercourse until Frank O'More rode one afternoon into the court, and informed his aunt that he had come to spend a few weeks at Westenried, as he began to fear a longer absence might cause him to be forgotten altogether.

During the first ten days Frank and Doris seemed chiefly to live for each other, walking, talking, riding, and boating, as much as possible apart from the rest of the family, and, when chance gave them companions, apparently unconscious of their presence. They spoke frequently in a language which, though ostensibly English, was nearly unintelligible to their hearers, using expressions not only familiar to their family, but even in their neighbourhood in Ireland. Is there, however, a large and united family who have not their own peculiar language, composed of children's words, remarks of grandfathers and grandmothers, old servants and favourite peasants, containing a world of meaning, or producing a crowd of recollections to the initiated ? The vocabulary of such languages is far more copious in Ireland than elsewhere, and was, in days of yore, more so than now, from the then habitually extensive hospitality, which brought the young people of wide-extending neighbourhoods into constant communication; when, therefore, we mention that *sobriquets* were usual among our branch of the O'More's, and then add to them the various Irish names of persons and places, Sigmund may be excused, notwithstanding his knowledge of English, for supposing that Doris and her cousin occasionally fell insensibly into what he imagined their native language, namely, Irish, and was surprised to find that the impression made on his ear so much resembled English, as far as hissing and chirping went.

The Director, who was accustomed to find Doris willing to receive instruction in German, and ever anxious to read the new works of Goethe and Schiller, began openly to accuse her of idleness and indifference to his favourite authors ; her laughing excuse that the books were not " on leave," and could be read when dear Frank was gone, in no way satisfying him.

Emmeran also, on perceiving that Doris would neither endeavour to convert him from his admiration of Napoleon, nor speculate with him on the inhabitants of other worlds, felt his vacation seriously curtailed of its usual amusement; and Sigmund became gloomy and discontented, in a manner that his father could only account for when Hilda's reserve yielded to Frank's cordial familiarity, and she became as unconstrained as Doris herself in her intercourse with him.

This monopolizing of both maidens on the part of Frank began at length to give umbrage, and the Director informed Hilda that he feared Sigmund would be seriously offended if she treated him any longer with such marked neglect.

" Why cannot he amuse himself with Mina Pallersberg as he used to do ? " was the careless answer. " I never was the least offended at his neglect, though it has been marked enough this long time. Mina says I have no right to expect his exclusive attention, or he mine, until we have been solemnly affianced."

"Unfortunately," observed the Director, " your mother wishes to postpone your betrothal for some time longer, but if you prefer it now, I am sure Sigmund will be the last person to object."

" Don't be too sure of that," cried Hilda, laughing ; " I have a great mind to let you ask him, just to hear what he will say."

" Nothing more easy," he replied, looking towards the open door of an adjoining room. " Sigmund," he said, slightly raising his voice, " Sigmund answer for yourself."

" I have no wish in any way to control Hilda," said Sigmund, coming slowly forward ; " we are, as she justly observes, not yet affianced, and if she prefer this young Irish adventurer to me, I believe there is no reason why she should not indulge the fancy ; that is, supposing O'More willing for her sake to resign his cousin Doris."

" There, uncle," cried Hilda, extrémely piqued and too unversed in the ways of the world to attempt any concealment of her feelings, " you see how he speaks to me. I am sure," she continued, with a vain effort to repress the tears that already stood trembling in her eyelids, " I am sure, had my father lived, he would never have compelled me to fulfil this—this—hateful engagement."

" You shall never be compelled by me——" began Sigmund, resentfully, while his father, much amazed at the apparent wish for release on both sides, hastened to interfere.

" Come, come, Hilda, this will never do," he said, half-reproachfully; "you have lately put Sigmund's patience to a trial, that, were I a young man, I should have ill borne, I can tell you. There seems to me, however, to be jealousy on both sides, and where there is jealousy there is love."

Hilda, who in her heart considered herself bound to fulfil the engagement made by her father, blushed deeply, and murmured some words indicative of a disposition to listen to any excuses or explanations that might be offered; Sigmund, however, walked to one of the windows in sullen silence.

"I think, Hilda," began the Director, after a pause, "you had better make some slight apology to Sigmund, not only for your late neglect of him, but also for the strong expression used when speaking of your engagement."

"I cannot do more than say that I should never have had an idea of not fulfilling my engagement if he had not shown himself so ready to break it off."

"I thought," said her uncle, smiling, "you accused him of paying too much attention to Mina Pallersberg?"

"Oh, I don't mind his paying attention to *her*," she answered, looking up, "that's of no consequence; but I don't choose him to forbid my liking Frank, when, as Mina says, he is himself quite downrightly in love with Doris."

Father and son looked at each other, and both coloured deeply.

The Director walked up and down the room for some time in silence, then seating himself beside his niece, observed, "It was very wrong of Mina to put such ideas into your head, my dear child, and I am sure, on maturer consideration, you will perceive that her suspicions are utterly without foundation."

"I don't think I shall," she answered, apparently more amused than angry. "Sigmund said yesterday that Doris was a perfect Saint Cecilia when playing the harp."

" Well," answered her uncle, " I think so too—a saint at least—almost an angel; yet I hope you won't think me for this reason 'quite downrightly in love.' "

Hilda laughed : " No, I don't, but Mina does."

" Indeed. It seems that Mina, to say the least, is a very injudicious friend, and not very safe companion for you. I really should like to know where she has acquired so much knowledge of such matters."

" In Munich, with grandmamma, but chiefly from Sigmund; he has told her all sorts of things, and she has told me a good many."

It would be difficult to describe the expression of Sigmund's face as he strode towards his cousin, and, laying his hand heavily on her arm, muttered, " What has she told you ? "

" What you told her, I suppose : at all events, enough to make my boating and riding with dear cousin Frank very excusable, even if you should not quite like it. Now, you see, Sigmund, I don't mind your paying attention to Mina; for as she says herself, it is only because she is a couple of years older than I am, and, after all, means nothing serious. But with Doris the case is different. Mina says you are making yourself ridiculous, for she knows, and so do I, that Doris would reject you without a moment's consideration."

" And is that all you fear ? "

" That is all, I assure you. She does not care in the least for attentions from you or any one. She says that being romantic and falling in love is absurd, so she has resolved never to marry, and when she is old enough intends to make a will and leave everything she possesses to Frank."

" Oh, indeed ! What a pity she happens to be half-a-dozen years younger than he is—not to mention his chances of receiving some ounces of lead either in his head or heart before the time comes for entering into possession of this inheritance!"

"There is no help for that, poor fellow! as he cannot leave the army at pleasure as you intend to do, though I do not think he would if he could."

"So much the better, as he is just fit for what he is, and nothing else."

"If you mean a perfectly intrepid cavalry officer," began Hilda, eagerly, "a beautiful rider—a—a——"

"I mean an Irish soldier of fortune, with all the faults of his nation."

"And the good qualities also," interposed Hilda.

"Well, perhaps so, but even they verge on faults, if not vices; he is good-natured enough to be easily led into folly; generous when he has nothing to give; gentlemanlike in his habits, which tempts him to extravagance; courageous, so that he is feared as a duellist——"

"You had better not go on, Sigmund," she exclaimed angrily, "or I shall be obliged to think you envious as well as jealous."

"And," asked their grandmother, who just then entered the room, "and of whom *can* Sigmund be either?"

"Certainly not of the person in question," he answered haughtily, while he bent his head with real or affected deference over the hand of the old lady and led her to an arm-chair.

"Hilda, my treasure, what is the matter? Who has vexed you?"

"They have been quarrelling, mother," said the Director; "but lovers' quarrels are said to be the renewal of love, and as jealousy was the cause on both sides, I am now convinced they are more attached to each other than we ever ventured to expect."

"I don't think I was jealous," said Hilda, playing with the long thick curls of her dark hair as they rested on the table beside her; "in fact, I am sure I was not."

"Nor was I," said Sigmund, "and you must not for a moment suppose that my father's reprimand was at my instigation."

"Then it seems we have been quarrelling for nothing," cried Hilda, laughing, and extending her hand, which he lazily approached, raised carelessly to his lips, and then, without speaking another word, slowly sauntered out of the room.

"In my youth," said the old lady, shaking her head, and with it the perfectly fashionable but indescribable half-turban, half-cap, that surmounted her slightly-powdered grey hair, "in my youth, young men were different. Your grandfather, Hilda, would have kneeled at my feet, and lingered at my side, after a reconciliation; but those good old times will never return; men have lost all sentiment, and are becoming from day to day more prosaic!"

CHAPTER XI.

THE SHOCK.

SIGMUND's sauntering step became a quick walk as he crossed the court and passed under the archway, and on the bridge his foot fell so heavily that it attracted the attention of Mina Pallersberg, and induced her to open and look out of the window of the room in her mother's apartments, which she always occupied when at Westenried. This was probably what Sigmund intended, for he turned round, raised his hat, waved it before him, and then, returning to the court, entered the garden, and walked through it and the orchard to the boat-house, where, folding his arms, he stood beside the entrance and awaited the arrival of the figure in white that he expected would soon reach the same place by a more circuitous route.   He did not raise his eyes as Mina approached, but when she stood beside him and looked anxiously in his face, he asked abruptly, "What have you said to Hilda?"   •

"To Hilda?"

"Yes; she informs me you have told her all sorts of things about me—and others!"

"Dear Sigmund, I was afraid she might have observed or suspected something, and so I——"

"You thought it necessary to lead her jealous thoughts into another channel?"

"She was not jealous, Sigmund—could not be, for she does not care more for you than you do for her."

"I tell you she does, and not half an hour ago renewed her engagement with me, when I gave her an opportunity of making herself free if she had desired it."

"And you *have* renewed it?"

"After a manner, yes—it was unavoidable."

"And without thinking of me? Oh, Sigmund!"

"It was no betrothal—we are just where we were yesterday; but you deserve this, and more, Mina, for having brought Doris's name in question. Of her Hilda might be jealous; of you, never."

"Not even when you fulfil your promise to me, Sigmund?"

"I tell you never," he repeated.

"I believe you are right," she said, colouring deeply; "Hilda will never be jealous of either of us. With her beauty, rank, and fortune, she will easily find some one else that she can like as well, or better, than she does you;

besides which, I do not think her capable of a strong attachment to any one."

"Then why did you try to persuade *me* she liked Frank O'More ? "

"She likes his attentions, and told me repeatedly that he was the dearest, handsomest creature she had ever seen in her life! Vanity and love of admiration make her wish to attract him."

"He is her cousin," began Sigmund.

"So are you," she interposed, quickly.

"Yes; and I think her as much attached to me as she can be to any one," said Sigmund, decidedly; and he believed this, for men are wonderfully tenacious on such subjects; "not," he added cynically, "not attached as you are, Mima, for interest and affection in your case go hand in hand."

"Sigmund, how can you be so cruel! " she cried, clasping her hands.

"And how," he retorted angrily—"how could you dare to say that I loved Doris ? "

"Because you do—I know you do," she cried, passionately. "I have no fear of Hilda, even with the prospect of a betrothal; but Doris has fascinated you and all at Westenried—my father, mother, the Director himself."

"So you informed Hilda, it seems; but the idea of the Director's being captivated is merely diverting."

"No, no, no," cried Mina, "it is dreadful."

"I tell you it is diverting," he replied, "and cannot in any way affect you."

"It can; for would not you be the most dangerous of rivals for him ? and will he not insist on your marriage with Hilda to remove all competition ? "

"What a head for intrigue you have, Mina—you might be two-and-thirty instead of two-and-twenty; but your

imagination is too wild on this occasion, and though he
certainly did his best to patch up my quarrel with Hilda
just now, I cannot bring myself to believe anything so very
preposterous. Be it, however, as it may, Mina, I must
forbid your enlightening my cousin on such subjects in
future. With regard to your own personal concerns, it is
unnecessary for me to recommend prudence."

"Quite," said Mina; "but surely we might find opportunities of seeing and speaking to each other more
frequently."

"If you can manage them without compromising yourself or me, I am sure I have no objection," he answered.

At this moment the sound of an approaching boat
attracted their attention. Mina retreated under the trees
of the orchard; Sigmund moved from the door of the boat-
house, careless whether or not he were seen; but leaning
against the sun-dried planks that formed the side, he saw
through an aperture of the warp wood the clumsy boat
paddled slowly into shade by the youthful soldier of whom
he spoke so slightingly, and thought, in spite of himself, so
highly. Not for any consideration would he have said that
Frank was handsome, but as he saw him standing in the
boat, his slight, perfectly-proportioned figure swinging
backwards and forwards, the afternoon sun glowing on his
animated countenance, he admired and hated him in nearly
equal proportions.

Unconscious of observation, Frank pushed the boat to
the low wall that served as landing-place, and said, while
assisting his aunt to land, "Tell Hilda she must come
directly, as we intend to cross the lake, and walk on the
Roman road until supper time."

"And I suppose, if she will not join you," said his aunt,
in reply, "I had better send some one to let you know."

"She *must* come," he answered, "and if not here directly

I shall go for her;" then, stepping over the planks, he seated himself in the stern of the boat between Doris and Emmeran, the latter continuing a conversation that, though hitherto apparently carried on between him and his aunt, had been intended for the edification of Doris herself.

"Granting that spirit is the sense of being——,"

"Bless me! are you still among the spirits?" cried Frank. "I hoped my aunt would have carried them all off with her."

"We were talking of spirit, not spirits," explained Doris.

"Excuse me," said Emmeran, "but spirit is composed of innumerable free and independent spiritual beings, each of which, apart from the whole, pursues its peculiar——"

"I tell you what," said Frank, "if you won't stop this bothering sort of talk, I'll go for Hilda!"

"Go," said Doris, laughing, "we dont want you."

This little speech gave infinite satisfaction to Sigmund; he watched Frank striding over the benches of the boat, and for some time paid no attention either to Emmeran's look of pleasure or the eager continuation of his explanation. When he again began to listen, he was rather amused at the topic of conversation chosen by his visionary brother, and the more so when he observed that he spoke in a rather pedantic and expounding style, evidently playing lecturer to the youthful but not unintelligent hearer, who opened a little wider her large pensive eyes while listening with an air of the profoundest attention.

"You must always bear in mind that we are not purely spiritual beings," he continued; "we are the union of an individual spirit with the most individual and highest state of nature—the organized human body! The spirit enters by this union into time; its eternity becomes henceforward composed of periods which we may call human lives. Am I clear? Do you understand?"

"Ye—es," answered Doris, hesitatingly; "you mean that your soul came into your body, and will remain in it during your life."

"I spoke of spirit in a general sense," he answered; "we shall come hereafter to the discussion of our "*I*," and "*not I*," and "*positive I*."

Doris nodded gently in acquiescence.

"The spirit is to a certain extent restricted, not to say imprisoned, by this incorporation, but gains on the other hand experience of the nature of matter. The union of spirit with matter is of short duration; the human form taken by the spirit falls as systematically back into the substance of which it was originally composed, as it increased and grew to perfection. This is quite clear."

"Quite," said Doris. "We grow up, and grow old, and——die."

"Exactly ; and death is the beginning of a new life for the spirit, that individual and independent continues to fulfil its destiny in eternity."

"You mean," said Doris, " in another and better world —in Heaven ? "

"Yes, I mean another world ; and may we not suppose that we have been in one before we came here ? "

"I don't know," she answered, thoughtfully ; "but in that case I think we should have some recollection of what we had seen and heard there."

"Why so ? What do you remember of your infancy ? What can you recall of your thoughts and acts at exactly this time last year ? Nothing, or next to nothing; but it does not follow that you did not think or act then, or that what you experienced is lost because you cannot bring it back to your mind distinctly. So it may be with the recollection of a former life ; if it were necessary for us to remember, we should do so."

"But it is at least remarkable," said Doris, "that of the millions of people who have lived in this world, not one has been conscious of having previously existed elsewhere."

"Are you sure of that?" he asked, earnestly. "*I* at least have had moments of vague recollections—floating uncertain visions."

"Oh, tell me all about them," cried Doris, eagerly.

"I cannot, for I was scarcely conscious of them at the time, and unable to recall them distinctly afterwards."

"Had you these visions in the long twilight of summer evenings?" she asked, in a low voice; "and were you alone in a large room gradually darkening, watching from the window the lengthening shadows of the trees upon the lawn—not exactly thinking, rather listening to distant sounds that brought fitful recollections of —— ?" She stopped.

"Of what?" he asked, quickly.

"Of places—and things—and people."

"That's it," he cried, eagerly; "places and people you were unable to name."

"But," said Doris, smiling, "my mother thinks I may have seen them during my infancy in Germany; and it is certain that all such recollections have ceased since I returned to this country."

"I rather think," he observed, slowly, "that as we grow older we lose these recollections—they are chased by the variety of other and newer impressions. Recall the events of your past life in this world, and you will find that only a few and not very important circumstances have had the power to make an indelible impression on your mind."

"In that I believe you are right," answered Doris. "I have a good memory, but on consideration I must confess that my distinct recollections are astonishingly few."

"And yet," said Emmeran, "when put together they form what we call experience. At all events, this view of life makes the occasional appearance of extraordinary genius less enigmatical, while it relieves one's mind concerning the otherwise unaccountably hard lot of so many of our fellow-creatures. The consideration that in the course of time each individual spirit——"

"Hallo!" cried Frank, entering the boat-house with Hilda, "hang me if they are not still grinding away at the spirits! Come now, Emmeran, be alive—take the oars and make yourself useful. I must sit aft, as I want to teach these girls to steer."

Emmeran obeyed, and was soon convinced that his presence was as much forgotten by his companions as if he had been Kuno the fisherman. And, in fact, the gaunt figure and pale grave face of the student, scarcely improved by the late addition of a moustache and beard of very yellow hair, was not likely to attract the attention of the young girls, when learning to steer from an instructor for whom they openly professed great affection, and to whose society on all occasions they gave a decided preference.

But there was another observer who by no means watched so calmly as Emmeran the group at the stern of the boat. In an uncontrollable fit of jealous rage Sigmund sprang into the boat-house, loosed the fisherman's punt, and pulled out into the lake with a vehemence that instantly attracted the attention of his brother.

"Sigmund is in furious pursuit," he observed, with a meaning smile; "shall we let him come up to us?"

"No, no," cried Frank, springing up and seizing his oars; let's have a race first."

And a race they had, which lasted for nearly half an hour, to the great amusement of both Hilda and Doris, when, having proved that they had a better boat and were

better manned, they lay on their oars and awaited the
"*Grand Seigneur*," as Frank called Sigmund, from his
frequent use of the word and constant enacting of what he
supposed its meaning.

"Your Serene Highness's pleasure?" said Frank,
raising his hand to his battered straw hat.

"Hilda," cried Sigmund, with compressed lips, "I
insist on your leaving that boat directly and returning
back with me to the castle."

"Why? for what purpose?" she asked, retreating as
much as the space would admit from his outstretched hand.

"Because I choose it."

"But I do *not*," she answered; "and if you have no
better reason, I shall certainly not go into your dirty wet
boat."

"It is not the dirt nor the water that prevents you,"
he retorted, angrily.

"You are quite right; I prefer my companions here to
you, when you are in such odious ill-temper."

"Rather say at all times," he suggested, with forced
calmness; and then added, "Remember our conversation
in my father's presence a couple of hours ago: either you
come into this boat, or——"

To the infinite surprise of all excepting Sigmund, Hilda
stood up, and, though indignantly refusing his assistance,
stepped into the punt and seated herself in the stern, with
a strong expression of displeasure on her beautiful features,
while Frank, who had been with difficulty prevented by
Doris from interfering, now pulled off his jacket, rolled it
up, and, having drawn the boats close together, placed it
beneath her feet.

"Thanks, dear Frank," she said, with heightened
colour; and either to show her sense of the contrast between the young men, or to punish or provoke Sigmund,

she accompanied her words with a look of such unrestrained affection and approbation, that Sigmund, angry with himself for having demanded an obedience that gave him no satisfaction, more irritated than even Hilda supposed at appearing in so disadvantageous a light to Doris, now clenched his hands, and resolved to end the scene by a separation of the boats. He may have observed that Frank had scarcely regained his place, but he certainly was not aware that Doris's hand was still grasping the side of the punt, when he raised his oar, and with all the strength of a powerful man in a state of ungovernable rage, pushed the boats wide asunder. The punt reeled in a manner that made Hilda draw in her breath with a stifled scream; Frank staggered and fell on his face; while Doris, unable to steady herself from the unexpected shock, was instantly precipitated into the water. There was no danger for her excepting from the eagerness of the two swimmers, who instantly plunged to her rescue as she rose to the surface, each equally eager to be her life-preserver. Frank, however, fiercely pushed Sigmund aside, although the motion cost Doris a fresh immersion in the lake; but he finally brought her safely to the boat, into which, with Emmeran's assistance, he placed her, leaving his competitor to regain the punt at his leisure.

A remarkable silence was observed respecting this adventure, Doris's mother alone being informed by her of what had occurred. Between Frank and Sigmund a quarrel would have been inevitable, had not Doris informed the former that Sigmund had expressed great regret at the consequences of his violence, and requested her forgiveness; but evidently the mutual dislike only waited for an opportunity to explode, and Doris anxiously endeavoured to keep them apart until the ire of both gradually began to subside.

CHAPTER XII.

A HOLY-EVE ADVENTURE.

DURING the course of the ensuing week Doris and her mother heard, with a satisfaction which they found it difficult to conceal, that an encampment at Nymphenburg, near Munich, would oblige Sigmund to leave Westenried. They had found Frank very unmanageable, and all their efforts to induce him to be cautious or forbearing in his intercourse with Sigmund so utterly fruitless, that, had not Hilda joined them, and for the time being not only avoided Frank, but in a measure endeavoured to propitiate Sigmund, the continual skirmishing would undoubtedly have ended in open war.

"Joy go with you," said Frank, gravely bowing as Sigmund turned to take leave of him.

"Much obliged," he replied, haughtily; "but I cannot quite believe that *you* think joy will go away with me, or wish joy to accompany me. This"—he added, glancing suspiciously towards Doris, whose lips quivered slightly with a suppressed smile—"this is either Irish poesie or Garvagh wit, which I do not understand."

"It is only part of a foolish nursery rhyme," interposed Doris, quickly, not a little alarmed at the now flashing eyes of both; "Frank has said it to me a hundred times."

"Then he did not mean to——"

"Come, come, Sigmund," cried his father, who was already seated in the carriage; "if we intend to reach our quarters for the night before dark, there is no more time to lose."

The sound of the wheels was still audible, while Frank

exclaimed, "I suppose, aunt, that now, as Emmeran and I are not likely to quarrel, and Sigmund is quite out of the way, you will have no objection to our celebrating Holy-Eve as we used to do at Garvagh ? "

" None whatever," she answered; " you may melt lead and burn nuts to your heart's content."

" Oh ! I assure you we intend to attempt much greater things than lead-melting or nut-burning, for Doris has promised to show Mina and Hilda their future husbands' faces in a glass, if they have courage to look at them."

" I can answer for myself," said Hilda; " but Mina has no courage when she hears of anything supernatural."

" Doris says there is nothing to be feared," observed Mina; " she has promised not to use any sleight of hand to dupe or frighten me."

" Only a little mummery," said Doris, " such as going to the vaults on the island at midnight, and looking in the glass by the light of burning salt and spirits of wine."

" Don't you think," asked Mina, appealing to the countess, " don't you think she might play this conjuring, or whatever it is, in a less alarming sort of place ? "

" Undoubtedly. With a white quilt or a table-cloth, one of the attics would do just as well."

" But why a white cloth ? "

" To assist the burning salt in exciting the imagination and causing apprehension."

" It will cause none to me," said Hilda; " I am convinced it is some jest, and she will find herself mistaken if she thinks to amuse herself at my expense. I shall look in the glass, and see whatever is to be seen, depend upon it."

" I think you will," said Frank; " and after all, you are not at all likely to see anything frightful. Even a blue light could scarcely disfigure such features as she will——"

Doris's hand was on his mouth.

"Now, Frank, I really do not think I can employ you as assistant if you talk in this thoughtless manner."

"How do you know that I was not going to say she would see Sigmund's handsome face, perhaps even lit up by smiles that have been confoundedly rare of late?"

"Faces seen in this way," said Doris, with affected solemnity, "are seldom smiling and always frightfully pale."

"Pray," asked Emmeran, "did *you* ever look in a glass at midnight before All Saints' Day?"

"Yes."

"And saw," he continued, "or thought you saw, a black-haired, blue-eyed fellow, just like Frank here?"

"No matter what I saw," replied Doris, laughing; "let me show you the face of your future wife, if only to remove your incredulity."

"No thank you; there is but one face I should like to see in your magic mirror, and that one you are not likely to show me."

"What do you mean by that?" cried Frank. "Are we to understand that you are a despairing lover, while we supposed you a rhymer,—I mean to say a poet?"

"And why a poet?" asked Emmeran.

"Your love of solitude and moonlight led to the supposition; add to which your studious habits and the little lamp that may be seen burning at all hours of the night in your room."

"Any other evidence?" he asked.

"Yes, your ink never dries up like other people's; and the other day when you allowed me to write my letters in your room I saw——"

"What did you see? asked Emmeran, colouring.

"Something written, that looked amazingly like poetry."

"Which you of course read and laughed at!"

"Which of course I did *not* read," replied Frank.

"Written or printed verse can be known at a distance that leaves the words illegible, and you can scarcely require the assurance that I did not place it within reading distance."

"After all," said Emmeran, "what matters it? You would have laughed to find I had composed a soldier's war-song!"

"Not I!" replied Frank; "I should only laugh if you turned soldier yourself."

"Why so?"

"Because you're a scholar, and only fit for a learned profession."

I don't know that," observed Emmeran, musingly; "I can handle a sabre as well as any of you."

"But in our warfare, Emmeran, we have no padding for either legs or arms such as I am told is usual in your university encounters, and no friends to interfere when matters take a serious turn; and though I have no doubt you have had your rows and fought your student duels most creditably, it's not the real thing, and you had better stick to the pen, for which you have a decided predilection."

"One is so slighted, almost despised, in times such as these, if not in the army!" observed Emmeran, looking wistfully after the three girls, who had sauntered into the garden.

"Oh it's that, is it?" said Frank, laughing; "well, you're pretty right there; we are somewhat favoured in that quarter, undoubtedly."

"I wonder," said Emmeran, "is it the uniform or the profession itself that——"

"I don't know, and don't care," answered Frank; "but it is very agreeable, and I hope it may never be otherwise." And even while speaking he began to walk towards the garden gate, leaving Emmeran standing by the fountain in the middle of the court with folded arms, his head bent down and completely absorbed in the self-communing that was habitual to him whenever an opportunity offered.

It is not necessary to describe the melting of lead or breaking of eggs into glasses, that, according to German credulity, must be filled with water during the singing of the *Ave Maria.* The nut-burning was new to Emmeran, who was untiring in putting his constancy to some mysterious personage, whom he declined naming, to the proof in this manner. Subsequently, every achievable superstitious practice, both German and English, was tried to while away the hours until midnight; but a length they became tired, seated themselves near a window, observing that it was fortunate the night, though cloudy, would not be dark for their expedition to the island, talked as a matter of course of superstitions in general, and then glided naturally and imperceptibly into a discussion of all the ghost stories they had ever heard; which, as the Countess Waldering observed (when they thought it time to look at the clock), was the best possible preparation for Doris's magic mirror on the island.

"You will let me be the first to look into it?" said Mina, with some hesitation.

"Of course, if you wish it."

"And—and—if you please, a little *before* it strikes twelve o'clock."

"I don't know whether or not I can agree to that," said Doris; "the charm lies in the midnight hour, you know."

"I always suspected that Mina's courage would fail in the end," cried Hilda, laughing; "the fact is, she has heard that there is no danger of an apparation until after the clock strikes twelve, as it is from All Saints' Day to Twelfth Night that ghosts and goblins are supposed to be at liberty to make themselves visible."

"I dare say that is the reason that midnight is the time chosen in Ireland, also," said Doris; "but is it not curious, mamma, that though no one here knows anything of Holy-Eve by name, there should be so much resemblance in the superstition and the time chosen."

"You might have observed the same at Midsummer, Doris, when the bonfires were made; however, if you mean to be in the island to-night before midnight, you have no more time to lose; for my part, I wish we were back again and in our beds!"

A mass of clouds covered the sky and obscured the full moon, which nevertheless gave a sombre steady light that penetrated through the branches of the nearly leafless trees of the orchard, dimly glimmered on the surface of the lake, and made the wooded hills beyond dark and prominent.

Silently they rowed in the calm melancholy autumn night to the island, and when there Doris and Frank were much too busy with the preparations for their mummery to observe the anxiety of Mina or the unusual gravity of Hilda.

"I wish, Doris, you would let Mina look in your glass before midnight," said her mother; "you have time enough if you choose to do so, and it is ungenerous your trying to increase her alarm after she has confessed her want of courage."

"Don't spare *me!*" cried Hilda; "let me if possible, stand before the glass while the clock is striking twelve!"

Doris laughed and disappeared with her lantern, followed by Frank carrying a basket. She led the way to the place where she had a few years previously spent a night with her mother, and Frank having been in the island during the morning, she found a roughly constructed table on which she deposited her glass, and then began to seek proper places for her dishes of salt and spirits of wine.

"Oh, Frank, this is delightfully horrible!" she exclaimed. "If Hilda can stand here alone and look in that glass without feeling uncomfortable, she has more courage than I have, that's all!"

"I think she has more courage than most girls," he said; "and we will put it to the proof, as she has boasted a good deal."

"I suppose I may bring Mina down now?" said Doris; "but you must go to the end of the vaults, beyond the stairs, where you can see without being seen."

And Frank, not unwillingly, withdrew to the place proposed, for exactly there he had deposited a beard made of black lamb's-wool and an old hussar jacket that he had found in a chest in one of the attics. He had, however, no intention of masquerading for Mina, and having accoutred himself in the jacket, which was easily concealed by his cloak, and thrust the beard and a black handkerchief into his pocket, he followed his cousin up the steps, and reached the boat just as Mina was leaving it with her.

"Remember, Doris, that Mina must not be left alone in the vaults," said her mother; "and the sooner you bring her back the better."

"For every reason," said Frank, "but especially because your blue flames are wasting their brightness on the damp vault walls, and it will soon be midnight."

"Oh, come then," cried Doris, taking Mina's hand and springing up the bank; "we shall be back directly."

"I wonder," observed Frank, soon afterwards, "I wonder you can sit freezing in that boat. Walking up and down the island is so much pleasanter!"

"I thought you intended to assist Doris?" said his aunt.

"No, thank you! this is nothing new to me, and the vaults are confoundedly cold."

He walked up and down, it must be confessed, a little ostentatiously, disappearing occasionally for some minutes, and then returning to propose their going in a body to release Mina from the apparitions she so much dreaded.

In the mean time, Doris led her half-willing, half-reluctant companion down the steps, and with some difficulty induced her to approach the glass.

"You must hold my hand and walk with me, Doris."

"Of course, if you wish it."

They stood before the glass.

"Well, what do you see?"

"Nothing."

"What! nothing at all?"

"Nothing."

"Not even your own face?"

"N—no."

Doris looked in the glass and perceived that Mina's eyes were shut firmly.

"Oh, if you close your eyes you will certainly see nothing; but all you have to see is your own face. Should you ever marry, you belong to your husband, and your face, being part of yourself—is *his!*"

"Is that all?" cried Mina, turning round almost angrily in the sudden revulsion of feeling; "is that all?"

"I thought," said Doris, smiling, "you would be glad to find my conjuring a mere play upon words."

"But I am not glad," said Mina; "for though terribly frightened, I should, after all, have looked in the glass, and I hoped or expected to see *him* or his shadow!"

"Well, look again," replied Doris; "if you really wish to be frightened, perhaps your imagination may conjure up something. *I* can show you nothing but your own face, and made all these preparations merely to try your courage and amuse you."

Quite reassured by these words, Mina looked straight into the glass, but almost instantly covering her face with her hands she uttered a half-suppressed scream and then burst into tears.

" What is the matter ? " asked Doris, anxiously ; " did you fancy you saw—"

" No ! no ! no ! it was not Sigmund—"

" Sigmund ? "

" Yes—no—that is—he was in my mind ; but I only saw my own face, as I have often thought of it—corpse-like—deep, deep under water ! "

" Let us go ! " cried Doris, much alarmed ; " you are talking so wildly that I cannot allow you to stay here any longer."

" Doris ! dear Doris ! you must first promise not to tell that I named—that I thought of Sigmund."

"I feel bound to be silent," said Doris, gravely, " for you spoke under the influence of terror caused by me. And now you must assist me to dissuade Hilda from coming here ; she might, after all, be frightened, and I will not undertake the responsibility."

The efforts to dissuade were unavailing, for Hilda was quite resolved to look in the magic glass.

"I shall not go with you," said Doris, "for Mina only saw her own face, and was completely terrified."

" I don't want or wish you or any one to go with me," replied Hilda, resolutely.

" Then make haste," rejoined Doris, " or else you will find yourself in the dark, which will certainly not be pleasant."

While they were speaking Frank had had time to hide himself in one of the vaults, and watched soon after the descent of Hilda. For a moment the quivering blue lights seemed to make a disagreeable impression ; but, without giving herself time to think, she walked quickly up to the glass and gazed steadily at the beautifully-regular features that even the ghastly colour thrown on them could not disfigure. Now, so standing alone at midnight before a glass and looking fixedly into it—be it Holy-Eve or not— is very soon anything but agreeable. One's own eyes become full of alarming intelligence, and seem those of some one else, piercing one's inmost thoughts. Taking, therefore, the place and light into consideration, Hilda's courage was very surprising; but she had had enough, and was just going to turn away, when she perceived the glass reflect a figure that seemed distant, and in the expiring light so indistinct that it might be mistaken for a shadow. It was a hard trial for the poor girl; her knees trembled, and she stretched both hands forward and grasped the planks on which the glass was placed; but still she looked steadily before her, and contemplated the pallid face of what appeared to her a wounded soldier, across whose forehead and nearly concealing one eye a broad black kerchief was bound, while the lower part of his face was covered with a thick short beard, leaving only a small portion of cheek visible.

While still gazing and doubting the evidence of her eyes, one of the lights flared wildly upwards and, previous to extinction, showed her for a moment the slight figure of an Austrian hussar; the other burned so dimly that she could scarcely any longer distinguish the outline of her own face, still less the apparition beyond. The fear of being left in utter darkness gave her courage to turn round and hurry towards the stone steps, up which she rushed, and then seated herself on a stone in the ruin beside which Doris had left her lantern.

Some minutes elapsed before she felt composed enough to descend to the boat; when she did so Frank was seated in it with the others, like them wondering what on earth could detain Hilda so long. He supposed she was unconscious of the lapse of time while admiring her pretty face in the mirror.

"Not exactly," she answered, stepping into the boat, "for I never liked my face so little as in that glass, and never wish to see it in such a light again."

"But in seeing it you saw your future husband's face," said Doris.

"That would be curious, for it was not Sigmund," she replied; "but I shall know him when I see him, at all events."

"Good gracious, child! what do you mean?" cried her mother, hastily. "Have you been terrified into the idea that you have seen an apparition?"

"I was not much frightened," answered Hilda; "in fact, only a little uncomfortable, until I saw the black-bearded hussar looking at me."

"This is some trick that has been played upon you," said her mother, starting up; "if Emmeran had not been sitting in the boat, and Frank walking up and down within sight of us the whole time, I should have accused them of having attempted to put your courage to the test. We must search the vaults instantly."

"I have seen enough of them for this night," said Hilda, seating herself beside Mina; "but I hope you may find somebody or something that will clear up this mystery."

"You, of course, expected to see Sigmund?" observed Mina, in a low voice.

"I expected to see my own face, and I saw it, and very corpse-like it looked; but what put an Austrian hussar into my head I cannot imagine, and one not in the least resembling any of those I used to know in papa's

7

regiment long ago, though the uniform was precisely the same."

"The woodranger has a black beard," suggested her mother.

"But he has small eyes and a snub nose," replied Hilda. "No, dear, it was certainly *not* the woodranger, who could not know anything of our intention to come here, and would not, at all events, venture to take such a liberty."

"Suppose he had been desired to post himself in the vaults?" suggested her mother, looking suspiciously at Emmeran and Frank. "I wish it were so; it would be more satisfactory."

"I believe," said Emmeran, turning to Frank, "*we* must now insist on a search, and the sooner the better. My conscience is clear, and I don't choose to be suspected."

Frank threw the folds of his mantle more carefully over his shoulder, and followed him to the vaults, accompanied by Doris and her mother.

Every nook and corner were searched, but without success, and they were preparing to return to the boat, when the light suddenly fell on something shining that lay on the ground. The countess picked it up eagerly, and held it to the candle of the lantern.

"How's this?" she exclaimed; "this ring is mine, or rather was mine, until I gave it to your stepfather, Doris. It served as guard to his wedding-ring, and well I remember his annoyance at having lost it one cold day, when he supposed he must have drawn it off his finger with his glove!"

Frank put his hand into the pocket of the jacket, and felt that a glove was in it! Should he confess, or should he not? that was the question. His aunt's agitation as

she recognized and examined the ring, pointed out her
initials inside, and showed how it could be contracted and
enlarged, dismayed him ; he feared also her displeasure for
having attempted to frighten Hilda, and—was silent.

From that time forward the ghost of Count Waldering
had undisturbed possession of the vaults on the island,
Frank's circumstantial confession, made some years subsequently, obtaining no general credence, as it was supposed
he merely invented a plausible story to satisfy his aunt and
silence the ghost-seers.

How many tales of haunted places have had less
foundation than the Holy-Eve prank of this young lieutenant of dragoons!

CHAPTER XIII.

THE SINGULAR BETROTHAL.

THE succeeding winter was spent in Munich, Doris and
her sister presented at Court, and allowed to enjoy the
gaieties of the Carnival without reserve. They gained
some knowledge of the world, became perfectly conscious
of their personal advantages, and were as thoroughly
dazzled and delighted with the then dancing, flirting,
French-speaking society of Munich, as might be expected.
Scarcely, however, had the recreations of Lent commenced,
when a journey to Ulm became necessary, in order to take
possession of the very considerable property which Hilda
had inherited from a grandaunt, of whose sudden death
they then heard.

This grandaunt had married, half a century previously,

the only son of one of those families called " patrician," in
the free town of Ulm.   He proved the last of his race, and
his arms, reversed in the usual manner under such circumstances, may be seen to this day on a bronze monument in
the beautiful cathedral of the town.   His wife and sole
heiress—by birth a Waldering, and possessed with the
mania for name and family which seems, with the exception of Turkey, to prevail all over Europe—had not only
left Hilda all she had promised her, but also everything
else she possessed in the world, with the solemn injunction
to fulfil her engagement to her cousin Sigmund as soon as
circumstances would permit.

Sigmund, then, as a party concerned; the Director, as a
man of business; and the dowager-countess, with her companion Mina Pallersberg, because they did not like being
left alone,—accompanied Hilda, her mother, and Doris, to
Ulm, and soon found themselves comfortably lodged in the
old patrician house, near one of the gates of the town, that
a few months later became the centre of important military
events.

The then threatening aspect of political affairs, however, appeared to them like a distant thunderstorm; they
hoped it would blow over, or at least not materially interfere with their plans and prospects.   Emmeran, greatly
against the wishes of his father and grandmother, had
lately entered the Bavarian army.   Sigmund, however,
about the same time, had retired from the service, and they
would have been perfectly satisfied with him had he been
a little more attentive to his cousin Hilda; while, however, daily discussing her affairs with his father, and
continually proposing improvements on her property, he
apparently forgot herself altogether, or seemed to consider
her as merely a part of what would be his at any time he
chose to appoint during the ensuing autumn.

At the rear of the Waldering house there was a small shady grass-garden, ending in a parapet wall, that had been built to confine the encroachments of the Danube; and under the trees a brick summer-house, that, according to the fashion of the time, was tastefully built to represent a Grecian temple. Here the family spent the greater part of the warm days of July and August, and here it was that Doris and her mother bravely undertook the political defence of the Austrians against the attacks of the Bavarians and French, in the persons of the Director and Sigmund—the old countess being neutral, Hilda purely Bavarian, while Mina Pallersberg was openly accused of the not uncommon meanness of siding with whichever party was most strongly represented. Here also they received frequent visits from Frank O'More, whose regiment was quartered in the neighbourhood, and laughed at his predictions of a concentration of troops in the town; his advice to them to return to Westenried or Munich being scoffed at by the Director as the opinion of a subaltern officer, who could not know any of the plans under consideration at head-quarters.

The fact was, Hilda's affairs made their presence very necessary at Ulm for some time longer, and, in the idea that they could leave the town whenever they pleased, they lingered on, from day to day more interested in the efforts made to repair and fortify the works on the neighbouring heights, where, in process of time, not only the garrison, but the inhabitants of the town and the peasants in its vicinity, were day and night employed in thousands. Never before, and perhaps never since, was Ulm a scene of such reckless gaiety as just then. At every hotel possessed of rooms sufficiently spacious for the purpose, there were balls without the intermission of a single night; and Frank, naturally wishing to partake of these festivities, and enjoy as much as possible the society of his relations, soon managed to have himself billeted in their house. He informed them of this arrangement one afternoon in the garden, and added, laughingly, that he was glad to perceive Sigmund was the only person to whom his presence would be an annoyance.

" Rather say a matter of indifference, Frank," observed his aunt.

" Anything but indifferent, dear aunt; can you not see that he is as jealous as ever ? "

" Jealous ! Of whom ? "

" Of me."

" For what reason ? "

" Because Doris likes me, and intends to marry me as soon as I am a colonel."

" I really was not aware of this arrangement," said his aunt, laughing; and looking towards her daughter, who was leaning on the parapet near them, " You have forgotten to ask my consent, Doris."

" I thought," she answered, smiling, " it would be better to wait until Frank had made up his mind whether he liked me or Hilda best; he has been rather wavering in his allegiance lately."

" Wavering ! " repeated Frank; " no, Doris, not for a moment ! I love you, and you alone; but you must allow me to *admire* Hilda, she has grown so wonderfully beautiful during the last year."

" You cannot admire her more than I do," said Doris, gently.

" Now, that's exactly what I knew you would say," continued Frank; " and, as you have no objection to my liking Hilda next best to you, we may as well tell my aunt our plans for the future."

" *Your* plans, Frank, if you please."

"Very well. My plan is this—you see, dear aunt, I cannot marry Doris for ever so many years; but she doesn't mind that—rather likes waiting, I believe."

"Oh, indeed!"

"Yes; I assure you she thinks ten years hence quite time enough; and, as I have nothing but my profession, I cannot give it up, you know; would not, however, if I could, as long as there is work to be done, or a chance of obtaining a Theresian Cross!"

"Or a bullet to cool your restless ambition," observed his aunt, quietly.

"Half-a-dozen bullets, if the reward be *the* Cross," he answered, gaily.

"And half-a-dozen it may cost you, Frank—perhaps your life!"

"Very possibly," he answered; and the more so as I am more likely to use my arm than my head in the effort to obtain it."

"Dear Frank, what *do* you mean?" asked Doris, moving nearer.

"I mean that few things are more difficult to obtain than a Theresian Cross, and that, though there are various ways of trying for it, mine must be some act of personal courage, as I fear my hand is readier than my head when on a field of battle."

"I think you might be satisfied with your promotion and the medal you have already received for personal bravery."

"No, Doris; nothing will satisfy me but this Cross, of which I have as good a chance as any one, for it is given without the slightest regard to religion, rank, or any other circumstance. This highest of all military decorations will confer on me the title of Baron, and you shall then choose a new name for me."

" Why not keep your own ?" asked Doris.

" Well, so I can, if you wish it ; but when one's own is not famous in any particular way, it is usual to take a name indicative of a—a—what a fellow has done, or something of that sort.''

" If that be the case," said his aunt, " I think we must wait until the fellow has been and done it."

Frank laughed. " Perhaps you are right," he said, good-humouredly ; " and there is not much chance of my having an opportunity of distinguishing myself just now, for every one says our position here is untenable. For my own part, I hate the idea of being shut up in a town, and would a thousand times rather meet the French at once, or retreat, if absolutely necessary, while it can be done creditably ! ''

" But," observed his aunt, " Captain Pallersberg thinks it is now too late to retire to the Tirol, and says we may very soon expect the French in our neighbourhood. The Director, however, has just informed me that, as the Walderings are Bavarians, we have personally nothing to fear."

" I hope, however," began Frank, " that you and Doris are not going to side with the French ? "

" By no means, Frank ; but women are privileged cowards, you know, and in case of the worst we cannot be expected openly to proclaim ourselves champions for Austria."

" I will," said Doris ; " at least whenever I can do so without making myself ridiculous."

" That's right," cried Frank ; " and I can assure you that, with the exception of Napoleon himself, there is scarcely a Frenchman who will think it necessary to take umbrage at your calling yourself an enemy."

At this moment Hilda entered the garden, and came towards them, exclaiming, " I thought, Frank, you were obliged to remain some days longer at Forsteck about the horses required for your regiment ? "

" Well, so I am, and I only came here to-day to report progress. A corporal and five men are with me in your gardener's old tower ; we have turned his cow out to graze, and taken possession of her quarters for our horses."

" I wonder you did not prefer Forsteck, for yourself, at least ? "

" Of course I should, if you were all staying there ; but what should I do alone in those great, grand rooms ? The gardener's tower, with its two pigeon-holes on each story, suits me famously, as I have my men above and my horses below me at night."

" And concerning the aloe at Elchingen, Frank, did you make inquiries about it ? "

" All right ! it is blowing magnificently. They have placed it in a sort of half-ruined chapel, near the monastery, and crowds of people from Ulm come daily to see it and wander afterwards to the inn, where roast chickens are still to be had by those who have money to pay for them ! "

" Now, mamma," said Hilda, " suppose we were to make an excursion to-morrow to see this blossoming aloe. You know aloes only blow once in a hundred years, and grandmamma and Mina wish to see it ; and you could all go in the carriage, and Doris and I might ride with Sigmund, and Frank could join us for an hour or two at Elchingen, and——"

" And—and—and," said her mother, laughing ; " you need not be so very eager, as I have not the least intention of opposing your plan."

" Then, Frank," said Hilda, " you must promise to join us."

" Of course, if those tiresome peasants of yours do not

detain me. Have you any commands for the gardener at Forsteck ? "

" Some flowers ; but you will be sure to forget to bring them to me."

"If I do, I promise to return to Forsteck for them, and give you leave to talk of my negligence for years to come ! "

" I only talk of your neglect of *me*, Frank; for if it were Doris who wished for flowers, you would bring them as certainly as I stand here, notwithstanding your habitual carelessness."

" And if I forgot them," he answered, " she would not think it worth speaking of."

" Perhaps so ; but as I am not Doris, I intend to exact the attention due to me."

" And, Doris," he rejoined gaily, " has given me leave to pay you as much as you desire."

" I know she has : she told me she had no right to object."

" That is not exactly the state of the case now," said Frank, with heightened colour, " for we have just entered into an engagement for ten years."

" Is this true ? " asked Sigmund—advancing from the gate of the yard into the garden and walking straight towards Doris—" Is this true, or is it one of your cousin's intolerably perplexing jests ? "

"I declare I scarcely know," she answered, smiling; " but if Frank chooses to consider himself engaged, I have no objection, as he is satisfied to postpone the discussion of the matter for such a length of time ! "

" Oh ! is that all ? " said Sigmund, turning towards the river; and then adding ironically in a low voice, " and this he calls an engagement ! "

" This is not all," cried Frank, roused to a vague feeling

of jealousy, and a good deal chafed at Doris's too apparent self-possession and caution; "this is not all; and I now demand a straightforward serious answer to——"

"Now, Frank, don't get into a passion for nothing," expostulated Doris.

"I am not in a passion," he answered, with quivering lips, "I am only in earnest, and very earnest, for once in my life! Doris, darling," he added, stretching forward both his hands, "is it, or is it not to be?"

And, without a moment's hesitation, Doris placed her hands in his and answered, "As you will, Frank; I only wished to leave you at liberty, because I doubted your constancy bearing the test of time, as I am quite sure mine will."

"Doris, don't say that."

"I would not if you had not compelled me," she replied; "and now go and be satisfied with having forced me to make a confession before witnesses, with which you might either have dispensed altogether, or asked for less imperiously and publicly."

Frank blushed as deeply at this reprimand as Doris herself had done while giving it; and murmuring something about being a hot-tempered fool and not worthy of her, he left the garden.

"A truly singular betrothal!" observed Sigmund, filiping some loose stones from the wall into the river.

"Doris," said her mother, gravely, "I trust you have not acted from impulse on this occasion, and overseen the importance of your promise."

"No, mamma, not at all. Frank and I have been intimate from infancy, and learned almost to like each other's faults. An engagement may serve to steady him, and I should have awaited his decision, at all events."

"You are quite right, Doris," said Hilda, warmly,

" for he certainly is the dearest, bravest, handsomest——"

" You had better not go on," cried her mother, laughing, " or Sigmund will be jealous."

" Not the least danger," he observed, without looking
up. " Hilda makes no secret of her preference for Frank,
and I feel and know as well as she does that our marriage
is but the fulfilment of a family compact. Fortunately,
our long intimacy and engagement has taught us, if not to
like, at least to tolerate, each other's faults, so perhaps,
after all," he added, shrugging his shoulders, " our chance
of happiness is as good as Frank's and Doris's."

" I hope so," said his aunt, gravely, as she turned
from them to follow Doris, who was walking towards the
house.

" Yet there is a great difference——" began Hilda,
hesitatingly.

" Perhaps so, if well considered," he replied.

" Let us consider well while there is time, Sigmund,"
she said, leaning on the wall beside him. " I fear, in fact,
I am sure, you are not at all attached to me, as Frank is
to Doris. You merely wish with my fortune to give the
Walderings their former position in the world ? "

" And you," he replied, calmly, " wish merely to share
that position, and preserve your name and rank."

" My father's wishes have weighed with me far more
than you suppose," said Hilda.

" Sufficiently to stifle your love and admiration for the
' dearest, bravest, handsomest ' of cousins ? " he asked,
ironically.

" No," said Hilda, courageously, though blushing intensely ; " but Frank has never thought of me, not more
than Doris of you ! There is no cause of jealousy for
either of us. so we may put that out of the question, and

only consider if it would not be better to break off an engagement that is becoming worse than irksome to us both?"

"You amaze me, Hilda, for just at this moment my engagement to you is less irksome than it has been for years, and yours to me ought to be the same."

"I do not understand——"

"Then I will speak as plainly as yourself: as long as Doris and Frank were free we might have entertained hopes, and——"

"No, Sigmund, Frank has openly professed his attachment to Doris ever since I knew him. Had not this been the case, I should never have consented to our betrothal before we left Munich. It is, however, not yet too late to make you free." Here she drew from her finger the ring he had given her when they had been affianced; but Sigmund only took it for a moment in his hand in order to replace it on hers, while vehemently declining the proffered freedom.

As they soon after left the garden, the door of the temple-formed summer-house was hastily opened, and Mina Pallersberg descended the steps carrying a large piece of tapestry-work, in which a nice observer might have discovered that the chief implement of industry, a needle, had been forgotten. Flushed and agitated, her first impulse was to follow the retreating figures. Even Sigmund's name was uttered in a low panting voice, but she suddenly turned round, retraced her steps to her former place of retreat, and was there found an hour afterwards, to all appearance working diligently, by a servant who came to inform her that the French papers had arrived, and the dowager-countess greatly wished to have them read to her.

CHAPTER XIV

A RIDE IN SEARCH OF A BOUQUET.

THE Walderings spent the next day at Elchingen, and, after an early dinner, visited the aloe, which is still well remembered by many of the then inhabitants of Ulm. It was a magnificent plant; and, with a couple of others less advanced in years, completely filled the chapel in which it had been placed. Both Doris and Hilda received from the gardener one of the pendant blossoms that grew thickly on the numerous long stalks; the others, less favoured, purchased small phials of the sap, which the Director immediately surmised to be honey and water, as no plant could have furnished Ulm with such a quantity of sweet juice and be still in so flourishing a condition.

"For so grand a plant the flower is insignificant," observed Doris; "but I am glad I have seen it."

"Many flowers, too, are prettier," said Hilda, examining hers attentively. "And," she added, suddenly raising her head and turning to Frank, "and, now that I think of it, where is the bouquet you were to bring me for the ball to-night? Forgotten, of course, as I predicted!"

"No, and yes," answered Frank, laughing. "The flowers were ordered by me yesterday evening, and brought this morning by the gardener. I placed them with the greatest care in water to keep them fresh, then went to examine a score of horses—received a despatch from headquarters ordering me to conclude my business as soon as possible, as there was no longer a doubt that the French were approaching our neighbourhood—mounted my horse without returning to my room, and so the flowers were forgotten."

"Don't suppose I expected you to remember them," said Hilda, turning from him; while Frank, perceiving that she was offended, followed, and, to obtain pardon, completely devoted himself to her for the remainder of the afternoon. He was not only forgiven, but soon reinstated in her good graces; and when he was obliged to return to Forsteck, she accompanied him to the yard to look at his new horse—told him she would dance with him if he could manage to come to the ball, and "she would give him another trial: he might bring the bouquet with him!"

"I think," said Mina Pallersberg, who had not left Hilda's side during the afternoon,—"I think it would be better if we all went home by Forsteck; it is very little out of the way, and you might ride on before the rest and see if your bouquet be really on Captain O'More's table, as he asserts."

"Of that there is no doubt whatever," answered Hilda, quickly; "but I should like the ride with Frank, and have a great mind to run back and ask mamma and grand-mamma's leave."

"Ah, bah!" cried Mina; "if you ask them, they will make all sorts of difficulties! Ride on before, and they will follow, you may depend upon it. Shall I say you will meet them at the cross roads?—or that they will find you at home before them? You can easily manage one or the other."

"Very easily," said Hilda, already wavering. "Frank, what do you say?"

"Don't ask me," he replied, "as of course I should like to have you with me anywhere, but quite especially on that tiresome, long, straight road."

"Then I don't see why I should not go."

"Nor I," he replied, "unless the fear of displeasing Sigmund deter you."

" But," suggested Mina, " I can tell Sigmund you hoped he would follow you."

" Yes, dear, do ; and with Doris for a companion he will enjoy himself supremely."

Mina forced a smile.

" I hope we shan't get a blowing-up for this frolic," said Frank, as Hilda's horse was led from the stable.

" From whom ? " asked Mina. " Have you not told me repeatedly that cousins might go anywhere together ? "

" Oh well, so they can in England," he answered ; " but people here are so ridiculously prudish that one never knows what one may do."

" It seems Captain O'More fears Sigmund's displeasure more than you do, Hilda," said Mina ironically.

Frank carefully raised his cousin to her saddle, and half smiled.

" Or," she continued,—" or is it Doris's disapprobation that he dreads ? "

This had more effect. Frank's colour mounted to his temples.

Hilda laid her hand on the mane of his horse as he was about to mount, and said earnestly, " Would you hesitate to take Doris with you to Forsteck ? "

" Not for a moment," he answered, vaulting into his saddle.

" And she would go with you ? "

" Undoubtedly ;—that is, if she felt inclined. And why not ? We have taken longer rides together both at Garvagh and Westenried."

Hilda smiled, nodded to Mina, and let her horse bound towards the gate of the yard that a servant held open, and in a few seconds she and her cousin were out of sight.

It was singular that Mina made no mention of Hilda's

desire that her sister and Sigmund should follow her, when informing the Walderings of the excursion in search of a bouquet.

"I never heard of anything so foolish and giddy!" cried the old countess, fanning herself vehemently, though the large room in which they were sitting was anything rather than warm. "Really quite improper, and enough to irritate Sigmund beyond measure."

"Oh, not at all," he said shrugging his shoulders; "I am really so accustomed to Hilda's open preference of Frank O'More, that I now scarcely perceive the most marked demonstration of devotion on her part. If Doris be satisfied with Frank——"

"I see no reason for displeasure," interposed Doris; "why should they not make a short excursion to obtain a bouquet for this evening's ball?"

"For every possible reason," said the Director severely. "Had you all gone together, and openly, even without consulting us, it would have been merely a pardonable *escapade;* but a—a—an elopement of this kind is highly reprehensible! You agree with me, I am sure?" he said, turning to his sister-in-law.

"I cannot attach much importance to their riding home by Forsteck instead of returning with us," she answered quietly; "excepting perhaps, that as the evening is cold and damp, a prolonged ride may give Hilda a cold."

"And I," said Doris, "have often, very often, been out longer and later with Frank, and nobody called it an elopement, or seemed to think it at all extraordinary."

"Excuse me," said the Director, "but I can assure you I very often felt inclined to express my disapprobation at Westenried, and was silent only because I supposed it a peculiarity of Englishwomen to—to—"

"To make use of their cousins?" interposed Doris,

8

laughing. "That is actually the case; and only imagine my having had seven such cousins as Frank to obey my orders for so many years at Garvagh! It was enough to make a tyrant of me for life; and would, perhaps, had I not come to Westenried and seen Sigmund exact implicit obedience from Hilda on all occasions. It is only lately that she has ventured sometimes in trifles to dispute his authority, though I think she likes having her own way even better than I do!"

"I must say," observed the Director, "that the last winter spent in Munich has not improved her."

"Nor me, perhaps?" asked Doris.

"Nor you," he answered gravely; "you have both become too conscious of your personal advantages, and in a manner emancipated yourselves from all control."

"My poor mother," cried Doris, smiling, "what a pair of worthless daughters you have got!"

"I am quite satisfied with you both," answered her mother rising, "though I begin to wish that Hilda had at least gone to Forsteck an hour or two earlier; she will have to ride hard to reach home before dark."

In the meantime Frank and Hilda gave themselves no sort of concern about the waning daylight; they rode on at a hard trot, talking and laughing merrily, so that the long straight road was passed over unobserved, and they were surprised when they found themselves close to the small tower at the end of the extensive orchard of Forsteck, where Frank had spent the last fortnight. At the door, which was slightly ajar, a dragoon stood waiting, or rather peering out in expectation of the arrival of his captain.

"All ready for a return to Ulm?" asked Frank as he was about to follow Hilda up the narrow winding staircase.

"Captain, a word, if you please," said the man, opening his eyes so wide, and looking towards Hilda with such an

expression of amazement and dismay that Frank with
difficulty repressed a smile.

"You and the men can remain here to-night," he said,
turning back for a moment; "but don't forget to offer five
guineas more for the bay mare at the mill before you leave
in the morning; and—a—Huber—what do you mean by
bringing the horses in here? We are going to mount again
directly."

"The road to Ulm will not be safe for the Countess
Hilda, Captain, as there is a detachment of French reconnoitring in the neighbourhood."

"Confound them!" cried Frank. "Why didn't they come
in the morning when we were alone? How strong are they?"

"Six-and-thirty light horse and an officer."

"We have munition," murmured Frank, "and some
days' provision too. If I only had Hilda safely in Ulm!
What *am* I to do with her?"

He had not time to consider; for, while one of the horses
still stood in the doorway, they heard the approach of cavalry,
and before they had time to close the door several men had
dismounted and rushed tumultuously into the tower.*

Frank sprang up the stairs into his room, where Hilda
was calmly arranging her bouquet—seized his pistols, took
down a musket from the wall, and, telling her hastily
neither to look out of the window nor open the door if she
heard a noise, he returned to the staircase in time to assist
the corporal, who was nearly overpowered by numbers.
Three times he fired with such astonishing rapidity, and so
effectually wounded his adversaries, that they threw down
their arms and began a hasty retreat. Some of his men,
who had been in the upper story, now hastened down the
stairs; others hurried from the stable, and the door was
soon effectually barricaded.

* Fact.

Hilda had not remained so passive as Frank had expected; she stood at the door of the room, and now exclaimed, " Frank! they have found the gardener's ladder, and placed it against the staircase window."

Before he could reach it, the head of an adventurous youth became apparent through the small round panes of glass.

" Shoot him, captain," cried the corporal, grimly.

" I'd rather not," said Frank; but he suddenly threw open the window, seized the ends of the ladder, and, in spite of the struggling Frenchman, dashed both with all his force to the ground.

" Now let us look at the windows in my rooms—they can be reached in the same way as this, and we have the two doors to defend also. Huber, post a man at each, and one of you go upstairs to look out. Hilda, can you load a gun?"

" No, Frank, but I can learn."

" That's a dear girl, I knew you would make yourself useful; I wish you were at home, though, with all my soul, but that can't be managed now."

And they ran up the stairs together.

" Now, look here, Hilda, while I load these pistols. I say, Huber, what's that noise below stairs?"

" An attack on the stable door, captain," shouted the corporal.

Frank loaded, then made a bound to the window near him, and fired.

" Give me the other pistol, Hilda."

She obeyed, and a horrible yell from below, mixed with shouts and imprecations, followed the second shot.

" They're going at last," he said, slowly retreating into the room; but even while he spoke the carbines of the whole troop were discharged in the direction of the window. A couple of bullets struck the ceiling, and sent down a shower of mortar; and while Frank threw his arms round Hilda to shield her, another swept the unlucky bouquet from the table beside him, shivering the glass, and dispersing fragments of flowers in all directions.

"They are retreating," shouted the man from the upper story—"retreating with five wounded."

"In what direction?" asked Frank.

"Ulm."

"They must have mounted the hay-cart to fire that last volley," cried Frank, turning towards the window.

"Oh, Frank, dear Frank, don't stand at the window again; it is much better to let them go away quietly."

"And," he said, turning round—"and better for you to go to the top of the tower, in case they should return here. One of those bullets might have killed you, Hilda!"

"Or you," she answered, quickly, "especially the one that hit the bouquet. I suppose," she added, anxiously—"I suppose we must now wait until it is dark before we return home?"

"Longer than that, Hilda," he answered, beginning to reload his pistols.

"I don't mind waiting," she observed, "or riding at midnight, if necessary; but you know, Frank, how dreadfully uneasy mamma would be, and I will run any risk rather than alarm her."

"The risk of being taken prisoner by the French?"

"Yes. My uncle says we have nothing to fear. I am a Bavarian, you know."

"And what am I?" asked Frank, laughing.

"You think, then," she asked, "there might be actual personal danger for you, if taken prisoner?"

"Rather beforehand," he answered, "as I should certainly fight hard for my liberty. But it was not our lives those men wanted just now, Hilda; it was prisoners—if possible, an officer who could give them information: you understand?"

"I believe I do; but on account of my mother and Doris, we must at least send the gardener to Ulm."

"Of course, if he come here; but I cannot risk or spare a man to look for him, dear Hilda, as we are barely enough to defend the place, and may be attacked again before morning. Don't, however, make yourself unhappy; I am sure Pallersberg will miss us at the ball to-night, and send or come to relieve us."

"And I am sure mamma will send for him at once," said Hilda.

"Most probably," he answered, closing the outside window-shutters carefully, and afterwards the window itself. "I should think," he continued, "she will scarcely hesitate in a case of this kind."

"In any case, Frank; for there is no one of whom she thinks so highly as Captain Pallersberg."

They were just then in complete darkness, but Frank was striking a light with flints and the other materials then necessary for the now so simple operation; and when his candle was lighted he held it low for the purpose of making the staircase visible, up which he led the way, while saying, "You will be much safer in the attic, Hilda, and as soon as I have examined the doors and windows, and given some directions, I shall come up and sit with you."

The tower, which was the last remnant of what had once been a castle, and was only separated by extensive gardens and an orchard from the new residence, had very thick, rough walls, a narrow stone staircase lighted by extremely small windows, two rooms on each story, and attics almost quite unfurnished, in order to have place

enough for seeds, bulbs, flower-pots, and gardening implements.

"We'll carry up some things to make you comfortable
by-and-by," said Frank, pushing all the carefully-sorted
seeds from the deal table, and drawing a stool towards
her; "and, after all, it will not be worse here than in the
vaults of the Chapel-island, where you were obliged to
take shelter from your friends, the French, some years
ago!"

"They are neither friends nor enemies just now, Frank.
We intend to be neutral, because our Crown Prince Louis
is still in Paris."

"Don't imagine," rejoined Frank, "that Napoleon will
allow you to be neutral, no matter how much you may
wish it—say allies, and you will be nearer the mark."

"Well," she said, "and why not? My uncle says the
Austrians have no right to compel us to join them, or
force us to commence a new war after all we have suffered."

"But I tell you," said Frank, seating himself astride
on a plank supported by blocks of wood, "I tell you you
are too weak to defend yourselves and preserve your neu-
trality, and we have promised to guarantee the inviolability
of all your possessions at the conclusion of the war!"

"Oh, indeed! You will allow us to retain what we
already possess! But *we* don't choose to have the law laid
down to us in that way, I can tell you!"

"Don't you?" cried Frank. "I suspect you'll learn
to find the commands of a French Emperor harder than
were ever those of a German."

"I don't think we shall," retorted Hilda, delighted to
find herself talking like her uncle, and able to irritate her
cousin. "Your Emperor required us to give up all independence, and put our army altogether under his orders.'

" Of course," said Frank, " and Napoleon will do the same."

" My uncle says——"

" I don't want to hear what your uncle says," cried Frank, starting up so energetically that the wooden supporters of his plank rolled to the other end of the room, " Why can't you give your opinion as Doris does, instead of making a parrot of yourself, and repeating other people's words ? Have you no ideas of your own, Hilda ? "

" Plenty," she replied, her voice trembling with anger and mortification ; " more than you will like to hear, perhaps. Taking you as a sample of an Austrian officer, one can quite understand a refusal to serve under them, and I don't require to learn from my uncle what everybody knows—that you are likely to be defeated in this war ! Prussia is neutral, the Russians ever so far away, and the French are here, and commanded by Napoleon, whose name is an army in itself ! "

" I need not ask what your hopes and wishes are," said Frank, biting his lip, " but I trust I shall live to hear you speak differently."

" Of what importance are the words of a parrot ? " she asked, ironically.

" Hilda, I am very sorry. I really did not mean——"

" You meant what you said, and were so rude that I should be very glad if you would go away, and not annoy me with your company until you come to take me home."

" You shall be implicitly obeyed. I have no wish to force my society on you or any one," said Frank, leaving the room in high dudgeon.

Before he was half-way down the stairs he felt the absurdity of quarrelling with his youthful cousin because she happened to have adopted the political opinions of her uncle, and the man to whom she was about to be united in the course of a few weeks. He turned round, and with hasty steps remounted to the door of her room, but found it bolted from within, and no entreaties on his part could induce her to open it, or even reply to his apologies.

The fact was, Hilda did not choose him to see that she had indulged in a hearty fit of crying, which was renewed as he again began to descend the stone steps. " I—knew —he did not care for me," she sobbed ; "but I—did—not —think he supposed me a mere repeater of other people's words—an idiot ! I will show him that I have ideas—and opinions—and—and—a will of my own, too ! Oh, how I wish I had not come here with him ! What will mamma say ? and my uncle ? And Sigmund, who is so jealous and suspicious, will of course think, and perhaps say, that I wanted to have a *tête-à-tête* ride with Frank ! And even Frank himself may imagine—but no—he only called it a frolic, and it would have been nothing else but for these odious French soldiers, who are just now really my enemies, though I have been foolish enough to quarrel with Frank about them ! "

CHAPTER XV.

WHAT PEOPLE SAID.

MEANTIME the Walderings drove homewards, at first quickly enough, then obliged to pass slowly different detachments of cavalry, and finally they were detained for more than an hour at the gate of the town by the entrance of troops into it. During their absence their house had assumed the appearance of a barrack : the court, offices corridors, and apartments were filled with soldiers. In the drawing-room a swarm of officers had assembled, talking loudly and gesticulating eagerly; and when Sigmund and his father advanced into the midst of them, they were at once informed that twenty thousand men were that night to be quartered in Ulm, and no householders could be spared the infliction of additional soldiers being billeted on them. They would, however, answer for the good conduct of their men, and that nothing in or about the house should be injured.

"May I ask," said the Director, looking round the disordered room, where caps and hats and swords and sabres lay in heaps, and even Doris's harp had been turned into a cloak-stand, "may I ask the cause of this sudden influx of military?"

The answer was more intelligible to Sigmund than to his father, who, however, understood that some dislocation of troops had become necessary in consequence of the approach of Ney and Soult at one side and Napoleon himself at the other; while Doris and her mother, still lingering near the door, heard with dismay that detachments of cavalry had been seen that afternoon reconnoitring in the neighbourhood of Elchingen.

"We have just come from Elchingen, and have heard nothing of the kind," observed the Countess Waldering.

"Nevertheless," answered one of the officers, "it is reported that Ney is in that direction; but," he added, on perceiving her alarm, "but the information may not be correct."

"Let us send for Captain Pallersberg," she said, anxiously.

"Pallersberg is not in Ulm just now," answered another officer, coming forward; "but if you will tell me the cause of your uneasiness, perhaps I can be of use."

She related that her daughter had made an excursion to Forsteck for some flowers, and she feared she might find it difficult to return home.

"Forsteck!" he repeated; "that is where O'More has been for the last ten days collecting horses, and he told me yesterday he intended to return this evening. Mademoiselle will meet him there, and could not have a better escort."

"Of course she will have his escort," said the Director; "but he may be overpowered by numbers."

"Then," replied the officer, smiling, "we must hope that he will defend himself in the old tower until we can send troops to raise the siege."

"This is no jesting matter," said the Director, testily. "O'More is so reckless that he might blow up the tower if unable to defend it, or make some wild sally that might cost my niece her life!'

"Oh, mother," cried Doris, greatly agitated, "let us go to Forsteck and save her, or share her fate!"

"Not for the universe!" cried Sigmund, suddenly roused from a state of apathy that had appeared unaccountable to them all excepting, perhaps, Mina Pallersberg, whose eyes had been fixed intently on him alone. "Why," he continued, "why should you incur danger for Hilda's wilful and wild conduct? And of what use could you be? I will go myself to Forsteck, and defend her from the consequences of an indiscretion that I shall scarcely be able to pardon."

"Sigmund!" cried Doris, as he passed her, "Sigmund! do not judge Hilda too harshly. I am convinced she expected—hoped we should follow her. Is it not so, Mina?"

"Very probably," she answered coldly.

"No, Doris!" he said, bending down towards her, and

whispering eagerly, "no! she wished to be with Frank, and will gladly brave the danger if shared with him; and I—I—interfere now wholly on your account, for it is torture to me to see you suffer a moment's uneasiness."

Doris drew back, equally surprised and shocked at his vehemence, while his grandmother, tapping him on the shoulder with her fan, observed, "Go, *mein Schatz*, you are the best emissary that can be employed on this occasion. Should you fall into the hands of the French, there is no danger either for you or your *fiancée*, and your presence will save her from all the scandalous reports and town talk to which her *étourderie* would give rise should she be unable to return home before her absence is observed."

Sigmund shook off the approval-tapping fan, not, perhaps, quite pleased to have his ride to Forsteck placed in so unhazardous a light, and left the room without answering.

The others followed, and when the door had closed on them the officers looked at each other meaningly, and then made some knowing grimaces.

"He has carried off the heiress, by Jove!" exclaimed one.

"Always thought he'd do it," said another.

"It's the way of these Irishmen," observed a third, "and is a famous stepping-stone to promotion. O'More's always in luck, at all events—continually getting into scrapes that would ruin other fellows, but which invariably turn out to his advantage. Now, were one of us at Forsteck, we might be overpowered, taken prisoner, and perhaps on our way to France before any one here would think it necessary to make an effort to save us; but O'More goes off with a young heiress, and the whole town and garrison will be in alarm a few hours hence."

"Alarm or not," said an elderly officer, who was

buckling on his sword preparatory to leaving the room, "it will be some days before we shall have time to think of him. The Archduke Ferdinand is expected, the movement of the troops must be completed, and then perhaps a retreat into Tirol taken into consideration."

"The Marshal will not listen to the word 'retreat,' though our forces do not amount to the half of the French," observed a youthful lieutenant. "He says the Russians must be here before long, and we can hold out until they come."

"Or," said the other, striding towards the door, "or until the town is bombarded."

That 5th of October was an intranquil night in Ulm, though, to the honour of the Imperialists, it must be observed that scarcely any European army could have been suddenly quartered in like numbers on the inhabitants of a town of such limited dimensions without giving cause for bitter complaints. So exemplary, however, was their conduct that not one serious transgression is on record.

At the most brilliant and most crowded of the balls that evening, the Walderings' absence was observed, and the family having hitherto occupied a prominent position on such occasions, Hilda's unfortunate ride, with many additions, soon became the chief topic of conversation. Some laughed, and talked of *étourderie*; others looked sagacious, and suggested that as the young countess had shown plainly enough how greatly she preferred Captain O'More to Count Sigmund, the ride might have been a bold stroke to break off her engagement to one cousin in order to be at liberty to marry the other. It was singular that none seemed to think the near relationship of Frank and Hilda sufficient to render their being prisoners together for a few days a mere matter of annoyance and probable personal danger; though, in point of fact, the connection is considered nearer in the Roman Catholic states of Germany than in England, as is made evident by a dispensation from the Pope being absolutely necessary for the marriage of such relations.

Doris and her mother found a melancholy consolation during the night in thinking that Sigmund was with Hilda, and that they could return home together the next morning without much danger, even supposing the French in the immediate neighbourhood; but when neither they nor any tidings reached home during the early part of the day, maternal anxiety overcame all other considerations, and refusing steadily Doris's entreaties to be allowed to accompany her, the countess drove off alone to Forsteck, while the Director went to head-quarters to seek whatever assistance could be procured. The former was met and sent back by a French patrol long before she had reached her destination; the latter was informed that an order had already been given for some squadrons of cuirassiers to clear the country in the direction of Elchingen. This may have been done; but the prisoners in the Forsteck tower were not released until Captain Pallersberg returned to Ulm at the end of the week, and was given permission to reconnoitre in the neighbourhood. A detachment of Frank's own regiment risked a détour to the tower, and brought him and his cousin back in a sort of triumph after a successful skirmish with some French horse, in which it was declared that Hilda had behaved with astonishing heroism, and that having made every evolution with perfect precision, she had not embarrassed them in the least.

Her explanation that her horse had learned to stand fire and knew his duty was not allowed to detract from her merit, and like a general surrounded by a numerous staff, she galloped through the streets to her home. There she raised her hand, in playful military salute, to her beaver hat, from which the long feather had actually been shot away an hour previously, and then disappeared under the archway, to spring to the ground and be clasped in the arms of her mother and sister, whose pale anxious faces formed a strong contrast to her sparkling eyes and wild state of excitement.

"Oh, my dear mother!" she exclaimed, as they mounted the stairs together, "I have been in a state of despair——"

"I can easily imagine it, my poor child," said her mother, interrupting her with a caress. "What apprehension and anxiety you must have endured during the last six days!"

"On your account and Doris's, dear mamma—more than I can express."

"It must have been a great relief to your mind when Sigmund joined you," continued her mother, leading the way to the drawing-room. "We only heard from him to-day to say he would return this evening. Why is he not with you?"

"He did not come to us at all, mamma; though Frank suspects he might have done so had he wished it."

"What do you mean, dear Hilda?"

Sigmund was intercepted on his way to us, and made prisoner by a Captain d'Esterre, who took him to Gundel-fingen."

"How did you hear that?"

"This Captain d'Esterre allowed him to send a peasant with a note to desire me to keep Frank quiet, as there were French patrols between us and Ulm."

"Mamma," said Doris, "that French captain is Louis d'Esterre, I am quite sure."

"Very probably; but go on, Hilda. Why did you not send the gardener here?"

"Of course I did, and he attempted to get to Ulm several times with a letter from me hid in baskets of fruit and vegetables, but was always found out and sent back again. Frank suspects that Sigmund was at the bottom of it all."

"In what way?"

"He says he must have been perfectly explicit with this Captain d'Esterre, who undoubtedly is the French emigrant who lived so long at Garvagh, otherwise we should certainly have been attacked more frequently and forcibly. Frank said from the first they only wanted a prisoner who could give them military information, and he is sure that Sigmund told all that was necessary. Frank and I had a desperate quarrel about politics; but I could not attempt to defend Sigmund, it is so abominable his telling about the incompleteness of the works round Ulm, and Marshal Mack's indecision concerning a retreat into Tirol!"

"Frank is by no means certain that Sigmund has done so," observed her mother.

"He says there can be little doubt of it; otherwise this D'Esterre would have considered it his duty to turn back and take us prisoners—disagreeable as it would have been to him. He thinks also that Sigmund could have obtained permission to return to Ulm, had he desired it, and ought, at all events, to have made an effort to come for *me*, instead of writing hypocritical letters deploring my equivocal position, and fearing that people might put a false construction on what he could assure me he still tried to consider mere *étourderie* on my part! Did you ever hear anything so absurd? Frank told me not to make myself unhappy, for that people had other things to think and talk about just now."

Perceiving her mother and sister look very grave, Hilda added, "And you think so too, mamma?"

" I wish I could—but it is not so, Hilda ; you have been talked of, and judged most unkindly."

" In what way ?—what could they say ? "

The Director, who had been standing unperceived in the doorway of an adjoining room, answered severely, " They said you preferred Frank to Sigmund, and had eloped with him *à l'Anglaise.*"

Hilda seemed overwhelmed with consternation at these words. Pale and trembling, she caught the back of the nearest chair, and gasped, " I—could not—foresee—that I —that we—should be imprisoned. He—I—we never thought——"

" Very likely not," said her uncle ; " but other people view this affair most unfavourably, and I should scarcely be surprised if, after so flagrant a breach of decorum, Sigmund should no longer think himself bound to fulfil his engagement to you."

" I shall not ask him," replied Hilda, haughtily ; " he might have told you that I proposed breaking it off the day before we went to Elchingen."

" Your position is now quite different from what it was then," replied her uncle ; " and you will have reason to be grateful to Sigmund if he can be induced to save you from the only alternative that now remains to silence slander and preserve your reputation."

" And what is the alternative ? " she asked, quickly. " For, though Sigmund's opinion is henceforward a matter · of indifference to me, I am ready to do anything to prove myself blameless in the eyes of others."

" That is no longer possible," said her uncle ; " and therefore I advise you to appeal to Sigmund's generosity, and——"

" Anything rather than that," cried Hilda, vehemently.

" Then," said the Director, " you have but to explain

9

the state of the case to your cousin Frank, who will see at once that he cannot do otherwise than—propose to—marry you himself ? "

" No, no, no!—never, never ! " she cried, passionately ; and then, rushing forwards, she threw herself on her knees beside her sister, and burst into tears.

The Director left the room, and a long and painful pause ensued, during which Hilda's slight figure shook with convulsive sobs, and was only prevented from falling prostrate on the ground by her sister's supporting arm.

" That speech about Sigmund was quite unnecessary," said Doris, addressing her mother.

" I don't care about it," interposed Hilda, raising her head with evident effort ; " for I had resolved, at all events, to break off my engagement with him. I never liked, and now almost hate him. Without having made an effort to save me from the consequences of my thoughtlessness, he will now condemn, and be the first to injure me in the eyes of the world, though he knows as well as you do that under Frank's protection I was as safe—far safer—than in his ; for Frank would have perilled his life to save mine. Oh ! mother, speak to us, but do not say that Doris and Frank must be sacrificed to save me from ignominy ! "

" Ignominy is too strong a word," said her mother, coming towards her ; " but I greatly fear that all the distressing trials to which a blighted reputation is liable will be your portion, my poor child! if Sigmund cannot be induced by his father to fulfil his engagement to you."

" Do not name him," cried Hilda, waving her hand impatiently, with an expression of strong aversion ; " had I the power now, I would refuse him ten thousand thousand times ! Has he not told me, without an attempt at reserve, that he cannot love me as he does Doris ? and did he not listen with perfect indifference to my confession that——" Here she stopped suddenly, clasped her hands above her head, and hid her face on her sister's knee.

And Doris's pale features became perfectly white, while her eyes sought her mother's in expressive interrogation. A compression of the lips and two or three sorrowful inclinations of the head denoted immediately afterwards that she had received a confirmation of long-entertained suspicions, and then, bending down, she whispered, "You told him, dear—that you loved Frank ? "

Hilda's fingers seemed to clasp tighter, but she did not move or make an attempt to answer.

During the pause that ensued they became aware of Sigmund's arrival by hearing him speak to a servant in the ante-room.

" I cannot let him see me in this state," cried Hilda, rising hastily from her kneeling position, and pushing her dishevelled hair from her face, " It will be better to write than to speak to him ; for I might say more than is necessary, and he might answer what I never could forgive or forget."

When Sigmund opened the door, he saw the three retreating figures in an adjoining room ; but, though he spoke, not one of them stopped, answered, or even looked round as if conscious of his presence.

CHAPTER XVI.

WHAT DORIS DID.

BEFORE Frank again saw his aunt and cousins, he had become unpleasantly acquainted with the calumnies to which Hilda's detention in the tower at Forsteck had given rise

Her position, as sole heiress to one of the oldest patrician families of Ulm, had been sufficiently conspicuous to make her words and actions the subject of discussion to the inhabitants of the town and its environs, in a manner of which neither she nor her nearest relations had had the slightest idea; so that her uncle's words were, in fact, but an echo of the rumours that had at first been whispered and then loudly and unreservedly repeated during her absence. If the officers of the garrison of Ulm thought her in the right to prefer their daring handsome comrade to the not very popular Count Waldering, the mode of expressing this opinion was highly offensive to Frank, who considered Hilda's name compromised by their jests and insinuations: angry words had ensued, satisfaction had been demanded and given with a promptitude peculiar to those times. Commanding officers had business more important than making minute inquiries concerning the wounds of men whose lives were daily exposed to danger by the immediate vicinity of the enemy, so that Frank, quite unmolested, defended the fame of his cousin at the point of his sword no less than four times in one week, while a duel with pistols had only been frustrated by a cannon-ball having killed his adversary a few hours before the time appointed for the meeting.

It would be difficult to describe the recklessness with regard to human life then prevalent; but Captain Pallersberg at length thought it his duty to interfere in the most effectual manner by informing the Walderings without reserve of all that had occurred.

Now Frank's refusal to resign Doris, and his unceremonious manner of declining to discuss "the elopement," —as both the Director and Sigmund persisted in calling the unlucky sojourn at Forsteck—had led to scenes that had ended in his first leaving the house and then abstaining altogether from even visiting there. Doris now wrote to request his return to them, saying that any appearance of a quarrel with him would only serve still more to injure Hilda, who, however, insisted on his ceasing to consider it necessary to defend her either in word or deed, and, to prevent further conflicts, they had resolved to leave Ulm for Tirol, if the removal were still practicable.

Frank found this note on his table in Pallersberg's room as they entered it together late at night, after a sharp engagement with the army of observation under Ney. The Imperialists had forced the French to retreat with great loss of men and baggage; and Frank and Pallersberg, having afterwards formed part of the escort of some hundreds of prisoners, who, after much delay and difficulty, had been quartered in the Latin school-houses of the over-filled town, were among the last to reach their rooms, a good deal fatigued, but still in a state of considerable exultation.

"From Doris!" cried Frank, eagerly taking up the note, seating himself at a table, and drawing a candle towards him.

"Pallersberg," he said, after a pause, "it seems that some infernal gossip has been unnecessarily communicative concerning me, for Hilda forbids my further interference in her affairs."

"I am very glad of it," said Pallersberg, "for your Quixotic encounters have been anything but advantageous to her."

"I have, at least, insured silence on the subject of the tower at Forsteck, Pallersberg."

"Silence in your presence, yes, and that may be a satisfaction to you; but what advantage is it to her? Can you silence the inhabitants of Ulm and its neighbourhood for miles around? Can you silence the garrison or the Bava-

rian *chevaux-légers* officers now at Elchingen, or even Sigmund Waldering himself?"

"He's a scoundrel!" cried Frank, "a sanctimonious
scoundrel, who won't fight!"

"Oh! you've tried him, have you?"

Frank was silent.

"Sigmund has many faults," said Pallersberg, "but
want of courage is not one of them. Believe me, the fear
of displeasing your cousin Doris alone influenced him on
this occasion."

"Doris?"

"He loves her," said Pallersberg, "has loved her for
years."

"I know that," answered Frank, "every one loves and
admires her, as a matter of course; but all I can say is, if
a cousin or even a brother of Doris's said half as much to
me as I did to Sigmund, when speaking about his conduct
to Hilda, I——"

"You," interposed Pallersberg, "you would have given
yourself the satisfaction of either shooting him, or being
shot by him, without for a moment considering the consequences to the cousin you professed to love."

"Now, don't preach to-night, Pallersberg, for I'm very
tired," said Frank, stretching out his legs, "and so hungry that I feel rather inclined to be quarrelsome than otherwise."

"I am sorry to hear that," said Pallersberg, "for I
must give you my opinion of the state of your affairs before
we part company."

"Part company! what do you mean?"

"I mean that you must return to the house of
your aunt or your cousin, whichever you choose to
call it."

"Ha! what's this?" cried Frank, referring to Doris's

note; by Jove, "you're the fellow who revealed my mis-doings to my aunt and Doris!"

"Yes," said Pallersberg, quietly, "you see in me the 'infernal gossip' who wished to prevent you from losing your own life, or taking that of others unnecessarily."

"Halt!" cried Frank, angrily; "no,—go on; you may say what you please."

"I believe I may," continued Pallersberg, "for besides being the 'gossip' you would also find me a 'sanctimo-nious scoundrel,' if an occasion should present itself."

"Do you mean that if I provoked you, you wouldn't——"

"I would not," said Pallersberg.

"On account of my aunt, I suppose?" said Frank.

"Just so; I can scarcely imagine your inducing me to do anything that would make me forfeit her esteem."

"All right!" said Frank; "I wish we had something to eat."

"And I," said Pallersberg, with some annoyance, "I wish you would listen to what I have to say without remind-ing me that you are still a boy!"

"Go on, then, old fellow," cried Frank, laughing; "you're a man, but I suspect just now as hungry as I am!"

"Shall I ask the people of the house if they can give us anything?" said Pallersberg, turning to the door.

"No; I'll hear you out, and have done with it. What has my aunt desired you to say to me?"

"Nothing; I was about to give you my own opinion—"

"Out with it, then," cried Frank, impatiently.

"And offer you some advice."

"Offer as much as you please, but don't expect me to take more than I like. For instance, if you were to advise me to give up Doris and stop the evil-speaking, lying, and slandering of the inhabitants of Ulm by marrying Hilda, I should simply say no!"

" And I," said Pallersberg, " should remind you that on all occasions, and especially when these inhabitants of Ulm were present, you paid such marked attention to your cousin Hilda, that Sigmund's patience astonished me as much as it did other people, and I never doubted that the detention at Forsteck would be used by you both as an excuse to break off a previous engagement, the fulfilment of which had so evidently become irksome."

" You mean Hilda's and Sigmund's," said Frank ; " but mine with Doris——"

" Was not known," answered Pallersberg ; " was not even suspected. Mademoiselle O'More has never shown the slightest preference for you in public that is not perfectly consistent with your relationship ; while Hilda has unconsciously betrayed her feelings to all the world ! I can assure you, Frank, that under other circumstances I should be the last to urge your marriage with her, or, indeed, any one, until you have become steadier."

" That," said Frank, " was precisely what I meant when I told Doris she must wait until I was a colonel."

" And," asked Pallersberg, " and she made no objection to the arrangement ? "

" None whatever ; was quite glad of the put off, I suspect ; Doris is not a marrying girl ! "

" And you are satisfied with this quiet passionless sort of regard ? "

" Why not ? it is very convenient just now."

" And for the sake of a person whose indifference you acknowledge, our beautiful young heiress is to be made unhappy for life ! "

" Doris is not indifferent ; she does not parade her affection, that's all. And the short and long of the matter is, I won't marry and give up my profession for any woman in Christendom."

"You need not give up your profession," suggested Pallersberg.

"I know better," said Frank; "Doris could never be induced to move about with a regiment."

"Of course not," replied Pallersberg; "you would not ask, nor would she ever propose such a thing. Hilda thinks differently—is willing to accede to any arrangement you may propose."

"You would find it difficult to convince me that she said so," replied Frank, ironically.

"Her mother seemed to have no doubt on the subject, and authorized me to speak to you."

"And," asked Frank, colouring deeply, "and was Doris present when my aunt said this?"

"No, we were alone; but what matters it? Has not Mademoiselle O'More released you from your engagement to her? Has she not (I must say nobly) declared that she will not be an impediment to her sister's happiness?"

"Yes," said Frank bitterly, "it was some such fine phrase that drove me from the house."

"To which, however, you will now return, for appearance' sake," said Pallersberg, persuasively.

"For appearance' sake!" repeated Frank; "will my return be really of use to Hilda?"

"Most undoubtedly," replied Pallersberg; "not only your return, but, if possible, your appearance with her in public and avoidance of anything like disunion with her family."

"You may be right," said Frank thoughtfully, "and I am certainly bound to do all that I can. Yes, Pallersberg, I will go, and at once, though I would far rather storm one of the enemy's batteries, than mount the staircase of that old corner house just now."

He threw his cloak over his shoulders while speaking the last words, and strode towards the door.

" Will you not make some change in your dress before meeting your aunt and cousins ? " asked Pallersberg.

" No ; but tell Hans to pack up, and follow me as soon as he can."

" Halt, Frank ! you really have no idea how wild you look, bespattered with mud and blood."

" Can't help it," said Frank ; " the other coat may be dry, but it is in no better condition than this one ; and, in short, I don't know where to find it. At all events my aunt can look upon a uniform in this condition without disgust ; and dear Doris must put aside her fastidiousness, and learn to brave the hardships of a siege, for leaving Ulm, as she proposes, is now out of the question. I shall have to tell her that there is much more likelihood of her sharing the rations of horseflesh they talked about at the head-quarters this morning."

" I hope we may get them, Frank," said Pallersberg ; " horseflesh, or anything that will enable us to hold out until the Russians arrive."

" I would rather fight out, than hold out," said Frank. " The Archduke says if we are not strong enough to give battle, there is no use in crowding the town with cavalry ; and, if he leave Ulm, I hope we may be commanded to go with him."

" Not much chance for you, Frank, for, since your proficiency in French has been discovered, you may expect to be employed continually as scrivener and interpreter. But now return to your relations without further delay ; it is so late that they may have already left the drawing-room."

" Just what I should like," answered Frank, hurrying down the stairs into the cold wet streets.

The entrance to the Waldering house was open, and a soldier who stood before the door was speaking to others employed within, where the vaulted space at the foot of the staircase had been converted into a stable.

"Halloa, Korinsky!" cried Frank, to a young officer who was passing him with a hasty salute, "do you know if Klenau's wounds are dangerous?"

"No,—yes; that is, I don't remember. My brother has just died, O'More; and, as they want his bed, poor fellow! I have proposed removing him to the garden. May we not leave him in the pavilion there until morning?"

"Of course, of course," said Frank; "I hoped his wounds were not mortal, as he kept his saddle after the charge."

A few steps further on Frank drew aside to let the officers pass who were carrying the body of their comrade down the stairs; and, as he mechanically raised his hand to his forehead, while gazing at the lifeless figure, it would have been difficult to decide whether the grave salute was intended as a greeting for the living, or a mark of respect for the dead.

He found the entrance-door of the first story still open, the light in the ante-room extinguished; but, on groping his way to the drawing-room, perceived not only a small night-lamp burning, but beside it a wax taper, which he thought had more than probably been placed there for him. Men—especially young and houseless men—are not very observant of the appearance or furniture of rooms; but as Frank raised the taper, and looked round him, he was unpleasantly struck by the dreary aspect of the once cheerful apartment; so much so that he found it difficult to convince himself that the chairs, tables, and curtains were unchanged. He did not perceive that the costly parquet floor, formerly polished and bright as a mirror, was now soiled and rayless; that the various ornaments of an elaborately rococo-furnished room had been removed, and that not a trace of the books or work of his aunt and cousins remained; but the green baize cloth thrown over a marble table, and the ordinary writing materials strewed upon it, indicated plainly enough that the room had been used as an office, and was deserted by its former inhabitants.

He walked as noiselessly as possible along the stone corridor to his room, opened the door softly, and suddenly found himself in the presence of a young man, who, with arms spread out on a table, held in his clasped hands a small green leather case, and gazed on the miniature portrait that it contained so earnestly, that he did not look round until Frank stepped into the room, and almost stood beside him.

" D'Esterre ! "

" François ! "

And Louis d'Esterre sprang up and embraced Frank with that unreserved demonstration of affection that our countrymen reserve altogether for women. Frank, however, had been long enough from home to submit with very tolerable composure to a succession of kisses from a bearded mouth ; he did not feel disposed to return them, but, waiting until the *epanchement* was over, he stretched out his hand, saying, " Well, old boy, what has brought you here ? "

" The chance of war," answered Louis, shrugging his shoulders. "Taken prisoner, I bethought me of *le Comte Sigismond de Waldering et—ma foi—me voilà !* "

" Speak English, Louis," said Frank, "and don't remind me that you are a Frenchman—if you can help it."

" *Non, mon ami ;* I have not forgot that English so agreeably learned in your hospitable house, and," he added, glancing towards the miniature on the table—"and this evening I have had much remembrances of those happy times with *cette chère et charmante* Doris ! "

" So it was her picture you were adoring just now ? "

" Well guess ! I have stealed it from the *salon,* and will keep it if I dare."

" You had better ask permission," said Frank, greatly irritated at no longer having the right to insist on its restitution.

" She say," exclaimed d'Esterre, in a sentimental voice —" she say we are *ennemis,* but she call me *Louis !* "

" Did she expect me this evening ? " asked Frank, abruptly.

" Oh, yees. Did you not find the *bougie* and her *petit billet* telling you about the *chambre ?* "

" *Petit billet ?* " repeated Frank. " I must go and look for it. Good-night !"

He left the room far less quietly than he had entered it, and returned to the drawing-room, where he wondered greatly how he could have overseen a note so evidently placed to attract attention—the light from the lamp actually falling brightly on his name written in large, distinct characters.

He seated himself on the sofa, and read :—

" I am sure you will come, and I hope you may find and read these lines before going to your room, which we have been obliged to give to Louis d'Esterre, who was brought here by Sigmund. Mamma's dressing-room has been prepared for your reception, but, if you are not too tired, I wish you would wait where you find this note until all is quiet in the house, as I shall then make an effort to see you for a few minutes alone."

Frank extinguished his taper, leaned back in the corner of the sofa, gazed drowsily at the lamp for a few minutes, then opened his eyes suddenly to their fullest extent, and looked round the room as if determined not to yield to the fatigue that was overwhelming him, forced himself to sit upright for a short time, and finally murmuring, " She won't mind," stretched himself at full length, and almost instantly was fast asleep.

So fast asleep that the sound of booted and spurred feet treading heavily not only on the stairs but in the room above, the closing and locking of doors, and even the entrance and approach of Doris herself, failed to rouse or disturb Frank until she placed her candle on the table, and, retiring behind the sofa on which he lay, fixed her eyes steadily on his face, when an expression of uneasiness passed over it, he breathed quickly, moved, and the lightest touch of her hand was sufficient to waken him completely.

" I ought not to have asked you to wait for me, Frank," she began, apologetically: " you must be so dreadfully fatigued."

" Well, I have undoubtedly had some hard work," he answered, smiling—" under arms and mounted nearly two-and-twenty hours ! Nothing less would have made me fall asleep, Doris, when I expected to see you ! "

" I should not have been so unreasonable," she continued, " were it not that this is the only time I can see you alone without exciting the suspicions of Hilda."

" Suspicions ?—Hilda ! "

" Yes, dear Frank. She fears I may be tempted to betray her, and I am about to do so—it is our last chance."

" Now, Doris, dear, speak plainly and straightforwardly —you know I am a bad hand at enigmas."

" To speak plainly, then, Frank, I must begin by reminding you of that unfortunate adventure which your late injudicious interference has only served to make still more known to every one in Ulm and its vicinity."

" I hope you are not going to talk again of that cursed old tower, Doris," he began, impatiently.

"Not of the tower," she said, quietly, "but of your and Hilda's imprisonment in it."

"S'death!" he cried, starting up, and beginning to stride up and down the room; "have I not told you, and my aunt, and every one, that I cannot be made answerable for that? D—— the tower, and everything belonging to it! May the French pillage, plunder, blast it to atoms— raze it to the ground!"

"All to no purpose," said Doris; "the destruction of the tower will neither deprive people of memories nor speech."

"It seems, however, Doris, that your memory is not what it used to be, or—" he said, stopping opposite her— "or you would recollect all I said on this subject when we parted not quite amicably about a week ago."

"I have not forgotten," she answered, seating herself on the sofa, and with a slight gesture inducing him to take the place beside her; "I have not forgotten, but I did not think it possible you would persist in your refusal when you were convinced that my resolution to break off our engagement was irrevocable. It seems, however, that we do not yet know each other."

"I am learning to know you," said Frank; "learning also to believe Pallersberg when he calls your regard for me quiet and passionless. Oh, Doris! if you really and truly loved me, you *could* not resign me to any one—not even to Hilda."

"I would not—I could not, Frank, if—if I had not discovered that Hilda loves you devotedly, and as passionately as—as you can possibly desire."

To Doris's surprise, Frank appeared neither astonished nor dismayed at this communication, which she expected to have had the same effect on him as on herself. An air of bored consciousness was, however, expressive enough;

and a sudden revulsion of feeling made her exclaim, "Frank! if you knew this before you went to Forsteck, you have acted with unpardonable selfishness, and are far more to blame than I believed possible."

"I knew nothing, and never thought about the matter," said Frank; "the people here and Pallersberg have been talking; but I hope they and you are mistaken."

"We are not mistaken—there is no doubt whatever."

"It is an infernal business altogether," said Frank, "and I shall end by becoming a victim to circumstances over which I had no control."

"Then you consent?" cried Doris, eagerly.

"I—suppose—I *must;* but it will prove a complete reversion of the order of things if Hilda have to make advances to me, and I try to return her affection—when I can."

Doris stood up.

"Stay, Doris; you cannot expect me to make this great sacrifice unconditionally. You must hear my stipulations. In the first place, I will not give up my profession——"

"You need not," she said, faintly.

"Nor will I live with Hilda for the next ten years."

"I dare say she will—of course she must—consent to this also," replied Doris.

"You would," said Frank; "but then your regard for me, I am now convinced, was merely that of one cousin for another."

"If it were not hitherto," said Doris, her voice faltering in spite of all her efforts to conceal her emotion—"if it were not hitherto, it must be so henceforward."

"Doris! Doris!" he cried, passionately, "you would show more feeling for me if you knew how much I value a kind word or look from you! Dispose of me as you will," he added, putting his arm round her, "but let me hear once more that you *have* loved me, *do* love me, and will *ever* love me! Say that, in resigning me to satisfy the prejudices of the world, you feel not only for me, but with me."

"I can say so, Frank, most truly," she answered, while large tears fell fast from her eyes in confirmation of her words.

"I believe you," he said, rising; "and ask no more. My aunt would call me selfish to wish it so, Doris; but love is selfish, and I love you, and have loved you more than I ever knew—till now."

"Let us hope, Frank, that time will reconcile——"

"No, Doris," he cried, interrupting her; "time will make no change in me."

"It will," she said, gently, "in you and in me also; and Hilda will never be quite conscious how much her happiness has cost us; for I am sure, Frank, you know me too well to think of attempting to prove your affection for me by an ostentatious neglect of her."

"As your sister," he answered, "and as my cousin, I liked her; but as a wife forced upon me, I hate her."

"I am sorry you think it necessary to say so," observed Doris; "but you know, dear Frank, it is not in your nature to hate any woman, and," she added, with a trembling smile—"and especially one so young and singularly attractive as Hilda."

Frank, like all men of action, ever more influenced by his feelings than his understanding, threw himself impetuously at her feet, and raising his clasped hands, exclaimed, "Hear me, Doris! I will give Hilda my hand and name at your command; but I swear by Heaven that neither ten years hence nor ever shall she be more to me than—— "

"What madness is this!" cried Doris, interrupting him.

" Can you for a moment doubt that I desire her and your happiness ? Let me assure you that every effort on your part to conceal your repugnance to this marriage I shall consider and value as a proof of personal regard for me."

Frank could not bring himself to believe this, but, feeling suddenly the choking sensation in his throat that usually precedes an outburst of grief, he made no attempt to speak, let his head sink on his knee, and remained perfectly motionless until Doris bent down and pressed her lips on the only part of his forehead that was visible. Perhaps he felt her tears—she saw his chest heave violently—heard a sound that resembled a suppressed sob, and hurried from the room, agitated and shocked at an exhibition of feeling for which she had been totally unprepared.

CHAPTER XVII.

MARRY IN HASTE, AND REPENT AT LEISURE.

After a few hours' repose, the inmates of the Waldering house were once more up and beginning to move about in the twilight of a foggy morning. Drums were beating and trumpets sounding in a manner as intelligible as speech to military ears, and among the first who hastened to obey these calls was Frank. He had seen his aunt for a few minutes while breakfasting, had confirmed his promise of the previous night, and given his aunt leave to make any arrangements she pleased, as far as he was concerned, but declined remaining longer in a house where the Director and Sigmund considered themselves at home.

"This house may be yours to-morrow—to-day, if you wish it, Frank," she had suggested, quickly.

"A few ounces of lead from a well-handled French musket would be more acceptable to me just now," had been his muttered answer when leaving the room.

And long had been the consultation afterwards between Doris and her mother as to what Hilda might be told, and what it would be absolutely necessary to conceal from her, for some time at least; the result being that they would inform her that Frank had agreed to the marriage, but, as he would not consent to give up his profession, and could not expect her to move about with him under existing circumstances, it had been arranged that she was to remain with them until the war was ended.

While Doris went to make this communication to Hilda, her mother entered the adjoining room, where Sigmund and his father were still lingering over their breakfast, and though quite aware that the Director's exasperation concerning Hilda had been the work of his son, and that she had latterly observed an unconcealed diminution of his anger, she was nevertheless a good deal surprised to find her present intelligence received by him with a look of blank disappointment.

"I rather expected you to rejoice with me at the prospect of so satisfactory a termination to this unfortunate affair," she said, looking from one to the other.

"Well—yes—I suppose it's all for the best," said the Director, embarrassed; "but a—I must say Sigmund has been hasty in this business, and now that I am convinced of poor dear Hilda's innocence——"

"Of that," said his sister-in-law, interrupting him, "I believe even Sigmund had no doubt."

"None whatever," said Sigmund; "but as I could not induce other people to take my view of the case, you must acknowledge there was no alternative but breaking off our engagement."

"Perhaps so, but it might have been done less violently," observed his aunt, "and, at all events, with some
consideration for her and our feelings."

"I should have acted otherwise," answered Sigmund,
"if Hilda had not irritated me by her open preference for
Frank, and made me the laughing-stock of Ulm ever since
we have been here."

There was much truth in this remark, and she turned
to her brother-in-law while observing, "Recriminations are
useless, and I am sure you will agree with me in thinking
that the sooner now this marriage takes place, the better."

"On that subject," cried Sigmund, eagerly, "there can
be no doubt whatever; for O'More is so thoroughly a man
of impulse that any delay would be a risk."

"On him we may rely," she answered, with a sigh;
"but I think if Hilda be given much time for consideration,
she will refuse to accept the sacrifice her sister has made
for her."

"All this may be very fine," said the Director, testily;
"but I must say, if things had remained as they were, it
would have been pleasanter in the end for us all! Sigmund would have had Hilda's fortune to put his affairs in
order; Frank O'More would not have been encumbered
with a wife, and we should have had the undisturbed enjoyment of our charming Doris's society for years to come;
whereas now Hilda will wish to live in Austria, in order to
be near her husband, and you and Doris will follow her."

"We have at present no plans of the kind," she
answered; "and I am even inclined to think that the
state of our finances will compel us to reside for some time
at Westenried."

"Ah!—ah!—that alters the case in some degree; and
with regard to the marriage, delay is useless if it be a thing
decided upon. We have only to substitute the name of

Frank O'More for that of Sigmund Count Waldering in the various documents already in my possession, and everything is in order. Permit me, however, to suggest some changes in the pecuniary arrangements, while reminding you that Sigmund's position and prospects were very different from this young Irishman's, who, a younger son and literally penniless, cannot possibly expect——"

" I don't know what he expects," she said, interrupting him ; " but I know what, under the circumstances, he may claim as a right, and therefore request that the arrangements may be precisely the same as proposed by you for Sigmund, with the exception of the double performance of the marriage ceremony,—one will now be sufficient, and I believe we may appoint the Protestant clergyman for this evening."

At this moment a servant entered, bringing the report from head-quarters which Sigmund had requested the officers then residing in the house to send him. It described the engagement of the previous day with Marshal Ney ; said that, from intercepted papers, no doubt could be entertained that the storming of the town had been projected ; mentioned that between eight and nine hundred prisoners had been taken, and commended the different regiments by name that had been engaged.

The Countess Waldering received at the same time a request to furnish ninety rations of soup, to be sent as soon as possible to the schoolhouse, where the French prisoners were in confinement.

She handed the paper to her brother-in-law, and asked, with a look of perplexity, " Is that an order for to-day, or for a time indefinite ? "

" I don't know," he answered ; " but you must send the soup to-day, at all events."

" Of course. Our stores, however, are nearly exhausted,

and there is hardly anything to be had in the town now, excepting potatoes and cheese."

The Director turned to his son with a rueful expression of countenance, and observed, "We shall come to the horse-flesh at last! Who was it that told us it tasted exactly like veal?"

"Pallersberg said so, I believe," answered Sigmund; "but if the French gain the heights round the town, a few shells will prove the impossibility of defending it for any length of time."

"You, of course, hope it may be so," observed his aunt, vainly endeavouring to hide her annoyance; "but you must allow me still to think it possible that the Russians may come to our relief."

"I did not mean to offend," said Sigmund, apologetically, "and assure you I only, as a *ci-devant* soldier, ventured an opinion which may prove altogether erroneous."

"I fear not," she replied, "as it is entertained by those who would rather think otherwise. However," she added, addressing the Director, "to go from great things to small ones, which more immediately concern us, I suppose I may depend on your making the necessary arrangements for this evening?"

"Undoubtedly. But allow me to propose insuring the appearance of the bridegroom, who may chance to be on guard, or on picket, or whatever they call it. You had better consult with him, or send to Captain Pallersberg, and request him to bring O'More to the cathedral at four o'clock in the afternoon. As guardian," he continued, walking with her to the door, "I should like to protest against this hurried marriage, but——"

"But," she said, interrupting him, "you feel, perhaps, that you have no right to do so after having been the first person to propose it."

"It was at Sigmund's instigation that I did so," cried the Director. "His anger and jealousy were quite ungovernable."

"Not so," she observed; "he has long wished for a plausible excuse to break off his engagement, but would, perhaps, have chosen another time and less unfeeling means had he not had motives which made this opportunity, for various reasons, the most desirable ever likely to occur."

"Well," said the Director, as the door closed, "he has much penetration, but this time has rather overshot the mark, I believe."

"Not exactly," said Sigmund; "I certainly had no objection to a plausible excuse for breaking off my engagement to Hilda, whose preference for Frank is notorious; but surely mine for Doris cannot have been less well known both to you and my aunt, though neither of you chose to appear conscious of it."

"Would you have wished it otherwise, Sigmund, when Doris's indifference to you was so very evident? And can you suppose you have the slightest chance, now that this indifference will be converted into actual dislike by your conduct to her sister and its consequences to herself?"

"Dislike is more easily overcome than indifference," said Sigmund confidently. "Let Frank be married to Hilda, and leave the rest to me."

"I begin to wish you were all married," said the Director, as he walked to the other end of the room, and drew a chair towards his writing-table.

"All!" repeated his son, laughing; "who do you mean by *all?*"

"Every one, with the exception of your grandmother," was the answer.

"Yourself included?"

" Why not ?   Men older than I am have married, and will marry to the end of time.   My sister-in-law says that it is a pleasant infatuation of our sex to imagine ourselves capable of inspiring affection, even at the most advanced period of life."

" Ha !" cried Sigmund, " Mina Pallersberg once hinted that you—but the idea is preposterous ! "

" Quite so," said his father, without looking round ; " but Mina has a good deal of discernment in such matters, and says that your plans now are also—preposterous."

" Mina is a most intriguing, dangerous girl," said Sigmund, " and I wish my grandmother would send her home to her parents, or otherwise dispose of her."

" You were not always of this opinion," observed his father, drily.

Sigmund was silent.

" But," he continued, while arranging his papers—" but that you have overcome any feeling beyond good-will and regard for her now, is very satisfactory."

" I do not feel a particle of either," answered Sigmund, " and repeat that I think her a most dangerous and intriguing character. It is impossible to calculate the mischief such a person can perpetrate in a family like ours, so I hope when you wished us all married Mina Pallersberg was included, in which case I can only say, the sooner the better."

" Be it so," said the Director.   " As, however, Hilda happens to be the first, I must now take her affairs in hand, and without further loss of time.   It will be a dismal business altogether this marriage, and I wish it were well over !"

A few hours later the soup required for the French

prisoners was sent from the house—then an effort made to supply the billeted officers and soldiers with a repast, while the family assembled about the same time in a small sitting-room overlooking the garden, to dine, with a frugality to which they were gradually becoming accustomed. Hilda and Doris were not present—no one seemed to expect them or consider an apology necessary ; but when the Director saw his sister-in-law preparing to return to them, he drew out his watch and observed significantly, " I hope they are dressed, for we must soon be on our way to the Cathedral."

Scarcely had she closed the door when she heard the stamping of horses and the rolling of wheels on the paving-stones of the yard, and seeing a servant springing up the stairs to announce the carriage, she entered her room, not sorry to have a pretext for putting an end to the painful situation in which her rival daughters had been placed since the morning.

Doris was calm and self-possessed—perhaps the feeling that she was acting magnanimously supported her—while Hilda, conscious of a latent satisfaction at the prospect of a marriage with Frank under any circumstances, was thoroughly ashamed of her selfishness and felt deeply humiliated in accepting the sacrifice so unostentatiously made by her sister.

" Mamma," she said, hurriedly, " Doris says she thinks Frank will be quite satisfied if I leave him perfectly at liberty and do not interfere with his plan of remaining in the army. The idea of being forced upon him in this way is so dreadful, that did I not know how much he likes me, and had he not told me unreservedly a hundred times that he loved me next best to Doris, I——"

" Hilda ! " cried the Director, knocking at the door, " we are waiting for you."

" Doris," she said, clasping her hands, and kneeling before her sister, who was waiting to place a white veil on her head, " dear Doris, say once more that you forgive me."

" Rather let me again explain that I have nothing to forgive, Hilda. Your ride to Forsteck with Frank really requires no apology, and for what has since occurred you cannot be made answerable."

Somewhat consoled by these words, Hilda rose, drew her black velvet pelisse over her white dress, and, covering her face with her veil, followed her mother out of the room.

A few minutes afterwards they were on their way to the Cathedral, followed by the Director, his mother, and Mina Pallersberg, in another carriage. The way was not long to the beautiful building, and at the portal, just dismounted from their horses, they found Frank and Pallersberg. Notwithstanding the inclemency of the weather, a number of people had collected round the entrance, who unceremoniously followed them into the church, and even to the private chapel in which the ceremony was to take place, where, with faces pressed against the filagree-work of the iron gate that separated it from the main building, they wondered in whispers why there were so few friends present, and what made both bride and bridegroom look so deadly pale.

The marriage ceremony commenced : to Doris it appeared like part of a troubled dream, especially when the exchange of rings was to take place, and she knew Hilda had none, and was sure Frank had never thought about the matter : her mother, however, advanced, and quickly drew from her finger her own wedding-ring, gave it to Frank, and then put into Hilda's trembling hand the ring that had been found by them on the previous Holy-Eve in the crypt of the church on the Chapel-island. The midnight scene then recurred to Hilda's mind with painful vividness, and it was with a feeling of perplexity and consternation that she nervously placed the ring on Frank's finger, audibly drawing in her breath, and afterwards raising her eyes for the first time anxiously to his countenance. He, too, seemed startled, and a crowd of recollections brought a deep flush to his face and temples, until a glance towards Doris again deprived him of every trace of colour.

When they again stood before the door of the church, and as Frank, after having placed Hilda and Doris in the carriage, drew aside to allow Pallersberg and his aunt to pass him, the Director placed his hand on his arm, and whispered, " You will come back with us, O'More, if only for appearance' sake and to sign the papers ? "

"Impossible ! " he answered, beckoning to the soldier who held his horse. " I must return to the redoubt on the Michaelsburg."

He waited until joined by Pallersberg; they sprang on their horses at the same moment, raised their hands in salute, and dashed at full gallop across the open space before the Cathedral.

" Doris," said Hilda, with faltering voice, " he did not speak to me—scarcely even looked at me."

" My dear child," observed her mother, gravely, " you must have patience with Frank for a little while ; he may, perhaps, think it necessary to affect indifference towards you, in order not to appear fickle to Doris."

Hilda turned quickly to her sister: " Is this likely, Doris? You know him best."

" Oh ! very—likely," panted Doris, with a painful effort to smile, while vividly recalling poor Frank's anguish when they had parted on the previous night.

"I am sorry," said their mother, taking a hand of each, "very sorry, to see you both suffering so much. It will scarcely serve as a consolation to tell you that I was once in my life far more severely tried—far more thoroughly unhappy than either of you!"

"Do not for a moment suppose that I am unhappy, dear mother," cried Doris, hastily; "or Hilda either, though her sudden marriage may have confused and alarmed her."

"I do feel confused," said Hilda, "and I dare say Frank is the same; that unlucky ring, too, may have made an unpleasant impression on him."

"That is not probable," observed her mother, "as he knows it was worn many years by your father, and never considered unlucky. You must not become superstitious, Hilda."

"How can I help it," she asked, despondingly, "when I remember where and how we found that ring?—and Frank so pale, that he reminded me horribly of the apparition I saw in the vaults of the chapel?"

The carriage stopped, and the wedding party slowly ascended the stairs, on which a group of officers had assembled to congratulate Frank on what they chose to call his clandestine marriage. They lingered there, too, for some time, in expectation of his probable arrival on horseback, returning at last to their rooms in great astonishment at his non-appearance, which, to them, was perfectly incomprehensible, as they knew that, like themselves, he was that day free from military duty, and therefore his absence must be voluntary.

It was so, in fact, and Pallersberg had been obliged to connive at this breach of decorum, in order that the first outburst of Frank's wrath and despair might be vented on him, instead of the youthful bride.

CHAPTER XVIII.

FREEDOM IN CHAINS.

ABOUT this time the Archduke Ferdinand left Ulm, preferring a retreat of the most perilous description to the capitulation which the tardy approach of the Russians made every day more probable. Frank's hopes of leaving the town were frustrated by a wounded general, who had taken up his quarters in the Waldering house, choosing to retain him as aide-de-camp ; and in consequence of this he was not only obliged to be there continually, but, notwithstanding all his efforts to make it evident that his intercourse with the family was a matter of necessity, and not choice, frequent meetings, and even long discussions, soon became unavoidable, his near relationship causing him to be chosen as the bearer of requests or demands that would otherwise have been made by letter.

At first Frank thought it indispensable to affect a press of business and extreme haste when delivering his messages ; by degrees, however, he discovered that his aunt and Doris were perfectly unchanged in their manner towards him, and that the Director and Sigmund never attempted to dispute any requisition made by him, no matter how unreasonable it might appear to them; but it was not until he brought a demand for the Waldering horses to remount some cuirassiers, that he perceived a sort of whispered appeal made to his neglected bride, as she sat somewhat apart from the others at a distant window, when the acquiescent motion of her head, and the words, "Of course ; why ask me ? " suddenly, and not agreeably, reminded him that she was proprietress of the house, and all that it contained.

For the first time since their marriage he addressed her directly while saying, half-apologetically, "We only require the carriage horses, Hilda."

"And why have you not taken them?" she asked, looking up, and blushing deeply.

"Because I have received orders to purchase, not take," he answered, resuming the air of distant politeness, which he considered expressive of his determination not to be won by her efforts to conciliate; "But," he continued, "I suppose your uncle or cousin will be better able to name a price than you."

"The horses are yours, Frank," she rejoined timidly, "to sell or dispose of in any way that you think proper."

Poor Hilda! She meant to please, and gave dire offence. Frank was irritated at being offered as a gift, when he came to purchase. He would not at that moment have accepted anything from her under any circumstances; so he turned abruptly to Sigmund, and asked him what he thought the horses were worth.

"Taking the present circumstances into consideration," answered Sigmund, "I suppose we must not venture to suggest as the price what they cost last year in Munich?"

"I should think not!" said Frank, laughing ironically; "rather a good deal less; for, though the bays are well enough, one of the greys must be fired for spavin before six weeks are over!"

"Spavin!" repeated Sigmund, looking towards his father. "Did you buy a spavined horse for Hilda?"

"Not intentionally," answered the Director, quietly; "but as you were not with us, and I am ignorant on such subjects, I was obliged to trust altogether to a horse-dealer."

"At all events," observed Sigmund, "it cannot be very evident, or I should have discovered it."

" I am ready to prove my assertion," said Frank, walking to the door, " and I hope you will excuse my driving a
hard bargain, for our funds are very low just now."

" Well! " exclaimed the Director when they had left
the room, " that is as remarkable an instance of perversity
as can well be imagined! "

" We must make some allowance for him just now,"
observed Doris. " You know he has been retained here
against his will; and he told mamma this morning that,
instead of receiving his promotion in his own regiment, as
he had hoped, he is appointed to the Hussars, now in
Vienna."

" Did he tell you the reason? " asked the Director.

" No."

" Then I can. It is in consequence of his various *passages d'armes* with his comrades about—about——"

" About me!" said Hilda. " No wonder he has learned
to dislike me! "

" Ah, bah! that won't last long," said the Director,
laughing; " and this change has served to prove that he has
many and powerful friends. Sigmund heard that there
were two other generals who would have taken him as
aide-de-camp, and not a single officer in his regiment could
be induced to bear witness against him."

" What! " exclaimed Doris, " not even those he had
wounded? "

" No. They were so chivalrous as to say that the provocation had been great, and that he had only acted as
they would have done in his place; besides, it was proved
that he had visited, sat up at night with them, and, I
believe, dressed their wounds! "

" Oh, how I like him for all this! " cried Hilda enthusiastically.

" Quixotic, as usual," said Doris—the expression of her

face giving anything rather than a disparaging meaning to the words.

"Courageous he is, at all events," observed the Director, "and disinterested, too, we must suppose, from his present effort to buy his wife's horses a bargain for these cuirassiers."

"He is quite right," said Hilda.

"I am glad you think so, my dear," said the Director, "and hope you may have reason to be equally satisfied with him in every respect."

"I am—that is, I should be quite satisfied if he were once more gay and like himself; to make him so, I could almost wish the Russians here and the French defeated!"

"Hear the youthful rebel!" cried the Director, laughing. "Four days married, and already a complete change of politics!"

"No," cried Hilda eagerly, "I am quite Bavarian still, and admire Napoleon as much as ever."

"And no doubt," interposed Doris, with some vehemence, "your admiration will be increased when Ulm is bombarded, and the country about is completely devastated."

"M. d'Esterre," replied Hilda, "told me that Napoleon will spare the town, as the burghers are known to be well disposed towards him."

"More shame for them!" began Doris.

"My dear girls," cried their mother, interfering, "you promised me to avoid this subject—the only one on which you ever disagree. Believe me, a few years hence you and all of us will think alike of this great general, but most perfidious and unscrupulous of men!"

The Director shook his head and smiled ironically; but thinking it better to avoid a useless discussion, he left the room, saying he had an appointment at the commissariat about forage. Doris and her mother soon after followed, on longer either thinking or speaking of Napoleon, but in deep consultation about the reception of additional troops that were to be billeted on them; while Hilda, the person, in fact, most of all concerned in these arrangements, pursued the occupation then universally prevalent in Ulm—the preparing of lint and bandages for a temporary hospital that had been established in what had once been and was still called the Wengen Monastery. The table before her was covered with long strips and narrow rolls of carefully docketed linen, heaps of fine and coarse lint, far more than enough to fill the basket placed beside her for their reception, but still she cut, and picked, and folded, only looking up for a moment when Frank suddenly returned to the room, apparently more surprised than pleased to find her alone in it.

"Sigmund declines receiving the money for the horses," he said advancing to the table; "and though I hoped to find the Director or my aunt here, you will do as well, or better than either, as the money is, in fact, yours." Here he pushed aside some of the lint and linen, and began to count his bank-notes in a most business-like manner.

"I have not purchased these horses for myself, Hilda," he said with some hesitation, "and therefore must beg you to sign this paper, acknowledging having received the sum of——"

He stopped, and Hilda looked up inquiringly.

"It is a matter of business," he added hastily, "and you know I must have something in the form of a receipt to show."

"I did not think of that," she said, rising so hastily that, in passing to another table where there were writing materials, her dress swept the carefully arranged notes to the ground. Then taking up a pen she inadvertently, and in a handwriting rendered almost illegible by agitation, signed the name of Waldering!

" That paper is of no use, Hilda; you had better ask the Director to write another," said Frank, preparing to leave the room.

" Oh, stay—I see my mistake now. Can I not write the—the other name underneath ? "

" No ; I would rather have the Director's signature."

" But you are not offended—not angry, I hope ? "

"Not in the least. I think it is very probable you prefer the name of Waldering, and if so you can resume it whenever you think it advisable to do so."

"Frank ! " she exclaimed laying her hand on his arm, "do you mean what my grandmother proposed this morning? Do you wish for a—a divorce ? "

" I have been told," he answered, " that there is no great difficulty in obtaining one in this part of Germany, and, should you desire it, I shall be ready at any time to meet your wishes; the proposal, however, must come from you or your family, for I have no legal cause of complaint, and no object to gain, since Doris is lost to me for ever ! "

" No legal cause of complaint ! " repeated Hilda. " I do not understand these things, Frank ; but Doris told me that if we did not ask you to leave the army, and that I returned to Westenried with my mother until the war was over, you would be satisfied."

" Yes ; those were my *stipulations.*"

" Before our marriage ? " she asked quickly.

" Undoubtedly ; otherwise I should never have consented."

" And I thought they were concessions on my part—made, however, most willingly at Doris's instigation."

" Call them concessions if you like," said Frank ; " I only insist on their being understood and adhered to, undeviatingly."

" Of course," said Hilda, a good deal alarmed at the

irritated tone of his voice—" of course; and if mamma should go to Innsbruck instead of Westenried, have you any objection to my accompanying her ? "

" Go where you please, and do what you like," he answered, turning away. " I make no pretension to authority in a union that is merely nominal."

Long after he had left the room, Hilda stood with hands tightly pressed together, flushed cheeks, and eyes resting on the closed door with the steady, abstracted gaze of profound thought. It was a long reluctant retrospect, producing much self-condemnation and regret, but was soon succeeded by a strong revulsion of feeling, made at once evident by the parted lips, quick audible breathing, and flashing eyes. Pride and resentment had gained the ascendency, and when Sigmund soon after entered the room, she walked to the window, bent over her parcels of linen while packing them into the basket, and then stooped to collect the scattered bank-notes, in order to place them again on the table.

" I wish, Sigmund," she said, with that apparent composure by no means uncommon in even very young women in moments of great mental agitation—" I wish you would put this money aside until my uncle returns home."

" But did not Frank give it to *you ?* " he asked.

" Yes. It happened, however, that a receipt was necessary, and when he placed one before me for signature, I thoughtlessly wrote ' Waldering ' instead of——"

" Ha ! ha ! ha ! capital !—as nice a manœuvre as could well be imagined !"

" It was nothing of the kind, Sigmund—a stupid mistake, only excusable when one takes into consideration how often I have signed the name of Waldering to similar papers since I came to Ulm. Pray send Frank a written acknowledgment this evening, or he will suppose me as negligent as I was thoughtless."

"Stay, Hilda—one word. Did not this little scene lead to a reconciliation with Frank? Believe me, I wish it most sincerely, for his conduct is such that I begin to fear you will feel irritated instead of grateful for my indirect influence in promoting your marriage."

"I neither feel the one nor the other, Sigmund," she answered, with forced calmness. "You had motives for your actions that Mina has since explained to me at some length."

"Just like her," he observed, bitterly: "and she has explained to Doris also, as a matter of course. I hope, however, she pointed out to *her* the great pecuniary sacrifice I made in resigning you?"

"Do not fancy you resigned me," said Hilda, eagerly seizing the offered vent for the anger rankling at her heart. "One would really suppose I was a thing to be taken or refused at pleasure! Frank's chivalrous conduct during my eight days' imprisonment would have made me love him had I never cared for him before, while your double-dealing on that occasion turned at once the little regard I ever felt for you into scorn!"

"If," said Sigmund, with ironical gravity—"if my humiliation can serve to raise your husband in your estimation, I can almost rejoice in it; but you have no right to scorn me for having promoted your marriage with this 'dearest, handsomest, bravest,' and, as you now tell me, most chivalrous of men! On the contrary, I have every reason to expect you to assist me in return by pleading my cause to Doris whenever an occasion offers."

"Plead for yourself; it will be in vain——" began Hilda; but at that moment Doris appeared at the door to remind her that it was time to go to the hospital.

"I am sorry to tell you," she said, as they walked away together, "that all the rooms and even the corridors of our Wenger Monastery Hospital are now filled with wounded, and the poor men complain more of cold and hunger than of their wounds. There are no mattresses, no cooking utensils, and a great want of linen and other necessaries. A printed request has been sent to all the inhabitants of the town for assistance, and mamma desired me to ask you if you object to her sending whatever we can spare?"

"How could I object?" said Hilda. "Is it not a duty to give everything we possess on such an occasion?"

"Mamma says she was sure you would think so," continued Doris; "but as the Director was of opinion that valuable wine such as you have in the cellars here would be thrown away if given for hospital use, we thought it better to consult you."

"Did my uncle say he would not allow me to give it?" asked Hilda.

"No, dear. You forget that since your marriage he has no further control, and Frank will certainly make no objection."

"I shall not ask him," said Hilda, with a decision quite unlike her usual manner; "he makes no pretension to authority in a union that is merely nominal."

Doris stood still and looked at her sister. "Did he say this, Hilda?"

"Yes, Doris, and at the same time told me distinctly that I might go where I pleased and do what I liked."

"Dear Hilda, I am so sorry!—but you will see that in time——"

"In time, Doris, I shall learn to enjoy my independence, and the first use I make of it will be to send all the wine in this house to the hospital!"

CHAPTER XIX.

SOLDIER'S WORK.

THE situation of the inhabitants of Ulm became every day more deplorable. During the last month soldiers had been quartered in all the houses, latterly to the amount of a hundred and fifty and even two hundred in those of very moderate dimensions. For the troops in and about the town rations both of bread and meat had been furnished in hundreds of thousands, causing millers, bakers, and butchers to be almost exclusively employed in the service of the army. All communication with the surrounding country was cut off; there was no market, and latterly no possibility of supplying the crowded town with provisions; beer could no longer be procured, bread seldom in sufficient quantities, often not at all; and at length high and low were alike reduced to the consumption of the still remaining stores of cheese and potatoes.

The unusual inclemency of the weather greatly added to the general discomfort; wild storms of biting sleet succeeded the rain that had previously fallen in torrents; the cold increased, and the ground in the vicinity of the hastily thrown up intrenchments became a thick clammy mud, not only impeding progress, but injuring uniforms and destroying shoes and boots in a manner that made a proclamation necessary commanding the attendance of all the shoemakers in Ulm to mend and make exclusively for the garrison.

It is difficult to imagine how the French, burthened with arms and provisions, managed to toil over roads rendered so nearly impassable by rain, and burrowed by the

passage of artillery and baggage-waggons ; but the chances
of fatigue and exposure to the weather were not on any
occasion taken into consideration by Napoleon when moving
his troops, and therefore, in spite of all impediments, the
presence of the main army soon became known in Ulm,
when the inhabitants heard the booming of cannon in the
direction of Elchingen and the rattle of musketry in their
immediate vicinity.

With the succeeding military movements we have no
concern, excepting in so far as they were evident or important to the inmates of the Waldering house, the situation
of which, not far from the Danube gate, made them witnesses
of the first engagement which took place within sight of
the walls of Ulm : this was when a column of French
cavalry, halting at some distance on the Memmingen road,
sent forward detachments to attack the Austrian pickets
there stationed, and a skirmish commenced which increased
to a conflict that lasted the whole afternoon.

The Director, Sigmund, and their friend d'Esterre
mounted to the roof of the house to watch with similar
hopes and feelings the progress of the engagement, while
Doris and Hilda, peering through a small window in the
loft, followed with anxious eyes the lines of moving infantry, the charges of cavalry, the march of reinforcements
from the town, and the wreaths of smoke that preceded
the report of musketry, without in the least understanding
what was going on.

"It does not look so awful as I imagined," observed
Hilda, "perhaps because the rain makes everything so
indistinct."

"Yet," said Doris, " it is horrible when one thinks that
they are trying to kill each other, and that every shot we
hear may cause death !"

At this moment Frank, mounted on Doris's horse,

galloped at full speed across the bridge in the direction of the combatants.

"They have sent him with orders," cried Doris, clasping her hands, "and he will be sure to get into danger."

"And you," said Hilda—"you have lent or given him Brian Boru?"

"Neither," answered Doris, quickly; "when his horse was wounded I proposed his taking him, but he assured me Brian was too light for a charger, did not stand fire, and I know not what else."

"And now," rejoined Hilda—"now he prefers him to *my* Selim; a freak not unlike his buying the carriage-horses, and paying—paying *me* for them, Doris!"

"I always feared he would be guilty of some such absurdities," said Doris, in a low voice. "Have patience, dear Hilda, and believe me all will go right at last."

"Not if he see his power, Doris, and continues so well assured of my affection. He now thinks that I will submit humbly to any amount of arrogance on his part; but he is mistaken, and I hope before long to show him that I feel conscious of the independence he so rudely conferred on me."

"But, Hilda, you have told me that you like this arrangement, and remain quite willingly with mamma and me."

"And so I do; I even find his ' stipulations,' as he calls them, quite reasonable and judicious; but when they are not disputed, why make a display of his indifference or dislike to me? Why give Sigmund opportunities of pretending sympathy and offering consolation?"

"Why, indeed!" said Doris; "he is perverse—ungenerous—and I shall tell him so the first opportunity that offers."

"Not for the universe!" exclaimed Hilda, hastily; "I will not have him ordered to treat me with politeness!"

" Perhaps you are right, Hilda; but at all events, when you judge him, take into consideration the state of agitation and anxiety in which he has lately been living. Believe me, he is not like himself just now !"

" To you, Doris, he is precisely what he ever was, and I only require him to be again the same to me. Am I un-reasonable ?"

" No, dear, no, and if you will only allow me to speak to him——"

" I will *not*, Doris; the time for the interference of friends is past, and having received his orders to adhere undeviatingly to these stipulations, I can only obey and console myself with——" She paused.

" With what ?" asked Doris, anxiously.

" With the power to go where I please and to do what I like," answered Hilda.

Neither of them spoke again, though they remained for some time longer side by side watching and waiting for the reappearance of Frank, who had apparently joined a body of cavalry that had soon after charged the French. They waited in vain; various detachments of troops left the town, but none returned, and at length, the storm beginning to drive sheets of waving sleet between them and the com-batants, they turned shivering from the window and descended to the small sitting-room at the back of the house, which with two or three other apartments of equally insignificant dimensions, had latterly been all that could be reserved for the private use of their family.

The sisters seated themselves at different windows, and looked into the garden with its Grecian temple, and the turbulent flooded river beyond, and were quite uncon-scious of the approach of evening until the sound of numer-ous and heavily-treading feet in the corridors announced the return of the soldiers billeted in the house to their quarters

"Do you think," asked Hilda, "there is any use in making inquiries about him? The officers here are so very polite that I don't at all mind asking them: besides, they know I have a right to——"

At this moment the door opened, and the object of their mutual anxiety stood before them. Bespattered with mud and blood, his clothes completely wet through, he advanced towards Doris with a step so slow and reluctant, so unlike himself, that she bent forward alarmed, and exclaimed as he approached, "Frank,—you are wounded!"

Hilda sprang to her feet with an ejaculation of stifled terror.

"No, Doris, I am not wounded; I am not, I assure you!" he added, as she rose and, approaching him, pointed to the upper part of the sleeve of his coat, which hung dangling from his elbow.

"That was a lucky cut for me," he said quietly; "but it cost a French dragoon his life. You see the sleeve alone is injured."

"I see that the lower part of it is saturated with blood," she answered.

"Then," he said, raising his arm for inspection, "it is French blood that streamed down the blade and over the hilt of my sword."

"Oh, Frank, how dreadful!"

"Yes, dear, very dreadful—after it is over; but when charging the enemy one is impelled onward by some irresistible impulse that gives a feeling of absolute exultation in crushing and destroying every opponent. There is something horribly exciting in these fierce struggles. It is soldier's work, Doris, and will not bear quiet discussion. I came to speak of something else; to tell you that when carrying orders from the General I borrowed your horse Brian Boru——"

"I know it," she answered ; "for I saw you riding over the bridge."

" Can you forgive me for taking him, Doris, when I tell you that half-an-hour afterwards he was shot under me? His death was quick, for two balls in the flank and one through the body made him fall without a struggle."

" And you, Frank, and you ? "

" I managed soon after to pull a French lancer from his horse, got into his saddle, and returned to the attack."

" And the lancer ? " she asked, glancing suspiciously towards the blood-stained garments.

"He was a gallant fellow, and fought hard before he yielded."

" Oh, then," she said, with a sigh of relief, " you did not kill *him ?* "

Frank was silent for some moments, and then, in a low voice, answered, " Doris, on such occasions, if a man does not take life, he loses it ! "

She covered her face with her hands, as if to shut out the scene that presented itself, while Frank stood before her, his arms folded, his eyes bent on the ground, uncon- scious of the looks of intense admiration bestowed on him by his youthful bride, in whose idea he was at that moment the personification of all that was heroic, brave, and beau- tiful ! What did she know of the horrible carnage in which he had been engaged? She saw him, mounted on her sister's prancing Hungarian steed, conquering everything that came within reach of his sword. She cared not how many had fallen,—she forgot they were French, and, as she usually asserted, her allies. To her there was but one slight, graceful rider sweeping the battle-field, with arm upraised, like a destroying angel! She could hardly contain her annoyance when her sister observed,—-

"You were merely the bearer of orders, Frank, and need not have been engaged if you had not wished it."

"Very true, Doris; but—I can't resist temptation when it comes in my way, and besides, my regiment was there——"

"Your regiment is now in Vienna," she interposed.

"Well, then, my old comrades were there; and when I saw my own troop in motion——"

"Frank, you never waited for that; you volunteered at once!"

"Yes, Doris, of course; and I would do it again!" he answered, impetuously; "and any fellow in my regiment would have volunteered on such an occasion."

"Oh, Doris," exclaimed Hilda, "how can you take him to task in this manner?"

"You do not know what she means, Hilda," said Frank, unable to conceal his annoyance at her interference, "but I do; and she is right in the main, although a little hard upon me, as usual. Doris," he added, after a pause, "I am sorry, very sorry, about Brian, and any amount of reproaches on that score I shall listen to submissively."

"I have none to make," she answered; "your own horse was unfit for service,—what could be more natural than to take mine?"

"Or mine?" interposed Hilda, making an effort to speak in her former unrestrained tone and manner. "How often have you said that Selim might be a general's charger or the parade horse of a Turkish bashaw! Take him into your service now, Frank, as the first step towards his promotion."

"Hilda," he answered, with a frigid gravity quite foreign to his character, and with great effort, assumed for the occasion, "you ought to feel that, circumstanced as we are, I cannot possibly accept anything from *you*. I hoped

I had been sufficiently explicit on this subject not very long since."

Even in the gloomy twilight of the autumn evening Frank saw the painfully deep blush that spread over Hilda's face and neck while he spoke; and though the opportunity of exhibiting his complete renunciation of her in Doris's presence had been very acceptable to him, the words had no sooner passed his lips than he began to relent, and to wish the latter would openly undertake the part of mediating, and enable him with a good grace to consent to a cessation of hostilities calculated eventually to lead to a satisfactory peace.

But he had gone too far; his words had reminded Hilda of all her previous resolutions, and made her ashamed of having been induced, by admiration of his personal courage, to place herself in a position that had given him an opportunity of rebuking and repulsing her again. She turned abruptly away, and left the room in silence more eloquent than words; and Doris, not at all disposed to mediate, stood up, exclaiming, "Frank, you will break her heart. Can you not see that she loves you ten times more than I ever did? Do you think that in her place I should have made so many attempts to conciliate you? I tell you, No! and one such repulse would have turned my affection into dislike, if not something stronger. I did not think you could be so ungracious and ungenerous; but it will at least serve the purpose of lowering you in Hilda's estimation—of making her see you as you are, instead of supposing you a demigod, as she does now!"

Before Frank had time to attempt an answer, Doris was gone; and, a good deal discomfited at the turn his affairs had taken, he sat down, placed his sword between his knees, his clasped hands upon the hilt, his chin upon his hands, and endeavoured, to the best of his ability, to form some plan " to set all to rights again, and make it up with both girls." Doris must be first considered. He did not attempt to dispute her superiority to Hilda—to himself— to every one; but he had a vague idea that she usurped a great deal of authority, and had been very hard upon him of late:—It is true she was always reasonable, always in the right; but surely she must be well aware that his affection for her was the sole cause of the conduct she reprehended so severely. He believed he had been *brusque* to Hilda—ungentlemanlike, in fact; and after all, if Doris really wished him to forget her, and turn to her sister, would it not?—yes—it certainly would be better to obey her. There was no mistaking Doris's manner, and she was evidently angry, and not in the least gratified by his conduct.—Here Frank sighed deeply, and then came various vivid recollections of Hilda's blushing eager efforts to turn the " winter of his discontent to glorious summer; " of unresisting submission to his stipulations, mingled, however, with some incipient fear of having tried her patience beyond endurance; but—had not Doris said that Hilda considered him a demigod?

The natural wish to see how Hilda's demigod looked just then, induced him to raise his eyes to the narrow glass between the windows, and the face reflected there, in spite of disordered hair and recent exposure to storm and sleet, was singularly handsome; it would also have been difficult to discover a fault in the well-formed figure, though the torn, stained, and bespattered uniform and mud-incrusted jack-boots were not exactly calculated to enhance its comeliness; nevertheless, as he stood up, and placed his hand on the marble slab of the *console,* he was anything rather than satisfied with his appearance—made some useless efforts to improve it, as people foolishly will do when conscious

they have previously been seen to disadvantage—hoped the
sunless evening, and consequently sombre room, had prevented his cousins from minutely observing his dress, and
then, murmuring something about even a demigod requiring soap and water, he turned away thinking, for the first
time in his life, more of Hilda than Doris.

CHAPTER XX.

" To eat horseflesh, or not to eat horseflesh ?
That is the question."

FRANK's intention of being reconciled to Hilda was frustrated by public events of such importance that he only
occasionally found time to think of, and regret, a procrastination that might eventually increase his difficulties. It
had by degrees become evident that the twenty-five thousand Austrians in Ulm were surrounded by the whole army
of Napoleon, and that the unfinished works beyond the
walls could not be defended for any length of time. The
French, with only a few days' provision in their knapsacks,
spread over the surrounding country like a swarm of
locusts, and soon caused a dearth that, reducing them to
half-rations, and the unfortunate inhabitants in their neighbourhood to utter destitution, made the reduction of Ulm,
and a movement elsewhere, a matter of absolute necessity.
The only change in the weather was from snow and sleet
to torrents of rain ; and under these circumstances the
heights round the town were attacked, carried by storm,
and the Austrians, overpowered by numbers, obliged to
retreat within the walls.

This engagement lasted without intermission during a whole afternoon, the incessant sound of no longer distant cannon and musketry alarming the burghers so much that they began to fear a bombardment; and, when a few large balls actually strayed into the streets, they thought it time to put the cellars in order, that they might serve as places of refuge for their families.

The Austrians posted cannon on the walls, barricaded the gates, and partially destroyed the bridges. A French officer, with bandaged eyes, and preceded by a trumpeter, was admitted into the town, and taken to the Golden Wheel, where the generals were assembled, but his proposal to them to capitulate was at once rejected.

From that time forward all the inhabitants of Ulm were kept in a state of feverish anxiety; but the disquietude was greater in the Waldering family than elsewhere, for it was a house "divided against itself"—the friends of one half being the foes of the other. Hilda, under the influence of her indignation against Frank, now sided completely with her uncle and Sigmund; while Doris and her mother, fully informed by Pallersberg of all that had occurred beyond the walls and at the Golden Wheel, only ventured to speak unreservedly to him or to Frank of their hopes and fears for the future.

"Do you think," asked the Countess Waldering one morning, as Frank was about to leave the room where he had in vain lingered in the hope of seeing Hilda—"do you think that Marshal Mack really believes the Russians to be so near us as Dachau?"

"I don't know," he answered; "at all events, he tried to make the French officer think so when he proposed a truce of eight days, to which it is impossible for Napoleon to consent, as he is wholly unprovided with supplies for his army."

"The provisions here will scarcely last so long," she observed.

"Mack seemed to think we might subsist on our three thousand horses," replied Frank.

"That proves, at all events," said his aunt, "that he is perfectly aware of the state of the town; the burghers, however, will not be well satisfied with his proclamation,—have you seen it?"

"No, but I know the purport."

"You ought to read it," she said, pushing the paper towards him.

And he read as follows :-

"In the name of his Majesty I render responsible, on their honour and their duty, all the generals and superior officers who shall mention the word 'surrender,' or who shall think of anything but the most obstinate defence—a defence which cannot be required for any considerable time, as in a very few days the advanced guards of an Imperial and a Russian army will appear before Ulm to relieve us. The army of the enemy is in the most deplorable situation, as well from want of provisions as the severity of the weather, and it is impossible that the blockade can be maintained beyond a few days.

"Our ditches are deep, our bastions strong; should provisions fail, we have more than three thousand horses, on which we can live for a considerable time. I myself will be the first to eat horseflesh———"

Frank paused, then placed the paper on the table.

"Well," said his aunt, inquiringly—"well, what do you think?"

"I think he will not eat the horseflesh," he answered.

There was something in the tone and manner in which these words were pronounced, so like Frank's former self, that Doris—who had lately made him feel her displeasure

12

by marked avoidance, and had been sitting at a work-table, apparently heedless of his presence—now looked up, fully expecting to see a gleam of his usual mirth playing on his countenance; but Frank was absently drawing lines on the painted floor with the point of his scabbard, and appeared profoundly dejected.

"So the chances," continued his aunt, "are, that we shall have to surrender?"

"Decidedly—unless the citizens of Ulm can be persuaded to allow the town to be reduced to ashes. The French are in possession of the heights, and a four-and-twenty hours' bombardment will complete the work of destruction."

"What were the terms of capitulation offered?" she asked.

"The garrison to lay down their arms, and become prisoners of war, with the exception of the officers, who receive permission to return to Austria with arms, horses, and baggage. Should it come to the worst," added Frank, "I shall cease to regret my appointment to another regiment, as General Laudon has promised to allow me to leave Ulm in whatever way I can as the bearer of despatches."

"And," asked his aunt, "have you formed any plan of escape?"

"I think of floating down the Danube on one of the wood-rafts until I get beyond the French lines," he answered; "but as long as there is anything to be done here, I have no intention of leaving."

"Have you anything very important to do, just now?"

"Yes—I must give orders about the interment, or I should rather say the burial, of our dead."

"Pretty much the same thing, Frank, is it not?"

"No; for the poor fellows must be consigned to the water of the Danube."

"For goodness' sake, Frank, take care that none are

thrown into the river who are merely in a state of insensibility !—such things often happen."

"I know it," he answered gloomily, "and will do my best to prevent any murderous mistakes. And now, Goodbye until evening."

When Frank returned some hours later, he was informed that all the family had gone to a loft on the top of the house to look at the French watch-fires on the heights round the town. He followed them there, groping his way up the last narrow flight of steps in total darkness, and then stopping at the entrance, surprised to find not only those he sought, but also a number of the officers quartered in the house, standing in groups near the small windows that projected from the roof. The loft was very spacious, and but dimly lighted by a lamp placed on a huge mangle near the door, so that it required some time to discover that the beams and shingles of the roof were visible, and that baskets, boxes, trunks of various dimensions, and a curious collection of old furniture, were heaped along the low walls at each side.

Frank approached his aunt, who, with Doris and Pallersberg, were standing at the window nearest him, and they silently drew back to enable him to lean out and see the hundreds of fires that burned with lurid flames on the Michaelsberg and all the heights around.

"We may expect a bombardment to-morrow," observed Pallersberg ; "and I have just been recommending your aunt and cousin to retreat to the collar as soon as it commences."

"Perhaps it would be expedient," said Frank, turning round, "though I do not think this house very dangerously situated. At all events, a good supply of water up here will be necessary, and we may chance to require those shrivelled leather buckets I have so often laughed at when

I saw them dangling above our heads in the vaulted passages below stairs."

"But," observed his aunt, "if we retreat to the cellar, who will attend to the house in case of fire?"

"The men quartered here, and who are not required elsewhere," he answered; "we have plenty of water, and plenty of hands to work. I suspect that will be our chief occupation to-morrow, unless Napoleon really wishes to destroy the town, which we must suppose he does not as it belongs to an ally."

"Then, I think, dear Doris," began his aunt, turning to her daughter, "if we can be of no use——"

"None whatever," interposed Frank; "and Hilda will of course go with you."

"I cannot answer for her, Frank; she has become rather wilful lately."

"Where is she?" he asked quietly.

"At one of the other windows, with her grandmother and uncle. Your unkindness, Frank, has made her turn altogether to them, and she has now so completely adopted their views of public affairs that, for the present, I think it better to avoid useless opposition."

"The political opinions of a girl of seventeen are not of much importance," said Frank; "but why hers should be so different from yours and Doris's I cannot well understand."

"You forget, Frank, that she is a Waldering—that she has been engaged to Sigmund for several years, and was to have been married to him this month. Would it not have been worse than folly had I tried to make her think differently from him and his family on a subject that is so continually discussed? A few kind words from you would have far outweighed all she has heard from either her uncle or Sigmund, and her personal enthusiasm for Napoleon could easily have been damped had you given yourself the slightest trouble to identify her interests with yours.''

Frank moved away in silence, walking towards that part of the loft where Hilda was standing. She and her relations were listening to encomiums and anecdotes of Napoleon, volubly poured forth by Louis d'Esterre, who ended by an instance of the marvellous munificence of his Emperor.

" Pshaw ! " cried Frank, at length turning on his heel. " It is very easy to give away other people's property and be generous, when it costs nothing ! "

" *Notre cher François se fâche, naturellement,*" said Louis, shrugging his shoulders, and continuing his discourse as if no interruption had taken place.

The Walderings saw Frank no more that evening, nor the next day until the afternoon, when the expected bombardment actually commenced. It soon became evident to all who had doubted the fact that the French, from their position on the Michaelsberg, could, and perhaps would, completely destroy the town if any delay in the capitulation should provoke them to do so. Cannon-balls were seen flying over the houses or heard hissing past the windows at first with more awe than alarm by the inhabitants ; but when the bursting shells killed and wounded several persons, and caused fire to break out in various places, the consternation became general. It is probable that this commencement of hostilities against the town was intended as a mere demonstration of power on the part of the enemy, for at the end of an hour the firing ceased as suddenly as it had begun, and hopes were for some time entertained that a capitulation was in prospect. No step towards it, however, having been taken, the cannonade commenced again, and so much more effectually that in most houses a retreat to the cellars became necessary.

Many balls and bombs had passed over the Waldering House and fallen into the Danube; but, excepting the dowager countess and her companion Mina Pallersberg, no one could at first be persuaded to seek safety underground, or believe in immediate danger in rooms where officers and men appeared to come and go precisely as usual. The Director wandered uneasily about the staircase, and occasionally followed Sigmund and Louis d'Esterre to the loft, where, reconnoitring from the windows at both sides with their telescopes, they vainly endeavoured to make him understand what was happening or likely to happen. It was while they were there that a shell struck and soon after exploded on the shingled roof, causing it instantaneously to ignite, so that, had not soldiers been both in the house itself and in the immediate neighbourhood, and all well supplied with the requisites for extinguishing the flames, there was every probability that, instead of the roof, the whole building and all in its vicinity would have been burnt to the ground.

When the alarm and confusion caused by this incident had subsided, the Director insisted on his sister-in-law and her daughters retiring to the cellars, where he accompanied them, explaining at some length the folly of people who could be of no use exposing themselves to the danger of mutilation or death. Having descended, candle in hand, to the vaults, they were not a little surprised to find themselves surrounded by a number of friends and acquaintances, who from more exposed parts of the town had sought refuge with them; and it happened that many of these, not having seen Hilda since her marriage, took the opportunity of formally congratulating her, and with a mixture of interest and curiosity commenced making inquiries concerning her plans for the future.

In order to escape explanations that were as embarrassing as unnecessary, and exclamations more irritating than sympathetic, Hilda at length took refuge on the cellar steps, and there remained alone and anxiously listening until she had convinced herself that for some reason or other the firing had ceased ; then she ascended to the fresh air above ground, venturing first under the vaulted entrance to the house and afterwards to the gate, which, being partly open, enabled her to look into the street.

Detachments of soldiers were marching past, crowds of people moving to and fro, and strangers speaking to each other without the slightest reserve, so that when Hilda joined some citizens standing in a group just outside the house no one appeared at all surprised, or hesitated for a moment to give her unasked all the information in their power.

" You see, Miss, they've stopped for the present, though no one knows anything of a capitula'ion as yet. A great many houses were burning half an hour ago, but the soldiers prevented the fire from spreading or doing much mischief. In the Hirsch and Frauen Street and about the Cathedral there was most danger, and there even the officers themselves worked at the pumps and buckets."

" And the hospital ? " asked Hilda.

" A black flag was hoisted there, but it's not easy to give such fireworks the right direction, and they say a shell burst in one of the large rooms and injured most of the wounded who were in it."

Hilda suddenly remembered that just then was the hour in which she and Doris were usually in the habit of sending or going to the hospital with lint and linen. She thought it very probable that the fear of exposing themselves to danger might deter many families that day from fulfilling their promise of delivering regular supplies ; how necessary, therefore, was it that an effort should be made by some of them! Would the quantity that she could carry be of sufficient importance to justify the risk incurred? Her mother had often said that the fear of not doing much ought never to deter any one from endeavouring to do the little within their power, and that if every one thought and acted so, great things would be accomplished.

She returned into the house, and on the impulse of the moment ran up to the sitting-room, packed in a large bundle all the lint and linen prepared by her mother, her sister, and herself during the last twenty-four hours, hurried with it down the stairs and past the entrance to the cellar, where she greatly feared encountering some one who would have a right to expostulate with her; but, excepting some soldiers, no one was there, and with an indescribable feeling of buoyancy she carried her load through the crowded streets to the hospital, and had there the satisfaction of hearing that her effort had not been in vain, as the greatest embarrassment had prevailed in consequence of the usual supplies not having been sent.

Had Hilda had time to go into the room in which the shell had exploded a couple of hours previously, she would have been more alarmed on leaving the hospital to find that the bombardment had recommenced, and that these fiery messengers were again flying whistling through the air. Few people excepting soldiers were now in the streets, and they were occupied preparing bivouac fires, as the closing day was unusually dark and chilly. Hilda walked on quickly, vaguely alarmed at the booming, hissing noise, and the report of distant explosions, until she reached the Cathedral; there she paused and looked round before crossing the open unsheltered Place. Most of the soldiers stood under the gateways of the adjacent houses, and those occupied without looked up frequently and shouted to each other at intervals. The shells that during the day had been visible in the form of black balls of iron, now appeared like fiery meteors with blazing tails most beautifully brilliant, first ascending to a certain height, and then gradually descending to the spot where they were destined to execute their work of destruction.

When Hilda saw these dangerous missiles sweeping majestically over her head, she felt extremely unwilling to venture across the Munsterplatz : on the other hand, the necessity of reaching home before it became quite dark made it unavoidable that she should do so without delay. A shed had been erected in the middle of the Platz by some masons employed in repairing the Cathedral, in which bricks, lime, and sand were sheltered from the weather, and towards this shed, as if it were a place of safety, Hilda walked as quickly as she could until the sound of loud calls of "Halt!" induced her to stop for a moment and look round : she saw the soldiers she had just passed all returning quickly to the houses, and only an officer, who, to her great annoyance, had closely followed her from the hospital, was rushing onwards, his cloak no longer concealing his face and person, but so flung backwards in order not to impede his progress that she instantly recognized Frank, and, greatly irritated at his having watched and frightened her unnecessarily, she resolved to run on to the next street and enter a shop where she and her family were well known.

" Hilda! Hilda!" he shouted, in a voice that was hoarse from alarm, but which she supposed denoted angry command ; and instantly resolving not to obey, she pursued her course until she perceived that a shell was actually descending in the direction of the shed towards which she was so madly hurrying. She saw it strike the earth, whirl round, burrow in the ground, which it seemed to excavate; but before it burst and the havoc commenced, and while she stood almost paralyzed by terror, she felt herself encircled by a strong arm and drawn with great violence to a considerable distance, where, though partly sheltered by a wall, Frank's efforts could not altogether save her from the blows of splintered wood, pieces of brick, stones, and a shower of lime and sand.

Hilda remained perfectly quiet until she perceived that Frank relaxed his grasp of her arm; then she asked, with a great effort to conceal her terror, if the danger were over?

"For this time, yes," he answered; "and I now wish to Heaven you were safe at home!"

"So do I," she said, shaking off the lime and sand that powdered her blue casimir dress; "but you need not come with me," she added, "for I am not in the least afraid of being alone."

"So I perceive," said Frank, a good deal piqued, but greatly admiring her courage. "It is, however, so late that I must insist on accompanying you to the Danube Gate. Will you not take my arm?"

"No, thank you."

They walked on for some time in silence, frequently passing the watchfires of the soldiers, and avoiding as much as possible the clouds of smoke, illumined by sparks and flashes of flame, that were wafted to and fro in the streets.

"The wind is rising," observed Frank; "I fear we shall have a stormy night, in every sense of the word."

"Very likely," she answered; "and I should think these fires must be very dangerous with so much wind to blow the flames in all directions."

"Perhaps so," said Frank; "but they are indispens-able."

"As to the bombardment," she continued, "that will not last long, or do much injury to the town."

"Indeed!"

"Captain d'Esterre says they will only fire for an hour or so, at intervals, to convince your generals that further resistance is useless."

Frank did not at all like hearing such painful truths from Hilda's lips, pronounced, too, with scarcely concealed exultation; and he therefore answered, rather scoffingly, "Of course, Louis—I mean Captain d'Esterre—must be right; and I should be glad to hear any other words of wisdom that he may have uttered. Your memory, I know, is good."

Her memory *was* good, and carried her back to the attic in the tower of Forsteck, where Frank had derided her want of judgment, and upbraided her with the continual repetition of other people's opinions. The recollection made her blush until her cheeks tingled; she had spoken to him merely to prove her self-possession and indifference to his presence, and he had convinced her that a word from him could chafe her beyond endurance. No reply occurred to her; and even had it, she could not at the moment have articulated without bursting into tears of anger and morti-fication. To avoid this, and fearing she might other-wise betray her feelings, she yielded to the impulse that prompted flight, and, while Frank waited for an answer to a speech he half regretted having made, she sprang from his side, and was actually out of sight before he had re-covered from his astonishment.

As a matter of course, he instantly started in pursuit, and, forgetting for the moment all the anxiety that had preyed upon his mind for weeks, he rushed along the streets

in a state of eager excitement, that increased whenever he
occasionally caught a glimpse of his fugitive bride.   He
nearly overtook her when she was passing a large fire, as,
in order not to attract attention, she there slackened her
pace to a quiet walk, but he was obliged, for appearance'
sake, to do nearly the same.   Nevertheless, he evidently
gained ground, and, by one great effort, came up to her
just before she reached a bivouac so near her home that
the light from the fire was reflected in all the window-
panes, and the carved oak gate of the Waldering house
was made distinctly visible.

Frank caught her arm, drew her towards him, and
panted some incoherent assurances that he had not intended to give offence.   She did not answer, or even listen
to him, but, struggling with violence to release herself
from his arms, pushed him from her with a gesture of
abhorrence, and then ran on to the watchfire.   He followed
with long strides, accompanying her to the open gate,
beside which he stood until she passed him and entered
the house.

CHAPTER XXI.

MORE AT ODDS THAN EVER.

THIS state of affairs could not last much longer, and during
the course of the ensuing day a convention was signed, by
which the fortress of Ulm was to be given up, and the
whole garrison to lay down its arms, if not relieved by a
Russian or Austrian army before the end of another week.
In the meantime a detachment of French troops were
allowed to enter the town, put in possession of the Goeck-

linger and Frauen Gates, and quartered in the houses already crowded with Austrians. The bridges were repaired with wood, the communication with the neighbourhood re-established, and, as a matter of course, all the French prisoners restored to liberty.

Louis d'Esterre made some very polite and appropriate speeches when taking leave, concluding with a fluent, low-toned declaration of devotion to Doris, as she stood a little apart from the others at a window, disconsolately watching some French chasseurs taking possession of the Grecian temple in the garden. She listened patiently, or rather apathetically, and when he ceased speaking quietly held out her hand, saying, " *Adieu, Louis! Je ne puis pas badiner aujourd'hui.*"

Sigmund, who was within hearing, laughed unrestrainedly.

Louis d'Esterre shrugged his shoulders, and laughed with him. " *Hélas!* I am the enemy to-day," he said, bowing over her hand; " but I still will hope my lofe will be returned."

At the foot of the stairs he met some chasseurs of his regiment, who greeted him enthusiastically, and, following them into the garden, he saw what he supposed the cause of Doris's displeasure. Not only was the temple filled with French soldiers, but a clump of rose-trees and flowering shrubs had been torn up by the roots, to make a clear space for a large fire, the fuel for which was being carried in armsfull from the adjacent woodhouse.

"I cannot prevent that," he murmured; "nor this either," he added, as some flower-pots containing valuable plants were pitched out of one of the windows of the temple; "the men have no time for gardening just now." A moment after he caught a glimpse of Frank through the branches of the nearly leafless trees, as he was sitting ou the low wall at the end of the garden, gazing thoughtfully into the river, and did not even move when Louis, advancing quickly towards him, called out, "*Holá François!*"

"My name is Frank," was the answer.

"*Je comprends*—the tongue is unpalatable——"

"Very," said Frank, without looking up, though he felt D'Esterre's hand on his shoulder, and did not for a moment doubt that the young Frenchman was looking at him kindly.

"I have got private notice, Frank; our *Empereur* will not—cannot wait until the 25th. If you have arrangement to make, do not delay."

"He *must* wait!" cried Frank, vehemently. "If I were in command, I would not yield an hour before the time stipulated."

"But you are not in command, *mon cher*, and—and—for what good to prolong this state of things? Your marshal has agreed to surrender—to-morrow."

"Where? when?" cried Frank, starting up.

"At Elchingen, two—three hours ago."

"Unconditionally?" asked Frank, impetuously.

"*N-o-n*—Ney is to remain here until the 25th."

"Do you mean," cried Frank, "that all the other troops are placed at your disposition for ulterior operations?—at once?—without even a week's delay?"

"We have only gain five days," said D'Esterre, half apologetically, "and it is vain your expecting the Russians, for they have not indeed reached Bohemia; this, and the state of the neighbourhood, and want of provisions——"

"Reasons enough, I suppose," said Frank, again seating himself on the wall.

"And you, *mon ami*, may rejoice——"

"I should like to know for what?" cried Frank with a grim smile.

" That you are no longer a Hohenlohe dragoon ! "

" You mean that, not being included in the capitulation, I am spared to-morrow's humiliation, and may soon use my sword again. Yes; that *is* a consolation."

" Ah, ha ! *notre chère* Doris had reason when she said, ' What is, is best ! ' and now, adieu ! "

" Farewell," said Frank, " I hope that when we next meet it will be under pleasanter circumstances. Forgive my *brusquerie* during the last few weeks, D'Esterre ; you know I have had both public and private griefs enough for a whole life ! "

" Adieu ! O'More ; we have no time to talk or think of either griefs or joys just now. Adieu ! "

Frank turned towards the river, and seemed to watch some men constructing a large raft from the remains of several others that had been prepared to float down the Danube to Vienna some days previously. The wood had been required for temporary sheds and other purposes, but enough was left to make it still worth while to undertake the toilsome drift. Large trunks of carefully-barked trees were firmly lashed together, and furnished with rudders and a hut resembling a miniature log-house. Frank whistled shrilly, and a man in leather boots that partly covered his thighs looked round, and soon after, with the assistance of some others, brought the raft under the garden-wall.

" To-morrow afternoon," said Frank, " between twelve and two o'clock, I shall be ready. If you can manage to be here at that time, so much the better ; if not, tell one of the Elchingen boatmen to take me up, and I can follow you down the river."

The man touched his cap, and then brought the raft back to its former moorings ; while Frank, slowly rising, prepared to go into the town and obtain minute information concerning the capitulation.

The first person he met confirmed D'Esterre's statement. The capitulation had been actually signed at Elchingen, and the garrison were to march out of Ulm the next day and defile before Napoleon with all the honours of war previous to laying down their arms. Now, though there was not a youthful Austrian lieutenant who had not long been aware that, with five-and-twenty thousand men in an ill-fortified town and surrounded by Napoleon's whole army, there was nothing else could be expected than a surrender at discretion, the universal grief and mortification was boundless. Not one undertook the defence of the unfortunate commander, and few, in that ill-starred hour, attempted even to vindicate the unavoidable and long-foreseen capitulation, which competent judges have since pronounced an inevitable consequence of a previous error— the having neglected to retreat into Tirol while it was still possible to do so.

The preparations for this parade were singularly tranquil, and the French quartered in the town, with that tact and good feeling which even their bitterest enemies must acknowledge them to possess, avoided so effectually giving umbrage to their irritated or sullen foes that not the slightest quarrel or disorder took place.

The next day, when Pallersberg came to take leave of Frank, he found him walking up and down the deserted drawing-room in the Waldering house in a state of restless excitement. His aunt and Doris stood at a window looking into the street—not to watch the inhabitants of the town hurrying eagerly towards the Michaelsberg to be present at what was to them merely a grand military pageant, but in order to wave a farewell to the numerous officers and men who had so long been quartered in their house, as they dejectedly assembled on the open space beneath.

"This is a bitter parting, Frank," said Pallersberg; "but if anything could reconcile me to your having left our regiment, it would be that you are spared what we must endure an hour hence!"

"I am not spared!" cried Frank, vehemently. "I feel it here! I shall feel, and in imagination see it all as distinctly as if riding beside our poor fellows, not one of whom I am ever likely to see again!"

"Who can tell?" said Pallersberg, with forced cheerfulness; "imprisonment is not death! Come, Frank, leave Ulm as soon as you can, and do not let your thoughts rest upon an event which you can neither avert nor ameliorate. I see you are prepared for your journey, or voyage, whichever you choose to call it; nothing can be better adapted to a raft than those waterproof boots, and, indeed, your whole dress, which, I suppose, is sailor fashion. An hour sooner or later makes no difference. Step on your raft when I mount my horse, and let us wait until we meet in Vienna to talk over this day's disaster. Come——"

"I must take leave of my aunt—and Doris," said Frank, hesitating.

"Do it quickly, then; it is unlike yourself being so dilatory."

"But I want—I wish—confound it, Pallersberg, you cannot expect me to go off without speaking a few words to Hilda!"

"Then make haste," answered Pallersberg, "for I saw her horse saddled as I came into the house, and she never keeps Selim waiting."

"Her horse!" exclaimed Frank, changing colour. "Her horse! and saddled? In the name of all the fiends, where is she going to ride on such a day as this?"

Pallersberg, who perceived the consternation his words had caused, hesitated, and then stammered something

about a natural wish for exercise after such long confinement:—the Director would probably choose some quiet
road."

" He will *not!* " cried Frank, violently; " you know he
won't. They are going to the Michaelsberg to witness
this accursed parade—to feast their eyes on the anguish of
our officers and the despair of our men! By Heaven, she
shall not go! " And, breaking from Pallersberg's detaining hand, he rushed down the stairs and reached the
vaulted passage below, while the horses were still stamping
impatiently on the wood pavement.

Sigmund had just vaulted into his saddle, the Director
was slowly mounting, and Hilda, drawing up the reins with
one hand, bent over Selim's arched neck, and with the
other arranged his long waving mane. She had just been
given her whip, and was looking round to see if her uncle
were ready, when Frank, pale with suppressed passion,
rushed forward, laid his hand on her bridle, and, in a hoarse
whisper, asked where she was going?

"To the Michaelsberg—to see Napoleon," she answered,
fearlessly, her cheeks flushing and her eyes flashing.

"You shall not go—I insist on your dismounting
instantly," he cried, laying his hand impetuously on
Selim's bridle.

The horse reared so frightfully that he threw his arm
round her, fearing an accident.

" Keep off, Frank—take your hand from my bridle—I
desire—I insist——"

He obeyed, but placed it heavily on the neck of the
irritated animal, while he looked up and again indignantly
commanded her to dismount.

"No, I will not; you have told me 'to go where I
please and do what I like,' and this is the first use I make
of my liberty."

Though the quotation of his own words was by no means calculated to restore Frank's equanimity, it at least reminded him that he ought to remonstrate rather than command; but he enforced his few unintelligible words of angry expostulation by a strong grasp of the bridle, and Hilda, instead of listening to him, raised her whip, and a moment after it descended with a sharp whistling sound on Selim's neck and Frank's retaining hand. With one wild bound the horse carried her through the gateway, and was immediately heard galloping madly over the pavement of the street, while Frank, unprepared for the shock, was dashed against the wall with great violence, and staggered along it until he came in contact with Pallersberg's shoulder, on which he leaned until the Director, riding up close to him, bent down and whispered, "Don't leave Ulm, Frank, until after our return this evening. You had better make it up with Hilda, for though she may be self-willed, you have been far more so."

Doris and her mother, who, standing at the foot of the staircase, had witnessed this scene in silent dismay, and Pallersberg, who knew not whether to reproach or console his friend, now watched him as, standing upright, he fixed his eyes for a moment on his hand, across which a broad crimson welt was very conspicuous—the fingers closed convulsively, the clenched hand was raised. Frank struck his forehead violently, and then, without uttering a word, he sprang through the court into the garden, where, vaulting over the wall, he suddenly disappeared.

When Doris, her mother, and Pallersberg followed, the raft on which he had alighted was already in the middle of the Danube; but they saw him leaning on the low roof of the hut erected on it, his head buried on his outstretched arms, and apparently so indifferent to all around him that the violent rolling and frequent immersion of the raft as it

entered the current of the flooded river was totally unheeded by him.

"I am sorry I was the cause of this rude parting," said
Pallersberg, when taking leave; "but my head was so full
of other matters that I quite forgot how unlikely it was
that Frank should know of the projected ride."

Long after Pallersberg was gone, Doris and her mother
stood leaning on the wall, gazing in the direction where
the raft had disappeared. It was a continuation of Doris's
thoughts when she observed that "Hilda's determination to
see Napoleon was most unfortunate."

"It is very natural," said her mother, "and quite to be
expected, after all she has lately heard of him. The day
chosen for the gratification of her curiosity is certainly
most unfortunate as far as Frank is concerned, and partly
excuses his extreme violence."

"Do you think," asked Doris, "they can ever be reconciled after what has just occurred?"

"Yes, Doris; the actions of both were violent, but
without lasting consequences, and the words few and not
easily recalled. Such deeds make less impression than a
very few bitter words."

"True," said Doris; "but the bitter words have not
been spared either."

"Then we can only hope," rejoined her mother, "that
when Frank recalls this parting he will scarcely wonder
that Hilda did not obey commands so peremptorily uttered,
and take into consideration that this is her first offence,
while he has treated her since their marriage with the
most unnecessary rudeness, affecting an aversion that it is
quite impossible he can have felt."

"I am afraid, dear mother, the motive of his conduct
was a wish to prove the depth of his affection for me."

"I can understand that, to a certain extent," answered

her mother; "but he need not have been so absolutely repulsive."

"I think," said Doris, hesitatingly—"I fear that dear Hilda made too many efforts to conciliate. She let him see how much she loved him, and few men—I mean Frank —in short, mamma, it is better never to let any man know the extent of one's regard; they only presume upon it and become tyrants."

"Excellently argued, Doris, and that you will act so I have no doubt; but Hilda loves Frank——"

"Well, so did—so *do* I, mamma."

"Yes, my dear, calmly and rationally, as a cousin who has been a brother to you."

"Oh, mamma, a little more, or else I could not have promised to marry him even ten years hence!"

Her mother shook her head, "As you *have* loved, you will, and may love him as long as he lives, Doris."

"I should be glad to think so, mamma—and Frank?"

"He must be given time, and Hilda will, I hope, have patience and forgive him."

"I am sure she will," said Doris, "and far more easily than I could."

"That's it, Doris; Hilda will submit to almost any amount of ill-treatment from him because she loves him— not rationally as you do, but passionately."

At this moment they heard the sound of distant military music. It was the bands of the Austrian regiments marching out ot Ulm to capitulate, and the gay strains sounded sad, as all music does when heard by the sorrowful.

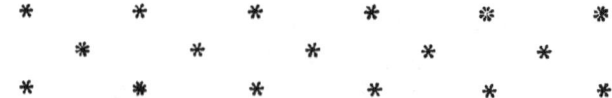

In the mean time Hilda, when joined by her uncle and

Sigmund, rode quickly on, through the Frauen Gate, towards the Michaelsberg, where about thirty-six thousand French had taken their position—the cavalry between the town and the hill, and so facing the infantry that the space between was left clear for the capitulating garrison. The weather was as clear and fine as it had previously been inclement, and the greater number of the inhabitants of Ulm swarmed through the gate, and sought places where they were likely to have a complete view of a scene alike pompous and painful.

Hilda was the only lady on horseback in the field, and her black velvet habit and plumed hat caused some sensa- tion—attracted also the attention of Louis d'Esterre, who immediately procured a place for her whence she could see Napoleon and all else likely to interest her. They were soon surrounded by a number of French officers, friends of D'Esterre's, and while Hilda laughed and talked with them, no one could have supposed that she was more depressed and hopelessly unhappy than she had ever been in her life. Her heart and thoughts were with Frank, and, from the moment it occurred to her that he might have left Ulm before she reached home, she forgot everything in the strong desire to return to the town, to see him again, and at least part peaceably from him. Not for any considera- tion, however, would she have allowed her uncle, still less Sigmund, to suspect she entertained such thoughts ; on the contrary, when Napoleon, followed by his numerous, bril- liant, and somewhat theatrical-looking staff, arrived from Elchingen, and was received with shouts and music, she pressed forward with quite as much eagerness as the others ; and as, immediately afterwards, the Austrian garrison marched through the Frauen Gate, she joined the crowd closing round the spot where the Emperor had halted, surrounded by a host of French and Austrian generals, all of whom were men of celebrity, whose names have since become historical.

Under the appearance of perfect serenity, Napoleon concealed the exultation he undoubtedly felt—he spoke politely to the Austrian generals of the chances of war—said that though so often victorious they must expect to be sometimes vanquished, and assured them of his earnest desire for peace! They bowed gravely; but as their troops defiled before the conqueror, many a hand raised in salute concealed eyes moist with tears of bitter resentment, or glowing with suppressed rage!

For the French army, and especially for Napoleon, that military pageant was an intoxicating spectacle, and, undisturbed by a knowledge of the future, he enjoyed his triumph. He could not foresee that on the succeeding day his fleet would be completely destroyed by Nelson at Trafalgar; still less could the idea present itself that exactly eight years from the capitulation of Ulm—on the same day of the month—at the same hour—he and his army would be flying from Leipsic, after having met with a far greater disaster; while those very regiments now marching sullenly past him would, when reorganized and under the command of an Austrian general at that moment close beside him, eventually assist in dethroning him, and procuring a peace that he would have no further power to disturb.

CHAPTER XXII.

The Austrians left Ulm, and a French garrison under General Labassée took their place. Marshal Ney also made the town his head-quarters for a week or ten days, during which time the ball-rooms of the hotels were again put into requisition, and a sort of mild moral compulsion used to induce the wives and daughters of the residents to appear at the "Golden Stag," "Baum Stark," "The Wheel," and elsewhere; that many were concealed in cellars, and still more sent off privately to visit distant relations, became subsequently known. Nevertheless, as a German woman can on an average dance twice as much as any other, the balls were gay enough, and before long all the young ladies were unanimous in declaring that when dancing quadrilles the French officers were inimitable, but in waltzing perfectly execrable.

Hilda, on her return from the Michaelsberg, had immediately walked into the garden, and straight to the wall where Frank had been seated three hours previously. Leaning over it, she glanced hastily across and down the river, raised her hand to shade her eyes from the glow of sunset, and looked intently again and again, as if unwilling to believe that the raft she sought was no longer there, then turned slowly away, and as she gathered up the folds of her habit, her eyes fell on her small gold-headed riding-whip, just then a so unpleasant remembrancer that, without a moment's hesitation, she jerked it into the Danube. How much sorrow and regret she flung away with the whip it would be hard to say; certain it is that she not only returned with perfect self-possession to the house, but even thought it necessary to prove her stoicism by stopping a moment in the yard to speak to Sigmund as he stood with folded arms inspecting the operation of hoof-washing.

Hilda asked no questions about Frank, and for a long time sedulously avoided naming him. She was at first unwilling to accompany her uncle and grandmother to the balls given by the French officers, but a few jesting remarks of Sigmund's made her suppose it absolutely necessary that she should be seen in public, and that people should know she was perfectly happy.

In strong contrast to these festivities were the sufferings of the poorer inhabitants of the town, who, absolutely impoverished by the number of soldiers billeted in the houses and the increasing prices of the commonest necessaries of life, had latterly been at times in actual want of food; but it was not until after the capitulation had restored communication with the neighbourhood that they became aware of the total destruction of all the fields and gardens in the vicinity. It was necessary to make excursions to the places where the army had only remained a day or two, or where engagements had taken place, to form an idea of the state of wretchedness to which the people were reduced. That the generals disapproved of and endeavoured to prevent all excesses is beyond a doubt; but where an army of upwards of a hundred thousand men, only carrying provisions for a day or two with them, literally overspread a country, the consequences must be ruin to the inhabitants. In the province of Swabia, to which Ulm belonged, there were more than a hundred districts where the people were deprived of food, furniture, farming implements, cattle, and even the necessary grain for seed. In the villages in which the troops had been

stationed, houses had been pulled down to furnish fuel for
the watchfires, and the inmates in a few hours reduced to
beggary; and few parts of the country had suffered more
fatally than that in which Hilda's newly-acquired property
was situated. After her first ride to Forsteck with her
uncle, she seemed to have no thought beyond that of procuring money to alleviate the universal distress. He
greatly approved of her subscribing a larger sum of money
than most of the other patrician families, but he could not
at all understand her determination to give the inhabitants
of Forsteck all the wood they required to rebuild their
houses, and he positively declined to assist her in selling
out of the Funds at a heavy loss. At last he complained
of her to her mother, and recommended a return to Westenried without delay.

"If she really cannot do anything more for these unfortunate people," was his sister-in-law's reply, "I shall, of
course, propose our leaving Ulm."

"You must not *allow* her to do anything more," he
said, decidedly; "it would be unpardonable if we permitted a girl of seventeen to squander her fortune in this
manner, and people might say I neglected to warn her
because she had not married my son. It is scarcely an
hour since she sold her horse to a French officer without
consulting any one!"

"Sold Selim!" cried Doris; "for what purpose?"

"To assist a miller at Forsteck whose wife and children came here yesterday and whined and whimpered for
an hour in her room. I never heard of such extravagance."

"This is not extravagance," said his sister-in-law; "it
is charity, and the purest instance of generosity I have
heard of for a long time. I do not imagine that Hilda
could have made a greater sacrifice than selling Selim."

"She will not be able to replace him for a good while," said the Director, grimly; "but, as I said before, she cannot do more for these people than she has done. It was her and ⁓ ⁓ wish that the greater part of her funded property should be settled upon Frank—and so——"

Here Hilda entered the room, followed by Mina, who seemed to be expostulating with her, for she said, when closing the door, "But you know, Hilda, your grandmother will not go to the ball without you, and I am actually engaged for all the quadrilles."

"I am sorry to interfere with your amusement, Mina, but I do not intend to go to any more balls. Mamma and Doris were quite right to stay at home. It is very unfeeling of us to dance and feast while the poor people about us are weeping and starving."

"Your staying at home will not do them any good," persisted Mina.

"I know that; but in thinking of them I have lost all interest in balls, and all inclination to dance."

"Oh, I understand what that really means," cried Mina, laughing; "but why cannot you dance quadrilles with the French, and keep the waltzes for our own people?"

"I don't choose to dance again with either French or German," said Hilda, decidedly.

"I suppose," observed Mina, rather sarcastically, "that Doris has been giving advice, and pointing out the impropriety of——"

"No!" cried Hilda, interrupting her, petulantly; "I have learned at last to think and speak for myself."

"With a vengeance!" exclaimed the Director, who was walking up and down the room, his hands, as usual, clasped behind his back.

"I wish I had done so sooner," she continued, with

some excitement; "for a little of what mamma calls firm-ness of character would have saved me, and some others, much grief and endless regret."

"I hope, however," said her mother, "that this newly-acquired firmness will not occasionally degenerate into obstinacy."

"No, mamma—never!"

"Your self-reliance makes me doubtful," said her mother, smiling.

"And I am more than doubtful," interposed the Director; "for, after explaining the absolute necessity of new roofing this house, and of repairing the damage done at Forsteck, and new stocking the farm there, she still expects to have money for every one who asks for it."

"Oh, no, uncle! I quite understand all you said to me this morning, and expect nothing from you now but papers covered with long rows of figures, accompanied by still longer lectures on economy."

"And what," said the Director, testily, "what is the use of my lecturing when I have no power to control? It is monstrous to think that a girl of your age can make ducks and drakes of such a property!"

"I don't intend to make ducks and drakes of it," answered Hilda, demurely; "I was not even aware, until now, that I was so completely at liberty."

"Your husband," he replied with emphasis, "is the only person to whom you are henceforward responsible in such matters."

"Then," said Hilda, "as he declines all concern in my affairs, I must beg of you to continue your guardianship until I have learned to understand something of business myself. I will even promise not to be unreasonable and extravagant for a long time to come; and, if you and mamma wish it, will put myself out of

temptation by leaving Ulm to-morrow, and going at once
to Westenried."

"Westenried!" exclaimed Mina, "you will die of *ennui*
there, after the gaiety we have enjoyed here."

"Gaiety! enjoyment!" repeated Hilda; "God in His
mercy defend me from such gaiety for the rest of my life!"

"And mine," said Doris, in a low voice.

"We shall not die of *ennui*," observed their mother;
"on the contrary, I am convinced the tranquillity of Westenried will be most welcome to us all after the harrowing
scenes we have witnessed here. Let us return there as soon
as possible."

The journey home (which now could be made in six
hours) required then three whole days. The Director, his
mother, and Mina, proceeded no further than Munich; but
Sigmund chose to go on to Westenried with the others,
and it was late on the evening of the third day as the
heavily-packed carriages rolled slowly into the court. The
hall-door and staircase were decorated with wreaths of fir-
tree branches, enlivened by the last asters of the season
placed at intervals, and the word "WELCOME" was conspicuous over the entrance to their apartments on the second
floor. Old Mr. Pallersberg followed them up the stairs,
while his wife remained with Sigmund on the first floor,
giving his servant various directions and a good deal of
unnecessary assistance.

"If you had only let me know that you were also
coming, Count Sigmund," she said, with ill-concealed
annoyance, "you would have found your rooms heated, and
everything in order; but I shall put all to rights when you
go upstairs to supper."

" I shall not go upstairs to supper," said Sigmund.

" And why not ? "

" Because I am not invited."

Madame Pallersberg looked at him inquiringly.

" Have you forgotten the changes that have taken place ? " he asked, " and that my position in my aunt's family is quite different from what it was ? "

" Well, no ; but she is your aunt still, and Mina wrote us that everything had been amicably arranged as far as you are concerned."

" Oh, very amicably," said Sigmund ; " but I can neither go to supper to-night, nor to dinner to-morrow, without an invitation ; so you must keep house for me."

" Beginning," she said, " to-morrow, I hope ; for, after having lived so long on potatoes and cheese, you really must have some of the magnificent turkey I have provided for the supper upstairs. Mina wrote, however, that, with all the starvation at Ulm, it was an uncommonly gay and sociable place."

" I believe she amused herself very well," said Sigmund; " the Austrian and French officers paid her a good deal of attention, and Mina likes that sort of thing."

" Well, I suppose it's natural at her age," said Madame Pallersberg ; " but I would rather hear of one proposal of marriage than of a score of admirers. I cannot help fearing, Count Sigmund, that our Mina has been a little spoiled by the grand people she meets at your grandmother's; they have given her quite a hankering after fine names and rank. I spoke to her several times when she was last here, and told her that counts and barons were often very poor, and would not, or could not, marry her, as she had no fortune ; while those who were rich would never condescend to think of her at all."

" And what did she say in answer ? " asked Sigmund.

"Not much : that generally speaking I was right, but that there were exceptions to all rules. There is no doubt, however, that she was very much out of spirits when here, and I latterly began to fear——" here she paused, and looked hard at him—" in fact, I strongly suspected she was suffering from an ill-placed, hopeless attachment."

"Bless my soul!" cried Sigmund; "you don't mean to insinuate that she, too, was captivated by the irresistible 'cousin Frank?' You know, of course, that both Doris and Hilda were over head and ears in love with him?"

"No, Count Sigmund; I thought of a more natural and probable attachment."

"You mean Emmeran? I have never observed anything of the kind; but it is hard to judge where such great intimacy exists."

"If it be Count Emmeran," she said, gravely, "I hope he will act honourably, and not raise hopes that must be disappointed, nor make promises that he cannot perform."

Just then her husband appeared at the door, and announced himself as the bearer of an invitation to supper, not only to Sigmund, but also to his wife.

"Well, I *am* glad you are to have a slice of that turkey," she said, leading the way upstairs; "how you will relish it after the potatoes and cheese of Ulm!"

CHAPTER XXIII.

ANOTHER HOLY-EVE.

THE tranquillity of Westenried proved acceptable to all its inmates; and, after receiving from Pallersberg an account of the battle of Austerlitz, and assurances of Frank's safety, the. succeeding peace of Presburg and its consequences furnished deeply interesting and constant subject of con- versation during the winter. Bavaria became a kingdom on the 1st of January, 1806; and in the following August the Emperor Franz II., resigning the crown of the Holy Empire, with the declaration that, under existing circum- stances, he could no longer consider himself Emperor of Germany, assumed, as Franz I., the title of Emperor of Austria, and the German Empire thenceforward belonged to history.

During the ensuing autumn the Director, his mother, and Mina Pallersberg, returned to Westenried; and when Emmeran joined them for a short time in October, they were (Frank's absence excepted) precisely the same party that had been there together two years previously. The same, yet not the same, for much was changed in that short time. Sigmund, who had only been absent for a few weeks in winter, had managed by degrees to regain his former intimacy in his aunt's family. Hilda openly avowed that she liked him infinitely better as cousin than as *fiancé*; and Doris whose mind was just then completely engrossed by Dr. Gall's newly-discovered system of phrenology, either seemed, or really was, unconscious of the fact that he had resumed his previous position by tacitly substituting her for Hilda.

The arrival of his grandmother and her companion Mina caused Sigmund great annoyance, as he well knew how difficult it would be to conceal his present hopes and plans concerning Doris from either of them. From his grand- mother he only apprehended being forced into premature explanations; but to Mina he had some years previously made a promise of marriage, should any chance ever release him from his engagement to Hilda. In Ulm he had assured her repeatedly of the impossibility of ever obtaining his father's consent, and would now unhesitatingly have told her the truth, that he no longer entertained a thought of fulfilling a promise so imprudently made, had he not feared an explanation and appeal on her part to Doris. This induced him to continue to temporise. He avoided Doris, spent most of his time shooting and fishing; and so it happened that Hilda and her sister resumed their walks, and rows on the lake together, and unconsciously recommenced the confidential intercourse that had ceased by mutual consent on the day that Frank had left Ulm. *His* name, however, had never been mentioned until one afternoon towards the end of October, when, as they walked together in the garden, Doris observed—

" This is the anniversary of your wedding-day, Hilda; I wish you many happy returns of it."

" Thank you, dear," she replied; " I am, at all events, very much happier than this time last year."

" I suppose," continued Doris, " that hearing of Frank's promotion gave you great pleasure ? "

" Of course it did."

" And a—Hilda—mamma and I were considering this morning if it would not on this occasion be advisable for you to write a few lines of congratulation, by way of commencing some sort of communication with him, and just on this day——"

" No, Doris; neither this day nor any other. I should despise myself if I ever again made the slightest advance to him ; and I am quite sure you would not do anything of the kind were you in my place."

" I don't know that," said Doris; " it makes an immense difference when one is actually married, and I do believe I should consider it a duty to make every effort to gain his heart after having accepted his hand."

" Very likely you are right, Doris—you generally are

14

—but I can bear no more repulses, and the next overture must come from him."

" But," suggested Doris, " it may be long before you meet if you trust to chance, or let things take their course."

" How long ? " asked Hilda.

Doris was silent.

" You think," said Hilda, " that he may wait until the end of the time stipulated—the whole ten years ? "

" N—o," answered Doris, reluctantly ; " I cannot think he will have resolution to absent himself so long from us— he is too warm-hearted."

" It is a pity, Doris, you had not studied Dr. Gall's system of phrenology before Frank left us ; we could then have balanced his organ of firmness against his warm heart."

Doris stopped for a moment, and looked keenly at her sister. That Hilda had gradually regained her former gaiety had long become evident, but that she could actually speak of Frank with smiling lips and a cheerful voice was, nevertheless, rather surprising.

" I believe your organ of firmness is very consider-able ? " said Doris.

" I thought," rejoined Hilda, archly, " that people generally called firmness, when possessed by women— obstinacy ? But you need not explain. Call it what you please, Doris, I have resolved not to accept the pity so universally offered me, and to banish Frank altogether from my thoughts."

" But can you do so, Hilda ? "

" Why not ? I have nothing to remind me of him, and I still hope we may be able to prevent my mother from commencing a correspondence that I am convinced will only make matters worse. He does not want to hear of or from us, for Mina told me it was out of consideration for me that her brother's last letter was not read aloud, because in it he mentioned that Frank had led the gayest possible life among the most fashionable people in Vienna during the Carnival—making himself, as usual, remarkable by all sorts of wild exploits, and unreservedly paying attention to every handsome woman he met. He is now on a visit somewhere in Hungary, where, by all accounts——"

"Mina need not have told you all this," said Doris, hastily.

"I am very much obliged to her," rejoined Hilda; "she has made my task much easier. I can scarcely imagine a better remedy for my foolish infatuation about Frank than the certainty of his not being worthy of the admiration and ardent affection I felt for him."

"But, after all," said Doris, quietly, "what has he done? The war is over for the present in Austria—why should not people begin to enjoy themselves again? Frank learns Polish and Hungarian dances—is liked as a partner, and invited to balls—he rides well, becomes intimate with his comrades, and goes to spend a few weeks with some of them in some out-of-the-way place where a number of gay people are assembled—where is the harm in all this?"

"None—to you, Doris, or your rational affection; but I—I feel jealous—horribly jealous of all these handsome women who have made him so utterly forget me."

"That was what I feared," said Doris; "and, therefore, I avoided mentioning this letter, though I can assure you it was, written lightly and kindly, and without any intention of provoking either anger or jealousy. Mina forgot to tell you that no *one* person is especially mentioned, and you well know that Frank is both naturally and habitually attentive to all women. If this be your only reason for not writing to him——"

"No, Doris," she answered, resuming suddenly her former cheerful manner; "this is only one of my many and good reasons for not writing; "but, were I to do so, it would be impossible to resist the temptation to tell him that Sigmund had been appointed to his place, and was now playing the part of friendly, rational lover to you, with the prospect of a marriage ten years hence."

"A marriage with Mina Pallersberg, perhaps," said Doris; "she told me, soon after her arrival here, that she and Sigmund had been definitively engaged from the day of your marriage."

"From the day of my marriage?" repeated Hilda, slowly.

"Yes, dear; it seems he has been for years conditionally engaged to her."

"Impossible!" cried Hilda—"quite impossible!"

"It is certainly not creditable to either," continued Doris; "but I believe Mina spoke truth when she told me he had promised she should be his wife if any chance ever released him from his engagement to you."

"Oh, Doris, this is quite dreadful. I did not imagine that any one could be so deliberately wicked. Do you know that, during the whole time of my engagement to Sigmund, Mina endeavoured to prejudice me against him —that she contrived to make me jealous of you—that, with motives which I now understand, she encouraged my admiration for Frank, and on innumerable occasions made arrangements and remarks tending to promote disunion among us all; but so acting and speaking, that she was the very last person likely to be implicated should quarrels ensue. I can even recollect that she was the proposer and encourager of that fatal ride to Forsteck——"

"We must be just," said Doris, "and remember that Mina could not possibly have foreseen such consequences."

" She foresaw a violent dispute with Sigmund, at all events," replied Hilda ; " and that was sufficient, as I had previously given him cause enough for jealousy, and tried his patience so often, at her instigation, that a few angry words might even then separate us. All her plans have succeeded, and she now only informs you of this engagement to prevent you from accepting Sigmund, whose wishes and intentions we all know, though they seem to have escaped your observation."

" Not exactly," said Doris ; " but I have tried to avoid so disagreeable an explanation."

" You mean to reject him ? "

" Undoubtedly."

" At all events," said Hilda, with heightened colour, "that is an easier task than to bear rejection, of which I have had such bitter experience."

At this moment they passed behind an edifice constructed of large rough stones, decorated inside with shells, and denominated " The Grotto," and heard Sigmund, in a loud and impatient voice, exclaim,—" There is no use in talking any more about it, Mina ; all stratagems are fair in love or war, you know, and I may as well end the discussion by confessing that I never for a moment entertained a serious thought of fulfilling so absurd and imprudent a promise. Let me again advise you to accept the proposal of the Forester of Waldering, or, indeed, any one your parents may recommend— —"

Doris and Hilda walked quickly on.

" Do you think she is really and deeply attached to him ? " asked Hilda ; "for," she added with a sigh, " in that case I could feel for her, and think her conduct more pardonable. One is so selfish—so very selfish—when under the influence of such feelings."

"I cannot imagine any one loving Sigmund for himself," answered Doris.

"If ambition influenced her," said Hilda, "she is justly punished, and we need not waste any commiseration on her."

A few days later the Director sent to invite Doris, Hilda, and their mother to dine with him in his apartments, and while they were sending a message of acceptance Sigmund and Emmeran entered the room and laughingly informed them that, as it was their father's birthday, they might prepare speeches and expect champagne!"

"And I only thought of Holy-Eve," said Doris.

"Is it indeed Holy-Eve?" cried Emmeran; "then I shall certainly burn nuts, as I did two years ago: do you remember?"

"Yes," answered Doris, laughing; "but I believe you were rather unfortunate, for the nut representing your ladylove always hopped off."

"While I," said Emmeran, "or rather my nut representative, burned and glowed to a cinder, and will do so still!"

"For the same mysterious personage?" asked Doris.

"The same—then, now, and for ever!"

"And you will not tell us her name?"

"No; but I should now like to look into your magic-glass at midnight, if you will go again to the island."

"Not for any consideration," she answered, gravely; "for though I do not at all believe that Hilda saw an apparition in the vaults, it is certainly remarkable not only that chance obliged her to give Frank the ring we found there, but also that *he* is now in the regiment in which her father served in his youth, and wears the very hussar uniform that she asserted she saw on the shadow in the glass!"

"That is very curious," said Emmeran; "I must ask Hilda more about it."

And he walked into the next room, while Doris, looking out of the window, fixed her eyes on the island and seemed to forget that Sigmund was beside her until he asked, "if she had ever looked in a magic-glass?"

"I have played all these Holy-Eve tricks, as they are called, in Ireland," she answered; "but either I am not superstitious or not imaginative,—I never saw or heard anything. Even lead when I melted it, and eggs when I broke them into glasses of water, failed to take a form that would admit of a surmise; it always seemed as if the fairies were resolved to strengthen me in my resolution to remain unmarried; and a young lady learned in such matters having informed me that the best security of all against marriage was to read the form of solemnization as it is printed in our Prayer-book, beginning at the words 'Dearly beloved,' and ending with 'amazement,' not missing a syllable or looking up, and commencing exactly as the clock struck twelve on Holy-Eve, I did so, and she gave me the satisfactory assurance that the ceremony would never be performed for me. I thought of this and of Frank just now, and find that events have confirmed her words in a manner that, to say the least, is very singular."

"Singular it would indeed be, if you remained much longer unmarried," said Sigmund; "and I feel bound as loyal knight to assist in breaking the spell cast on you by this midnight sorcery. An English clergyman might easily be found, Doris, to read this service for you—and me——." He paused, and then added, "May I hope it will be so?"

"No."

"And why?"

"I do not like you well enough."

" Have you any other reason ? "

" Perhaps I have ; but that is sufficient."

" It is not ! " he cried, catching her hand to detain her. " You must tell me if Mina Pallersberg has been speaking to you ? "

" *You* spoke very loudly to her in the garden yesterday," answered Doris, " and when I passed the grotto with Hilda I heard you say you had never entertained a thought of fulfilling your absurd and imprudent promise to her."

" And what was that promise ? " he asked, quickly ; " or rather, how could you have understood what I meant if she had not previously explained ? "

Doris attempted no answer.

" Then it is as I suspected," he said, vainly endeavouring to conceal his agitation ; " and now you must hear my explanation."

" I should rather not," said Doris ; " you cannot deny having made the promise."

" I made it conditionally when there was not the slightest chance of what has since occurred taking place, and long before I ever saw you. Listen to me, Doris : Mina's intrigues to disengage me from Hilda have been diabolical. I saw through but permitted them, because I wished to have you free and to be at liberty myself."

" Then you were her accomplice," said Doris, " and now, having confessed that you indirectly assisted in separating me from Frank, how can you expect me to give you his place in my regard ? "

" *His* place ! " exclaimed Sigmund ; " I do not want it, I do not wish for it ! Your regard for him was mere habit, like mine for Hilda—a brotherly, cousinly, affectionate, most laudable sort of regard ; but I will venture to aver that as yet you have not an idea of love as I understand it."

"Perhaps not," she answered. "You loved Mina well enough to give her what you call a conditional promise of marriage; on Hilda you bestowed an habitual affection that served as foundation for a solemn betrothal, and for me you profess a regard that stimulated you to aid in destroying my best chance of domestic happiness in this world! Let us not quarrel, Sigmund: I hope before long to be able to forgive both you and Mina as thoroughly as Hilda does; but more than that I cannot promise."

Just then the others entered the room, and it was agreed that at this birth-day dinner they would all appear in full dress; even Emmeran was enjoined to put on his uniform, and desired to request Madame Pallersberg to wear her new cap with the scarlet topknot.

"She has sent us one of her famous chocolate tarts," he said, laughing, "and on it there are a couple of clumsy sugar-hearts as decoration. I puzzled long before I discovered that they might perhaps be intended to represent her and her husband's hearts as 'Friendship's offering' to our Director. My father was wonderfully pleased at the discovery, and walked up and down the room rubbing his hands and laughing heartily."

When they assembled at dinner-time, Sigmund forced himself to appear as cheerful as the rest of the party, and made his father the longest and most elaborate of congratulations on the completion of his three score of years.

The dinner lasted long, and a good deal of champagne had been consumed before the Director found himself sufficiently exhilarated to make an oration that had evidently been prepared, and which some of those present, as was afterwards ascertained, were awaiting in nervous anxiety. He commenced by handing Sigmund a written document, containing a formal resignation of Westenried and all its appurtenances to him; then declared his intention of be-

stowing personally on Emmeran the sum of money that he
was hereafter to receive as inheritance, and, while his two
sons still gazed at him in speechless astonishment, he added
that, " having provided for them, he felt at liberty to take
a step that would materially conduce to the happiness of the
rest of his life—he had found an amiable and accomplished
companion——." Here he rose, and approaching Mina,
took her hand, bowed over it, and then presented her to his
family as his future wife !

The reader may imagine the effects of these words on
all present; even the Pallersbergs, though not surprised,
seemed fully to share the universal embarrassment, mixed
with much anxiety. Mina changed colour rapidly and
glanced furtively towards Sigmund, on whom, in fact, all
eyes were fixed, and he seemed to think it incumbent on
him to answer, for, with features working convulsively and
after several vain attempts to articulate, he at length stammered : " Has this—this very unexpected—arrangement—
been made to-day ?"

" Oh, no !" answered his father, cheerfully ; " that document in your hand will prove that the resolution has been
long formed."

" And *her* consent ?" asked Sigmund, with a forced
smile.

" Was given, I may say willingly given, before we left
Munich."

Sigmund started from his seat, and strode towards
Mina. " Your consent was willingly given ?" he said, in a
voice of suppressed rage.

Mina did not answer ; she turned her head away, and
clung to the Director's arm.

" Have you," continued Sigmund, sternly—" have you
for once in your life told the truth—the whole truth ? And
does my father know that even yesterday you——?"

Mina's agitation became so great that the Director turned angrily towards his son, and asked what he meant by openly insulting a person who would soon be a member of their family?

"If," said Sigmund, with a sneer, "if you are not completely blinded by your passion for this young lady, I think a few minutes' conversation with me will make the future relationship very problematical."

"Do not believe what he says," cried Mina, bursting into tears. "He does not wish you to marry again, and intends to traduce me!"

"Sigmund," said the Director, earnestly and quietly, "I did not at all anticipate this violent opposition to my marriage on your part, and must remind you that you have less right than any one to interfere on this occasion. I have put you in complete possession of your uncle's property, and only reserved my own small fortune, my profession, and subsequent pension for myself. In no way, therefore, can my marriage concern you; and I not only decline any advice you may intend to offer, but insist on your making an apology to Mina for the very improper expressions you have just used concerning her."

"I will not apologise," said Sigmund, haughtily, or ever see or speak to her, should she succeed in persuading you to make her your wife!"

"Be it so, Sigmund; you are fortunately not necessary to our happiness," answered the Director, seating himself again at the table.

An angry retort hovered on Sigmund's lips; but perfectly aware that by self-possession alone he could make an impression on his father, he bent down towards him, and, with the assurance that he had not meant to offend *him*, formally requested an hour's conversation the next morning, and hoped to be excused if he absented himself for the remainder of the evening.

"More than excused," replied the Director, without looking round. "I am well aware that sons seldom approve of their fathers' marrying again, but if ever a man had a right to do so, I may say I have!"

Sigmund left the room, and great efforts were made by all to restore the previous cheerfulness, but in vain ; every one was more or less embarrassed, and the party broke up in consequence at an early hour, the Director assuring Mina and her parents, as he accompanied them down the stairs, that they should never again be subjected to such rudeness, and that Sigmund's conduct would only serve to hasten the marriage he had opposed with such unexpected violence.

When Mina soon after entered her own room, she found on the table a carefully sealed note, containing but the one line :—

"Meet me at the willow-tree, in the orchard, at midnight."

And, with eyes' riveted on the order she dared not disobey, she sat deliberating anxiously until the short day drew to a close, and the words of the dreaded appointment became illegible.

She heard her father's step on the drawbridge, and looked after him as he walked towards the inn where he usually spent a couple of hours every evening, and then she joined her mother, and listened to her indignant remarks about Sigmund, and praises of the Director, while they both worked at the *trousseau* that had been in secret progress for many weeks— Madame Pallersberg being herself so loquacious that her daughter's silence was quite unobserved. At length they separated for the night, and soon after Mr. Pallersberg returned home. Mina heard him carefully lock the castle gate, ascend the stairs, and enter his room, the door of which she passed two hours later on tiptoe, a shawl drawn tightly over her shivering figure, and her head covered with a black lace scarf.

The night was dark, notwithstanding the myriads of stars in the cloudless sky ; but when her eyes had become accustomed to the obscurity, she easily found her way across the court, and into the garden and orchard.

The willow-tree was not far from the boat-house, close to the lake, and with boughs extending far over the surface of the water into which the pendant branches dipped unceasingly—just then with some violence, as they were blown to and fro by the autumn wind. The lake was dark and ruffled, and the outline of Sigmund's figure indistinct, even when Mina stood almost close beside him.

" Sigmund, be merciful," she said, in a low voice of entreaty, "and do not deprive me of my last chance of—of—"

· " Of becoming Countess Waldering," he said, interrupting her,—" father or son, it is all the same to you ! But no ; I had almost forgotten—you preferred me yesterday—perhaps to-day—or even now ?"

" Oh, Sigmund ! if you had ever loved me, or any one, you could not be so cruel !"

" It is precisely because I love that I have resolved to punish you for interfering with my best chance of happiness. You told Doris of my promise to you. In return I shall tell my father what you have said and written to me. He shall know all—all—to-morrow, and I leave you to judge if he will afterwards think it necessary to fulfil any promises he may have made you."

" Spare me, Sigmund ! Spare me ! I see that without your consent I cannot become your father's wife, but for Heaven's sake give me back my letters. I believed you implicitly when you assured me you had destroyed them and even now cannot think it possible that you will use such means to betray me! Be satisfied with having deprived me of an establishment such as will never again be offered me."

"Then you resign all claims on my father?"

"I cannot help myself."

"But in these same letters," continued Sigmund, "you have mentioned my grandmother in a manner that will cause you to forfeit her friendship and protection in future."

"Sigmund, what I wrote was but a continuation of my conversations with you."

"My words, fortunately, are not written," he observed, cynically.

"Must I then return to my parents?" she asked. "Do you condemn me to live over the gateway of the castle for the rest of my life?"

"By no neans," he answered. "I consider you so dangerous, that I should make it a point with your father that you were never to enter his apartments here."

"Are you in earnest, Sigmund?"

"More so than I ever was in my life when speaking to you," he answered.

"And what is to become of me? Do you know that are making me homeless?"

"You have made me the same," he cried, fiercely. "By your means Westenried has become odious to me on the very day it was put into my possession. Your infernal machinations first separated me from Hilda, and then made Doris dislike me. I have now my revenge, and I enjoy it."

"You will drive me to despair!" she said, in a low, wailing voice. "I wish I were dead, and in my grave. Have mercy!" she added, clinging to him, though he tried to push her from him—"have mercy, as you hope for mercy; for, if you do not relent, you will force me to end my life in the lake!"

"The old story!" he answered, laughing ironically. "How often have you threatened to take this plunge, and haunt me for the rest of my life? I do hope, however, you have no fancy of the kind just now, as I should be under the necessity of saving you from drowning, and the water must be most confoundedly cold on such a night as this!"

The taunt gave Mina courage; she flung her shawl from her shoulders, and, with a loud wild cry, sprang into the lake.

The moment Sigmund recovered from his astonishment he followed her; but the night was so dark that he could not see her when she rose to the surface, and it was in vain that he afterwards swam about, panting her name and grasping everything he found floating on the water.

It was long—very long—before he could believe that the unfortunate girl once loved, and latterly so intensely hated, had actually been driven by him to commit suicide. As he again stood under the willow-tree, breathless, and with clothes from which the water poured in streams, he for a moment—for one horrible moment—felt himself a murderer; the next—such is the perversion of the human heart—he found excuses for himself, and soon after the blame rested chiefly on his victim. By what mode of reasoning he came to this conclusion is of no importance to us; it was probably not very satisfactory, as he stamped repeatedly on the ground, and ended by muttering that " he was not the first man who had broken a promise of marriage, nor was he likely to be the last. He had not believed her threat of drowning herself; and if the night had not been so dark, and the lake like a pool of ink, he could easily have saved her life. He had done his best, at all events, and there was no use in standing there any longer."

And then he turned away, fully resolved never to betray his share in this catastrophe.

Nor did he ; but enough blame rested on him to cause
a conflict with his father on the ensuing day that served
effectually to estrange them for ever.

———

CHAPTER XXIV.

THREE YEARS LATER.

AFTER the events related in the foregoing chapter, Westenried became a disagreeable residence to all the Waldering
family.   The Director and his mother returned to Munich,
Sigmund went to Paris, and Emmeran, when obliged to
join his regiment, then quartered at Innsbruck, easily
persuaded his aunt and cousins to accompany him there.

The peace of Presburg had given Tirol to Bavaria, and
in its beautifully situated capital on the Inn not only
Bavarian troops were stationed, but many Bavarian families
had established themselves.   Doris's mother, though
possessed of some houses in what was then a suburb, but is
now a part of the town of Innsbruck, was unwilling to
inconvenience tenants who had occupied them for many
years, and therefore took a suite of apartments in a more
central, and what was then considered a more desirable
situation, which she furnished in the newest and most
ponderous Egyptian style.   Sphynxes, with profoundly
serene faces, formed the sides of sofas, eagles' heads and
necks the arms of chairs, gilt mummies supported marble
consoles, serpents wound themselves through the intricate
draperies of curtains, and alligators and pyramids strongly

predominated in the ornaments strewed about the rooms. This description of furniture was at that time considered pure English from being an inspiration of the Prince Regent, and for some years successfully rivalled the meagre fashion of chairs and tables commonly called "*Style de l'Empire.*"

In these apartments Tiroleans and Bavarians met as on neutral ground, and all allusion to the war raging in other parts of Europe was avoided if in any way calculated to lead to unpleasant political discussions. But the misfortunes of Prussia, the millions exacted by Napoleon after the battle of Jena, and the unreasonable contributions levied in Hamburg and Lubeck, were spoken of freely enough, as well as the losses of the Russians and the frightful sacrifice of human life caused by the insatiable French conqueror.

When Napoleon prohibited any kind of commerce and communication with Great Britain, and even decreed that every British subject found in the countries occupied by his troops or those of his allies should be made prisoners of war, Doris took counsel of her numerous Bavarian and Tirolean friends, and received from them the most satisfactory assurances of protection, coupled, however, with the advice to change her name for a German one as soon as possible in order to be prepared for all emergencies.

There was much laughing and jesting on this subject, unmixed with any apprehension of approaching danger. If people surmised or suspected that the defeat of the French in Spain and Portugal might encourage Austria to make another effort to relieve herself and Europe from the tyranny of France, it was generally supposed that Tirol was not likely to become the seat of war, as, even for the passage of troops the country was singularly ill-adapted, and military men declared that it would be difficult to find a plain of sufficient dimensions in any of the valleys to serve either as a field of battle or for the encampment of a regular army.

Under these circumstances, it was by no means surprising that the officers of the Bavarian regiments at that time in Innsbruck should endeavour to make the time pass as pleasantly as possible, and that the carnival of the year 1809 was as gay as can well be imagined in a provincial town.

Private masquerades were of frequent recurrence, for the Bavarians were, and are to this day partial to such entertainments; and the Walderings and some others gave general invitations to their acquaintances to assemble on stated evenings in their apartments, adding a request that the guests would appear masked, costumed, or in domino.

These assemblies amused Doris and Hilda extremely, and guesses concerning the identity of the masks promoted conversation long after such guests had left them.

"I wish," said Hilda, one night when Emmeran was taking leave in his usual reluctant manner, although he had passed the whole evening with them; "I wish you could find out who wore the Roman costume this evening, and looked so picturesque and dignified; his silence and evident wish to avoid you makes me suppose him one of the officers of your regiment."

"That is not very likely," answered Emmeran; "as there was certainly nothing in his appearance at all familiar to me."

"Of course not, in such a dress, and with a half-mask and false beard; but," she continued, "suppose the same figure in your uniform, and try to recollect if any one of your officers has a head shaped like his, or such hands and feet."

"There are a good many of his height among us," said Emmeran, thoughtfully; "but not any of them could stand as he did. I could almost suspect him to be——"

"What?"

"An actor—a tragedian, or something of that sort."

"So," exclaimed Hilda, "a man must be an actor if he can stand and walk gracefully in a toga!"

"Well," he replied, "I should say it required some practice or study; at least, I know I could not do it."

Hilda laughed. "Oh, Emmeran, if you only would *try*," she said, eagerly; "do pray get a toga, and come here on Thursday as a Roman. Doris and I will put you into all the attitudes."

"And at the same time laugh at my awkwardness?" he rejoined.

"If you choose to make us laugh, you can do so undoubtedly," she said; "but I do not see why you cannot manage a toga, and lean your elbow on the stove just as well as any one else."

"If Doris and my aunt also think it would be amusing to see me in such a dress," he observed, "I can go to the people who hire out masks, and perhaps get the very same costume you saw this evening."

Doris said she did not think there was anything particularly entertaining in a Roman mask; she was sure the person who wore it that evening had only wished to show his figure to advantage.

"And perhaps," said Emmeran, "you also think that as I have not at all a graceful figure, I had better avoid the tunic and toga?"

"Not if you like to wear them, Emmeran. I dare say there were more Romans with figures like yours than such as we saw to-night; had we been in a circus, I should have expected to see him throw aside his well-draped toga and spring on the back of the first galloping horse within his reach."

"Well, Hilda, what do you say to that?" asked Emmeran.

"Nothing. I only hope you will appear here on Thursday evening as representative of what the Romans really were, or"—she added with an arch smile—"or what Doris supposes them to have been!"

"The colour of my hair would be more appropriate for a Goth," said Emmeran, smiling; "and this fellow's black head was a perfect 'Titus.'"

"Perhaps it was a wig," suggested Doris.

"Then," said Hilda, amused, "you had better get one like it, with beard to match."

"Why not?" said Doris; "the Romans painted and dyed their hair, and I believe in later times wore wigs also."

"Very true," said Emmeran; "and as light-coloured hair was admired at Rome, I might wear my own if I can procure a beard of the same colour. At all events, while inquiring about the toga, I can try to find out who wore it this evening."

"Pray do," said Hilda, "and then we shall see who made the best guess. I suppose him an officer; you think him a tragedian. Doris says he resembles, or might be, a circus rider; and mamma, dear, what did he appear to you?"

"A coxcomb!" answered her mother; and while Hilda laughed and Doris smiled, Emmeran buckled on his sword and slowly left the room.

During the course of the next two days the silent Roman mask became the subject of conversation in many families, and induced an unusual number of people, both masked and unmasked, to appear at the Walderings' on the following Thursday. Great was the satisfaction of the assembled company to find the toga-ed figure standing, carefully draped, on the spot described; while Hilda and Doris were not a little amused to see many walk up and stare and discuss the posture and dress, as if Emmeran had been placed there for exhibition.

"So," observed an old lady, adjusting her spectacles and gazing upwards, "so this is the Emperor Titus."

The figure shook its head slowly.

"Therese, did you not tell me it was Titus?"

"No, grandmamma; I said that a head with short curled hair is the newest fashion, and is called a 'Titus.'"

"Then what was that story your brother told us of the Emperor who so often said that he had lost a day?"

"My friends," said Emmeran solemnly, "I have lost many a day."

"I thought this mask wouldn't speak," cried a young man advancing; "make him talk and we shall soon discover who he is!"

"The voice is feigned," said one.

"The hair is false," said another.

"No, the hair is his own, and only the nose and forehead are masked," observed a third.

At this moment a pilgrim, with a long white beard, advanced slowly into the middle of the room, affecting great age, and leaning heavily on his staff, but the moment his eyes fell on Emmeran he stood upright, strode a few steps forward, and then, as if suddenly remembering his assumed character, bent down his head and tottered on to the nearest chair.

Doris, Hilda, and their mother had been expecting the arrival of this mask, as, though Emmeran had not been able to ascertain the name of the person who had worn the toga on the former evening, he had heard that a pilgrim's dress had been ordered for a future occasion, and there was every probability of his appearing in it at their house.

And now this pilgrim sat, leaning on his staff, slightly bent forward, his eyes peering eagerly through the mask, but, as Doris soon discovered, almost exclusively watching her and her family. Who could he be? There was only one person who might wish to enter their house masked, in order to see them without the necessity of making himself known; and as the thought of Frank flashed through her mind, she recalled the figure not only of the Roman mask, but also of an Armenian—a blue domino—and a Greek, who had all more or less excited their curiosity, in different places, during the last week or two, and deliberated whether or not he were likely to recommence his intercourse with them in this eccentric manner.

Meantime Emmeran grew heartily tired of the dignified posture in which he had been placed by his cousins, and perceiving they had ceased to watch him, he flung his toga, in a more military than graceful manner, over his shoulder, and sauntered into the·adjoining room, where he found Doris surrounded by a number of clamorous guests entreating her to play some Irish airs on the harp.

"Ask my sister," was her answer; "Hilda plays them quite as well as I do, and far more willingly."

"I suppose," said Emmeran, as the others returned to the larger room in search of Hilda, "I suppose these national melodies remind you too forcibly of Ireland and ——Frank."

"They make me melancholy, for some reason or other," she answered, "though I really do not think that Frank has much to do with it. His quarrel, by letter, with my mother, was most unfortunate, as it has completely estranged him and so long prevented his making any effort to be reconciled to Hilda; nevertheless, when you told us that this pilgrim mask was supposed to be a stranger, and mentioned his extreme anxiety to conceal his name, I could not help thinking of Frank, who alone might venture to come here uninvited and unpresented ; and the very possibility of his being in that pilgrim's dress would have made playing the harp just now a very painful effort to me."

"I am sorry to hear it," said Emmeran, "for I hoped you could meet him with perfect equanimity."

"You mistake me," said Doris, slightly colouring, "it is only the mystery that disconcerts me; for if the pilgrim were to walk in here, take off his beard, and really prove to be Frank, I think—indeed I am sure—I could play as long as he or any one chose to listen. How fortunate that Hilda has no suspicion!" she added, as a light hand passed over the strings of the harp, and lingered on some of the upper ones that required tuning.

She was right. Hilda had no suspicion. She thought it so natural that a mask should make a mystery of his name, at least until the carnival was over, that she did not even recollect the pilgrim's presence, still less perceive his movement, as the request was made to her, or his start as she prepared to comply with it. But Doris and Emmeran were more observant; they knew how great Frank's surprise would be to find that Hilda had acquired an accomplishment, which not only his love of music but also national feelings made him value highly. They knew also her secret intention of surprising him, when an opportunity should offer, and now she was about to do so with an unconsciousness of his presence that was most advantageous to her; for even Hilda's courage might have failed had she been aware, or even thought it possible, that the pilgrim who now stood masked before her was Frank !

Never, however, did she play with more self-possession and feeling, never more willingly, than just then ; and the long-robed pilgrim, forgetful of his staff and venerable beard, stood gazing at the charming performer with folded arms and head erect, a foot, on which a spur could easily be imagined, unconsciously marking the time, while an occasional movement of the head and figure proved the irresistible impression made on him by the music.

When Hilda ceased, stood up, and pushed the harp aside, he drew back, joined a group of dominos near the door, and with them soon after left the room.

In order to preserve his incognito, Emmeran thought it necessary that evening to retire with the other guests, so that Hilda, Doris, and their mother were alone when about to separate for the night.

"After all," observed Hilda, "Emmeran looked better than I expected; he is neither an Apollo nor a Hercules, but I dare say Doris was right in supposing that more Romans may have resembled him than the man who was here on Monday. What a difference dress makes! I should never have noticed the pilgrim of to-night had not Emmeran told us he was the Roman mask on Monday."

"I suspect he is more than that," said Doris. "Do you remember the Armenian, the blue domino, and the Greek who was at Madame d'Epplen's and seemed to watch and follow us wherever we went?"

"Perfectly," said Hilda; "and on consideration the Greek and Roman have a strong resemblance in hair and figure. As he was so often at the Epplens', perhaps he is some Bavarian who has brought her a letter from her husband; he may even be an officer in Colonel d'Epplen's regiment, and she can in that case tell us all about him."

"Let us defer the discussion of this not very important subject until to-morrow," interposed their mother, with difficulty suppressing a yawn; "I confess I am more sleepy than inquisitive just now."

"Suppose, however, dear mother," said Doris, "that I had some reason for thinking it possible that the Armenian, the Greek, the Roman, and to-night's pilgrim were one person, and that person——Frank ? "

Her mother stopped, turned round, and repeated the word " Frank ! "

Hilda leaned on the chair nearest her, and listened attentively to all her sister's reasons for the supposition.

"You may be right or not, Doris," she said, in a low voice; " I only know that I am thankful you did not tell me your suspicions while he was here."

"This is worth investigating," said their mother, "and if Frank really be here we can send Emmeran to him, and——."

"No, dear mother," cried Hilda, eagerly interrupting her; "I have long forgiven Frank all he said to me, and wrote to you, but I can never consent to the slightest advance being again made to him."

"Remember, Hilda, the opportunities are few ;—this is the first that has occurred since your marriage, that is, during the space of nearly four years."

"True," said Hilda, "I have been forgotten, or worse than forgotten, all this time; but, were it twice as long, I would not seek a reconciliation."

"Have you any objection," asked her mother, "to my proposing a meeting and explanation with him ? "

"None whatever as far as your personal quarrel is concerned, but I do not wish my name to be mentioned."

"It will be impossible to avoid naming you, Hilda, for our quarrel, you know, was altogether about you, and my wish for a reconciliation wholly on your account."

"Then, mamma, I must entreat you earnestly to let the matter rest. Believe me, if you make advances to Frank he will only accept them as far as you and Doris are concerned, and you will subject me to an additional mortification that when it is too late you will wish you had spared me!'"

"What ought we to do?" asked her mother, turning to Doris, who stood musing near the candle she had just lighted.

"Nothing," she answered, quietly. "Frank has come to our house masked, and taken such precautions to remain unknown that I think we had better respect his incognito and not even make inquiries about him."

"Quite right," said Hilda. "If any one understands Frank thoroughly, it is Doris;" and she walked towards her room humming one of the Irish melodies she had played on the harp an hour previously.

"Doris, I don't at all like your advice on this occasion," observed her mother, as soon as they were alone. "If we do not make some effort to bring Frank and Hilda together, they may live on in this way for years."

"And if they meet they may quarrel," replied Doris.

"Not likely," said her mother, "for Hilda is even more attractive than she was at Ulm, and Frank will soon discover that a few years have given her too much knowledge of the world to quarrel with him as she did there."

"There are so many ways of quarrelling," suggested Doris.

"But," continued her mother, "I believe we may take it for granted that she is as much attached to him as ever?"

"Of that I have little doubt," answered Doris; "but from some remarks she made about Frank I suspect she has taken offence at the accounts which our injudicious friends have given her of his gay life both at Vienna and Prague. She looked so much more thoughtful than pleased when we were speaking of him just now that I almost doubt her wishing either an explanation or meeting just at present."

"That," observed her mother, "may be in consequence of their having parted in anger; but the embarrassment which they both must feel can only be removed by the good offices of friends and relations, and I shall therefore send Emmeran to Frank to-morrow."

———

CHAPTER XXV.

HOW THEY MET.

"I HOPE, Hilda," said her mother, late on the afternoon of the succeeding day, "I hope you will be glad to hear that Frank is coming to us this evening?"

"Certainly not, mamma, if you have requested the pleasure of his company."

"I sent Emmeran to him," she answered, in explanation, "and he found Frank as willing to come to us as we are to receive him. Doris's supposition that he was the Armenian and the Greek mask we met at the Epplens' was perfectly correct."

"And—— a—— in what character does he appear to-night?"

"This is not our evening for receiving masks, Hilda, and I do not intend to go to the Epplens'."

"Nevertheless, I must repeat my question, mamma, and again ask in what character does Frank come to us this evening?"

"He comes as my nephew, ——" began her mother.

"Of course," said Hilda, "your nephew, and Doris's cousin, and my cousin, too, because he cannot help himself, but——but—— "

"Hilda," said her mother, "you must be satisfied for

the present with knowing that he is willing to forgive and forget, and he hopes we shall do the same."

" Forgiving is easy, my dear mother, when there are faults on both sides. As I ought not to have consented to a marriage that I knew to be so much against his inclinations, so he, having consented, should not afterwards have treated me so unkindly. This, however, I can forgive, but I cannot and will not forget his assurance that he would make no pretension to authority, and that our union was merely nominal. I shall, therefore, be glad to see my cousin Frank this evening, but need not remain at home for the purpose. I dare say he will still be here when I return from the Epplens'."

It was, perhaps, to prevent expostulation that Hilda left the room, while her mother, turning to Doris, exclaimed in a tone of vexation : " I am sorry to perceive you were right,—my interference has been injudicious, and I now fear I shall bring them together only to give them an opportunity of quarrelling afresh. Perhaps we had better send Emmeran again to Frank."

" For what purpose ?" asked Doris ; " he cannot unsay your message, or even tell him we do not wish to see him."

" But, my dear girl, consider the consequences should Frank come here fully expecting a joyful reception from Hilda, and taking it for granted that she is willing to agree to any plan for the future he may think proper to propose!"

" He can scarcely entertain such expectations," said Doris, " however great his hopes of ultimate reconciliation may be. I always, however, thought it would be better to let him find out his errors, and correct them himself. Your well-meant interference after we left Ulm, dear mamma, only made matters worse ; and now that he feels a little natural curiosity, if not something better, to know how we are living here, believe me, instead of sending Emmeran to tell him that we had found him out in spite of all his disguises, and should be delighted to see him again, it would have been wiser to have waited until he made himself known to us, and asked, if after such prolonged neglect we, or rather Hilda, would consent to see him."

"You may be right, Doris, but something must be done, for Hilda is in a fair way to forget him altogether."

"That I doubt," said Doris.

"She never speaks of him," continued her mother.

"Neither should I, under such circumstances," replied Doris.

"And I fear," added her mother, "that she is even beginning to like the attentions of others."

"There is safety in the multitude of her admirers," rejoined Doris, "and if I know Frank at all, the admiration of others will only serve to increase his. Have you not said yourself that men not unfrequently value their wives as Jews and Turks do their jewels, in exact proportion to their worth in the eyes of the world? and some one else said he had known men who only cared for their wives when they were well dressed! Now Hilda is much admired and always well-dressed—Frank has been sent for —they are to meet to-night with all the advantages of increased experience; let us leave them to judge and act for themselves in future."

*　　*　　*　　*　　*　　*　　*

Frank came, and if unpleasantly surprised at Hilda's absence, he betrayed it not. The information that she was at the Epplens' seemed perfectly to satisfy him, and he talked for a long time in the most unreserved manner without even referring to her. Emmeran's presence was a great restraint; he had come with Frank and seated himself in his usual place, in perfect unconsciousness of being in the way, until he perceived his aunt retire to another part of the room, where, calling Frank to her side, she began a low, eager conversation that immediately attracted Doris's attention in a very remarkable manner. " I believe I had better go away," he then whispered, with a glance towards the speakers,—but as he rose, Frank looked at his watch, stood up also, and was taking leave with a promise to come the next day, when the door opened, and Ililda, brilliant in the light, white, gold-bordered drapery of a Priestess of the Sun, entered the room. Her face was covered with the silk mask that (representing the features of a youthful Peruvian) had secured her freedom of speech during the evening, and, without removing it, she first extended her hand to Frank, and then assured her mother and sister that the *soirée* at the Epplens' had been unusually gay. "Almost every one was masked," she added; "even little Babette had a costume *à la Tirolienne*, and would not betray any of the people she knew, though Colonel Dietfurt offered her immense bribes in the form of French bonbons."

"So Dietfurt was there!" observed Frank.

" Yes," she replied, sitting down and beginning to untie her mask with apparent composure; " he is everywhere, and uncommonly popular."

"And," continued Frank, "does he still proclaim his intention of raising the Tirolean conscripts and pacificating the country with only his own regiment and a few squadrons of cavalry ? "

" We are beginning to hope," she answered, " that no coercive measures will be necessary—that the inhabitants of Tirol will remember that they are now Bavarians, and that they cannot expect to be exempted from the military conscription which has now become the law of the whole land."

"I am surprised," said Frank, a little ironically, "to hear you speak at all of *Tirol;* I thought, as a Bavarian, you would tell me I was in the 'Inn circle.'"

"Well, so you are," she answered, taking her mask from her face, and looking at him with an arch smile; "and we hope you will like our 'circle' so well that you may be induced to remain in it for some time."

Frank smiled, put down his hat, and leaned on the back of the nearest chair.

"I must now tell you all about the masks," she continued, turning to the others. " What excited most interest was a group dressed as Tirolean peasants; and among them, Doris, there was a representative of that picturesque-looking man with the wonderfully long black beard we saw so often in the streets lately. I almost think it must have been the man himself."

"My dear Hilda," cried her mother, "how can you imagine a peasant as a guest in the drawing-room of Madame d'Epplen!"

"One seldom sees such interesting figures in a drawing-room," replied Hilda, laughing; "even the bearded mask resembling him created quite a sensation."

"Perhaps," suggested Emmeran, glancing towards Frank, "perhaps this man is sufficiently interesting to make you wish me to procure the dress and appear in it here to-morrow evening?"

"You could not wear it, Emmeran," she replied; "for this man's shoulders are twice as broad as yours. The costume is that of a peasant of the valley of Passeyer, where he is innkeeper, freeholder, and horse-dealer. His inn is called 'The Sands,' perhaps because the river Passeyer made incursions and deposited sand on his land. They say it is rather an insignificant place; but I shall certainly visit him there when we go to Meran next autumn, as we could easily ride or walk to 'The Sands,' if we remained the night there."

" This man's beard is procuring him celebrity," observed Frank, unconsciously raising his hand to the long moustache he had carefully cultivated since his change of regiment. "Now," he added, "if I were at liberty to let my beard grow, I should perhaps have a better chance of becoming remarkable than in any other way; it would soon cover half my face, and might induce people to talk about me."

" They do talk about you," said Hilda, colouring, "quite as much as you could desire. Old General Kinkel and everybody know who you are, and what you are, and why you came here."

" All that was in my passport," said Frank, with a smile that seemed inclined to turn into a laugh ; "besides which I was subjected to the cross-questioning of the military authorities here, who elicited more than I wished or intended to tell, if I could have helped myself."

" Was it necessary to be so very explicit? " asked Hilda.

" I should have been sent back to Vienna, if I had not," he answered. " You see, Hilda, your friend Napoleon is still my enemy; he is displeased with some of the military movements in Austria, fears another effort for freedom, and General Kinkel has received private information that *all* Austrian officers now coming to Tirol are emissaries of the Archduke John ! My loquaciousness alone procured me permission to remain at Innsbruck ; but I am well watched, and have the certainty that all my letters will be opened and carefully inspected."

" The Bavarians never open letters," cried Hilda ; " do they, Emmeran ? "

" I .have nothing to do with letters," he answered,

"but as Austria is certainly preparing for war, and emissaries from the Archduke have undoubtedly been here, the less Frank writes about. military matters, or the state of public feeling in Tirol, the better. But, now, tell us something more about this landlord of ' The Sands,' whose name I know is Andrew Hofer."

" So you have heard of him, too ? "

" Of course; he is a great man in his valley, was one of the deputies sent to the Archduke John after the peace of Presburg, and is supposed, like all the Tirolean innkeepers, to be an incorrigible Austrian."

" That is," said Doris, " he is a patriot in the best sense of the word."

" It is natural that you should think so," said Emmeran; " but it is pretty generally understood that the innkeepers are dissatisfied about the duty on wine; it is also well known that at the target-shooting matches last summer all sorts of opposition to our government was planned, and that these landlords have not only concealed, but aided the flight of our conscripts on several occasions."

" They were quite right," said Doris: " why should they assist in delivering up their countrymen to be formed into regiments for Napoleon's use ? Have you not told me yourself that he has required 30,000 men from Bavaria, and not left you enough to defend Tirol for a week in case of a war ? "

" Yes, Doris, I said so, but—you need not have repeated it before Frank."

" No, indeed," said Frank, laughing; " for I am as well aware of it as you or any officer of the garrison of Innsbruck. Come, Emmeran, we need not play at enemies here; I can assure you that any information you could give me 1 knew before I entered your ' circle,' such as the number of men here, at Halle, and elsewhere—that some

16

of the burghers of Innsbruck are not unfavourable to
Bavaria, but that the peasants are supposed to be loyal—
that is, Austrian—with heart and soul. I should be glad
to find out that they would give their bodies also in case
of a war—and this hiding and flight of the conscripts looks
rather like it."

"I don't know that," said Emmeran; "the Tiroleans
will take up arms to defend their country, if necessary;
but they hate the uniform and discipline of a regiment, and
you know it has hitherto been one of their privileges never
to be employed out of their own land."

"That was the Austrian law," said Frank, "and they
seem not to have forgotten it. Now, if that fellow with
the beard were here, I daresay he could tell us all about
it."

"No doubt of that," said Emmeran; "we don't quite
like his mysterious journeys in all directions, on pretence
of buying and selling horses : people even say he has been
in Vienna lately—perhaps you saw him there ? "

"And if I did," said Frank smiling, "you don't suppose
after what you have just said, that I should tell you so ? "

"I wish I knew him," interposed Doris, "for I should
like to advise him to shave off his beard; it will be sure, in
times like these, to bring him into trouble by making him
a marked man."

"He would not shave off that beard for you nor for any
one," said Hilda; "they say that a wager with some friends
was the cause of his allowing it to grow. It happened that
one evening a beggar, with a similar beard, came up to
them, when they were sitting drinking wine together before
the house on the Sands; and, as Andrew Hofer had not
been long married, these friends asked him what his wife
would say if he took it into his head to let his beard grow
to such a length ? He replied that she had no right to

prevent him, and that he could let his beard grow in any way he chose. They laughed, jested, and finally betted a yoke of oxen that he dared not remain a year without shaving: he gained the wager, and has preserved his beard ever since!''

"He is right," said Frank: "it saves time, a vast deal of trouble, and soap; and I can only say that, if his patriotism equal his beard, I shall be happy to make his acquaintance. And now," he added, turning to his aunt, " I believe that I ought to say good-night, but I shall accept your invitation to take up my quarters in your house to-morrow, for you have fully convinced me that it is absolutely necessary to do so, if only for appearance' sake, and to prevent people from talking about what does not concern them. Good-night!''

"Halt, Frank! we can go together," cried Emmeran.

But Frank had no inclination to wait until Emmeran had buckled on his sword and made arrangements for a walk to Wiltau on the following day. Before a convenient hour for the latter had been decided upon, Frank had descended the staircase, and was already in the street making long strides towards his hotel.

As he passed the sentinel posted at General Kinkel's house, he perceived the man leaning on his musket and looking after a couple of peasants who were walking with a Capuchin monk at the other side of the street, and conversing in the low, undemonstrative manner peculiar to the Tiroleans. The sentinel followed the three receding figures with a vacant stare, little supposing that they were men of whom he would soon hear much and often; men whose names would become of note in the history of their country, and over whose graves monuments would be erected, before which not only Tiroleans, but even foreigners, would stand and speak of them and their deeds with enthusiasm. Frank

could not know this either, just then, but he recognized in
the broad-shouldered peasant Andrew Hofer, the innkeeper
of the Sands, and, while looking at him, scarcely observed
the muscular figure and intelligent face of Joseph Speckbacher, or the red-bearded monk Joachim Haspinger, whose
brilliant eloquence and personal courage made his subsequent fame little inferior to that of his companions.*

Frank walked quickly on, but stopped under a lantern
that hung suspended by a chain across the street, drew out
his watch, and, while winding it up, said, in a low, distinct
voice, as they passed him: "Andrew Hofer, either shave
off your beard or return to the Sands; you have attracted
attention and are watched."

And the three men moved on as if they had not heard,
or that the information in no way concerned them.

Frank was still standing under the lantern, when he
was overtaken by Emmeran.

"You might as well have waited for me, Frank; and
regulated your watch where you had light to see what you
were about."

"No, Emmeran, I could not stand it any longer.   The
self-possession of that Priestess of the Sun quite overpowered me."

"And astonished me not a little," said Emmeran; "but
you must allow the mask was very well chosen, and a proof
of Hilda's complete acquiescence in your wishes."

"Hang me if I have an idea what you mean, or what
she meant either," said Frank, impatiently.

---

* Hofer's remains were brought from Italy, and interred in the Hof-
church at Innsbruck.   Speckbacher has been given a place beside him,
and his funeral was celebrated with great pomp in the year 1858.
Haspinger, with all his wonted energy, accompanied the Tirolean
Chasseurs to Italy as Field Chaplain in the year 1848, and died of old
age a few years since at Salzburg.

"You know," observed Emmeran, "that a Priestess of the Sun is supposed to have made a vow to live unloved, and, if possible, unloving, until her thirtieth year, at the end of which time she is free, or, rather, expected to marry and become a useful member of society."

"Nonsense," cried Frank, half laughing; "say, rather, that this dress showed her beautiful figure to advantage, and you will be nearer the mark."

"That may have influenced her, too," said Emmeran; "for the white gauze draperies and the spangled veil, and even the gilt suns on her head and girdle, were singularly becoming!"

"Well," said Frank, "I thought her——all she wished to appear and a coquette into the bargain; but I suspect she was affecting a nonchalance she could not have felt, for I am quite sure I saw her hands tremble when she untied her mask."

"How could it be otherwise?" said Emmeran; "remember the manner in which you parted, and her odd position in consequence of your eccentric stipulations."

"My aunt need not have told her of them," said Frank.

"I understood," replied Emmeran, "that Hilda had heard from you yourself that her marriage was merely nominal. Doris gave hopes of your coming to your senses and settling down quietly in ten years or so; but my aunt seemed to think that a meeting would set all to rights, and hoped you would not think of postponing your reconciliation with Hilda so long, or even until the war was over. And she was right; for it is hard to say when that will be, as it seems never to cease now-a-days, and may break out here before long. Is this the case?"

"I shouldn't wonder if it were," answered Frank; "the present state of affairs is not likely to last."

"I suppose," continued Emmeran, "I must not press

this subject; but I hope a time will come when we can speak to each other as unreservedly as we used to do at Westenried."

"The time will come, and soon," replied Frank, as they stood before the door of the hotel; "but while waiting for it you need not look at me so reproachfully just as if you thought me an emissary of the Archduke's or a——spy!"

"Frank!"

"Now, don't try to appear as if you had not entertained some such suspicion. Can you not believe that I asked and obtained leave of absence for the sole purpose of seeing my aunt, Doris, and Hilda?"

"Nothing could be more natural, at all events," said Emmeran.

"As to the state of public feeling in Tirol," continued Frank, "it is as well, or, rather, far better understood in Vienna than here. I have had, therefore, nothing of importance to ascertain, nothing to discover, and no new acquaintances to make. That I have chiefly associated with people already known to me and who are staunch Austrians is not surprising, as I can speak to them of hopes that would be offensive to you, and, in fact, I should never have entered a Bavarian house here if it had not been to see those nearest and dearest to me without restraint."

"I am very glad you are not here officially," observed Emmeran.

"So am I," rejoined Frank; "and if it be any satisfaction, or even a relief to your mind, I can give you the assurance that were I able to send a letter to Pallersberg with the certainty of its reaching him unopened, it would contain no information beyond the assertion that I have found everything precisely as we were led to expect."

"Are you, indeed, so very well informed?" asked Emmeran.

"So well," answered Frank, turning back for a moment as he was about to enter the hotel, "so well, that I cannot submit to be questioned by any one. I ask for no information from you, and you must expect none from me. Let us talk of my aunt and Doris and Hilda,—the Director, or even your grandmother ; but not a word of politics or the discontent of the people here, the movements of our armies, or——Napoleon Bonaparte ! "

CHAPTER XXVI.

WHAT WAS DONE FOR APPEARANCE' SAKE.

MIDNIGHT was long past and Hilda still sat before her toilet table in deepest reverie. She shivered occasionally —for the room had become cold, and her dressing-gown was of very light muslin—but she felt no inclination either to go to bed or to open the door leading into her sister's room, which, by mutual consent, was always left ajar during the night.

"I am sure Doris is still up," she murmured at length, rising slowly ; "waiting perhaps for me to open the door and speak of Frank ! "

Doris, however, was apparently not waiting, at least she had extinguished her light and was in bed.

"Good night, Hilda ! I am not asleep," she said in a cheerful voice.

And Hilda advanced into the room, stood beside the bed, and stooped down to kiss her.

"How cold you are, and how dreadfully pale ! " cried Doris, as a gleam of light from the adjoining room fell on her sister's face.

Hilda turned her back to the door.

"You are not ill, I hope?" said Doris, raising herself on her elbow.

"No, I am only cold, but I do not like to go to bed until I have asked you if——if my mother said anything to Frank this evening."

"Yes, she spoke to him alone, and at some distance from me, just before you returned home."

"I thought so," said Hilda; "her anxiety that we should be reconciled is so great that she cannot be neutral; and I am sure she told him of my resolution to abide by his stipulations, and requested him to have patience with me."

"She had not time to say much," observed Doris, "for Emmeran, supposing himself *de trop*, almost immediately stood up, and Frank seemed glad of the interruption; I am, however, surprised at your objecting to her saving you the annoyance of an explanation."

"Because I am convinced she will say too much, Doris; try to excuse me, perhaps, which I consider quite unnecessary. What did he say, dear, when he heard I was at the Epplens'?"

"He said nothing, but I suspect he was disappointed if not vexed."

"And you, Doris,—how did you feel when you saw and spoke to him again."

"Very glad; very happy."

"No recollections of Ulm? no regrets?"

"No dear, nothing but a desire for your mutual happiness."

"Now, Doris, answer me truly, and without reserve; do you think he has conquered the preference for you that made him so inexorable to me?"

"Quite," replied Doris, calmly; "I never doubted that he would; and I am much mistaken if he will not like you all the better now for the barrier he has himself placed between you."

"Dear Doris, do you indeed think this? you who know him so well! And may I hope that you approve of my resolution to make no more humble advances as I did at Ulm?"

"He will expect nothing of that kind now," said Doris; "you have only to receive him graciously, to listen to his excuses patiently, and then to pardon magnanimously."

"I should like," said Hilda, "to punish him a little first; but then, I am sure, you would take his part, and not mine."

"I have always taken part with you, Hilda, excepting the day you struck him with your riding-whip."

"Oh, Doris, don't remind me of that. I wonder did he think of it this evening?"

"Scarcely," she replied; "for we avoided speaking of Ulm before you came, and afterwards, you know, we talked of nothing but the Tirolean masks. But I must say, Hilda, I think you have punished him enough by giving him so cool a reception this evening, and advise you not to be too hard upon him to-morrow, when he professes sorrow for the past, and makes promises for the future."

"I don't know what he will do or say," observed Hilda thoughtfully, "but I suppose we shall have some explanation before long. I wish it were over, and that I had said nothing I should regret afterwards. I have composed a great many speeches, but when the time comes to make them, shall probably forget them all."

"And have recourse to tears?" suggested Doris.

"No," said Hilda, firmly; "what I have to say will not bear that sort of accompaniment. If Frank only gives me a few days to overcome my embarrassment——"

"A few days!" cried Doris, interrupting her, "you do not know, Frank, if you think he will give you a single day. Prepare your speech for to-morrow, Hilda, and go to bed now as fast as you can."

The next day Hilda thought she perceived a determination on the part of her mother and sister to leave her alone in the drawing-room, about the time that Frank was expected, and, therefore, remonstrated with the latter when she saw her retiring with her work in her hand.

"I shall stay here if you wish it," said Doris, "but I think it would be far better if you had your explanation without witnesses."

"I cannot agree with you, Doris. Frank had no consideration of this kind in Ulm, and scorned and slighted me openly enough!"

"But," said Doris, "I am convinced that even in Ulm he began to repent."

"The result of his repentance," observed Hilda, ironically, "was, however, the letter to my mother, complaining bitterly of having been inveigled into a marriage against his will!"

"Remember her letter to him, Hilda; could anything be more severe?"

"Perhaps not; but he deserved to hear the unpleasant truth from some one."

"Now, Hilda, if you are going to repeat any of these truths to him this morning, you really must excuse my declining to hear them, or witness the quarrel that will inevitably ensue."

"I don't intend to quarrel."

"As if it were possible to avoid it!"

"Stay with me, Doris, and you shall see."

Doris hesitated.

"I do assure you," she continued, half laughing, "I

do assure you he shall find me a perfect Griselda—obedient to a fault."

" Now, Hilda, what do you mean ?"

Before she could answer, the door opened, and Frank, advancing into the middle of the room, wished them "good morning," adding, the moment the door was closed: " Well, here I am, as my aunt says, for appearance' sake, and as we are to appear a thoroughly united family in public, I propose a short rehearsal of our parts in private. May I kiss you for appearance' sake, Doris ?" he asked, approaching her with a smile.

She understood this as an appeal for a precedent, and, drawing him towards her, answered gaily, " For old affection's sake as often as you please, my dear cousin."

A moment after he stood by Hilda, bent down towards her, and whispered, " May I ?"

" Yes, my dear *cousin*, for appearance' sake as often as you judge necessary."

Frank evidently did not like the manner in which permission was given, availed himself of it, nevertheless, and then " hoped, as she laid so much stress on the word *cousin*, he might consider himself entitled to all the privileges of that singularly privileged relationship."

" Undoubtedly, Frank," she replied. " I only used the word to convince you how perfectly I remembered all you said to me at Ulm."

" I am sorry to find your memory so retentive," he observed, biting the top of his cane in evident embarrassment. " Emmeran gave me distinctly to understand we were mutually to forgive and forget."

" I can forgive with all my heart, Frank," she answered, smiling ; " and shall soon forget everything but——your stipulations. The fact is," she added, bending over her tapestry-frame so that her long curls fell on her cheek, and partially concealed a deep blush, — "the fact is, I now value highly the permission you gave me to go where I please, and to do what I like; and I have become so perfectly satisfied with our nominal union that I can await in perfect contentment the time fixed by you for its termination."

Hilda spoke so low that Frank had to stoop down until his head was quite close to hers, in order to hear what she said, while her mother, who just then opened the door of her room, supposing their conférence had come to an amicable conclusion, advanced towards them, and began eagerly to express her satisfaction that their estrangement was at an end; but the moment Frank raised his head she saw her mistake, for his face was pale, and his lips quivered when he tried to smile.

"What is the meaning of this?" she asked, turning reproachfully to her daughter.

Hilda looked up, pushed back her hair from her face, and with difficulty repressing a smile of triumph, replied, "I believe Frank is surprised to find that I have learned to make my duty my delight, and can obey his commands with pleasure."

Frank stood up and raised his hat from the table; his aunt laid her hand on his arm, and said apologetically, "Come, Frank, you must bear Hilda's wilfulness as she has borne yours,—with patience. I thought I said enough yesterday evening to make you understand that she had not yet been able to forgive without reserve."

"I assure you," interposed Hilda, demurely, "I have not only forgiven without reserve, but also expressed my deference to his wishes in the most satisfactory manner. Frank understands me perfectly."

"Yes," he said, slowly, "I understand that I have been brought here on false pretences."

" That was mamma's fault," said Hilda, hastily ; " both Doris and I thought it would be far better to let you find your own way back to us."

" It *would* have been far better and pleasanter for us all," said Frank; " but," he added, turning to his aunt, " the question now is,—having come here for appearance' sake, must I remain with you?"

" It will have a very odd appearance if you do not," she answered.

" Then," he continued, " then we must mutually agree to a complete cessation of hostilities."

" Nothing can be more desirable," she replied.

He looked towards Hilda.

She nodded her head two or three times in smiling acquiescence.

" And——and——," he added, no one is to know—not even Emmeran is to be told that I have been made a fool of in this way."

" If," said his aunt, earnestly, " if you do not yourself complain or explain to him, he shall never hear from us that you misunderstood my message."

Frank walked to a window, and while he stood there in grim displeasure, Doris and her mother left the room.

A long silence ensued. Hilda heard some very impatient movements—a drumming on the window, and at last the muttered words, " There he is already coming down the street."

She knew he meant Emmeran, and wished to say they expected him to walk with them to Wiltau ; but from the moment she had been alone with Frank her courage had deserted her, and finding herself unable to speak unconcernedly, she remained silent, secretly rejoicing at the prospect of a speedy interruption to so disagreeable a *tête-à-tête.*

Frank's impatience visibly increased; he strode towards the door, then back to the window, and seemed still irresolute what to do until he heard Emmeran's footsteps in the anteroom; then, urged perhaps by the fear of exposing himself to ridicule, he sprang suddenly across the room, shoved with all his force one of the heavy arm-chairs close to Hilda, flung himself into it, put his arm round her, seized her hand, and as the door opened, bent down his head, and whispering, "We must do or say something for appearance' sake," allowed Emmeran to suppose he had interrupted a scene of joyful reconciliation.

The moment Hilda recovered from her astonishment, the supreme absurdity of their situation provoked an inclination to laugh that she found it difficult to suppress. Frank thought there was triumph in her mirth, and drew back with such evident displeasure and mortification that Emmeran, supposing himself an intruder, stammered an apology, and prepared to leave the room.

"Pray don't go," said Frank, rising, and almost immediately recovering his self-possession; "Hilda and I are not lovers, you know, and people who have been so long married ought not to be put out of countenance so easily. Our *tête-à-tête* has lasted quite long enough, I assure you."

"I came by appointment——" began Emmeran.

"Yes," interposed Hilda, "and we shall be ready directly for our walk to Wiltau. Frank will, I hope, go with us, and tell us something about Vienna and his friends there. Perhaps," she added, stopping for a moment at the door, "perhaps he will find that we know more of *his* sayings and doings than he does of ours."

"I dare say," said Frank, carelessly, "that Pallersberg's letters to my aunt kept you tolerably *au courant.*"

"There were others who have been far more communicative," she replied; "and," here she raised her finger, playfully threatening, "and you may expect to be taken to task some day when we have nothing else to talk about."

They were all soon after on their way to Wiltau. Frank immediately drew Hilda's arm within his, and whispered gaily, "It is all for appearance' sake, you know," walked on with her alone.

Doris and her mother looked at each other inquiringly, while Emmeran smiled, shrugged his shoulders, and observed, "Is it possible you expected anything else?"

CHAPTER XXVII.

LOVE OR HABIT?

"WELL, Doris," said Frank, one morning when he found himself alone in the drawing-room with his cousin, "all this is very pleasant; Hilda is charming, my aunt kindness itself, and you,—precisely what I expected; but here I am nearly at the end of my leave of absence in exactly the same position as when I entered the house. Hilda may like this sort of thing, and we have certainly been flirting away at a famous rate lately, but I think it is time to be serious now. Couldn't you give her a hint that the next advance ought to come from her, seeing that I am '*en penitence,*' as old Madame Fredon used to say."

"Remember Ulm," answered Doris; "recall the manner in which you received her advances then, and——have patience."

He did remember Ulm, and thought of the painful midnight parting from the cousin by whom he now sat, apparently in very nearly the state of calm self-possession she had then predicted time would give them both; and then he recalled the vision of a trembling childlike bride whom he had scorned, whose advances he had spurned, and was reasonable enough to check his natural impetuosity and answer quietly : " The recollection of Ulm is not calculated to make me patient, at least not with myself, Doris ; for I am now convinced that I ought either to have braved you all and persisted in my refusal to marry Hilda, or having yielded, to have done so with a good grace. Hilda must, however, have told you that I latterly made advances to her in Ulm that were singularly ill-received."

Doris looked up inquiringly.

" The day of the bombardment, when I accompanied her home from the hospital, she would not listen to my really penitent apologies, but pushed and pommelled me in the street, and you and others saw her a few days afterwards lash me pretty freely with her horsewhip."

" She has long got over all that kind of impetuosity," said Doris, smiling.

" Yes," replied Frank, " she seems to have taken a leaf out of your book, and to have profited so well by your instructions, that she is more than a match for me now."

" Have you any objection to her resembling me ? " asked Doris.

" I believe I would rather have her as she was at Ulm," he replied ; " we should suit each other better, for I begin to think, Doris, that it is not judicious for a man to choose a wife so superior to him as you would have been—I mean as you certainly will be—whenever you condescend to bestow your hand and a moderate portion of dispassionate regard on——on whomsoever my words may induce you to think at this moment ! "

" I think of no one," said Doris quietly.

" Don't you ? " said Frank, laughing ; " then what on earth brings Emmeran here every day ? "

"Habit," she replied.

"Habit!" he repeated; "then habit seems in a fair way to make you necessary to his happiness."

"It is not impossible that he may think so," she answered, "at least for some time; but change of scene and occupation enable people, especially men, to conquer such fancies with wonderful facility."

"I protest against the word 'facility,'" said Frank earnestly; "but if you speak from experience I dare not contradict you."

"Yes, Frank, I speak from experience, and you have had far more than I, if the half of what we have heard be true."

"What have you heard?" he asked, colouring.

"That there have been houses which you have frequented quite as habitually as Emmeran does ours, and that you have had fancies which you made no effort to conceal as he does."

"I cannot live without the society of women," said Frank; "and if you knew more of the world you would scarcely blame me for seeking it among people whose manners and habits most resemble those of my home."

"I do not blame you, Frank, if you never forgot that you had neither hand nor heart at your disposal."

"Well," he said, leaning back in his chair and looking up to the ceiling, "well, it was pretty generally known that in a fit of enthusiastic deference and devotion to one cousin I had bestowed my hand on another, and was not particularly happy in consequence; as to my heart, Doris, to tell the truth I did not well know what to do with it at first, and I confess that I became intimate in some pleasant houses, acquired habits rather resembling Emmeran's here, and assiduously endeavoured to banish Ulm and all that occurred there from my memory."

17

" So we heard," said Doris dryly.

"You did not mind," he said, bending forward, " for your affection for me was merely ' habit,' I suppose."

"It was habit," said Doris, laying down her work and fixing her eyes calmly on his face, " but it had grown with my growth and strengthened with my strength ; it was the affection of nearest relationship, and what it was at Garvagh, Westenried, and Ulm, it is now and will be as long as I live."

" Allow me to speak as plainly as yourself, Doris," he replied warmly ; " and in extenuation of my conduct at Ulm, let me tell you that my affection for you was more than habit —it was love—a passionate first love, Doris.   You and you alone were ever present in my mind when I longed for pro-motion, glory, and a Theresian cross ; for with all your good sense, my dear cousin, you could not conceal from me your value for the ' bubble reputation,' and I would have sought it at the ' cannon's mouth ' to win your heart.   Even as a boy I was quite aware you liked me all the better for the reckless deeds that so often brought me to grief during the holidays at Garvagh."

Doris could not deny this.   She well remembered that her preferring him to all his brothers had first been caused by his protecting her from the attack of an angry bull, having drawn the animal's attention to himself while she and his much older brother Henry sought safety in flight ; she was conscious, too, that his hard riding, desperate driving, and wagers as wild as perilous, had found favour in her eyes, and that at a later period she had in her heart made excuses for less pardonable proofs of courage even while compelling herself to utter words of reproach.

" I believe," she said reluctantly, " I believe all women admire courage as a manly quality, and one that they seldom have the good fortune to possess themselves."

"So much the better," said Frank; "I don't think courage at all necessary for a woman excepting when on horseback;—for men it is indispensable, but is so common, dear Doris, that he who possesses nothing else is poor indeed! I am afraid you think this is my case, and if Hilda be of the same opinion, the sooner I join my regiment again the better."

While Frank was speaking Hilda had entered the room, and he named her just as she stood opposite him with her hand on the back of her sister's chair.

"Don't you think, Doris," she said, bending forwards and speaking in an audible whisper, "don't you think he wants us to contradict him?"

"He wants more than that," answered Doris, laughing; "but we won't spoil him with flattery like the ladies of Vienna and Prague."

"And Innsbruck, too," said Hilda; "our friends tell me that I can form no idea of his sudden popularity here."

"That," said Frank, "is easily accounted for when you remember that I am an Austrian officer; believe me, Hilda, my popularity here is altogether political."

"And elsewhere?" she asked.

"I am not aware of any," he answered. "Colonel Bereny and General Vacquant gave me introductions, and people were kind and hospitable, perhaps in consideration of my being so far from my own country and kindred."

"We have heard that some were more than kind," persisted Hilda, with heightened colour; "that in one house you were every day and all day!"

"I was aide-de-camp, and had my horses there."

"And now?"

"I am no longer aide-de-camp," he replied, laughing,

" but I am every day and all day at General Vacquant's house. Have you any objection ? "

" Oh no, not the least. I suppose, Frank, that six years hence, when the war is quite ended, you will be a general ——or at least a colonel ? "

" The chances are in my favour just now," he answered.

" And then, Frank, we, too, shall have aides-de-camp, shan't we ? "

" Perhaps *I* shall," he said, colouring very perceptibly.

" And they will have their horses in our stables," she continued ; " and be every day and all day in our house ? "

" That will depend upon circumstances," he replied ; " for though I should have no objection to a quiet, steady fellow such as I am——"

At this moment a servant entered with a note which had been sent from a neighbouring hotel.

Frank's colour deepened as he read, and an expression of intense annoyance passed over his features.

" No answer," he said, looking up for a moment; " I shall call in the course of the afternoon." Then twisting the note round his fingers, he turned again to Hilda, and continued—" What were we talking about ? Was it not of the time when we should be living together——"

" No, we were talking of aides-de-camp," she said, quickly ; " and I wish to bespeak one who can ride, drive, walk, talk, sing, and dance with me. I should like him to have a good deal of general information, a decided predilection for England and everything English, and, if he be a Hungarian, so much the better, as I can take advantage of the opportunity to learn his language ! "

" I shall attend to your directions," said Frank, " and when the time comes seek a Hungarian answering this description. With regard to the language, if you have any fancy for it, I can give you some instruction beforehand myself; for when I was appointed to my present regiment, I was obliged, as a matter of course, to learn it."

" We heard so," she observed, pointedly; " and from all accounts were led to suppose that you found the wife of your Colonel, Madame de Bereny, an extremely agreeable instructress."

"An extremely agreeable acquaintance, or rather friend," he replied; " but for the Hungarian language I had a master every day for a year."

" Perhaps, then, you only frequented her house so assiduously in order to acquire fluency in speaking ? "

" Not exactly," said Frank, rising with the evident intention of leaving the room ; " I liked both the Colonel and his wife, had a general invitation to their house, and felt as much at home there as I do here."

" Perhaps more ? " suggested Hilda, with some pique.

" That might easily be," he answered, in the same tone, while closing the door.

" Well, Doris, I hope you are now convinced that all we have heard is true ? "

" No, Hilda, I am much more convinced that all my misgivings about your jealousy were well founded; and I am sorry you have betrayed yourself to Frank."

" I could not help it, Doris ; everything he does, everything he says, convinces me that his coming here was a mere duty without a particle of inclination, excepting, perhaps, to see you again! He tried to hate me at Ulm, and I believe failed in his efforts ; he is trying to like me now, perhaps, and seems equally unsuccessful ! "

" I am quite sure, Hilda, he likes you as much as any reasonable woman could desire."

" But I am not reasonable on this subject," said Hilda.

" I am glad you are aware of it," observed Doris, " for

Frank seems to think so too, and expects the next advance to come from you."

"He may wait long for it," replied Hilda.

"I hope not," said Doris; "remember you are his wife, and that an effort to conciliate on your part is the most natural thing imaginable."

"Oh, very likely; but I shall never attempt anything of the kind again, and I hope you will explain this to him."

"No, dear, I do not at all like this office of mediating, which you both seem so determined to force upon me. Frank requested me to tell you that he expected you to yield a little now; you say he may wait a while. I hope he may do so, and not relax in demonstrations of affection that ought to have removed all your jealous doubts."

"They have not removed them," said Hilda; "I believe all that I have heard, and am as convinced as I was before he came here that he consoled himself for your loss and altogether forgot me in the house of this Madame de Bereny."

"As far as I am concerned," said Doris, "he is more than consoled, for he has just given me to understand that he now knows I was not at all a person calculated to have made him happy."

"Dear Doris, did he say that?" exclaimed Hilda, with irrepressible exultation: "did he indeed say that—and to you?"

"Something to that purport, at all events," answered Doris. "But, oh, Hilda!" she added, reproachfully, "can it be possible that all this time you have been jealous of me too?"

"No, Doris, no; that would be too unreasonable! No, not jealous,—certainly not in the common sense of the word; but how could I be sure that Frank would not again see and feel your superiority to me and every one?' How could I be certain that his first love would not return with double force?—Oh! Doris," she cried, suddenly covering her face with her hands, "I know you must hate and despise me for this weakness."

"No," said Doris, sorrowfully, "I rather pity you; and greatly fear, if you cannot conquer it, you will not only make yourself unhappy, but also weary and worry Frank beyond endurance."

"Doris," cried Hilda, petulantly, "it is easy for you to reprove and warn,—you, with your calm, cousinly affection for Frank, and your phlegmatic friendship for Emmeran! What can you know of jealousy?"

"Nothing," answered Doris, "excepting that I do not consider it a proof of love."

"Don't you?" said Hilda; "but I do, and intend to put Frank to the test by it."

"I advise you not, Hilda, for I suspect his education and habits would rather prompt him to demand explanations from the supposed rival than from you. Remember what occurred at Ulm before your marriage."

"This is intolerable!" cried Hilda. "Here have I been all this time, never venturing to dance twice at a ball with the same person, never receiving morning visitors, and giving up riding because our escort had become too numerous, while Frank has been amusing himself morning, noon, and night at this Madame de Bereny's, not to mention all the other demi and demi-semi flirtations of which we have heard."

"I don't believe the half of what we have heard," said Doris, "and advise you to judge of Frank for yourself. Just determine to suppose yourself not yet married to him——"

"That I can do very easily," interposed Hilda.

"And," continued Doris—"and also suppose Frank merely a person from whom you had reason to expect a proposal of marriage——"

" Well, Doris, that seems to me exactly my position during the last three weeks, but he will not propose; he says everything but that!"

" Probably," said Doris, "he fears another repulse; and, indeed, you refer so continually to the foolish stipulations made by him at Ulm that I do not wonder at his cautions."

" It seems," observed Hilda, "that Frank and I are doomed to be at odds like all the rest of the world. I could almost suppose that I represented Bavaria, and Frank Austria; we are at present observing each other and manœuvring, but a very little provocation on either side would again cause an open declaration of war."

" Avoid that," said Doris, "if you possibly can."

" Yes, dear, I mean to do so; but you, being France, ought to help Bavaria——"

"Not I," said Doris, laughing; "I am England, and side with Austria. Emmeran may, if you like, represent France——"

And just at that moment they heard him speaking to their mother in the adjoining room, the door of which he had partly opened.

" How often one thinks and speaks of people who chance to be near us!" observed Hilda.

"Emmeran has brought some one with him," said Doris, turning her head in the direction of another voice that just then named Hilda in eager inquiry.

" It is Sigmund!" said Hilda. " What can have induced him to come here? If you are the attraction, Doris, I hope you will occupy his attention exclusively, for there is no one whose observation I should dread so much; he will watch every look and weigh every word until he find out the hollow truce between Frank and me. If I had only refrained from mentioning this odious Madame de Bereny to-day——or if Frank could at all conceal his feelings——but there is no chance for us; this time to-morrow Sigmund will know everything we wish to conceal, and we shall not have even an idea of the motives that induced him to come to Innsbruck!"

———

CHAPTER XXVIII.

CROSS PURPOSES.

SIGMUND received a very cool reception from both Doris and Hilda, a frigid bow from Frank, when they met at dinner, and all three declined speaking French, or appearing in the least interested in his adventures during his two years' sojourn at Paris. The most touching anecdotes of Napoleon's magnanimity, the most amazing accounts of the splendour of the French Court, having failed to elicit a remark from Hilda, he at length turned to her and observed: " Well, Hilda, my father was right when he said you would soon become a staunch Austrian. O'More's politics are yours now, of course; so I scarcely know whether you will be glad or sorry to hear that we are again on the eve of war."

" I am sorry, very sorry," said Hilda; " but Frank has been too little with me to have had any influence on my political opinions, so you may consider me quite Bavarian still."

" Indeed! Then perhaps you get the Augsburg paper

regularly, and know what is going on in the world; most people here seem in utter ignorance of everything, excepting that the conscription is unpopular, and that the peasants' sons have fled to the mountains to avoid being enlisted."

"There are more things unpopular than the conscription," interposed Doris; "but we have no means of showing our discontent at present otherwise than by confiding our presentiments of evil, and repeating prophecies of war, to whoever will listen to us."

"If you have had any presentiments," said Sigmund, "it would interest me extremely to hear them." And he glanced, while speaking, from Doris to Frank.

The latter appeared wholly occupied with the fruit on his plate, and did not even look up.

"I have a strong presentiment," answered Doris, "that this state of affairs cannot last:" and the scarcely perceptible colour in her cheeks deepened to a bright pink, as she continued: "of course we shall have war, never-ending war, until all make common cause with England against France."

"Nothing less probable than that," said Sigmund, shrugging his shoulders. "Is not Austria just now preparing to invade Bavaria, in order to resume the power and privileges formerly possessed by the Emperors of Germany?"

"That is your view of the case," said Doris; "I may be allowed to think that Austria only wants to free herself and others from French thraldom, and to recover her lost territories. Tirol, of course, first of all."

"I, for one," said Sigmund, "should have no objection to resign Tirol, which is a burthen to us—a superstitious, unruly people, whose demands it is impossible to satisfy."

"Superstitious they may be," said Doris; "but they

are a loyal and courageous people, and Austrian to their heart's core."

"You think, perhaps," said Sigmund, again glancing towards Frank—"you think that in case of a war, they will rebel and join Austria?"

"I don't know—I hope they may."

"But, in that case, Innsbruck is no place for you, my aunt, or Hilda, and I can only trust you will all return with me to Westenried."

"We have nothing to fear," said Doris. "Mamma and I will be a protection to Hilda from the 'rebels,' as you call them; and she and Emmeran must defend us in return from the French, who, of course, will make their appearance soon after the first cannon-shot."

"If O'More do not urge you to leave Innsbruck," said Sigmund—and this time he fixed his eyes steadily on Frank —"there is probably nothing to be apprehended. I consider his allowing you to remain here a sort of guarantee for the peace of Tirol."

Frank did not choose to take the least notice of this speech, and continued his occupation of carving a double eagle out of a piece of orange-peel.

"General Kinkel said something similar to me yesterday," observed Hilda; "but I told him that Frank never interfered with our plans or movements, and, as well as I could judge, seemed to consider Innsbruck a very suitable and pleasant place of residence for us."

"If you gave the General such an assurance, Hilda, it must have been very satisfactory to him," observed Sigmund.

"I should rather think," said Hilda, "it must be a matter of perfect indifference to him where we lived."

"Very likely, at any other time," said Sigmund; "but just now General Kinkel may naturally suppose that O'More would use all his influence to induce you to leave Innsbruck, if there were the slightest chance of a rebellion."

" There is none," said Hilda confidently ; " but even if there were, I really do not know to what place we could go."

" To Westenried," answered Sigmund ; " nothing would give me greater satisfaction than being able to persuade you to return with me to Bavaria."

" No, Sigmund ; mamma intends to wait until you are married before she again resides in her apartments there."

" That is unfortunate," said Sigmund, with unusual earnestness ; " let me however hope I may be of use as escort to Ulm or Forsteck ?"

" I—that is we—dislike both places, and would not meet the people there now for any consideration."

" Indeed ! I was not aware of that."

" Besides," added Hilda, hastily, " it is absolutely necessary for mamma's health that we should spend the autumn in Meran, so you see if we were to leave Tirol we could only go to some place in Austria."

" That would never answer," observed Sigmund ; " for they say we are on the eve of a war that will end precisely like that of the year *five !*"

" May I ask who you mean by ' they'?" asked Frank, looking up at last.

" No, Frank, you may not," interposed his aunt, rising from the dining-table ; " nor may Sigmund continue to speak in inuendoes that only serve to irritate and remind us of our different political opinions."

" I assure you, dear aunt," began Sigmund, " I meant nothing offensive in supposing that O'More might be better informed of the state of Tirol than I am."

" Perhaps so," she answered ; " but I must insist on the avoidance of all political discussions. What is the use of perpetually quarrelling about the actions of people over

whom we have no control ? or angrily discussing events over
which we have had no influence ? Our want of unanimity
in politics is unfortunate ; but, as we are not likely to change
each other's opinions, I must prohibit the subject altogether."

" Be it so," replied Sigmund ; " after such a long separation we can be at no loss for conversation,"—and he took a
place beside Doris when they entered the drawing-room,
from which he never moved during the remainder of the
evening.

Frank and Hilda were unusually embarrassed in consequence of their conversation about Madame de Bereny, and
though the consciousness of being watched intently by
Sigmund's penetrating eyes induced them to speak to each
other occasionally, there was something in the manner of
both that immediately excited his curiosity and induced
him, after he had taken leave, to accompany his brother
home, instead of returning at once to his hotel.

Now, though Emmeran was not at all disposed to be
communicative, Sigmund elicited enough by means of cross-
questioning to confirm his suspicions that Hilda and Frank
were by no means on such good terms as they wished people
to suppose, and that Doris had not found any one to take
Frank's place.

" I rather expected by this time to find a rival in you,"
said Sigmund, carelessly.

" A rival ?"

" Yes, after a fashion. She might have got used to
your society, you know, and discovered that you are a good
sort of fellow in the main ; that would be enough in time
to induce Doris to marry you or any one, I should think."

" Thank you for the hint," said Emmeran dryly.

" It was no hint, Emmeran, it was merely a supposition, which I am glad to find without foundation. The
fact is, living in Paris is very expensive, and my finances

are at so low an ebb that I must again and seriously think of marriage. My father has never forgiven my interference about Mina—to hear him talk one would really suppose I had deliberately taken her life—so I have nothing further to expect from him; you have barely enough for yourself in these hard times; and, after having enjoyed so many years' liberty, I have no fancy to enter the army again: what then remains but matrimony? Now, as you sapiently observed this morning, I am not a man to come to Innsbruck without a motive——." Here Sigmund paused.

"Am I to understand," asked Emmeran, with wonderful composure, "that you have come here to propose to Doris?"

"No——I did not come for that purpose——but——I am inclined to think it would be my best plan now; her fortune would answer well enough, though I should be very glad it were larger, and that I had not to wait until her mother's death for the best half of it; however, I still like and admire Doris immensely, and when I take into consideration, that at the time she refused me so decidedly at Westenried, she had been strongly prejudiced against me by Mina, and had not had time to forgive my having aided and abetted in her separation from Frank, I think the present time far more favourable, and have little doubt of success."

"I never knew you had actually spoken to her of marriage," said Emmeran, "and cannot imagine how you had courage under the circumstances."

"It would certainly have been wiser had I been less precipitate in every way," said Sigmund; "but at that time I thought altogether of love, and not in the least of money, and a precious fool I made of myself!"

"Don't do it again," said Emmeran.

" No danger ; the chances that were mine at Ulm are lost for ever, but, as a marriage with Doris would now be an act of wisdom on my part, the effort must be made, and at once : to-morrow, perhaps, if an opportunity offer. I am sorry to interfere with any plans you may have formed, Emmeran, but you see I can't help myself."

"I have no plans, Sigmund ; I have never dared to tell Doris that I love her."

" More fool you, and all the better for me," answered Sigmund. " Good night ! Dine with me to-morrow, and you shall hear the result of my conference with Doris."

He nodded his head, and turned in the direction of his hotel, the way towards which led him back to a more central part of the town, and past the house where his aunt lodged. What more natural than that he should look up at the windows of the still lighted rooms, and speculate which was inhabited by Doris ? And he did look up, but only for a moment, as his attention was almost immediately attracted by the opening of a small door, made for the convenience of pedestrians at the side of the *porte cochère.* A man stepped into the street, and having turned round, and carefully relocked the door, drew up the collar of his cloak, pressed his hat over his brow, and walked quickly down the street.

Had this occurred elsewhere, it is more than probable that Sigmund would not have felt sufficient interest or curiosity to look a second time in that direction ; but an inmate and the possessor of a key to that house was well worth another glance, and that glance was sufficient to make him certain that the person now striding on before him was no other than Frank, who so short a time previously had haughtily bowed him a " good night," and then, bedchamber candlestick in hand, sedately walked with his aunt, Doris, and Hilda, along the corridor to his room !

Many wild conjectures passed through Sigmund's mind, but all were at fault when he discovered that Frank was actually going to the hotel where he himself lodged ; by walking a little slower, he allowed him to enter alone the still lighted entrance to the house, observed that he spoke a few words to one of the waiters, and then springing up the stairs, seemed to require no further directions.

The same waiter stood by the staircase as Sigmund approached it, civil and loquacious as such persons generally are, so that a question or two concerning the new arrivals soon procured the information that a Hungarian lady, Madame de Bereny, had arrived that afternoon, and was now in possession of the rooms adjoining his.

" And a——that gentleman who has just gone upstairs ?" said Sigmund.

" That is an officer in her husband's regiment. She sent to him immediately after her arrival, and he came for a short time to make arrangements for her, as her servants are all Hungarians, and speak very little German."

" I suppose," said Sigmund, " he has come here now to complete these arrangements ?"

" I am not quite sure of that," answered the waiter, " for he rather seemed to think our house too noisy for her, and recommended a removal to a private lodging."

" Quite a friend of the family," observed Sigmund.

" Without doubt," answered the waiter ; " for he knew all the servants by name, and the lady's lap-dog nearly went mad with delight when he saw him."

Sigmund walked upstairs to his room, opened and closed the door very quietly, and then threw himself at full length on a sofa.

Now this sofa was placed against the door of communication with the adjoining apartment, and it is probable that a similar piece of furniture was there also so placed, for Sigmund soon heard Frank and Madame de Bereny's voices in eager conversation. He could distinguish every tone and word, but——they spoke in a language unknown to him, which he naturally supposed to be Hungarian, yet felt exceedingly irritated at the lady not preferring German, French, or even English, which would have enabled him at once to ascertain all he wanted to know.

Sigmund, however, soon felt convinced that he knew enough to put Frank in some measure in his power, for were not this visit to Madame de Bereny a secret, assuredly some other hour would have been chosen for it. He resolved to see his brother in the morning, and cross-question him again about Frank and Hilda,—for he began once more strongly to suspect there was continued repugnance on one side, and pique, if not indifference, on the other. Such feelings, under the circumstances, were so possible, so probable, that he had, in fact, come to Innsbruck fully prepared to find it so ; and nothing but Frank's presence, and his being domiciled in his aunt's house, could have made him believe the contrary.

It was while Sigmund was with Emmeran at an early hour on the following day that Frank entered the drawing-room, and lounged on a sofa there, with a book in his hand, until the hour that Doris usually made her appearance. The moment he saw her, and had convinced himself that Hilda was not following, he started up and approached her, exclaiming, " Give me advice and assistance, Doris ; I am in a horrible dilemma."

" About what, Frank ? "

" Hilda is jealous, and——Madame de Bereny is here ! "

"And what has induced Madame de Bereny to come to Innsbruck?" she asked gravely.

"Her health. She is on her way to Meran."

"But," said Doris, "it is too early for Meran."

"Just so," he answered; "and therefore she intends to remain a short time here."

"A very singular arrangement, to say the least," observed Doris.

"Not at all," he replied; "her husband is likely to be in active service, and wishes her out of the way, as she is very delicate and cannot bear much knocking about."

"She knew you were here?" said Doris.

"Of course," he answered, "and expects me to make all sorts of arrangements for her."

"That is natural enough," observed Doris, "when you have been so much in her house."

"Quite natural," said Frank; "but do you suppose Hilda will think so?"

Doris was silent.

"You know she will not," he continued, "and Madame de Bereny wants to be introduced to my aunt and you and Hilda. I wish I had had the good fortune to have left Innsbruck before she came; nothing but the hope of a satisfactory explanation with Hilda has detained me latterly, and now I see no prospect of anything but a regular blow up."

"Perhaps you had better return to Vienna at once," suggested Doris.

"I can't, dear girl, until I have got lodgings for Madame de Bereny here and written about apartments for her at Meran. You have no idea how helpless she is! If she were only fairly out of that hotel it would be a great relief to me, for Sigmund's rooms are near hers, and in order to avoid meeting him I was obliged to call on her last night after you had all gone to bed!"

"And she received you so late?"

"Why not? she supposed we had had company, and it was not necessary for me to explain."

"You must be very intimate," said Doris.

"Very," said Frank; "quite like relations."

"And a——is she young and handsome?"

"I declare I never thought about her age," he answered, "but should think her a good deal older than either you or Hilda at all events. She is a very attractive woman, and her eyes especially are quite beautiful, just like yours, only the eyelashes are not so long and black."

"I wish," said Doris, "that for Hilda's sake she were much older and less engaging."

"Oh, well, so do I," said Frank; "but the question now is, do you think my aunt will object to know her?"

"I think it will altogether depend upon Hilda," answered Doris.

"Then," said Frank, "you must undertake to explain everything, and persuade Hilda to be good-natured and civil."

"And if she should decline the acquaintance of your attractive friend, Frank?"

"In that case," he answered, "I shall be under the necessity of using all my influence to induce Madame de Bereny to leave Innsbruck without delay."

"Do so, Frank," cried Doris eagerly; "it will be much the best plan."

"I would rather not," he said reluctantly, "for you see, dear, if I have not time to write and make arrangements about her lodgings at Meran I must go there with her myself."

" Nonsense, Frank! she could not be so unreasonable as to expect anything of the kind."

" She brought me a letter from her husband," he continued, "and he requests me either to establish her here under the protection of my relations, or——to take her to Meran."

" Then," said Doris, bending over her worktable, and diligently arranging its contents, " then it was not at his desire that you relaxed in your attentions to her and ceased to be his aide-de-camp ? "

" Not at all," answered Frank ; " my promotion would have obliged me to resign at all events, and it was Madame de Bereny herself who requested me to sacrifice the pleasure of her society in order to silence the slanderous tongues of her best friends and most intimate acquaintances."

" She was right," said Doris.

" Of course she was," rejoined Frank ; " we continue as good friends as ever, and more than ever enjoy a meeting when an occasion offers, for it is astonishing how difficulties of any kind enhance the value of intercourse. Hilda seems to understand this sort of thing perfectly, for her pride and prudery have made me more in love with her than I ever thought possible."

" I am glad to hear that," said Doris.

" Are you ? then you must listen to the rest of it. I never until yesterday even suspected that she was of a jealous disposition, and a more disagreeable discovery I could hardly have made, for my wife might have had almost any other fault with impunity ; but to weigh my words and looks to suit a jealous woman's fancy is a lesson I can never learn, and I am so convinced of this that I do not even intend to try."

" You always seem to forget," observed Doris, " how

little your conduct has been calculated to give her confidence to you."

"No, Doris, that consideration alone has enabled me to be 'like patience on a monument smiling at grief' ever since I came here."

Doris laughed.

"You may think it very amusing," said Frank; "but I can scarcely imagine a more absurd or irritating position than mine lately. As long as I thought Hilda was punishing me for my misdemeanours at Ulm, I was obliged to be patient; but I shall positively rebel if she intend to call me to account for my sayings and doings at Vienna, and take it into her head to be jealous, and jealous without cause, too!"

"Without cause!" repeated Doris; "can I with truth give Hilda this assurance?"

Frank hesitated for a moment, and then said, "May I speak without reserve——may I confess——."

"No, Frank," said Doris, rising, "I think you had better not; but do try and persuade this Madame de Bereny to leave Innsbruck."

"Dearest Doris," he cried, catching her hand as she was passing, and detaining her; "you mistake me altogether. I was not thinking of Madame de Bereny. Hilda could only gain by a comparison with her, or indeed with anyone I have ever known, excepting yourself. Of you alone, Doris, she might with some sort of reason be jealous, for I——I cannot help myself, I——. Now don't be angry," he added, colouring deeply; "all I mean to say,—all I have to confess is, that if Hilda will not teach me to forget, I am very likely to fall back into my old 'habit,' as you call it; in which case the remedy you recommended yesterday—change of scene and occupation—will become absolutely necessary for me."

At this moment the door opened, and Sigmund advanced into the room.

" I hope, Doris," said Frank, when he saw her about to leave them, " I hope you are going to tell my aunt and Hilda what I have said about Madame de Bereny; and while you are doing so, I shall just have time to write a letter to Pallersberg, and take it to the post."

CHAPTER XXIX.

A RETORT UN-COURTEOUS.

FRANK wrote, and Sigmund sat at no great distance with a book in his hand, over the pages of which his eye inquisitively followed the quickly-moving pen. The letter was so short and so hastily written, that commencement and signature alike required pressure on the blotting-paper before folding, and Frank pushed back his chair, and stood up while extending his hand for a wafer.

" If your letter contain any important information," observed Sigmund, " I recommend your using sealing-wax."

" Do you think it will make any difference?" asked Frank; " is there any chance of a letter from me to Pallersberg escaping inspection just now?"

" Not much if you use a wafer," answered Sigmund, " for of course there are people here who think you have eyes and ears, and may mention what you have seen and heard to a friend, especially if he be a military man."

Frank lit a taper, and sealed his letter.

At the door he met Hilda, and, forgetful of " appearances," and Sigmund's presence, he first formally wished her good morning, and then hoped she was satisfied with Doris's explanation, and would have no objection to see Madame de Bereny.

Her look of astonishment induced him to add, "Oh, I perceive you have not yet seen Doris — pray go to her, and let me speak to you when I return from the post."

He left the room without waiting for an answer, and Hilda, under the influence of anxiety and curiosity, was hurrying towards the door of her mother's room without noticing Sigmund, when he called out, "Come, Hilda, if your husband thinks it necessary to be so immensely respectful when saying good morning, I scarcely know what kind of obeisance will suit my more distant relationship."

"Frank does not breakfast with us," she said, as if in apology, "but he has evidently desired Doris to explain something to me, and therefore you must amuse yourself as you best can until our discussion is over."

"It seems," observed Sigmund, "that Doris is the medium of communication between you and your husband —when I came here just now he was probably giving her a message for you, but why doesn't he speak to you himself instead of desiring *her* to inform you that Madame de Bereny has followed him to Innsbruck?"

Hilda changed colour and breathed quickly, while she compelled herself with forced composure to ask if he were quite sure that "that was what Doris had to tell her?"

"There can be no doubt of it," he answered, "as Madame de Bereny's name was distinctly mentioned, and Frank asked if you were satisfied with Doris's explanation."

"There is nothing to be explained," said Hilda, walking to the window, and pretending to look out in order to conceal her agitation. "It is very evident that if he could speak to Doris on the subject, Madame de Bereny must be altogether to blame !"

"Nothing more likely," said Sigmund; "I have no doubt he is uncommonly bored by her coming here just now, and may even have told her so in his peculiarly candid manner when he went to see her at the hotel last night."

" You forget," said Hilda, " that last night we were all together in this room."

" Yes, until eleven o'clock ; but where were we at mid-night ? "

" Sigmund, that is not—that cannot be true."

" Well, perhaps not, Hilda ; at all events, I am sorry I said anything, as most probably Frank pleaded some other engagement to you."

" No," she said, regaining her self-possession, "I know nothing of his engagements. There is but little confidence between us—as yet."

" So I perceive," observed Sigmund, seating himself at the writing-table, and turning over the leaves of the blotting-paper.

" Some explanation, however, is absolutely necessary now," she continued, coming towards him, and leaning on the back of his chair.

" Then I think," he replied, " you had better apply to Doris, who is authorized to give it."

" But," said Hilda, " an explanation given by her, and mixed with excuses for Frank, will put me out of all patience ; she is absolutely blind to his faults."

" Indeed ?"

" Yes, and mamma also, at least when either of them speak to me of him. Now you——"

" I," said Sigmund, " have never been blind to his faults. I think him a wild, good-for-nothing fellow ; an insolent coxcomb, who thinks, where women are concerned, he has only to come, see, and conquer! Emmeran tells me you have been trying to show him that he is not quite so irresistible as he supposed, but how little you have succeeded you may see by reading what he has written in your paper book."

He took it up, and read with strong emphasis the following lines :—

"The 'lost one' is as devotedly and passionately attached as ever. The separation forgiven, and the intense desire for re-union beyond my most sanguine expectations."

"Frank wrote that in my book!" exclaimed Hilda, extending her hand for it.

"Not exactly, not intentionally. The fact is, Hilda, this is a letter to Pallersberg, written just before you came into the room ; the ink must have been quite wet when pressed on the blotting-paper, for the writing is perfectly legible on the other side."

Hilda drew back. "I misunderstood you," she said reprovingly, " and supposed Frank had written something in my book that he intended me to read. No temptation would have induced me to look at what he wrote to another person."

"Well, you have only listened to it," said Sigmund ironically ; "and I must explain that I should not have endeavoured to find out what he wrote to Pallersberg, had I not expected to obtain some very important political information couched in the metaphorical language which we have heard the Tiroleans use on such occasions."

"And then you intended to betray him!" cried Hilda, indignantly.

"I should not have betrayed *him* personally, because he happens to be your husband, Hilda ; but I do not deny that I intended to have made use of any information I might have obtained in this way, well knowing that Frank is good authority, and taking it for granted that he would not write if he had not a question to answer. It seems, however, that I was mistaken; he is evidently more occupied with you than with politics just now; and, believe me, I should not blame him in the least, did I not see how ill he requites the ' devotion ' and ' passionate attachment' of which he boasts with such arrogance."

Now though Hilda's affection for her husband did not waver for a moment, she felt herself just then in the position of a neglected and injured wife, and that Frank should have written so triumphantly to Pallersberg mortified her beyond endurance. She therefore allowed Sigmund to call her marriage a " sacrifice," and listened without interruption to his assurances that no act of his life caused him so much regret as having aided in promoting such a union.

There was far more truth in this last observation than Hilda suspected, and Sigmund was becoming eager and eloquent on the subject, when Frank's return caused a sudden interruption.

Sigmund ceased speaking, but could not altogether conceal his embarrassment; Hilda merely removed her hand from her eyes, and then covered them again without moving from the back of the chair on which she had been leaning; while Frank, who had entered from his aunt's apartment, and knew she had not yet seen Doris, slowly advanced, and gravely requested permission to speak to her alone in the dining-room.

" Rather, allow me to leave you together," said Sigmund, rising; "I have not yet seen either my aunt or Doris, and can take the opportunity of going to them."

" Hilda, I have much to say to you," began Frank, with unusual diffidence; " will you not sit down ? "

Hilda took the vacant chair at the writing-table, and, as her eyes fell on the blotting-paper, she hardened her heart, and regained perfect outward composure.

Frank advanced to the place where she had previously been standing, and, instantly following her glance towards the table, saw with dismay the counterpart of his letter to Pallersberg in thick, blotted, but perfectly distinct characters, exposed to view. The blood mounted to his temples and swelled the veins there while he exclaimed indignantly: " I need not ask who took advantage of my haste and carelessness to ascertain what I wrote to Pallersberg! I could perhaps have forgiven, even while contemning, such a means of obtaining what might be supposed important political information; but it was the act of a contemptible scoundrel to show the writing to you, and endeavour to incense you against me!"

" I am not in the least incensed," said Hilda calmly.

" Then you might be, and with reason," said Frank, " if I could not give you the solemn assurance that I never thought of you when I wrote those lines."

Hilda looked up amazed. " May I read them?" she asked, extending her hand towards the table, and drawing the book nearer.

Frank could not refuse, but felt instantly conscious that he had spoken thoughtlessly.

Hilda seemed to weigh every word; them placed her hand on the writing, and asked: "Of whom *did* you think?"

Frank made no attempt to answer.

" Of Madame de Bereny, perhaps?"

" No, on my honour," he replied, in a tone of extreme vexation.

" Excuse my supposing she might be this '*lost one*,'" said Hilda, with bitter irony. " That she is ' *as devotedly and passionately attached as ever,*' I have no doubt. I even remember hearing that a partial separation or diminution of intimacy had taken place——she might have '*forgiven*' this, you know ; and certainly nothing but a very ' *intense desire for re-union* ' could have induced her to follow you to Innsbruck ! "

" She has not followed me," said Frank ; " Madame de Bereny is on her way to Meran."

" And," continued Hilda, " do you think she would have come to Innsbruck now if you had not been here ? "

" I have no reason to suppose she would not," he answered. " My leave of absence is almost expired, and if she wished to see me here it was probably for the purpose of obtaining through me an introduction to you and my aunt."

" And you," said Hilda quickly,—" you have, of course, explained the impossibility of proposing anything of the kind to me ? "

" No," said Frank ; " I hoped, with Doris's assistance, to persuade you to do a kind action ; it need not be more than a formal interchange of visits ; and if you do not like her, you can avoid all intimacy."

" I shall avoid all intercourse with such a person," said Hilda, rising ; " and I am surprised to hear that Doris even listened to your proposal."

" I half expected this refusal," rejoined Frank ; " but think when you hear the consequences of a persistence in it, you will yield a little. The Berenys have been so very kind and hospitable to me, Hilda, that it is incumbent on me to pay her every attention in my power ; she has brought me a letter from her husband, in which he confides her to my care ; and if you will not see and know her, I must conceal the affront by persuading her to continue her journey to Meran without stopping here."

" Persuade her to go away by all means," said Hilda, angrily ; " the sooner the better ! "

" In that case," continued Frank, " Colonel Bereny has requested me to accompany her to Meran—and—I shall do so."

" Do what you like, and go where you please," cried Hilda, passionately, quoting his own words to her at Ulm ; and before she had time to repent her violence, Frank had seized his hat and left the room.

     *   *   *   *   *   *

     *   *   *   *   *

     *   *   *   *   *   *

" He only wanted an excuse to go off with her ! " said Hilda, vehemently, when her mother a few hours later read aloud a letter she had just received from Frank ; " and as to his advice that we should remove to Meran before the month of April, I consider it merely a *ruse* to draw us into an acquaintance with that odious woman."

" Rather a warning well worth consideration," answered her mother. " Frank has hitherto thought himself un-authorized to interfere with your plans, but in this letter he mentions expressly that some information which he has lately procured prompts the advice. I think we might go to Meran, and easily avoid knowing Madame de Bereny."

" As if," said Hilda,—" as if it were probable that you and Doris would not then cheat me into conciliating Frank by attention to her ! "

" There was a time when I might have been tempted to do so," said her mother ; " but I am now convinced that it was a great mistake my trying to force a reconciliation between you, and I shall never attempt anything of the kind again."

" Then, dear mamma, let us not think of leaving Inns-bruck until September, when change of air and ripe grapes will be necessary for your health; and, in the mean time, we may hope that the heat of a Meran summer will disgust Madame de Bereny with the climate, and induce her to return to her husband before we take up our abode there for the winter."

Emmeran was just then dining with his brother at the hotel, and waiting in vain for the expected information respecting Doris: he thought of nothing else; but it was not until they were about to separate that he asked Sigmund the result of his interview with her.

"The interview," he answered, smiling, "turned out an ordinary morning visit in presence of my aunt; but I did not wish it otherwise, as, in consequence of a conversation with Hilda, I had already determined to reconsider the matter, and observe carefully the state of affairs here before I again committed myself."

"A very wise resolution," observed Emmeran.

"I think it is," continued Sigmund, "though not in the sense you mean. Circumstances favour me singularly, and now make the success of a previous and better plan more than probable."

"Am I to be made acquainted with it," asked Emmeran, without any great demonstration of interest.

"I do not see why you should not," answered his brother; "I have long discovered that the most foolish act of my life was breaking off my engagement with Hilda, and may as well tell you plainly that on having ascertained that O'More had been upwards of three years absent without keeping up any sort of communication with his wife and notoriously leading a very gay life in Vienna, I came here for the purpose of advising Hilda to obtain a divorce from him, and then intended to urge her to fulfil her late father's and aunt's wishes by consenting to a marriage with me."

" Sigmund, are you mad ?"

" By no means ; perfectly sane, I assure you. Men and women marry from pique or to punish one another every day. You may, however, imagine my astonishment and disappointment when, on my arrival, I found the scapegrace himself here, and though evidently doing penance for his sins, apparently pretty certain of absolution ! When I left you last night, I had fully resolved to take Doris——"

" I suppose," said Emmeran, interrupting him, " you mean that you had some, perhaps unfounded, hope that she might be induced to take you."

" As you please," said Sigmund, laughing; " from such a charming stoic as Doris a man can submit to a moderate display of condescension. But to make a long story short, Emmeran, I consider my chances with Hilda infinitely better than with Doris, for besides the remembrance of our former long engagement, her father's wishes, and the injunction in her aunt's will, I shall have her jealousy, re-sentment, and desire of revenge on my side ! O'More has played famously into my hand during the last four-and-twenty hours, and has just crowned his misdeeds by going off publicly with Madame de Bereny !"

" Impossible !" cried Emmeran, starting up ; " this is some mistake—some misunderstanding."

" None whatever," answered Sigmund ; " I saw the fair Hungarian descending the stairs leaning, or rather hanging, on his arm ; she seems one of those women who are bewitch-ingly helpless when men like O'More come in their way ; she allowed him absolutely to lift her into the carriage, after which he handed in the *femme de chambre* as if she had been a maid of honour—you know that's his way—and then for propriety's sake, I suppose, seemed very much inclined to mount the box, or otherwise dispose of himself out-side, until a small very white hand was extended that drew him like a loadstone into the interior—and off they went!"

"And who," asked Emmeran, uneasily, "who is to tell this to Hilda ?"

"She knows it already," answered Sigmund, "but I have not yet heard how she bears it, for I only saw Doris."

"And what did Doris say ?" asked Emmeran.

"She informed me with the most perfect composure, that Frank had received a letter from Colonel Bereny requesting him to take his wife to Meran and establish her in comfortable lodgings there ; and then she added, that she feared they had scarcely a chance of seeing him again for some time as his leave of absence had so nearly expired."

"Oh, then it's all right," said Emmeran ; "and Hilda has been made to understand that Frank could not well refuse to escort the wife of his colonel to Meran if requested to do so."

"You may believe that if you like," rejoined Sigmund, smiling ironically, "but I know better what Hilda thinks and feels on this subject. She allowed me to speak in very strong terms of this husband of hers to-day, and had he not interrupted us, I should have pointed out how easily her marriage in Ulm could be annulled, and recommended her to think seriously of a separation; but it was as well I said nothing, for you who have studied law during some of the best years of your life, can explain to her all about Protestant divorces far better than I can. Give me your assistance on this occasion, Emmeran, and I cease at once to be your rival with Doris."

"I don't at all fear your rivalry," answered Emmeran imperturbably, "I know and understand Doris so thoroughly, that the moment you told me she had refused you at Westenried, I felt convinced she would do so here also ; for what has since occurred to make her change her opinion of you? of Hilda I am not so sure ; violent love is said to turn into violent hatred sometimes, and, though it is difficult to imagine such a thing——"

" Oh, not at all," cried Sigmund, interrupting him, " I can understand the change perfectly ; and Hilda has been deserted and neglected with an ostentation very likely to irritate a proud and passionate girl beyond endurance. I tell you, Emmeran, I only require time to make her discard him !"

" Don't be too sure of that, Sigmund."

" I shall not be precipitate if that be what you mean," answered Sigmund, " for the sacrifice of a few weeks—or even months if necessary, is not too much on this occasion ; and, in fact, I am rather at a loss to know what to do with myself just at present."

" I should have supposed," said Emmeran, " that there was a good deal of occupation for you at Westenried after so long an absence."

" I cannot deny that," said Sigmund ; " but I hate the place, and nothing is in order there since the Pallersbergs left it. By the by I was excessively annoyed at Hilda's establishing them at Forsteck after the insolent letter they wrote to me ; and one of my first acts when I marry her will be to send them an order to decamp."

" You will not find it easy to obtain Hilda's consent to that," said Emmeran, half-laughing ; " she is in constant correspondence with Pallersberg, and now understands the management of her affairs perfectly. Talk to her of her rights and rents, her woods, fields, and cattle, and you will be rather astonished, I suspect."

" Rather say disgusted," cried Sigmund ; " but I shall soon put an end to all interference on her part ; and the very first thing will be to get rid of those detestable Pallersbergs."

" I advise you," said Emmeran dryly, " to defer proclaiming this not very laudable intention of yours until—."

" Until what ?" asked Sigmund.

" Until the Waldering flag wave above the roof of Forsteck !"

CHAPTER XXX.

THE FATAL " NO."

SOME weeks elapsed before Frank wrote again; when he did so, the letter was from Vienna, addressed to Doris, and urged, in the strongest terms, a removal of the family to Meran, if that place were necessary for his aunt's health, but if not, to Forsteck or Ulm, where, as the fortifications had been destroyed, there was no danger of the town being again subjected to a siege, or their being incommoded in case of a war, excepting, perhaps, occasionally by the passage of troops.

This letter Doris had instantly taken to her mother's room and left with her and Hilda for discussion, purposely returning to her tapestry-frame, near one of the windows in the drawing-room, in order to avoid giving her opinion or advice. Hilda, however, soon followed her, and throwing down the letter observed, with evident pique : " As Frank has chosen you for correspondent, I must beg you to let him know that I do not see any necessity for leaving Innsbruck, even in case of a war, unless he can give less vague reasons for his advice. The passage of troops will not annoy us here more than at Ulm, and Innsbruck being also unfortified, we need have no apprehension of a siege;

if, however, you and mamma think otherwise, there is nothing to prevent you from going to Meran whenever you please."

"Hilda," said Doris, "you know perfectly well that we cannot leave you here alone."

"Why not?" she asked. "Am I a child still? Surely when a woman has been married as long as I have she may be supposed able to take care of herself. I am sure Frank thinks so, and if you write to him will care very little about *my* refusal to comply with his request; he will be only too happy to hear from you at all events, and has evidently, for this purpose, chosen you as the permanent medium of communication between us."

"I decline the offer," said Doris in a low voice, as she bent over her work.

"But you cannot refuse to answer such a letter as this?"

"Scarcely," answered Doris.

"I thought so," cried Hilda; "that entreating post-script for a few words from your 'dear hand' is irresistible, and the 'darling cousin' will 'resume her office of Mentor.'"

"Hilda, what do you mean?" asked Doris, looking up alarmed.

"I mean," she answered with suppressed vehemence, —"I mean that it is evident Frank loves you still and cares not at all for me!—I mean that I would give years of my life for such a letter from him!"

"Years of your life," repeated Doris; "but not a few hours to Madame de Bereny!"

"It was indeed folly to refuse that request," said Hilda, "for it only served to show him what a much more desirable and compliant wife you would have made him than I can."

"Am I to understand that you object to my answering his letter?" asked Doris, rising.

"Object!" exclaimed Hilda passionately—"how can I object when I have no other means of hearing of him? Rather tell him to write often and regularly!"

"No, Hilda; Frank shall never cause disunion between us if I can prevent it. My letter will forbid his writing to me again, and contain a request that he will either correspond in future with my mother or desire his friend Pallersberg to do so more frequently."

"Doris, I cannot consent to any such arrangements: you know Major Pallersberg writes chiefly about politics and literature, and only mentions Frank in the most cursory manner."

"With that you must be satisfied for the present," answered Doris, seating herself at the writing-table.

"Wait a moment," said Hilda imploringly, while she laid her hand on her sister's shoulder; "you understand, dear Doris, that I do not blame you in the least for what has happened——"

"I blame myself," answered Doris, turning round with a flush of anger on her cheek; "I blame myself for having ever, *ever* interfered! How can I justify so misusing my influence over Frank at Ulm? If I thought it necessary, I might have resigned; but I had no right whatever to dispose of him for life—irrevocably!"

"Not irrevocably," cried Hilda, greatly agitated; "write to him, Doris—tell him that I now consent to, and even desire, the divorce he proposed at Ulm. Sigmund says it can be obtained without any difficulty, and has offered to manage everything for me."

"Is it possible you have consulted Sigmund?"

"No; but he has contrived to discover all we intended to conceal from him; I knew he would when he came here, and if I must take his advice, I suppose I had better employ him."

"Do neither the one nor the other, Hilda; depend upon it he has some hidden motive for his interference; and though I do not in the least doubt his statement that you can have your marriage annulled according to German law, I am much mistaken if divorces can be so easily obtained in England, and you would scarcely desire to be free yourself while Frank continued bound to you."

"No—oh, no—quite the contrary!" cried Hilda; "my sole wish was to restore him to complete freedom; if, however, this cannot be effected," she continued, "I can only promise to endeavour in every way to conciliate him when we meet again."

"Why not begin at once?" asked Doris. "Take his advice about Meran, and go there next week, as he proposes."

"No, Doris; that would be too humiliating; you cannot expect me to follow and seek the acquaintance of the artful woman who has caused him to desert me in so open and scandalous a manner."

"I thought," said Doris, "you told me you had yourself dismissed him in the very words he used to you at Ulm?"

"Well, so I did."

"And if," said Doris, "if he now choose 'to go where he pleases, and to do what he likes,' who can blame him?"

"Not you, at all events," cried Hilda petulantly; "you think him faultless, and are ever ready to throw the blame of our disagreements on me. Doris!" she added, stopping for a moment at the door, towards which she had walked while speaking, "Doris, that was an ill-starred day on which you resigned him to me!"

"Ill-starred, indeed!" repeated Doris, as her sister

left the room, and then, leaning over the writing-table and supporting her head with her hand, she allowed bitter regret for the first time to mix itself with the painful re-trospect that drew large, reluctant tears to her eyes. "*He*, at least, has never reproached me," she murmured; "and yet he might well have done so lately, instead of asking me to plead his cause with this passionate and jealous sister of mine. I must not, however, despair or become weary of making efforts to reconcile them to each other— it is the only atonement I can ever make him."

She drew a sheet of paper towards her and wrote "Dear Frank,"—then paused to think how she could best soften Hilda's refusal to leave Innsbruck—looked up, and perceived Emmeran advancing towards her from her mother's room.

"I am the bearer of a message from Hilda," he said earnestly; "she begs you will forgive all she said just now, and desire Frank to write to you as often as he can or will."

Doris shook her head.

"I am afraid she has been very unreasonable and un-kind," he continued; "but she seemed really penitent, and told me your patience with her was perfectly incompre-hensible."

"Her words were less so," said Doris, "and my cor-respondence with Frank must end in this letter."

"I warned her not to employ me as emissary," observed Emmeran; "for any one and every one can say 'no' to me without difficulty. I am quite accustomed to the odious little word, and now never expect to hear anything else when I make a request."

"To others, perhaps," said Doris, smiling; "but not to me, for I cannot remember having often said 'no' to you, Emmeran."

"Many and many a time," he answered; "but you have forgotten your refusals because they were of no importance to you. I can, however, recollect a 'no' of some years since that made a fatal impression on me."

"You excite my curiosity," she said, pushing away her writing-paper; "where did I pronounce this fatal 'no'?"

"At Westenried."

"But when?"

"On the last Holy-eve we spent there."

"Don't remind me of that dreadful evening."

"It was before it had become dreadful," said Emmeran, "that I asked you to let me look in your magic mirror, or whatever you called it, and you refused at once, without a moment's hesitation."

"I believe," said Doris, "I should do the same now, and for the same reason."

"Of course you would," answered Emmeran, gravely. "It is only during occasional moments of infatuation that I ever suppose anything else possible."

She did not appear to hear him, but continued, musingly —"You know, Emmeran, at that time the recollection of what Hilda imagined she had seen in the vaults a year previously, and the curious circumstance of the ring found there being required for her marriage, had made an unpleasant impression on us all; but I believe you never heard that Mina, when alarmed by the flickering of the blue lights, fancied she saw her own corpse beneath the water of the lake. Now, though, as well as I can recall her words, the idea had presented itself to her often before, and I am quite convinced that the subsequent events would have occurred whether we had looked in the glass or not, yet you can understand my dislike to everything of the kind in future."

"Perfectly," answered Emmeran. "No one is free from a certain portion of superstition; it lies deep in the mind of all, and is at best but dormant in that of the most rational. At Westenried, however, I thought, and indeed still think, that the chief cause of your refusal was a suspicion that I might attempt to place the glass so that I sh uld have seen your face reflected in it, and perhaps have even cheated you into seeing mine!"

Doris did not choose to understand. "I have no doubt," she said, smiling, "that your plan to turn my pretended witchcraft into ridicule was well devised; but I had had more than enough of blue lights and vaults, and believe, that even seeing your well-known face and smart new uniform under such circumstances would have been anything rather than agreeable to me."

"I believe you," said Emmeran; "and can even recollect that when we met at dinner on that memorable day you did not bestow a single glance on the smart new uniform, though I had the folly to expect and wish you to do so."

"You are jesting, of course," said Doris.

"Not at all, I assure you."

Doris shook her head, and laughed incredulously. "I have since then had opportunities enough of becoming acquainted with your uniform," she said, "and can only hope you will pardon my saying that I prefer seeing you in any other dress."

"Indeed!" he exclaimed, with a look of such surprise and disappointment that she added;—

"I mean you look better in a morning or evening coat, or even a shooting-jacket. You know you were never intended for a soldier, and it is very evident that the uniform bores and the accoutrements embarrass you!"

"Very true," he answered; "but I thought you had a

great predilection for military trappings, that is," he added, on perceiving her look of astonishment, "I supposed you liked the profession of which they are the outward sign; and in fact, Doris, I should never have entered the army if I had not thought it the best or perhaps only means of finding favour in your eyes."

"Nonsense, Emmeran! you cannot make me believe that you gave up your former pursuits, and changed all your habits and occupations on my account?"

"Yet I did so, and without regret as yet, Doris; for has not chance so favoured me that I have enjoyed your society for more than two years without interruption?"

Doris began to perceive that there was something more than "habit" in Emmeran's regard for her; she even felt a sort of certainty that he was devoted to her in a manner that ought not to be trifled with. "A poor recompense, Emmeran, for such loss of time," she said, a good deal embarrassed; "and I now scarcely know whether I ought or ought not to give you the assurance that I have no sort of predilection for the army as a profession, nor for soldiers ——in general."

"Nor," he observed, "nor will you care to hear that I shall probably return to my former occupation as soon as the war is over, for I am now convinced that my time has indeed been lost—I must however say agreeably lost—here; and though I may not, as you say, be soldierlike, I am at least so much a soldier at heart that instead of remaining longer in garrison here, I shall endeavour to exchange into another regiment in which I am more likely to see something of active service."

"I hope you will not do any such thing," cried Doris, hastily, and feeling at the moment very strongly how necessary "habit," had made Emmeran's society to her; "we shall miss you dreadfully."

"Very flattering for me if you do," he answered, "and I am even selfish enough to hope it may be the case; but while talking of myself I have forgotten to plead for Hilda, —do, pray, grant her request, and continue your correspondence with Frank; let her hear of, if she cannot expect to hear from him."

"Dear Emmeran, I am really sorry to be obliged to refuse this request; but assure you I have reasons that make my correspondence with Frank quite out of the question——ask anything else——"

But Emmeran turned away in the direction of her mother's room, saying, with a faint smile, "That he had had refusals enough for one day, and would now leave her to write her letter."

CHAPTER XXXI.

NO ONE KNOWS WHAT A DAY MAY BRING FORTH.

BEFORE many days of the month of April had passed over, Hilda began to understand the purport of Frank's letter, and to wish she had been less determined in refusing to follow his advice. Although none but the initiated were aware of the powerful conspiracy formed by the Tiroleans to shake off a foreign yoke and return to their allegiance to their emperor, many circumstances had occurred to lead to the supposition that when the expected declaration of war became public, the peasants would take up arms and join any Austrian force sent into the country.

One evening as the Walderings were returning from a walk to Mount Isel, they perceived several groups of people standing on the banks of the Inn eagerly watching the progress of a strong plank that floated past on the surface of the water.

Sigmund and Hilda stopped and looked in the same direction.

"I had no idea," observed the former, shrugging his shoulders, "that a plank swimming on the river Inn was so unusual a circumstance."

"It is not the plank," said Hilda; "it is the flagstaff on it with the red streamer that attracts attention."

"And," suggested Sigmund, "which will, no doubt, furnish the superstitious people here with a '*pendant*' to the story you have just been telling me about the bloody hand portentous of war that was lately seen on the freshly scoured table of the inn in Sarnthal."

"But," said Hilda, "you will find it more difficult to give a satisfactory explanation of the red flag than the red hand. I know the hostlers of the country inns are frequently butchers, and the one at Sarnthal *may* have leaned on the table when fresh from the slaughter-house —but the carpenter who placed the flag on that plank had certainly some hidden meaning."

"Not," answered Sigmund, "not if he were a juvenile workman who, we may suppose, found a strip of red calico, or it may be a handkerchief of his grandfather's, and having nailed it either on the stick or crutch of that worthy relative, only required a strong board to complete the construction of the primitive plaything destined to excite the curiosity, fears, and hopes of the inhabitants of Innsbruck!"

Hilda shook her head. "I cannot help thinking that Frank would have given a very different explanation of that floating flag," she said, walking on to join her mother.

"He would most probably have declined giving any

at all, if the thing really have a meaning," muttered Sigmund, and, while speaking, his eye fell on a peasant-woman who had been standing close beside them.

"The less said the better," observed the woman, turning towards him for a moment with a look of mysterious meaning, and at the same time thrusting a slip of paper into his hand.

Sigmund opened and read the words, "It is time." The thought instantly presented itself that he had been mistaken for Frank, and, hoping to obtain some information by continuing to personate him, he looked round, intending to commence a conversation; but the woman was gone, and no one in the least resembling her within sight. A peasant stood alone at no great distance, still gazing after the now scarcely perceptible red flag, and Sigmund approaching him, repeated in a low voice the words he had just heard, "The less said the better."

The man turned from the river, and seemed very naturally to expect to hear more.

"*It is time*," continued Sigmund, emphatically.

"Time for what?" asked the peasant, casting a look of provoking intelligence first on the paper and then on Sigmund, who instantly perceived that a reply was expected which he could not give, and while he pretended to examine the paper he held in his hand, supposing he should find some other notice on it, the man continued with a shrewd smile and a glance westward, "By my watch and the setting sun it is six o'clock, and——supper-time for most people."

"It will not be six o'clock until to-morrow morning," answered Sigmund, putting the paper into his pocket and walking off, unconscious that his reply had produced a change in the expression of the peasant's face, followed by a few hasty steps after him, that were, however, suddenly arrested when he perceived Sigmund join his brother and cousins, and unhesitatingly exhibit the paper containing the three mysterious words.

Sigmund never knew that the peasant he had addressed was Joseph Speckbacher, "The Man of Rinn," as he has since been poetically called by his biographer, and at that time the person in all Tirol most capable of giving the information he required. Speckbacher was just then endeavouring to ascertain the strength of the Innsbruck garrison, and to him the floating flag on the river, and the words, "It is time," were full of meaning; they told him to hasten the preparations for the insurrection, to give notice to the inhabitants of the valley of the Inn, and encouraged him to concert with his followers the plan of taking the town of Hall by surprise, which he afterwards put into execution with equal subtlety and celerity.

The movements of the Man of Rinn were, however, only indirectly of importance to the Walderings, though their first serious apprehensions were occasioned by the signal fires which he soon after caused to be lighted on the surrounding mountains.

One of the most remarkable circumstances in this insurrection was the inviolable secresy observed by the thousands of initiated. The innkeepers, commencing with Andrew Hofer himself, were almost all deeply implicated; their houses during the frequent target-shooting matches served as places of assembly for the peasants, their cellars were used for the concealment of ammunition, and all injudicious outbursts of patriotism, or manifestations of disaffection to the ruling powers, which were of not unfrequent occurrence in such places, were alike supposed to be the effects of the Tirolean wine, which at that time the peasants drank in amazing quantities.

At length the long-expected declaration of war on the

part of Austria was made known in Innsbruck by the distribution of innumerable proclamations, printed in Vienna, and smuggled in some unaccountable manner into the country. Fires then blazed at nightfall on the highest mountains, the alarm-bells of the neighbouring villages pealed without intermission, and crowds of peasants assembling on the roads and on the heights round Innsbruck, successfully forced the Bavarian pickets from the Martinswand, Gallwiese, and Mount Isel into the town. General Kinkel and Colonel Dietfurt posted cannon on the bridges, and took every possible means with their limited garrison to quell the revolt, but with the exception of some wealthy Jews and a few burghers, they had no friends in the town, and found it impossible to prevent constant communication with the insurgents.

Sigmund entered his aunt's apartment late on the evening of this day; he brought a musket, a sword, and a brace of pistols with him, and declared his intention of remaining in their drawing-room during the night, as it was impossible to tell what might occur. The central position of their house enabled Emmeran to look in occasionally, and tell them what was going on, but after daylight they saw him no more, and Sigmund was at length sent out to procure information.

It was still early when he returned in a state of great excitement, and informed them that thousands of peasants were swarming in all directions towards the town, and that the Bavarian cannoniers had been little else than targets for the Tirolean riflemen, who aimed at them deliberately as if at a shooting-match. "The rebels," he continued, "have got possession of the bridges, and are now forcing their way through the triumphal arch, and every other entrance to the town; our men are fighting like lions, but they must be overpowered by such numbers."

"Is there no one," cried Doris, "to explain this to General Kinkel? Surely in a case of this kind any garrison may capitulate without disgrace."

"Dietfurt will not listen to any terms," answered Sigmund, "and was furious because Kinkel proposed evacuating the town if allowed to retreat unmolested. Some well-disposed citizens made their appearance near one of the bridges, and attempted to procure at least a short cessation of hostilities; but the peasants have no respect for flags of truce, they rushed down the Hotting hill, took the bridge and cannon by storm, disarmed our men, and chased the citizens before them into the town."

"And was no further effort made?" asked Doris.

"Yes," he answered; "in the Town-house, where I have just been, I hoped they might come to terms, but the insurgents insist on the garrison laying down their arms, and that, of course, is not to be thought of for an instant. If you have no objection to my leaving you," he continued, buckling on the sword, and filling his pockets with ammunition, "I should like to join Dietfurt, and have a shot at these traitors."

"If you go," said Doris, "I hope it will be to Emmeran. Think how dreadfully revolting such scenes and deeds must be to him——he ought never to have been a soldier!"

At that moment they heard cavalry galloping through the street, and Sigmund rushed to the window; he turned round however directly, for the steady tread and regular platoon fire of infantry became audible in another direction.

"We are in the thick of it," he cried, throwing open the doors leading to the back of the house; our men must be marching towards the hospital."

They all followed, and required no explanation to make them understand that the peasants had obtained possession of the hospital, and were firing from the windows, and rushing tumultuously from the gateway to attack the advancing troops.

A desperate conflict ensued almost beneath their windows, for the back of the house was only separated from the road by a small court-yard containing a pump and some sheds for wood. They could see distinctly the faces of the combatants, and how well known to them were those of the officers who now courageously led on their men to so hopeless an attack, Colonel Dietfurt the foremost of all, apparently in a state of frenzy!

The terrified spectators at the windows of the Waldering apartments soon saw and followed with harrowing interest but one actor in this frightful scene;—it was Emmeran—not the quiet, thoughtful, low-voiced man they had hitherto known, whose accoutrements were generally such evident incumbrances to him;—the sword he so gladly put aside whenever an opportunity offered was now brandished above his head, his eyes flashed, and Dietfurt himself was not more daringly reckless, more passionately eloquent in urging his men to charge. Though wounded he still continued to advance, until a ball in the side made him sink on one knee, while a stream of blood poured from his lips; but when some peasants approached to take him prisoner, he started again to his feet and continued the combat until overpowered by numbers and weakness he sank on the ground.

By this time Sigmund, who had rushed from the room and sprang down the stairs, was already in the court impetuously opening the small door of communication with the road; the others followed in wild alarm, and Doris would perhaps have pressed after him among the combatants, had he not almost immediately reappeared holding in his arms the apparently lifeless body of his brother.

"Shut the yard-door!" shouted the proprietor of the

house, who was leaning out of one of the upper windows; "shut the door, or we shall have the peasants in here firing from the windows of our rooms."

His words seemed about to be verified, for a number of men pressed hard upon Sigmund, whose arms, however, were no sooner at liberty than he drew his sword, turned upon them, and, forcing them back, pursued them into the midst of the combat. The yard-door was instantly closed by eager hands; but Hilda sprang forward and again threw it wide open, exclaiming resolutely: "I will not have him shut out; let him return to us."

And even while she was speaking, Sigmund staggered back and fell senseless at her feet.

· Then the door was firmly bolted; and the clashing of swords and loud report of firearms continued without, while the terrified inmates of the yard made vain attempts to restore the wounded brothers to consciousness.

"He is dead, quite dead, Hilda!" said the Countess Waldering, as she raised the hair from Sigmund's forehead and pointed to a double wound there; "it is useless trying to revive him." And she turned to Emmeran, who showed some signs of returning life.

Doris was sitting on the ground supporting Emmeran's head on her knee, and bathing his temples with cold water from a tub that had been placed near her. His uniform was covered with blood, and so was his sword, which he still grasped tightly, struggling convulsively whenever anyone attempted to take it from him, and causing a fresh loss of blood that immediately produced renewed faintness.

"Oh, leave it in his hand!" said Doris, "and send some one to the next house; perhaps the surgeon who lives there is at home, and could come to us."

"I cannot allow the house door to be opened just yet,"

said the landlord, who was now standing beside her; "the street is too full of riflemen."

"*You* have nothing to fear from them, Mr. Hartmann," interposed Doris, indignantly.

"No, mademoiselle, for myself nothing, but for my cellar everything, I can, however, send up to the roof of the house, and have no doubt that most of our neighbours are assembled on the leads there; it is not even improbable that we may find the surgeon himself among them; and I must say, when things take this turn, it is a far better and safer place up there than in a yard such as this."

"Hilda," said Doris, with an expressive glance upwards; "he will come instantly if you go yourself for him."

Hilda immediately ran into the house, followed by Mr. Hartmann, who begged her to wait for him, as she could not possibly open the door on the roof alone; while his wife, coming forward with an embarrassed air, "hoped that Count Emmeran's uniform would be taken off as soon as possible, as it might place her and her husband in a very unpleasant position; the blood-stained sword alone," she said, "would be sufficient to provoke the peasants to plunder her house should they now force their way into it."

Doris thought this exaggeration; but she bent down her head and whispered, "Give me your sword, dear Emmeran."

He evidently not only had heard, but also understood, what had been said, for he slowly opened his eyes, and when he perceived her hand extended towards the offending weapon, his fingers relaxed their grasp of it, and clasped instead the small cold hand that disarmed him, and which he feebly raised and pressed on the wound in his side, from which the blood still flowed profusely.

"Thank goodness," said her mother, "he can see and hear again; so, though perhaps too weak to move, I think if I were to send down a mattress, he might be carried up to Frank's room even before Surgeon Manhart comes here."

"I think so, too," answered Doris; "and the sooner we remove him from this place the better."

Her mother left the yard, followed by the assembled servants and other inmates of the house; and Emmeran instantly seemed aware that they were alone: "Doris," he said, in a scarcely audible voice, and she bent down her head towards him—"Doris!——I fear all is lost——I saw Dietfurt fall, and——" here he stopped, and she perceived the paleness of death again spread over his features as his eyes fell on the outstretched rigid form of his brother. With great effort he raised himself on his elbow, and panted: "Go to him, Doris——do not neglect him for me——I—I am quite well now, and——he may be only badly wounded ——poor fellow——"

A violent attempt to rise from his recumbent position produced a return of weakness, followed by a swoon, from which he only completely recovered when the surgeon began to probe his wounds.

CHAPTER XXXII.

UP WITH THE EAGLE !

WOMEN are frequently violent politicians in *words*, but fortunately very seldom in *deeds*, and therefore it will scarcely surprise the reader to hear that Doris's feeling of exultation at the complete success of the Tirolean insurrection, was almost turned into depression when, added to Sigmund's death and Emmeran's dangerous wounds, she heard of the number of Bavarians who had lost their lives in the course of a few hours. That most of the officers who had fallen were personally known to her only served to increase her dejection, and it was remarkable that Hilda listened at first with more interest than Doris could to the details given by their landlady of the street combats and other events that had taken place.

"Before eleven o'clock," said Madame Hartmann, pertinaciously addressing Doris in expectation of complete sympathy—"before eleven o'clock the enemy were killed, wounded, or taken prisoners."

"And Colonel Dietfurt?" asked Hilda; "is there any hope of his recovery?"

"People say his wounds are not absolutely mortal," answered Madame Hartmann; "but he has got a fever, and is delirious; they took him to the hospital, and are obliged to keep him in his bed by force: it is curious that when he saw the wounded peasants there he immediately asked them who had been their leader; and though they assured him they had none, he said that he knew better, and had seen him mounted on a white horse several times during the combat."

"Delirium, of course," observed Hilda.

"I suppose so," said Madame Hartmann; "but the people imagine it must have been St. Jacob, the patron saint of Innsbruck,* and they now suppose themselves quite invincible. Hartmann says it would be a very good thing if they had a visible commander, and he thinks they will chose Hofer, or Speckbacher, or perhaps Teimer."

"Who is Teimer?" asked Hilda.

"One likely to be of importance in times like these," she answered; "and fortunately both he and Baron Hormayer were at the University with Hartmann, and are

* Fact.

friends of his, which secures us a couple of powerful pro-
tectors in case of need. Teimer gave up his studies to
enter the militia, and has seen a good deal of service one
way or other; they say he is also an emissary of the Archduke's, and a friend of Andrew Hofer's. I had no wish to
have him in my house the last time he was in Innsbruck,"
she added, laughing; "but he would be a very welcome
guest just now."

"I don't think," said Hilda, "that under these circumstances Mr. Hartmann need have had any apprehension
about his cellars, or you about the presence of our poor
wounded cousin; but what may those expect who have no
friends to defend them?—the Bavarian families residing
here, for instance?"

"Well, I don't think they need be uneasy," she answered.
"From the peasants they have nothing to fear, though I
cannot answer for the mob of the town, you know. I
believe some parties of them have already commenced
plundering the warehouses of the Jews, on pretence of
recovering the plate and altar ornaments of the secularized
monasteries; and there is no denying that the cellars of the
wine merchants are still more or less in danger; so we can
only hope that Marshal Chasteler and the Austrians will
soon be here, as thousands and thousands of peasants are
still marching into the town, and no one knows where they
will take up their quarters."

Just then her husband came home, and informed the
hastily assembled inmates of the house that his friend
Major Teimer had arrived in Innsbruck, and as imperial
commissioner taken the command of the town.

"I hope, Hartmann, you asked him to come and stay
with us?" said his wife, in a sudden paroxysm of hospitality.

"Of course; but he has so much to do trying to preserve order, that we have little chance of seeing him for some time. There are the wounded on both sides to be taken care of, the prisoners and Bavarian functionaries to be protected—in short, so many arrangements to be made, that it was quite a relief to him when the peasants were induced to go in search of a wooden eagle that has been discovered in the Franciscan church, and afterwards amused themselves shouting, 'Long live our Emperor, Franz!'"

"And Marshal Chasteler, Hartmann, and the Austrians? when may we expect to see them?"

"We hoped that they would have been here this evening," he answered, with some embarrassment; "but—but——"

"Has anything happened?" asked his wife, anxiously; "the French, perhaps——"

"Yes," he said, "we have just heard from a scout that the French under General Bisson are marching towards us, and there is little doubt of the truth of his assertion, for the alarm bells are already pealing in the direction indicated."

"Oh, dear! oh, dear!" she cried; "and I thought we had gained such a victory! Perhaps the peasants will go off now and leave us to the mercy of the French!"

"No danger of that," said her husband, "for our people feel that they have gone too far to recede, and are already making preparations for the reception of the enemy; barricades have been erected at the triumphal arch; the streets in that direction are all blocked up, and every house and garden fit for defence will be occupied by our riflemen."

"I wish the Austrians were here, and the fighting over," said Madame Hartmann.

"So do I; but as there is no danger for the present,

you may go to bed, and sleep securely until morning."

The advice was good; but who could sleep with such noise in the streets at night—such incessant pealing of alarm-bells after daybreak?

Doris, Hilda, and their mother were frequently in Emmeran's room, and tried to beguile the weary, sleepless hours by informing him of all that was going on in the town. They were enabled to do so without difficulty, as Major Teimer was actually in the house with them, at first as guest, and some hours afterwards as fugitive, the people having begun to doubt the authenticity of his credentials, and refusing to obey any further orders given by him.

"This is very unfortunate," observed Doris, "for his orders and arrangements were exceedingly judicious; and I fear that even Tiroleans may commit excesses if long without a leader."

"That is very probable," said Hilda. "It is a pity they could not continue the worship of the Imperial Eagle a little longer—it was a harmless amusement."

"You have not told me about that," said Emmeran, looking towards Doris.

"I thought—I feared—you might not like to hear anything so fanatically Austrian."

"I like to hear everything, without reserve," he answered.

"In that case," said Doris, "I ought to have told you the meaning of the noise in the street this afternoon, when you desired me to look out of this window, for just then the people were carrying about in triumph a gigantic eagle made of carved wood that some one had discovered in the Franciscan church. The cries of 'Vivat' that you heard were addressed to this symbol of Austria, which, after having been paraded in procession through the principal streets, was at last placed with enthusiastic shouts over the gate of the post-office."

"Well," he said, on perceiving that she paused; "is that all?"

"Not quite, for the ladder that had been used for this purpose was held in its place by the peasants, who ascended it one after the other to embrace and kiss the eagle; and when any one remained longer than the time allowed, a jealous murmur reminded him that others were waiting to take his place; but I dare say you think all this very contemptible?"

"By no means,—genuine enthusiasm is never contemptible.   Pray go on!"

"Madame Hartmann assured me that many of those present had tears in their eyes when an old man who had fought bravely all the morning threw his arms round the eagle, and exclaimed, "Hurrah, old fellow, your feathers have grown again!"*

"You need not have hesitated to tell me all this, Doris," observed Emmeran; "none of us can now doubt the patriotism of the Tiroleans or their determination to remain Austrian; but they are probably not aware that the small garrison they overpowered yesterday morning are in daily expectation of French troops, who are on the march from Italy, and these may reach Innsbruck before the Austrians."

"There is no doubt of that," said Hilda, "for the French under General Bisson are now on Mount Isel, and it is to assemble the peasants that they have been ringing the alarm-bells so incessantly."

"Some of our troops must be with Bisson," cried Emmeran, trying to raise himself from his pillow.

"Major Teimer only spoke of the French——" began Doris.

* Fact.

"No matter ; I think if I could see the surgeon again he would allow me to get up."

"He would not," said Doris, " for he told me you were very likely to suffer from fever, and had no chance of being able to leave your room for weeks. You heard him say so, mamma ?"

"Yes," answered her mother ; "and I also heard him recommend perfect tranquillity and the avoidance of all mental excitement; but this last direction has been altogether forgotten, I think."

"Very true," said Doris ; "it is unpardonable our discussing such subjects in this room."

"Oh, my dear aunt !" cried Emmeran, beseechingly ; " do not condemn me to lie here listening to the shouts in the streets, the pealing of bells, and firing of signals, without being told what is going on——if you keep me in ignorance I shall inevitably become delirious !"

"Well, you shall hear all we can ascertain on condition that you remain quiet; and remember that happen what will you must resign yourself to be our prisoner in this room until your wounds are healed."

" Be it so," answered Emmeran, submissively ; " I promise to listen with perfect stoicism to whatever you may henceforward tell me."

A servant just then entered the room to say that Mr. Hartmann requested to see her.

"Doris," said Emmeran, but without moving or even looking at her, " are the rebels——that is, the insurgents ——I mean the peasants——"

" Or the patriots," interposed Doris ; " but you may call them what you please now !"

"Are they still in Innsbruck ?" he asked.

"Yes."

" And where have they been quartered ?"

" Some in the houses, but by far the greater number in the streets, and the fields and gardens beyond the town."

" Have they obtained any advantages elsewhere ?"

" Yes, I believe Speckbacher has taken Hall by surprise, and Hofer gained a victory near Sterzing."

" There will soon be some hard fighting," said Emmerân, " for Bisson is evidently surrounded by your——patriots, and will have to force a passage through the town."

" Or——capitulate," said his aunt, who just then returned to the room. " Major Teimer seems to think this inevitable ; and actually, some hours ago, procured an open letter from General Kinkel to this Frenchman, recommending him to send some one to ascertain the state of affairs here, the force and enthusiasm of the peasants, and the utter impossibility of avoiding a capitulation."

" Bisson is not likely to pay much attention to a letter so evidently written under compulsion," observed Emmeran.

" Don't be too sure of that," said his aunt, " for both a French and a Bavarian officer of high rank were immediately sent here, and Major Teimer has thought it necessary to retain them in the town."

" As prisoners ?" cried Emmeran, " impossible !"

" Well, I don't myself think it is right," she continued, " but Major Teimer says that 'necessity has no laws,' and he has sent back an aide-de-camp or soldier who was with them ; since then there has been some skirmishing, enough he thinks to convince the French of their dangerous position, and he is now going to Wiltau to propose a capitulation."

" Doris," whispered Emmeran, " if there were no Bavarians under Bisson's command, I shouldn't mind his having to capitulate. Napoleon only gave us Tirol in order to secure a free passage for his armies to and from Italy, and as he has not allowed us to reserve enough troops to keep possession of the country, he may take the consequences !"

"I am glad you begin to understand him," she answered.

"By the by," said her mother, after a pause, "Mr. Hartmann has just made an extraordinary request; it seems that General Bisson obstinately refuses to confer with any one excepting an Austrian officer, and as Major Teimer has no uniform here, Mr. Hartmann thought that perhaps we could lend him one of Frank's."

"What an idea!" cried Hilda indignantly, "and for such a purpose, too!"

"My dear Hilda, the chances are that if Frank were here he would put on his uniform and go himself to Wiltau! As it was, I could only regret that there was none to lend; so Major Teimer has borrowed one belonging to a pensioned staff-officer, who however is, unfortunately, a tall corpulent man while Major Teimer is small and slight."*

"At any other time," said Hilda, "and under any other circumstances, I really could laugh at such a masquerade."

"I don't think General Bisson will be at all inclined to laugh," answered her mother, "nor is Major Teimer at all a man likely to provoke laughter: he jested himself about the uniform, but said if it assisted him to compel the French to capitulate, it was all he required."

"At all events," said Hilda, "I am glad that Frank's uniform is safe in my wardrobe."

"So he had one with him when he was here," observed her mother, a good deal surprised.

"Yes," answered Hilda; "and forgot it in his hurry to leave us!"

"It is fortunate I did not know it," continued her mother, "for your refusing to lend it might have given offence, which is better avoided at all times, and very especially at present."

"My dear mother, it would have been of very little

* Fact.

importance, for I am convinced we shall have the French in the town a few hours hence."

"If so," interposed Doris, "they will enter it as prisoners!"

"Whatever may happen," said their mother, "I am sure you will agree with me in thinking that the expression of hopes or fears, triumph or despondency, ought to be avoided by us, in consideration that what gives satisfaction to one must cause disappointment to the other; and, at all events, I trust that regard for Emmeran will induce you to refrain from such discussions in this room for some time at least."

"No, no, by no means!" cried Emmeran, eagerly. "I should be very sorry if my presence imposed any sort of restraint on either of my cousins, as it would serve to make them avoid my room. I like to hear both sides of the question, and particularly desire to have an account of all that occurs at Wiltau from my bitterest enemy—from Doris herself!"

"But the doctor's directions, Emmeran——," began his aunt.

"I know what they were," he answered, "but am perfectly convinced that no tranquillity, mental or bodily, would now do me so much good as a long conversation with you about various things that are making me anxious and restless. Sit down beside me, dear aunt, and do not again leave me alone to work myself into a fever, as I did yesterday."

While she seated herself in the chair to which he pointed, Doris and Hilda walked through the open doors of the adjoining rooms until they reached a window with a small stone balcony, on which they stepped to look up and down the deserted street.

"I wish we were in some other part of the town," observed Hilda, "for we can see nothing here."

"I think we saw more than enough yesterday," answered Doris; "that scene at the gate of the hospital, and Sigmund's death, I shall never be able to forget."

"Nor I," said Hilda; "it was dreadful to witness, but we have the consolation of knowing that Emmeran rivalled Colonel Dietfurt in courage, and that Sigmund fell in the performance of a noble act——I am afraid I must say the only one of his life!"

"Hilda!"

"I mean what I say, Doris; his death was as chivalrous as his life was base and unprincipled."

"Let the recollection of his faults be buried with him," said Doris; "let us forgive, as we hope to be forgiven."

"Be it so," said Hilda; "I never knew how treacherous and unscrupulous he was until yesterday morning, when on this balcony, standing where you are now, he spoke to me, perhaps for the first time in his life, wholly without reserve."

"I think I know when that occurred," said Doris; "was it not just before he left us for the last time to obtain information? I saw directly that something was wrong, and even suspected what he had said to you."

"No, Doris, you could not imagine anything so perfidious."

"Yes, I can, Hilda; for since the day you told me he had proposed obtaining a divorce for you, and I perceived he had even ventured to urge you to consent, there could be little doubt about the motives that induced him to visit us, and remain so long in Innsbruck."

"And I only thought of *you!*" said Hilda; "it would have been so natural his making another overture."

"Perhaps so," answered Doris, "but in that case he would never have given himself so much trouble to irritate you against Frank."

Here they heard the distant report of a rifle, then another, and another, until they came in the quick succession of sharp skirmishing.

"I hate the sound of that slow firing," observed Hilda, "and especially those single rifle shots,—they denote the deliberate aiming of your Tirolean patriots, and every bullet takes a life!"

Doris did not like the idea suggested, and seemed inclined to leave the balcony.

"And I must say," continued Hilda, "that if Frank was aware of this impending insurrection, he might have been more explicit both in words and letters."

"I think," replied Doris, "he both said and wrote as much as he could venture to do under the circumstances— certainly enough to have induced anyone but you to leave Innsbruck!"

"My dear Doris, I did not understand half what he meant until yesterday, or I should have strongly urged, instead of merely proposing, that you and my mother should leave me here."

"That was out of the question, Hilda; but since poor Emmeran has been so badly wounded, we rejoice in your wilfulness, which, of course, was encouraged by a consciousness of having friends on both sides."

"I will not deny that the certainty of protection was a great relief to my mind, as far as you were concerned," said Hilda; "but, for my part, I should, at all events, have remained here, and for a thoroughly selfish motive — the wish to see Frank again."

"Do you suppose there is any chance of his returning here?" asked Doris.

"I may hope so," answered Hilda; "for he told me soon after his arrival that, if things turned out as he expected, he should, most probably, be in Innsbruck again before spring was over. Taking it, therefore, for granted that he was even then aware of the probability of this insurrection, it is evident that, if Austria gain the advantage in this struggle, Frank will come here."

"I hope he may," said Doris, stepping into the room, but lingering beside the glass door, while she added, "I wish he were here now, and in Major Teimer's place, compelling the French to capitulate."

"I think, instead of capitulating, they are marching into the town," said Hilda; "for the firing has ceased, and I hear distinctly the sound of distant music."

"It may be the peasants——," began Doris.

"No," rejoined Hilda; "it is good military music, and not the fifes and drums, violins and Jews'-harps, that we heard yesterday when the Tiroleans were celebrating their triumph."

Doris listened, and her countenance fell.

"The French are marching into the town," repeated Hilda, in a subdued voice; "this is not what Frank expected, and I could—almost—wish it were otherwise!"

And, in fact, it was otherwise; for the French then marching into Innsbruck were prisoners, and the cheerful military music wafted on the south wind towards the town was compulsory! the bands of the captured regiments having been ordered to enliven with their best marches the triumph of the Tiroleans.

A few hours later, the most minute particulars of all that had occurred became known, and nowhere more accurately than in the house of which the Walderings were inmates. Having heard Mr. Hartmann's, perhaps, exaggerated, account of the scene enacted at Wiltau, Hilda and Doris felt alike unwilling to be the first to communicate such intelligence to Emmeran, and requested their mother to tell him of the capitulation in the best way she could devise

Emmeran heard her without interruption. "This is a great humiliation for the French," he observed, as she ceased speaking, "a far greater than the surrender in Spain last year—Dupont had at least a regular army before him, and not a swarm of half-armed peasants!"

"My dear Emmeran, you must take into consideration the number of the peasants here, and—their rifles."

"I have reason to do so," he answered; "but I am glad Dietfurt did not; for I would rather be lying here, crippled as I now am, than have yielded without firing a shot. Even my poor brother's death cannot make me think otherwise."

"I shall not attempt to dispute the point with you, Emmeran; but you must forgive my rejoicing in a capitulation that has saved so many lives. As, however, soldiers have their own code of laws, perhaps you will be glad to hear that the Bavarians, under General Bisson, wanted to force their way through the town, and were in despair at the inopportune absence of their colonel."

"Where was he?" asked Emmeran.

"In Innsbruck. He and a Frenchman of equal rank were the officers detained here as prisoners yesterday."

"I remember you telling me," said Emmeran: "but I had no idea at the time that one of them was so well known to me. Can it, however, be possible that Bisson made no attempt to come to terms with this Major Teimer?"

"Of course he made repeated efforts," she answered. "He promised to pay for everything he required in the town (a great concession for a French general), and only demanded a free passage for his troops, to enable them without delay to join their Emperor at Augsburg. Major Teimer's answer was, that there was no alternative—they must lay down their arms and become prisoners of war.

The General even proposed marching, with both arms and ammunition following in baggage-waggons—in vain : Major Teimer was inexorable ; and the moment he turned away in displeasure, a signal was given, and the Tirolese fire recommenced. I imagine it must have been very effective, for even the French grenadiers showed symptoms of insubordination ; and when the peasants pressed forward, the officers surrounded the General and began to insist on surrender, their anxiety for a capitulation and horror of the mass of wildly-shouting riflemen being so great, that two of them actually signed their names *before* General Bisson ! "*

"Poor man !" said Emmeran, glancing towards the door, where Doris and Hilda were now standing; " even Doris would pity him did she know what awaits him in his first interview with Napoleon, and the court-martial that will inevitably succeed it."

" I do pity him," said Doris, coming forward; " so much so that, as far as General Bisson is personally concerned, I could not enjoy Major Teimer's triumphant recital."

" For my part," said Hilda, " I have taken an inveterate dislike to that Major Teimer ; he seemed, even by his own account, to have had no sort of consideration for the unfortunate old General, even when he saw him tear his grey hair, and heard him, with tears of despair, lament his loss of honour and military renown."

" Perhaps," suggested her mother, " Major Teimer may have felt without venturing to show his compassion. Had he been moved by his adversary's distress, he would have been obliged to grant him better terms."

" At all events," said Hilda, " I am glad he did not wear Frank's uniform."

* Fact.

"The capitulation is signed," observed Emmeran, with a sigh, "and is of such importance that I wish Frank had been here and worn his uniform himself. This act of Major Teimer's is of a description to entitle him to a Theresian cross, and I have little doubt that he will obtain it.* We cannot blame him, Hilda, for having gained a bloodless victory, and done his country an essential service."

"Oh, I am sure, Emmeran, if *you* think his conduct praiseworthy," observed Hilda, "I have nothing more to say!"

"It was, by all accounts," said her mother, "more praiseworthy than polite; but when General Chasteler arrives, Hilda, you will have an enemy whose chivalrous manners will give you complete satisfaction."

"Well, Doris," said Emmeran, "why don't you speak? I am waiting to hear from you how the peasants used their victory."

"Rather ask how they abused it," interposed Hilda; "all the soldiers were immediately disarmed."

"Of course they were," said Emmeran; "that was one of the stipulations, I suppose."

"Perhaps," said Hilda, "it was also stipulated that General Bisson was to drive into Innsbruck with Major Teimer in an open carriage, and that the bands of the regiments were to play their parade marches while on their way to imprisonment?"

"Scarcely," answered Emmeran; "but one cannot expect a display of fine feeling from a crowd of triumphant peasants."

"I think they behaved uncommonly well," observed

---

* He did, and became in consequence Baron of "Wiltau"—the name of the place where the capitulation was signed.

Doris; "no one was injured or insulted, although they were perfectly conscious of their strength and numbers, and had no authorized leader! One cannot on such occasions expect them to march into the town with the precision and order of a regiment of soldiers. They may have exulted too loudly, but it was loyal exultation, and their shouts were for their Emperor and the Archduke John."

"Not forgetting the Austrian colours and the eagle," said Hilda. "Only imagine, Emmeran: all the painters in Innsbruck are now employed turning the blue and white Bavarian colours into yellow and black, and carpenters have been set to work to take down the lions and exalt the eagles."

"That is not at all surprising," said Emmeran, quietly; "these emblems are of immense importance."

"Indeed! then I must tell you the fate of the lion that was on the palace."

"No, Hilda, pray don't," cried Doris, interrupting her. "Can you not see that these details are distressing Emmeran? the lion has been removed, and an eagle will take its place as a matter of course, and no further explanation is necessary."

"Doris—come here," said Emmeran, rather authoritatively—presuming, perhaps, on his helpless state and her undisguised sympathy.

And she came towards him, and sat down on the chair to which he pointed, and allowed him to take her hand and hold it fast, while he added, "Tell me what they did to the lion that was on the *façade* of the palace?"

She did not answer.

"I can make allowance for the wild exultation of peasants," he continued, "and your silence makes me, perhaps, imagine the insult greater than it actually was.

I suppose they dashed it to the ground and trampled on it?"

"No, no," cried Doris, colouring; "the lion was beyond the reach of any ladder they could just then procure, so—they—made a target of it, and—shot it down with their rifles."

"A thoroughly Tirolean idea," said Emmeran; "and if the lion must make place for the eagle, better so than otherwise."

"It was a tumultuous shooting-match," said Doris, "but one cannot expect refinement of feeling from peasants; we must be satisfied to find them disposed to treat the prisoners humanely, and willing to take the best possible care of the wounded."

"And," asked Emmeran, looking towards his aunt—" and is there any chance of a few hours' tranquillity for the burial of the dead?"

"There may be to-morrow," she answered, "and Sigmund's remains can be placed in the vault of the Sarnthal family until the time come for their removal to Westenried. I have written as you desired to your father, sent to inquire about Colonel Dietfurt, and requested Madame Hartmann to order mourning for us during the short time the shops were open to-day. Perhaps I ought to mention that there is a report in the town that another detachment of French have been seen on the march to Innsbruck, and most of the peasants are preparing to meet them on Mount Isel."

"A most fortunate report," observed Hilda, " even if it prove altogether false, for Doris herself must acknowledge that it is dangerous having so many thousands of peasants crowded together in a place like this, without even a nominal commander or any one having a shadow of authority over them or others."

"I should think so anywhere but here," said Doris,

" but I am so thoroughly convinced of the purely patriotic motives of this revolt, that I can feel no fear of the peasants committing excesses. There is far more danger of their going to their homes before the work of emancipation is completed."

"I hope you may be right," said Hilda, "and I trust you will not think me very ignoble and selfish if I also hope we may have a quiet night. I feel as if I could sleep until the day after to-morrow, were the church bells and patriots silenced for that short space of time."

"Let us take advantage of the present tranquillity," said her mother; "we have, at all events, talked far too much in this room to-day, and Emmeran will be better without seeing any of us for some time."

The night was as quiet as Hilda could have desired, and when the bells began to peal in the morning there was no cause for anxiety; instead of the French, Marshal Chasteler and the Austrian troops under his command marched into the town, accompanied by an enthusiastic multitude of peasants, whose patriotism found vent in the wildest demonstrations of joy and devotion.

CHAPTER XXXIII.

WHO MADE THE WORLD AT ODDS?

DORIS, Hilda, and their mother observed what is called respect for Sigmund's memory, by putting on deep mourning and living for some time in great seclusion; they did not say so, but they knew this was merely for appearance' sake, and made no other hypocritical attempts to feign a grief they could not feel. His name was never mentioned when they were alone, and Emmeran after some time learned to avoid a topic that so evidently imposed a restraint upon relations to whom, in the intimacy of protracted illness, he was becoming daily more attached.

The alarm-bells ceased to peal, firing and shouting were no longer heard in the streets, the peasants returned to their houses and worked in the fields and vineyards as quietly and unconcernedly as if their three days' insurrection had freed them for ever from a foreign yoke, while Marshal Chasteler employed himself in the organization of the militia, or rather of the voluntary *levee en masse* of the people for the defence of the country. Fortunately there was not much to be done, the laws of Tirol making it in such cases incumbent on every man between eighteen and sixty years of age either to take up arms himself or send a substitute. These men generally supplied themselves with provisions for a fortnight, and if their absence from home exceeded that time, whatever they required was sent afterwards by their parish, women and children being most frequently used as messengers.

A more military regulation of this force was attempted, companies and battalions formed, officers appointed, and the favourite Tirolean pike-grey colour chosen for the uniform; that was not, however, very generally worn, the peasants preferring the costume of their valleys, which, when dark-coloured, was peculiarly suitable to the mode of warfare subsequently adopted.

The Innsbruck newspaper was for some time completely filled with the Marquis Chasteler's addresses to the Tiroleans, and the Archduke John's proclamations and orders. To Doris and her mother these were deeply interesting, and one might have supposed they were the same to Hilda, as she sat carefully studying the double columns of the very diminutive ill-printed papers, had not an occasional remark served to prove that she wished to remind her mother and sister that her view of affairs remained unchanged.

"It seems there were 20,000 peasants here during the insurrection," she observed one morning to Emmeran, who had left his room for the first time, and was lying on a sofa in the drawing-room; "they are exceedingly praised in this proclamation of the Marquis Chasteler."

"And with reason," he answered; "I agree with Doris in thinking they behaved uncommonly well for men without a leader."

"It is a very good thing, however," she continued, "that they have all gone home again; a regular army, even of enemies, is greatly to be preferred to these patriots, with or without a leader."

"Especially," said Emmeran, "when the commanding enemy is such a man as Chasteler."

"Yes," said Hilda; "I like him because he visited Colonel Dietfurt, did all in his power to save his life, and has since had him buried with military honours; and I like him for the chivalrous act of sending back the embroidered bands of the captured colours, when he found they had been worked by our Princess Augusta."

"And," said Emmeran, smiling, "you like him most of all for calling here and talking of your father and Frank!"

"I thought him very gentlemanlike," said Hilda.

"So he ought to be," observed Emmeran, "for he is a descendant of a branch of the House of Lothringen, a grandee of Spain, and I know not what all besides."

"He calls himself a Tirolean in this proclamation," said Hilda, referring to the paper in her hand; "and mentions expressly that his country, the Netherlands, is lost to him;

but that having become naturalized here, he now considers the name of Tirolean his highest title."

"Perhaps you will do the same some years hence," observed Emmeran.

Hilda looked at him inquiringly.

"Well, if not expressly Tirolean, at least Austrian, which is the next thing to it," he continued; "for Frank will in the course of time undoubtedly add one more to the naturalized possessors of names beginning with O,—why not O'More, as well as O'Donnel, O'Reilly, O'Connor, O'Niel, and all the rest of them?"

"I rather think," said Hilda, "that if ever Frank become naturalized in Austria, he will endeavour to take the name of Garvagh; a permission of that kind is easily obtained on such occasions; and, when speaking to Doris of his annoyance at his father and brother having lately changed the old Irish name of 'Garvagh' into Beechpark, he said he should like to adopt it as surname if an occasion presented itself."

"Taking the name of an estate is very common in many countries," observed Emmeran.

"Very," said Hilda; "and Doris tells me there are quite as many officers with names of Irish places in the Austrian army as of those beginning with O; but they sound so much more like German than English, that only people acquainted with the meaning of Irish words can detect them, and, in a couple of generations, the derivation is forgotten. Do you remember, Doris, when you were reading the army promotions some time ago, the remarkably pretty names that you told me meant in Irish, 'the vale of thrushes,' and 'the old castle'?"

"Yes," answered Doris; "and the inhabitants of that old castle, which, however, is now a modern house, were very nearly related to the O'Mores of Garvagh. I recollect hearing that some great-great-uncle of ours had gone abroad, entered the service of the Emperor of Germany, married, and become gradually so estranged from his family that his children never attempted to keep up any correspondence with their relations in Ireland. That officer is very probably a descendant of Uncle Barry's, but may never have heard the meaning of his name, and might even be incredulous if it were explained to him."

"Well," said Emmeran, "Frank may purchase or otherwise obtain the right to call himself ' von Garvagh,' and I allow it is a name that could pass muster so well as German, that his great-grandchildren may be pardoned if they are unconscious of a relationship with the future O'Mores of Beechpark ! "

Frank's great-grandchildren did not seem particularly to interest Hilda ; she gathered up the papers, carried them to Emmeran, and observed that, as a Baron Hormayer had been appointed Intendant, which was probably a sort of governor of the county, and the Marquis Chasteler had gone to the south of Tirol, she supposed everything would go on quietly until the Bavarians returned to take possession of the land.

"It will be a very difficult thing for them to accomplish," he answered. "It is evident that the affection of the Tiroleans for their Emperor and his brothers is a sort of fanaticism ; they have heard of the Spanish guerillas too, and the riflemen here will rival if not surpass them. The inhabitants of a country in open insurrection are the most dangerous of adversaries, and if they systematically desert their villages and fly from us as they have begun to do, we shall be without provisions for our army, and have no means of obtaining any kind of information, which is of more importance than you can well imagine ! I must also tell you that no one who has not been on the mountains here can form an idea of the various footpaths known only to the peasants, who can on the same day harass our army in the rear, and a few hours afterwards meet us at the entrance of one of those innumerable narrow passes that in a less mountainous country would be considered impracticable. We shall gain no laurels here, Hilda; and, to speak from experience, I should say that rifle bullets and defeat were anything rather than agreeable."

"You have been particularly unfortunate," said Hilda.

"I have no right to say so," he answered, "for had one of the bullets penetrated a little deeper, I should not have lived to complain; nevertheless, as I cannot, like the French soldier, hope that a marshal's *bâton* is in store for me, or, like Frank, see a Theresian cross dangling perpetually within reach of my drawn sword, nothing but a perhaps false feeling of honour induces me to continue in the army. I have a sort of presentiment that I am one of those un- lucky mortals who may fight until they are cripples without ever rising beyond the rank of a subaltern!"

"I thought," said Doris, who was replacing the broken strings of her harp that had been untouched for several weeks,—"I thought you had quite resolved to leave the army, even before you received the letter from your father entreating you to do so?"

"Such is my intention," said Emmeran; "but not until the present war is over. I hope I shall be fit for service again before long; but I would rather be employed elsewhere than in Tirol."

"Why so?" asked Hilda.

"Because I don't like the kind of warfare we are likely to have here; and I cannot help admiring the loyalty of the Tiroleans to their Emperor. Our Bavarian Highlanders would protest, I hope, just as energetically, if Napoleon took it into his head to bestow them on Austria; in short,

Hilda, I feel as if I were fighting on the wrong side, which proves that Doris was right when she said some weeks ago that I had no business to be a soldier : as such I ought to fight when commanded, without considering the justness of the cause or my own feelings."

" I suspect Doris has changed her mind about your military capabilities," observed Hilda; " the engagement that we witnessed at the hospital has convinced us you can be a very daring, almost a fierce soldier."

" Not more so than any of the others you saw there," answered Emmeran ; " though I confess to having felt for a short time that fighting fury of which Frank has spoken to me, and which I am very much inclined to think proceeds from mere animal exasperation."

" Doris," cried Hilda, " do you hear his definition of courage ?"

" It was not a definition of courage," rejoined Emmeran, quietly ; " courage supposes a full consciousness of danger, with the power of judging how it may best be averted ; but this exasperation is a rousing of our worst passions, and is totally reckless of consequences."

" But," said Hilda, " it frequently leads to the performance of daring deeds that make men famous."

" Or," said Emmeran, " or, as the case may be, to dreadful deeds that make them infamous. I imagine that this sort of exasperation may be felt by murderers ; I have even heard that butchers in the act of killing ——"

" Now, Doris," cried Hilda, appealingly, " is it not dreadful—the manner in which he analyses his own and other people's feelings ! Here have I been for years supposing Frank's achievements quite heroic, — I had even begun to consider Emmeran himself a sort of second-best hero, and now he explains that both being in a state of animal exasperation, were little better than murderers or butchers in the act of killing!"

"I need not explain," said Emmeran, indolently, "for I know you understand that I speak of feelings that only lasted for a short time, and which I shall sedulously suppress if ever another occasion offer. You will, of course, despise me thoroughly when I assure you that I prefer the actual pain of my wounds to the recollection of those I inflicted."

"No, Emmeran; I do not know any one less to be despised than you are, nor, in spite of all you say, can I for a moment doubt your eminent personal courage; I have even very little doubt that, should any opportunities present themselves, you will be quite as subject to these paroxysms of exasperation as Frank."

"You may be right," he answered, thoughtfully, "I cannot answer for myself."

"You had better not," rejoined Hilda. "Suppose, for instance, you had been with Napoleon lately, and heard him give as parole, '*Bavière et Bravoure,*' do you think that your enthusiasm would have been less than that of others? Do you doubt that, led on by him, you would have acted otherwise than at the hospital gate?"

Emmeran did not answer; his eyes followed Doris, as she put down her tuning-key, and pushed aside her harp, and he waited until she was at some distance from them before he said in a whisper: "You ought not to have reminded Doris of the losses of the Austrians at Ratisbon; she has scarcely eaten anything since we got those newspapers from Madame d'Epplen—her face of dismay effectually quelled any enthusiasm I might have felt on the occasion, and there certainly was some truth in what she said about Napoleon personally commanding our troops, only to make them bear the brunt of the battle, and

enable him to save his own army as much as circumstances would permit. No one can admire Napoleon
as a general more than I do, Hilda ; but, as a man,
my regard and respect for him is much on a par with
Doris."

" I suspect her opinion is beginning to influence you on
many subjects as well as this one," said Hilda.

"I should not be ashamed to acknowledge it if it were
so," he replied ; " but I never was an unreserved admirer
of his like my father, Sigmund, and, in fact, almost all my
acquaintances. I still prefer a German to a French general, a German to a French '*parole*,' and might, perhaps,
have heard unmoved Napoleon pronounce the flattering
alliteration, ' *Bavière et Bravoure*.' "

While Emmeran had been speaking, his aunt had entered the room, and Hilda turned from him to meet her,
and exclaim, " So soon back again ! was Madame d'Epplen
from home ?"

" No,—she does not venture out now, as she naturally
fears an increase of the unpopularity of all Bavarians
when it becomes known that General Wrede and Lefebvre,
Duke of Dantzic, are actually on the march here !"

When Doris heard this she came towards her mother,
who continued, in answer to a look of eager inquiry, " The
peasants are already under arms again, Doris, and have
done their utmost to defend the mountain defiles,—when
their ammunition was exhausted they precipitated masses
of rock and felled trees on the invaders,—but it was all to
no purpose, the armies are advancing, and the efforts of
the people are in vain."

" Where is Marshal Chasteler now ?" asked Doris,
quickly.

" Marching from the south, they say ; but he will be
overpowered by numbers, and is personally in imminent

danger, as Napoleon has pronounced him an outlaw, and given orders that he is to be shot if taken prisoner."

"Oh, mother!" cried Hilda, "I cannot believe that Napoleon would do anything so unchivalrous towards the actual commander of an enemy's army!"

"You can, nevertheless, read it," answered her mother, "for it is printed in several of the papers that Madame d'Epplen's friends have contrived to send her from Munich. The wording of the death-warrant will please you as little as the act itself, Hilda; it is against ' *One* Chasteler,— a so-called general in the Austrian service, who was the cause of the insurrection in Tirol, and has been proved guilty of the murder of numerous French and Bavarians.' "

Here her mother took a packet of newspapers from her pocket, and began to search for those from which she had just quoted, when her eye fell on the following passage, and she could not resist the temptation to read it aloud with ironical emphasis.

"The victories of Napoleon the Great are not alone the wonder and pride of this century, but also materially conduce to the happiness and welfare of mankind. From the moment of conquest the vanquished people are under the protection of the Conqueror, the Hero, and the Sage, who seems chosen by Providence to give repose to all nations, by conferring on them a higher degree of independence.* The Emperor Napoleon is a father to all, father even to the people with whose army and princes he is at war—his care for the unprotected never ceases."

"Hilda, I leave you and Emmeran to read the rest, if you care to hear it, when I inform you that Vienna, after a short bombardment, has been obliged to capitulate."

---

* Verbatim from a newspaper of that period.

Without taking any notice of the effect her words had produced on her hearers, she continued : " Madame d'Epplen requested me to keep this information secret, as it might produce unpleasant feelings towards the few Bavarians still resident here, and she seems convinced that a week or two will decide the fate of Tirol, if not of Austria."

A servant opened the door to announce dinner.

No one moved.

Hilda bent down towards Emmeran, and whispered, " Is there any chance of the war ending with the capitulation of Vienna ? "

" Not the least," he answered.

" And you think there may be a battle ? "

" More than *one*, most probably."

" And Frank ?"

" Frank," answered Emmeran, " is by this time with the Archduke Charles—just where he would most desire to be."

" Oh, Emmeran, I cannot this time rejoice at the success of Napoleon ! can you ? "

" Perhaps I might, if—if Doris did not look so deadly pale and disheartened."

" Doris's anxiety is on a grand scale," said Hilda ; " she thinks of French ascendency and the enslaving of nations —but I," she added, with difficulty restraining her tears, " I only think of Frank, and if he be wounded or—or worse —I shall hate Napoleon as long as I live ! "

" It is scarcely just—your making him answerable for Frank's safety," observed Emmeran.

" Yet I do," she answered ; " for, as you would say yourself, he is the cause, though the remote one, of all that may happen. Would this war have ever been ?—or would there be any war at all if it were not for him ? "

Emmeran turned towards her evidently disposed to

discuss the subject; but Hilda walked quickly away from him, and not in the direction of the dining-room, which that day remained unoccupied.

CHAPTER XXXIV.

CONTAINING MORE FACT THAN FICTION.

IT is not our province to describe the military movements of the Austrians and Tiroleans on one side, and the French and Bavarians on the other, during the ensuing week or ten days. Horrible accounts of the burning and plundering of Schwatz reached Innsbruck, and considerably increased the desire of the burghers there for peace on any terms, so that when the Bavarian General Wrede not long afterwards entered the town, all the bells pealed, a crowd of anxious citizens met and accompanied him through the streets to the suburb called Neustadt, and there listened, with great humility, to his reproaches and threats of punishment in case of future insubordination. At the intercession of the Burghermeister he promised to spare the town, and in reference to Schwatz observed : "Other places have been less fortunate than Innsbruck—I wished to save Schwatz also, but a crowd of mad peasants threw themselves into the houses, and had the audacity to fire on my soldiers ; no means could be found to bring these wretches to reason—and the unfortunate town has in consequence become a heap of ruins ! I know the names of the most guilty here," he continued, "but His Majesty Max Joseph has desired me to show indulgence whenever it is possible, and I shall do so."

submit to be stared at, and he therefore drew her arm within his and moved forward.

It has been observed that some people have an instantaneous consciousness of eyes fixed intently on them; and either for this reason, or in consequence of some slight impediment in passing the threshold of the church, Doris suddenly looked up and saw close to her the pallid, agitated face of the officer from the mill. Doubt, consternation, and dismay were successively reflected in her expressive features,—while a hectic flush that passed across the invalid's cheeks seemed suddenly to confirm her worst apprehensions, and she grasped Emmeran's arm in a vain endeavour to make him stop, or at least retard his progress. For the first time in her life she found him inattentive to her wishes; he even drew her forward after she found voice to gasp out the words, "Wait—oh, wait a moment!" and he continued to stride on, though aware that her head was turned backwards, and nothing but his restraining hand prevented her from leaving his side.

"Emmeran," she whispered, breathlessly, "didn't you see him? Didn't you know him?"

"Yes, dearest; but you must restrain your feelings, both for his sake and for Hilda's—she must not be told that he is here."

Doris made a great effort, and regained her self-possession so completely that when they reached the house she was able to speak to her friends, and made a plausible excuse for leaving them by expressing a desire to change her dress. Her heightened colour and flurried manner when whispering a few words to Emmeran as she passed him was so natural that it excited no attention, still less that he should afterwards sit down beside his charming sister-in-law, and assist her to do the honours of the breakfast-table.

In the meantime Doris rushed up the stairs to her room, pulled the flowers and veil from her hair, threw a long grey travelling cloak over her shoulders, and, taking her bonnet in her hand, ran down the stairs and out of the house, not stopping for a moment until she found herself at the entrance of the mill. Fortunately the family were at their early dinner, and she was able to continue her journey uninterrupted to the part of the house in which the room she sought was situated.

She knocked with unhesitating impatience, and on receiving permission to enter, sprang forward with a stifled cry of anguish, and threw herself on her knees beside the couch on which her wounded cousin lay. "Oh, Frank! what a meeting!—what a parting is this!" was all she could utter before her pent-up feelings found relief in a passionate burst of tears.

Frank's lips quivered. "You know me, Doris, in spite of all disfigurement?"

She looked up for a moment, but immediately afterwards buried her head in the sofa cushion, and sobbed aloud.

"I understand you," he said gently; "I am indeed a frightful object to look at—and it is for this reason that I have kept Hilda in ignorance of my present state."

"No, Frank,—no,—it is not that—I am—and she will be—far more afflicted now than had she heard the truth at a time when her fears would have served as preparation for the shock. Your letters—your cheerful letters have deceived us completely—cruelly."

"No, Doris, darling, there was no cruelty to you, or Hilda, or my aunt, in this concealment. It was at first said that I was mortally wounded, then I nearly died or fever. Suppose Hilda had proposed coming to me."

"You need not suppose," said Doris, raising her head

and pushing back her dishevelled hair. "You may be quite sure she would have gone to you! And she will come to you now, and no longer hesitate to tell you how devotedly she loves you!"

"Not yet," said Frank, raising himself upright, while Doris seated herself on a footstool beside the sofa. "I cannot allow Hilda to be told either that I am here, or wounded, for I should doubt any demonstration of affection from her now, or at least not value it as I ought, from the suspicion that compassion alone prompted it! The thought is natural, Doris, after having so signally failed to overcome her pride at Innsbruck."

"Oh, Frank, how little you know Hilda's, or any woman's heart!"

"I know yours," he said, bending down and looking into her overflowing eyes until his own filled with tears. "I know yours so well, Doris, that were I even torn to pieces by a cannon-ball, like poor Louis d'Esterre, I could wish to see you without a moment's fear that you would love me less."

"Has Louis been so dangerously wounded?" asked Doris, with compassionate interest.

"He is dead!" answered Frank, "and I must speak of his death, as he sent you a message which I promised to deliver to you."

"You were able to be of use to him?" said Doris; "you consoled him in his last moments?"

"N—o," said Frank, reluctantly, "I—saw him during the battle of Wagram lying under a tree in a state I dare not describe to you—in short, mortally wounded—and should not even have known him had he not called to me. I dismounted, and he requested me to take from him your miniature, of which he confessed he had possessed himself without permission at Ulm, and ever since worn next his heart. You must forgive him, Doris—he loved you more than you supposed, and desired me to tell you so with almost his last breath, poor fellow!"

"Then you saw him die?"

"He asked me to shoot him, Doris—asked me to put him out of torture that must end in death—but I was a coward, and could not do it."

"And you were obliged to leave him in that state?" said Doris breathlessly.

"No; he persuaded one of our men to have compassion on him. I only heard the shot, Doris, but felt as if the bullet had struck my own heart too. It was a mental wound that will never heal, that will bleed whenever it is touched as long as I live!"

"How horrible!" murmured Doris, covering her face with her hands.

"I wish I had not spoken of him," said Frank, "but unfortunately he was in my thoughts when you came into the room, for I had been considering how I could manage to send you the miniature, that you might give it to Emmeran as a wedding present."

"It belongs to my mother," said Doris, "and if I give it to her now she will inevitably ask where I found it."

"Then," said Frank, "you must keep it yourself for the present, as I cannot give you permission to tell her. I wish I had resolution to leave the mill, but it is hard to resign the pleasure of sitting at this window and seeing Ililda so frequently, especially since my fears of being recognized by her have been nearly removed by Emmeran, who told me that she had resolved not to look at me again because I reminded her of the spectre she saw in the——"

At this moment a hasty step on the stairs, and immediately afterwards an unceremonious hand on the lock of the door, made Doris snatch up her bonnet from the floor; but

before she had time to put it on her head Emmeran
entered the room. "Doris," he said, half apologetically,
"I was obliged to propose coming for you, or else Hilda
would have gone to your room, discovered your absence,
and the consequences might have been fatal to Frank's
secret. Have you told him that he will soon see us again?
—that we return to Meran for the winter?"

"I have not had time to speak of our plans," she answered; "but am now sorry we cannot remain here altogether, as you might have visited Frank daily, and even I
could have managed to see and speak to him occasionally."

"We can do so when we come back," said Emmeran,
cheerfully; "and in the meantime Frank must take care of
himself, and grow strong and handsome again. I quite
approve of his former, and can perfectly understand his
present, motives for concealment."

"I can *not*," said Doris; "and I am sure that Hilda
would feel as I do, and only love him ten times better for
all these wounds." While speaking she pushed aside the
black bandage, raised the thick hair from his temple, and
kissed repeatedly the still red scar she had exposed to
view.

"Farewell, Frank!" she said, with difficulty restraining
her tears. "Farewell!—but only for a few weeks. I do.
not think I can wait until winter to see you again."

Frank stood up, embraced her in silence, looked after
her as she left the room, and then wrung Emmeran's hand
without making an attempt to speak.

"Emmeran, I cannot yet go to the drawing-room," said
Doris, stopping at the foot of the staircase; "it would be
impossible for me to think or speak of anything but Frank

at present; but my not yet having changed my dress, and Janet requiring directions about packing, will serve to excuse me a little longer."

The dress was changed, and Janet had carried off the wedding-garment, but still Doris lingered in her room, walking about uneasily for some time, until at last, throwing herself on her knees, she covered her face with her hands. It was so that Hilda found her at the end of half-an-hour, and though she stood up immediately, and forced a smile while listening to her sister's playful reproaches for having played truant so long, there was something in the expression of her face that made Hilda first hesitate, then stop suddenly, and at last, after a pause, exclaim, "Doris, what is the matter? Something dreadful has happened—"

"It might have been worse," she answered, turning away; "but even as it is I hesitate to tell you."

A horrible suspicion flashed through Hilda's mind; she put her arm round her sister, and whispered, "You are not unhappy?—you do not repent your marriage——?"

"No, oh, no!" said Doris, quickly. "It was not of myself that I have been thinking—it was of you and—of Frank."

"Dear Doris, how very kind of you! But indeed you must not look so disheartened about us, as I have now not the slightest doubt that our next meeting will unite us for life. Will you not come downstairs? I fear if you remain here any longer our friends may think——"

"Never mind what they think!" exclaimed Doris, with such unusual impatience, that Hilda was not only silenced, but so astonished, that she gazed at her sister in stronger interrogation than many words could have expressed. And she was understood, for Doris soon continued: "You may well be surprised, Hilda; but you must have patience for a few minutes. I have something that I wish to tell

you—that I believe I must tell you, though I know I am
not at liberty to do so. It is true," she added, rather
speaking to herself than her sister, "it is true that no
promise of secresy was exacted, and none made; but it
was understood—I know it was—and the reliance on my
silence was so great, that not even an injunction was given
me !"

" Now pray, Doris, don't excite my curiosity any further
if you have no intention of telling me your secret, whatever
it may be."

" It is not mine," said Doris ; "it is the secret of another
person, and mere sophistry my trying to consider myself at
liberty to divulge it. But I feel certain of pardon hereafter—pardon from all concerned—yet nothing could
overcome my scruples of conscience but a dread of the
responsibility of leaving you here for months in ignorance
of what so nearly concerns you."

" Then tell me all about it, Doris, and I will promise
any amount of secresy and discretion that may be necessary."

" Your words are well chosen," said Doris, placing her
hand on her sister's ; " I require both from you."

" Well, go on—I promise."

" Promise solemnly," continued Doris, "that nothing
—nothing will tempt you by *word* or *deed* to betray your
knowledge of what I am about to tell you. Remember I
warn you beforehand that you will be severely tried, and
that no entreaties by letter will induce me to release you
from your engagement."

For a moment Hilda hesitated—then looked intently
at her sister's grave face, thought suddenly of Madame de
Bereny, and ended by pledging herself to secresy as solemnly as was required of her.

" Hilda," began Doris, " did you see the wounded

officer from the mill standing at the door as we came out of church!"

"No," she answered, rather surprised at the question; "the effort to get through the crowd and overtake you and Emmeran prevented me from looking at any one, and I fortunately did not see him."

"But I did," said Doris, slowly; "I saw him distinctly, and was so near him that I could perceive his face flush and his eyes fill with tears as I passed. There was something in the expression of his eyes that attracted me even more than their form and colour, though both were familiar —very familiar to me."

"Some one we knew at Ulm?" suggested Hilda.

"At Ulm?—yes——" said Doris, completely perplexed by her unconsciousness.

"Not Major Pallersberg, I hope?" said Hilda. "Mamma would be so shocked."

"No," answered Doris, sadly; "but she will indeed be greatly shocked—as much as I was—but scarcely as much as you will be."

"Ha!" cried Hilda, suddenly alarmed; "but no—it is impossible! Oh, Doris," she added, with a trembling smile, "you have tortured me unpardonably!"

"No, dear Hilda, I have only prepared you for what you must hear, for what is bad enough, but might be far more——the wounded officer is——"

"Don't say it!" cried Hilda, vehemently; "this is some horrible fancy of yours——there may be a likeness —I will not deny it; but oh, Doris, you must not expect me to believe that the ghastly invalid at the mill is my noble, handsome Frank!"

Doris slowly moved her head in sad confirmation.

"It cannot be," continued Hilda, with increasing agitation; "you are—you must be mistaken. Doris, dear Doris, say that it is so; yon forget that I have received letters from him with the Znaim postmark on them."

"They were written here," said Doris; "and sent to Major Pallersberg to be posted there."

"How do you know that?"

"Emmeran told me so as we walked from the mill together, about half an hour ago."

"Then you have already been there—you and Emmeran have seen him?"

"Yes."

"Spoken to him?"

"Yes."

Pale as death, Hilda sat down on the nearest chair. Her doubts were at an end, her hopes that Doris might have been mistaken extinguished; but her grief was at first too acute for utterance, and she remained motionless, pressing her clasped hands on her heart, and breathing audibly, while her sister bent over her, suggesting every consolation that could be offered. "I am sure," she said, in conclusion, "you will at least acknowledge we ought to be thankful that *his* life was spared when tens of thousands fell!"

"Yes, dear," panted Hilda, "I am indeed very thankful."

"Besides," continued Doris, "Emmeran assures me that Frank's complete recovery is now merely a question of time."

"And care, Doris," cried Hilda, suddenly rousing herself; "and care! And you will release me from my thoughtless promise, and let me take care of him—won't you, dearest?"

"I *cannot*," said Doris, firmly, "for Frank will not have it so; he said he should doubt any demonstration of affection from you now, or, at least, not value it as he ought, from the suspicion that it was prompted alone by com·passion."

"How little he knows me!" cried Hilda, passionately.

"I told him so," continued Doris; "but men cannot understand us on such occasions, for even Emmeran said he approved of Frank's former, and perfectly understood his present, motives for concealment."

"I believe," said Hilda, "from what he once said, when speaking of Colonel Bereny, that I can guess his motives for silence in the first instance, but his reason for not seeing me now is as unjust as it is ungenerous."

"It seems so," answered Doris; "but when you take into consideration your former quarrels and misunderstandings, there is some excuse for him. Besides, it would be unreasonable to expect him to remain altogether unconscious of his great personal advantages, or their value in the opinion of most people, and must therefore forgive him if he attribute at least part of your regard to what the world has forced him to consider one of his chief merits. In short, Hilda, it is evident that he is unwilling you should see him in a state that he imagines would only cause you to pity him."

"This is a hard punishment for my pride and jealousy," said Hilda, "and proves that my letters have not made him forget either. I can now only hope that he is not so ill as he appears to be—that he does not absolutely require the care and attention he spurns so unkindly."

"He is greatly emaciated," answered Doris, "but I believe his wounds are nearly all healed, and the one on his forehead will scarcely be perceived when the scar is no longer red."

"And his arm?"

"Is only in a sling; perhaps he cannot yet move it, for the sleeve of his jacket was cut open."

" But he walks with a crutch, Doris—and I fear—I fear——"

Doris remembered that Frank had raised himself on the sofa with great difficulty, and had required a crutch when he stood up ; she turned away, saying, "I don't know—I hope not."

" Doris," cried Emmeran, knocking at the door, " the carriage is packed, and our guests are preparing to take leave."

" I am coming," she answered, tying on her bonnet and taking up her gloves.

" One moment ! " cried Hilda. " May I tell my mother ? "

" Yes, but only on the same conditions that I have told you—a promise of secresy, which I know she will keep. Tell her that I have betrayed Frank, not only to prevent you from leaving this house in order to avoid him, but also in the hope that, if circumstances favour you, means may be found to induce him by degrees to lay aside his incognito."

Doris spoke these last words as they descended the stairs together, and they were soon after in the midst of noisily sympathizing friends, who naturally supposed that Doris's heavy tearful eyelids and Hilda's colourless lips were caused by their approaching separation.

What occurred during the succeeding quarter of an hour appeared to Hilda like a feverish dream ; she heard the murmuring of voices without distinguishing the words ; she looked at her mother and wondered how she could smile so brightly and seem so happy, and then she followed the others when they descended the steps that led alike to the miller's wine-cellars and the gateway opening on the road. She felt herself embraced by Doris and Emmeran, saw the carriage drive off, forced a smile, and tried to appear interested in what was said during the procrastinated leave-taking of the assembled guests, but no sooner was the gate closed upon the last of them, than she turned round, flew up the stairs to her room, locked the door, and yielded to her painfully restrained grief without control.

Some time elapsed before her mother thought it advisable to follow her and propose a walk in the surrounding vineyards. Hilda opened the door, but turned away her head while saying that she did not feel much inclined to go out. Her mother drew her towards her, looked affectionately at her agitated face, and said, with a smile, "Your anxiety about Doris is unnecessary, dear Hilda. I wish I were as sure of your happiness as I am of hers."

"Of that," said Hilda, "there is no chance. My happiness was lost in the cathedral at Ulm; and I now know but too well that Frank not only never cared for *me*, but even doubts *my* affection for *him*."

"Have you heard from him again?" asked her mother, quickly.

"No, but I have heard *of* him; he does not want or wish to see me."

"Jealous again, Hilda!" said her mother, sitting down with a look of resignation. "Come, then tell me all about it, and as Doris is no longer here, I must take her place, and laugh at or scold you as the case may be."

"Rather say," answered Hilda, seating herself on a footstool, and placing her arm and head on her mother's knee, "rather say you will take her place and console me—if you can."

"I shall try to do so," said her mother, with a quiet smile; "and now tell me what you have heard *of* him."

But Hilda, in her turn, felt the difficulty of communicating ill-tidings to a person unprepared to hear them, and, when urged to speak, answered hesitatingly, " I ought to try to tell you, as Doris told me ——"

" Doris ? " repeated her mother, surprised.

" Yes, but first of all I must obtain a promise of secresy from you."

The promise was given without a moment's hesitation, and then Hilda suddenly raised her head, and in a few passionate sentences explained all.

CHAPTER XLII.

NONE SO BLIND AS THOSE WHO WILL NOT SEE.

HILDA's grief subsided by degrees into resignation. She spoke constantly of Frank, and found her mother not only a patient and indulgent listener, but even inclined to join her in any feasible plan likely to induce him to betray himself. For a whole week he kept more out of sight than ever, the most sultry weather no longer tempting him to seek shade beneath the chesnut-trees, or the mildest evenings inducing him, as had been his wont, to sit at the door of the mill until the darkness permitted him to limp unseen in the sheltered walks of the vineyard. Tired, however, of the confinement, he at length resolved to undertake some short excursions in the neighbourhood, and, as few can be made otherwise than on foot or on horseback, he first used the miller's little carriage to visit Lana and the Badl, and then hired one of his horses to ride to the castle of Tirol; it was seeing this animal undergoing very unusual ablutions that induced Hilda to make inquiries as to the cause.

"The colonel, ma'am, feels himself so much better that he is going to ride to Tirol."

"But is that horse safe?" she asked, with an anxious glance towards the fore-feet, which seemed somewhat impaired by heavy draught.

"Lord bless you, ma'am! the colonel's servant, as was here before you came, told us his master could ride any 'oss."

"I have no doubt of that," said Hilda, "but with a wounded arm and—and the leg——"

"You may be right there," said the man, looking up; "that leg is less than no use to him, and he knows it too, for he told me to bring a chair and a man to help him to mount, and to be sure to choose a time when no one was likely to see him."

"Are you—or is the man you spoke of, going with him?" asked Hilda.

"No, ma'am; I offered, but he wouldn't hear of such a thing."

"And," said Hilda, "if the horse makes a false step on those paved roads, and he has not strength to pull him up, what will be the consequence?"

"Bad enough, ma'am; but when I recommended him to look sharp, especially coming down hill, he said his right arm was still fit for service, and I needn't have no fears either for him or for the 'oss, ma'am."

Hilda went immediately to her mother and informed her of Frank's intention, adding a wish to follow him to the castle of Tirol, if it could be done without exciting his suspicions.

"Let us take chance for that," answered her mother, "and send at once for horses, but, as neither they nor the roads are likely to tempt us to go out of a walk, I propose that we engage peasants to lead them. We must not set out for at least half-an-hour after Frank, and can take Hans with us in case we should return late."

"Is there no danger of his recognizing Frank?" asked Hilda.

"I think not; but what matter if he do? I could almost wish that Janet had not gone away with Doris; she went so often to the mill, that a meeting with Frank in the end would have been certain, and equally certain that she would have known him, and would neither have made a promise of secresy nor considered herself bound to be silent under such circumstances. The question now is— can you now see Frank with the necessary composure, and if I am able to persuade him that we do not recognize him, can you speak to him as a stranger?"

"I will try," said Hilda; "I *must* try, as there is no alternative between avoiding him altogether or keeping my promise to Doris."

Before they set out on their excursion, Hilda received a letter from Frank, in which he informed her that he had at last obtained the object of his ambition—a Theresian Cross—was to be made Baron, and, if she approved, would take the name of More von Garvagh."

"These honours," observed her mother, "have probably already more than consoled him for his wounds; and I am convinced, if it were not for this eccentric concealment from you, he would be perfectly happy."

"And so should I," answered Hilda; "but you seem to oversee the unkindness of his requiring conceal-ment from me alone! Now, I should like to know," she added thoughtfully, "whether or not Madame de Bereny knew all this when she was here last week? Frank's letter bears the date of that very day, and he may have seen her—in fact he may have often seen her before we came to Meran."

" I don't think he did," interposed her mother, " for by all accounts he was too ill to go out when he first came here, and if she had ever been at the mill, the family there would have spoken of it."

" I hope you are right," said Hilda, "for without being supposed jealous, I think I may say it would have been very hard if he had consented to see her and refused to see me ! Do you think I ought to comply with her request, and let her know what he has written ? I fear a note or message will bring her here again."

" Let her come," replied her mother, " for if we could manage to make her meet Frank, her recognition of him would save us a great deal of painful acting."

" What a pity we did not think of this plan before," said Hilda. " It would have been so easy to have induced her to go to Tirol with us to-day."

" No, Hilda ! Let us first see him alone, and put our self-possession to the proof without witnesses."

" It will be a hard trial," said Hilda, " and I can only hope that circumstances will favour us."

An hour later they were on the road to the village and castle of Tirol, mounted on horses such as guides generally place at the service of strangers—quiet animals, whose only pace seems an eager walk that is generally supposed to be warranted safe. Hilda did not think it necessary to consider herself on horseback at all—she placed the reins in the hand of her guide and, heedless or unconscious of the beautiful scenery around her, indulged in a long retrospect, beginning at the early winter morning on which she had seen her cousin Frank as he stamped his feet on the snow-covered ground of the Chapel-island and laughingly shook the water of the lake from his dripping clothes, and ending with the spectral figure of her husband standing beneath the tree in the orchard ten days previously. It

"In Ulm, in the year 1805."

"Where is your husband now?"

"Near Vienna; perhaps he was at Aspern. I wish I could hear of him."

"Is he in the army?"

"Yes; in a hussar regiment."

"And the name of the Colonel of this regiment?"

Hilda paused, and then, with deepened colour, answered, "Bereny."

"Your husband's name?"

"Frank O'More."

A murmur of satisfaction from the assembled peasants rather bewildered than encouraged Hilda. The priest waved his hand majestically.

"There is nothing proved as yet," he said, solemnly; "any acquaintance of the young lady's might have stated these circumstances, which are probably well known to many people. Is not this the case?" he added appealing to Hilda.

"They are known to my relations and friends," she answered.

"Just so; a brother or cousin, for instance?"

"I have no brother."

"Then let us say, cousin; I think he said he was a cousin too!"

Hilda became uneasy; she feared that Emmeran might actually have had the rashness to attempt her rescue. Such an adventure was unlike an act of his; but what would he not do to spare Doris a moment's anxiety?

"Can you describe his appearance?" asked the priest.

"How can I, without knowing of whom you are speaking?" she rejoined quickly.

Folding his arms slowly, and fixing his eyes on her face

as if to watch the effect of his words, the priest at length thought proper to explain : " This man," he said, " has a passport, in which he is named Myer, horse-dealer ; and this he says was given him to facilitate his passage through various detachments of the French army.   That he is an officer and not a horse-dealer I have myself no doubt; but his coming here instead of going direct with his important intelligence to Andrew Hofer,—resigning to a brother officer who travelled with him the honour of being the first to announce the victory at Aspern, can only be accounted for by your actually being as he asserts—his wife ! "

" Do you mean," cried Hilda, " that this officer has said he is my husband ? "

" Yes," answered the priest; " and he imagines he has a right to demand your being set at liberty as well as himself, that you may return together to Innsbruck."

" Oh, let me go to him ! " she cried, endeavouring to pass without further questioning.

" Stay," he said with unruffled dignity, " you now know of whom I am speaking, and I therefore expect you to prove the truth of his assertion by giving a description of his person."

" He is *very* handsome——," she began hurriedly.

Some youthful laughter became audible in the lobby.

Hilda blushed crimson.

The priest looked in the direction of the door, frowned reprovingly, and then blandly observed, " There are different kinds of beauty ;—some think emaciated fair-haired men handsome, while others——"

Hilda stopped aghast.   Emmeran was fair-haired, and just then remarkably emaciated.   Confused, disappointed, and alarmed, she turned away, unwilling to expose her trembling lips and tearful eyes to so many observers; both, however, had been seen by the priest, and his voice was compassionate when he again spoke.

" I am very sorry," he said, " that these precautions are necessary ; but I really must request a description of your husband's person in order to remove the doubts of these people. Is he tall ? "

Hilda remained silent, and continued to look out of the window to which she had retreated, determined at least not to injure Emmeran by her evidence.

" Dark-haired ? " persisted the priest.

No answer.

" Perhaps you will at least describe a wedding-ring that he showed me, and which he said was peculiar enough to identify him ? "

Hilda turned round instantly, and, flushed with fresh hope, described the ring found in the vault of the Chapel-island.

" Quite right," observed the priest, referring to his paper of notes ; " and the name engraved inside you can, of course, also tell us ? "

" It was Waldering of Westenried," answered Hilda ; " the ring had been my father's, and the name was his."

" It would be impossible to doubt any longer," said the priest, in a loud voice, " and I do not hesitate to proclaim my firm belief of all that the Austrian officer has told me. Give him some of the best wine in the house to drink the health of our Emperor and the Archduke Charles, and then let him depart in peace with his wife whenever he pleases."

These words were followed by a tumultuous rush of peasants down the stairs. The priest stood for a moment, expecting, perhaps, some deferential movement on the part of Hilda ; but, on perceiving that she sat down, and leaning her elbows on the nearest table, covered her face with her hands, he strode haughtily out of the room, and turned the key in the lock, perhaps to remind her that she was a prisoner until he chose to permit her release.

———

CHAPTER XXXV.

A WHIM.

THE room was not improved in appearance since Hilda had first seen it, some hours previously. Disorderly rows of half-emptied wine-bottles and glasses stood on the long deal tables, broken crusts of bread were strewed around—wooden benches upset, and a strong odour of bad tobacco contaminated the atmosphere. Was it the latter which caused the feeling of suffocation that made her open a window and gasp for breath? She tried to think so, but was unfortunately given time to ventilate the room and convince herself of the contrary. There was much shouting, and probably drinking, below stairs—perhaps Frank could not get away from the people there? Still it was very possible that he was less anxious for a meeting than she was. "Should she let him perceive this? Certainly not. She would remember her promise to Doris never again to repulse him; but after all that had occurred, he could not expect any actual demonstration of rejoicing on her part." And Hilda drew up her slight figure to its most dignified height, and began deliberately to harden her heart.

This dilatoriness on the part of Frank was most injudicious — it gave Hilda time to remember that they had parted in anger, that he had braved her displeasure by going to Meran with Madame de Bereny, had in fact given her so much cause to be offended, that she imagined she had a right to expect some show of penitence on his part before she could forgive without reserve. A quick step on the stairs brought her cogitations to an abrupt conclusion, and made her heart beat so violently, that it was absolutely a relief when she became aware its direction was towards Madame d'Epplen's room. But the delay was short—after a few returning steps across the lobby, the key turned in the lock, the door of her room opened, and she started up to place herself rigidly in forced composure beside a chair, the back of which she grasped to keep her tottering figure steady.

And all this trepidation had been endured, and this great effort to conceal her heart-sinking made for—a chambermaid, who entered unceremoniously, bringing her the shawl and hat she had left in Madame d'Epplen's room.

" You're to put these things on, and be ready when he おus you," said the girl, throwing them on the table beside Hilda; "I heard him say he had no time to lose, for he wants to be with Andrew Hofer on Mount Isel early in the morning."

A sudden revulsion of feeling made Hilda disposed to rebel. "No; she would *not* put them on; she would not aid and abet in his joining Andrew Hofer. His sending such a message, or any message, was unpardonable ! "

The chambermaid collected a number of bottles and glasses on a tray, and while carefully carrying the clattering brittle ware out of the room, omitted to lock or even firmly close the door; and Hilda paused for a moment to consider should she return to Madame d'Epplen, or control her temper and await Frank's coming ? It is strange that it never occurred to her that he too might dread as much as wish for a meeting; and when the silence in the room permitted her to become aware that some one was passing the balcony with lingering, uncertain steps, she never thought of him, but stood deeply musing in the room until she heard her name pronounced in a very low voice, and on looking up saw him standing at one of the windows that opened into the balcony.

Hilda sprang forward in an irrepressible movement of joy, and found the window at which he stood fortified as it were with a nearly impervious row of those prickly cactus that so very frequently decorate such windows until the weather permit their removal to the balcony itself.

It is possible, however, that just then neither she nor Frank had any objections to the interposition of these plants; he peered through and over them without embarrassment, and Hilda's hand braved the danger of thorns in a hurried endeavour to find an opening through which it could meet his. The hand of course received a very satisfactory portion of kisses before it was withdrawn—and so the dreaded meeting was over.

"You will return with me to Innsbruck, Hilda?"

"Ye—es, if you wish it, though I have some qualms of conscience at deserting Madame d'Epplen."

"You need have none; I have explained who she is, and a few days hence you will see her again safe under Hofer's protection."

"That is—a prisoner?" said Hilda.

"Well, I suppose so. Chances of war, you know. I may be the same to-night if you do not assist me to pass the Bavarian pickets."

"But I hope, Frank, you have not put yourself into real danger on my account; for, after all, I do not think these peasants intended us any harm."

"I am sure they didn't," he answered; "but I could not endure the idea of your being a prisoner, and forced to wander about on the mountains against your will."

"It was very kind of you," said Hilda.

Frank laughed.

"I heard you sacrificed the pleasure of being the bearer of good news," she continued.

"Not exactly, Hilda, for I had always intended my comrade Stainer to be spokesman on this occasion, as he is a Tirolean and ran the risk from the purest patriotic motives;* while I, after having ascertained that there was no chance of further military movements for some weeks, proposed accompanying him in order to——return to Innsbruck. We were furnished with passports giving us the professions in which we thought we could best pass muster; Stainer chose to be supposed a landscape painter, and I——"

"The priest told me that you represented a horse-dealer," said Hilda.

"I do so still," he answered; "have you any objection to walk down to the valley with such an ill-dressed fellow?"

"None whatever—by moonlight," said Hilda gaily; "only let me first take leave of Madame d'Epplen, and tell her she need be under no further apprehensions either about me or herself."

A short time afterwards they descended the stairs together and left the inn amidst the respectful greetings of a dense crowd of peasants.

When out of sight and walking down the narrow road at a rapid pace, Frank told Hilda that he had met Janet on her way home in a great state of anxiety, had sent a message to his aunt by her, and then struck off at once into the mountains. "I had no difficulty in finding you," he added, "for an innkeeper who knew Stainer told me there was to be a meeting of riflemen in this direction to-night, and the party who took Madame d'Epplen prisoner were on their way here."

* Fact.

" I wonder what they have done with her horses," said Hilda.

" They are to be sent to Hofer* as soon as affairs have taken a decided turn."

" And when will that be ? "

" To-morrow or the day after, I hope."

" You don't mean to say, Frank, that you expect the peasants to gain any advantage over General Deroy ? "

" I mean that the general has not been left half enough troops to enable him to maintain his position, and that even his eminent military talent will scarcely save him from the fate of Bisson ! "

" I won't——I can't believe that," cried Hilda vehemently.

" Well, I daresay I am mistaken," said Frank good-humouredly ; " perhaps we shall be defeated, and I may be a prisoner of Deroy's, an inmate of the hospital, or a corpse for the churchyard about this time to-morrow ! "

" Frank, if I had known this, I would not have left the inn," she cried, stopping suddenly ; " but I can go back again, for you told me you could not well pass the Bavarian pickets without my assistance—and I won't assist you to peril your life unnecessarily ! "

While saying the last words she turned back and began a resolute reascent of the mountain. Frank followed reluctantly, in ill-concealed wrath, and with lips firmly pressed together. Hilda did not like this constrained silence, and when she spoke again there was even more deprecation in her voice than words.

" You can easily imagine, Frank, how much I must wish to return to Innsbruck and my mother. Believe me,

* They were used on state occasions by Andrew Hofer, during the imprisonment of Madame d'Epplen ; but he returned them to her in good condition at a later period.

nothing but anxiety for your safety would induce me to put myself again in the power of these peasants."

"Do not expect me to feel or feign any gratitude for this proof of regard," he answered, "or suppose me more in your power than I actually am. With such a passport as mine, and these clothes, I could easily satisfy the scruples of the officer on picket at the bridge; and I need scarcely tell you that there is nothing to prevent me from taking the same way to Andrew Hofer as the peasants to whom you are returning."

Hilda stood still, and the light of the moon, now high above the mountains, fell full on her agitated face as she exclaimed bitterly, "Oh, how could I be such a fool as to suppose that I had any influence! I see it all now—you have made a slight deviation from your way to take me with you, but that is all. I shall go back to Madame d'Epplen, and will not embarrass you with my presence when passing the officer on picket, or make any useless attempts to prevent you from crossing the mountains, should you prefer that mode of joining your friends."

"Hilda," said Frank, earnestly, "let me assure you that I have taken this opportunity of returning to Tirol solely for the purpose of seeing you again. We have been very foolish, and given people an opportunity of talking of faults on both sides, incompatibility of temper, and so forth; but as I believe in the main you rather like me, and as I have discovered, during our last separation, how very much I like you, I have fully determined to avoid disputes of any kind in future. Now, it is evident, that for this purpose one of us must yield, and, as you will *not*, I have resolved to do so completely, and without reserve. Half measures are, however, my aversion, and, therefore, with the exception of military matters and my duty as a soldier, I put myself completely under your command, and promise the obedience of a serf and the humility of a slave. Are you satisfied ? ”

Satisfied ! She was delighted—exultant ! But, with all her love of power, Frank's manly, unreserved confession of affection remained uppermost in her mind ; and when, blushing deeply, she placed her hand on his arm, and with a very bright smile assured him he would not find her so tyrannical as he supposed, she would have greatly liked to seal the proposed compact with an unreserved embrace.

That Frank himself felt strongly tempted to do so is more than probable—at least there is no other way of accounting for the sudden flush that passed across his face, and the outstretched arm that for a moment seemed in-clined to place itself in the proper position for a waltz round the small moonlit space before them ; but he re-frained, and with an affectation of modest reserve, though with eyes betraying more mirth than he perhaps intended, he drew back, saying, “I beg your pardon, Hilda, I had almost forgotten that I am under restraint, and dare not offer a caress, though I may hope to receive one occa-sionally when I deserve it.”

Frank was a good actor, and his words and manner instantly explained his intention to force her to make advances, which he could receive in whatever manner he pleased ; she concealed her annoyance, however, even while giving it vent, by instantly putting his patience and obe-dience to the test.

“I shall now return to Madame d'Epplen,” she said, “but must forbid your leaving the village to-night with the peasants who are about to join Hofer.”

Frank gravely bowed acquiescence.

“ Or,” she continued, with some hesitation, “ I believe I should prefer your taking me back to my mother—and then remaining with us.”

"Impossible, Hilda. If I reach Innsbruck to-night, I must join my comrades on Mount Isel to-morrow. All the officers now with Hofer are volunteers, and even my slight military knowledge may be useful, as I happen to be acquainted with the ground about the town."

"Oh, very well," she said, walking on; "if you think your absence more satisfactorily accounted for by being on the top of this mountain, I have nothing more to say."

"Not so," he answered, quickly; "it is that I consider myself obliged to remain with you when you are the prisoner of these peasants, no matter how well-intentioned they may be; but you are a soldier's daughter and a soldier's wife, Hilda, and ought to understand the dilemma in which you are placing me."

She did understand it perfectly, and fearing to exasperate him by an abuse of the power given her, turned round instantly. "I will not take upon myself the responsibility of leading you into danger," she said, slowly, "and therefore prefer giving you leave to do as you please in this instance."

"Thank you," said Frank, eagerly; "let us get on to Innsbruck as fast as we can; I daresay the little vehicle I bespoke is waiting for us already at the inn in the valley."

"Were you so quite sure that I would return with you?" she asked, with some pique, accepting, however, his offered arm with a very good grace.

"Well, yes; I thought giving you full power would have a good effect, and I was not mistaken. You would not like people to say that I had shirked an engagement when it came in my way, would you?"

"No one would dare to say that of you," she cried, indignantly.

Frank laughed, as if his apprehensions on that score were not very great, and Hilda clasped her hands over his arm while she continued : "But really, Frank, your fear-lessness is now so well known that you can afford to be more prudent, and you must promise to be so for my sake."

"I begin to think that I bear a charmed life," he answered, gravely, "for if ever wounds or early death were to be my portion, I ran my greatest risk lately at Aspern. Not an officer of my regiment escaped, so that when the last engagement ended I was in full command of the few men who could be mustered."

"Was Colonel Bereny also wounded ?" she asked.

"Dangerously, Hilda, and so hideously disfigured and crippled that death would be a release to him."

Hilda shuddered, and was scarcely conscious of the thought that prompted her next questions.

"Did you write to his wife? Has she gone to him ?"

"No. Vienna is still occupied by the enemy, and he knows too well the dangers and privations to which she would be subjected to allow her to join him. Men cannot have—cannot even wish to have—their wives with them under such circumstances."

"I should certainly go to you, Frank, if I heard you were wounded—no danger or privation should prevent me."

"And yet, Hilda, seeing you beside my bed in the ward of a military hospital would cause me more pain than pleasure."

"Indeed !"

"I should feel like poor Bereny, unwilling to let my wife run the risk of catching the fever always so prevalent in such places ; I should dread your seeing the horrible wounds——. But talking of wounds reminds me of Em-meran—how is he ? What a lucky fellow to escape the hospital, and have you and Doris to take care of him !"

" Doris did take great care of him," said Hilda ; "but you have no idea how gallantly he behaved in that un. expected insurrection."

" Oh yes, I know all about it, for my aunt wrote a full account of everything that occurred to Pallersberg. Sigmund's death surprised us, of course ; but we felt no regret, rather the contrary I am afraid, as neither of us had reason to like him, and there is no doubt that Emmeran will be a more worthy chief for the family of Waldering."

" I think he will," said Hilda.

" My aunt flatters herself also," continued Frank, " that his political opinions are gradually changing—his admiration of Napoleon quite on the wane."

" Doris's influence is great," said Hilda in a low voice.

" Of course it is," he answered, thoughtfully ; "but less in politics than you suppose. Emmeran is one of those who have been made adherents of the French by circumstances, national feelings, and personal connexions ; but he will see through the designs of Napoleon as clearly as any of us when the war is at an end."

" With all my heart I wish it were at an end !" murmured Hilda fervently.

" It is greatly to be desired," answered Frank, "even by those who most long for advancement, and can only obtain it sword in hand ! Such, you know, is my case ; but, after the frightful loss of life I have so lately witnessed, I can sincerely join in your wish. Perhaps peace in the world would promote the same in our family, or at least put an end to the political disputes which have for some years helped to disunite us ! A family more at odds than we have been in this respect it would be hard to find ! "

" Very true," said Hilda ; "but one cannot help having

political opinions, and it is hard not to express them when not only witnessing but actually suffering from the events taking place."

"I acknowledge," said Frank, "that it is sometimes very hard to be silent : I felt it so when last in Innsbruck and unable to give you warning of the coming revolt of Tirol; I feel it now, while exulting in a victory I scarcely dare to mention lest a quarrel might be the consequence."

"Tell me all about your victory, Frank; I should like to hear it."

He shook his head and remained silent.

"I should indeed," she continued, "and don't at all mind hearing that the French have been defeated. I only care for Bavarians now——you surely don't require me to forget that I am Bavarian as well as English, Frank ? "

No, he did not require anything so unreasonable, and the result was most satisfactory. The rest of the way down the mountain was beguiled by an animated account of the battle of Aspern, followed by a recital of Frank's subsequent adventures during his journey to Tirol with Captain Stainer as joint bearer of important intelligence that might have long been withheld from the public by a dilatory, timid, or ill-disposed post.

Frank had purposely made a deviation from the narrow road, and by taking advantage of a steep footpath not only shortened the way but managed to emerge from the wood at a small inn situated in the valley where he had ordered a peasant's market-cart and horse to be in readiness for him.

"I cannot propose your resting here, Hilda," he said, advancing to the closed door of the house, and knocking loudly, "for we have no time to lose ; but I must ask you to wait a few minutes while I metamorphose myself into a farm-servant, as in that capacity I shall have to drive you into Innsbruck."

The door was opened, and a sleepy hostler made his appearance; on recognizing Frank, however, he turned towards the stable, and brought out a horse ready harnessed, Hilda meantime sitting on a bench before the door, feeling strangely confused and happy. She scarcely observed a man who afterwards ran out of the house and spoke to the hostler, until she saw him take some dust from the road and deliberately throw it over his hair, and then dip his hands in the spring and rub them with some clay, during the latter operation taking care to give his nails a sufficient quantity of mud; but when the same man walked towards her with the bent knees and slouching gait of a mountaineer, she could scarcely believe it was Frank, so perfect was his personification of a peasant, so complete the change in his appearance that had been effected in the space of a few minutes.

"I should have looked better if I had borrowed a Sunday suit," he said, smiling at her astonishment; "but it would not have answered my purpose so well. I am afraid you think me very ugly and rather dirty in this guise?"

"Clay is clean dirt, Frank, and will, I hope, enable you to pass the Bavarian pickets without question. Won't you sit beside me in the cart? there is room enough on the seat for us both."

"You forget that I am Franz the hostler's son," he answered, laughing; "and I must sit on this plank at your feet and allow my legs to dangle in closest proximity to my horse's tail."

"An awkward place, Frank, if he were disposed to kick; and he has no blinkers, nor in fact almost any harness!"

"He wants nothing but traces to take us to Innsbruck," was Frank's reply, as he placed himself on what might be supposed the footboard of the seat. "You shall see how we drive in this part of the world," he added; and seizing the reins he flapped them up and down two or three times, while he muttered a few guttural words of encouragement, and the horse immediately started off at a good hard trot.

Strange to say, the road appeared shorter to Hilda in that jolting vehical by moonlight than when seated on the box of Madame d'Epplen's well-built carriage in the morning, and she could hardly believe they were approaching the much dreaded picket when Frank exclaimed, "Now, Hilda, here we are; tell the truth with reserve, and avoid delay as much as possible; you must take my purse and passport, however, for both would be encumbrances to the stupid lout I intend to represent for the next quarter of an hour;" and while speaking he rounded his shoulders, bent still more forward his head, and gave to his handsome features an expression of supremely dull indifference. When ordered to halt he did so slowly, contriving to pass the officer some yards, and then employed himself disentangling the lash of his whip while receiving the merited reprimand for his dilatory obedience.

Hilda fortunately happened to know the officer on picket, and told him of Madame d'Epplen and her own capture by the peasants, adding that she owed her release to the circumstance of her being the wife of an Austrian officer, and that she was now on her way home.

"And the name of the village where Madame d'Epplen is now detained?" asked the officer.

"We could not find it out," she answered, "for not one of the people there would tell us."

"Of course not. But," he added, pointing to Frank, "this smart coachman of yours may know it. I say, my lad, can you tell me where this lady came from?"

"Innsbruck," answered Frank, biting industriously at a knot in the lash of his whip.

"I mean where she came from to-night."

Frank named the inn where they had procured the market-cart; and the officer would have been satisfied if some one had not explained that the place named was in the valley and close to the river Inn.

"I am afraid you will find him very stupid," said Hilda.

"A Tirolean is more frequently cunning than stupid," replied the officer, "and his answers make me suspect he knows more than he chooses to tell. If it were not for the fear of inconveniencing you, I should like extremely to detain him until we find out Madame d'Epplen's place of imprisonment."

"Oh, pray let him take me into Innsbruck!" said Hilda; "my mother and sister must be in a great state of anxiety about me, and you can obtain the information you require from any good map. The village, I think, lies higher than what is called the Middle Mountains; but before any one can be sent, Madame d'Epplen will have left it, for they told her she must get up at daybreak, and it will soon be that now!"

"Very true," said the officer, looking eastwards; "and I have no one to send in pursuit, nor would it be of any use, for the peasants are assembling in thousands, and can do what they please just at present. Good night, or good morning, madame; I hope you may reach home without further impediment."

Not long afterwards they were rattling over the pavement of Innsbruck; and, turning into the street that ended their journey, Frank's eyes glanced along the fronts of the houses, and he exclaimed, "Just as I expected—neither my aunt nor Doris have gone to bed; their windows are open, and they are looking out for us. I hope some one will

24

come to hold the horse, so that I may go upstairs for a few minutes."

The entrance-gate was wide open, and the whole family assembled to meet them. Frank's dress when he unconsciously assumed his own manner caused a good deal of mirth, in which he joined, even while declaring that he had not time to amuse himself. He had left a uniform in Innsbruck, and now required it for immediate use.

" There are other clothes of yours here——" suggested Hilda.

"I must don the uniform nevertheless," he answered, laughing ; " without it the peasants won't obey commands, and I may have to make myself useful on Mount Isel a few hours hence."

" Hilda will give it you," said his aunt.

And Hilda turned reluctantly enough towards her room, followed by Frank, who lost no time in packing the uniform and whatever else he required into a portmanteau which he sent downstairs, and then said cheerfully, "Farewell, Hilda, for a day or two,—or more, as the case may be ; our next meeting depends so completely on the success of a cause to which you are ill-disposed, that I scarcely know whether or not you wish to see me again ? "

" Oh, Frank, how can you talk so ? "

" Is it not true ? " he asked ; " will seeing me console you for the defeat of the Bavarians now in and about Innsbruck ? "

Hilda struggled hard for composure. " If it were a French general or a French army——" she began.

"I perceive I shall only be half welcome," he said, good-humouredly ; " nevertheless, I hope to see you before long again. And now, dear Hilda, we must take leave, or rather you must take leave of me ; for you understood, of course, that when I promised obedience and humility, all demonstrations of regard must henceforward proceed from you!"

"Nonsense, Frank."

"I am serious, Hilda; you have openly scorned me before all the world here, and I now, as a sort of compensation, expect you to make love to me with equal ostentation."

"I am sure you expect nothing of the kind, Frank; you know, as well as I do, that it would be very un—un— maidenly!"

Frank's colour mounted to his temples: "Perhaps, then, Hilda," he said, hesitatingly, "we had better make some arrangement for occasions like the present; for instance—I have, you know, promised to obey you implicitly, and if you order me to kiss you, or anything of that kind, I'll do it!"

"I am afraid you must wait a long time for any such order from me, Frank," she replied, secretly enjoying his embarrassment, and with difficulty restraining a laugh.

"Oh, as long as you please!" he retorted, with some pique; "I renew my promise of obedience to any extent, and only wish we had more time to expend on this sort of foolery. Remember, the next proposal must come from you; meantime, adieu!"

Hilda followed him to the door, and watched with some chagrin his unreserved leave-taking of her mother and sister; the moment, however, that he turned to the stairs, she ran back into her room, and threw one of the windows wide open, just in time to see him spring into the market-cart, and then, looking up towards her, flourish his hat in the air.

"He is not offended, after all," she murmured, with great satisfaction; "and when he comes back he will perhaps have forgotten this tiresome whim!"

CHAPTER XXXVI.

A VOW.

HILDA was still in her mother's room talking over the events of the last four-and-twenty hours, when Emmeran returned from a mountain in the neighbourhood, where as a person well acquainted with the country, he had accompanied General Deroy when reconnoitring in that direction. As Emmeran's absence had prevented him from hearing of Hilda's imprisonment, he listened with equal surprise and interest to all she had to relate, seemed to consider Frank's arrival and the account of the battle of Aspern very important intelligence, and said that, though much fatigued, he would return to head-quarters and report the information he had obtained.

"Stay!" cried Hilda; "you must first give me the assurance that no pursuit of Frank will be attempted."

"Do not be uneasy," he answered, smiling; "you have not told me what direction he has taken, and I do not want to know it. Frank's words admit of no doubt;—Napoleon has lost a battle, and to us the certainty that we can entertain no hopes of reinforcements from Lefebvre may be of great consequence."

"Then," said Hilda, "Frank was right after all when he said a capitulation was inevitable; he spoke of General Bisson, who was nearly in the same position, you know, last April——."

"Deroy is not Bisson," said Emmeran, confidently; "though Fefebvre has certainly put his military talents to a hard proof by leaving him such an insufficient force to keep possession of a country like Tirol. This second insurrection has been kept nearly as secret as the first, and we find it utterly impossible to procure any sort of information concerning the movements of the peasants. I, therefore, felt no sort of uneasiness about you —— but then I never dreamed of your going beyond our outposts with Madame d'Epplen !"

" I ought not to have done so," said Hilda; " as it has turned out, however, it is of no importance. A night's rest lost, that's all."

" Take a day's rest instead," suggested Emmeran, preparing to leave the room; " I shall do so, too — if I can."

Hilda thought the advice good, and slept until disturbed by the report of cannon in the direction of Mount Isel. The continuation of such sounds soon roused her completely; and, on going to her mother's room, she found her and Doris in the state of restless anxiety that she remembered they had all felt so frequently at Ulm. The recollection, too, of what they had witnessed from their windows during the former insurrection recurred vividly to their minds, and materially aided their fantasy in bringing before them the scenes being enacted beyond the town ; so that, unable to cheer each other, they spent the greater part of the day in wandering despondingly from room to room, making futile attempts to employ at least their hands when the combat seemed to flag, and listening at intervals to the marvellous and improbable accounts of victory reported by their landlord and the Austrian servants in the house, which were immediately and stoutly contradicted by Hilda's Bavarian domestics, whose information, however, was chiefly obtained from soldiers in the act of carrying their wounded comrades to the hospital.

It was undeniable that General Deroy was in a critical. position, for, in addition to the whole country being in insurrection, and volunteers daily increasing the numbers of his opponents, his hopes of receiving supplies of ammunition were extinguished, in consequence of all communication with Bavaria having been cut off. These facts being well known to the Tiroleans and the Austrian officers commanding on Mount Isel, they towards evening proposed a capitulation on the same terms that had been accepted by the French two months previously.

But General Deroy was neither intimidated by his difficulties, nor urged to yield by his officers, as his predecessor had been; he refused to capitulate, and would only agree to a four-and-twenty hours' truce; which, however, was declined. The day had drawn to a close during the negotiations, and, by mutual consent, hostilities ceased on both sides with the waning light; the Tiroleans and Austrians trusting that the next day would bring them complete victory.

It was on the evening of that day that Emmeran noiselessly entered the drawing-room in his aunt's apartments and walked straight to the sofa on which Doris was sitting.

"We heard you were safe," she said, looking up with a smile; "but how fatigued you must be! And they tell us nothing is decided, and that the combat will begin again to-morrow. We must not, therefore, think of asking you any questions, for you ought to go to bed and sleep as long as you can."

"I believe you are right," he answered; "and you would, at all events, feel little interest in hearing of our various attacks and repulses on Mount Isel. At present we have neither lost nor won, and may think ourselves well off if matters remain so."

"You are talking enigmas," said Hilda, coming towards him; "what do you mean?"

"I mean that we are in as perplexing a position as can well be imagined, and that we have a great deal to do, and very little time to do it in," he answered, drawing out his watch; " so that I can scarcely allow myself two hours' rest, and should then like you to give me some supper before I leave you again."

" Only two hours' rest for an invalid such as you are!" exclaimed Hilda.

"I wish it were twelve instead of two," he answered; " but I have no time to play invalid now, and must be at head-quarters before midnight."

"In that case," said Doris, placing her watch on the table before her, " we must order you to bed at once; and I will promise to waken you when it is time to get up."

" Thank you," said Emmeran, cheerfully; " with you on guard I have no doubt I shall be fast asleep in five minutes."

Hilda followed him out of the room.

"Emmeran," she said, earnestly, " may I ask why you must leave us again at midnight ? "

He whispered the three words, "We must retreat;" then placed his finger on his lips, and closed the door of his room.

And Hilda returned to her sister, and watched her pale, anxious face, without venturing unpermitted to repeat the words that had tranquillized and pained herself in nearly equal proportions.

Emmeran was wakened, supped in haste, received with evident satisfaction a parcel from Hilda, out of which the neck of a field flask protruded, and took leave.

" Doris," he said, lingering beside her for a moment, ' my usual soldier luck attends me this time also—Frank will in the course of the coming day appear as conquering hero, while I——"

"Dear Emmeran," she interposed, eagerly, "there are cases where a capitulation is both honourable and humane. Why not save life where the sacrifice of it is useless?"

"That is what we intend to do," he said, bitterly.

"Let us rejoice it is to be so," she continued; "and that we may not expect another day of strife and bloodshed."

"You may rather expect a day of triumph," said Emmeran; "and if, during the course of it, you bestow a thought on me, it is all I can reasonably hope."

"Will you not return to us?" she asked, looking towards Hilda, and evidently surprised at her silence.

Emmeran shook his head.

"I thought," she continued, "you would perhaps remain here, as hitherto, an invalid prisoner on parole."

"I am, in fact, no longer an invalid, Doris; and General Deroy did me the honour to say he required my services."

"That alters the case," she said, extending her hand.

"You'll think of me sometimes, Doris?"

"Very often, most probably."

"And regret my absence?"

"Undoubtedly."

"And wish for my return?"

"Most assuredly."

"I suppose I must be satisfied," he said, turning away.

"I think you ought," said Hilda, "for I do not know any one of whom she will so often think, or so much wish to see again, excepting, perhaps—Frank."

He had slowly progressed towards the door while she was speaking, stood outside until she ceased, and then closed it without attempting an answer.

The knowledge which Emmeran had acquired of the

country about Innsbruck during his three years' residence there proved of eminent service during the arrangements made for the retreat that had become absolutely necessary, and which General Deroy judiciously undertook during the darkness of night. Favoured by the noise of the rushing waters of the flooded river and the blasts of a strong wind, the movements of the troops were unobserved, and at daybreak the Tiroleans perceived with amazement, that excepting the pickets, who had shared their wine very freely with them during the night, not a Bavarian soldier was to be seen !

Some faint attempts at pursuit were made, some skirmishing attempted at the places which they passed, but the order of the retreating force was so complete, that little loss and no delay was caused ; and as the Tiroleans, like the French Vendéans, and the Scotch Highlanders in 1745, invariably supposed the contest ended when the invaders were chased from or voluntarily evacuated the country, they soon desisted, satisfied that Tirol was again Austrian, and Franz their Emperor.

The importance and advantages of the insurrection in Tirol for Austria now began to be felt and understood, and addresses from the Emperor and his brothers to the people were, in the form of letters, published in the Innsbruck papers. For this second emancipation of the country, as well as for the victory of Aspern, which soon became publicly known, a solemn *Te Deum* was celebrated in the Franciscan church, at which the civil governor, Baron Hormayer, the officers who had fought on Mount Isel, Hofer, Speckbacher, and the martial monk Haspinger, were present—also Doris and Hilda; and the latter made no attempt to conceal the curiosity and interest with which the peasant leaders inspired her. She had listened with eager attention to Frank's praises of Speckbacher's natural military genius, to his description of Peter Haspinger, ever to be seen where the contest was raging, his massive crucifix serving at one moment to console the dying, the next either as weapon or as *bâton* to lead the riflemen to a charge. For Hofer Frank felt a sort of personal regard, which Hilda began unconsciously to share, when chance, or perhaps some innocent manœuvring on the part of her relations, had brought her frequently into contact with him. His picturesque appearance undoubtedly had its weight with her as well as others, and she soon discovered that one of his greatest charms was his being such a perfect representative of a Tirolean peasant.

Andrew Hofer's immense popularity among his countrymen was partly owing to his retaining his peasant habits and manners even after he had been invested with the highest authority by his Emperor; the Tiroleans were jealous and watchful in this particular—preferred seeing him on foot, though he was a good rider, and looked well on horseback, and would have been much offended had he made any change in his dress. There is also no doubt that his being as uninstructed, simple-minded, and superstitiously religious as themselves, rather increased than lessened the respect shown him; he was one of themselves —their representative—the reflection of his glory fell full on them—and though there were few of the other and more talented leaders who were not conscious that they could take his place, not one of them ever succeeded in being even supposed his rival. Fortunate for Tirol that it was so, for never had insurrectionists a more humane leader—fortunate also for the invading armies that could feel certain the prisoners and wounded left in the country would be treated with consideration and kindness.

Meantime Frank had not forgotten his whim, as Hilda expected—on the contrary, the continuation of it seemed to have become a trial of power on his part, and his aunt having resolved never again to interfere, he was allowed to decline "keeping up appearances" without the slightest opposition. He came to them regularly every morning as visitor, but only accompanied them in their walks or drives when especially invited by Hilda. A stranger might have supposed him a timid lover waiting anxiously for encouragement that was ever given with provoking reserve; but Hilda interpreted otherwise his proud humility and ostentatious obedience—she detected many a glance of mirthful saucy triumph that was wholly unobserved by others, and which tempted her to punish him more frequently than was perhaps quite judicious, considering the short time they were to be together.

Frank had not the least idea that the course he was pursuing would prove less irritating to Hilda than to himself; and, had he not been her husband, the case might have been different; but, feeling certain of his affection, and unable to find the slightest cause for jealousy, she was perfectly satisfied, and amused herself by tempting him to forget his resolution whenever an opportunity offered.

"I have received a letter from Pallersberg," he said one morning soon after he had taken his accustomed place beside her.

She looked up anxiously. "I hope you will not have to leave us sooner than you expected, Frank?"

"I believe I must,—there is nothing more to be done here,—the French have had only too much time to recover their losses and receive reinforcements, and the Archduke thinks the sooner we are able to give them battle again the better."

"And is there no chance of peace?" she asked despondingly.

"That," he replied, "is a question which Napoleon

alone can answer. At present war is the order of the day, and I must join my regiment. Pallersberg tells me that poor Bereny has just died of his wounds, and there is a letter enclosed which I must either forward or deliver to Madame de Bereny in Meran."

"Forward it, Frank," said Hilda, with heightened colour; "no one can expect you to undertake the part of a near relation on such an occasion!"

"But her near relations are all in Hungary," he said, pleadingly, "and most of his also, and with those in Vienna no communication is now possible. It is very hard for a woman in her state of health to receive such intelligence unprepared."

"Very hard," said Hilda; "but I do not see why you should be the person chosen to inform, or rather to console her."

"Probably," suggested Frank, "because I am an intimate friend, and just now very near Meran."

"I think," she rejoined, "it would be quite sufficient even for an intimate friend in your place to write a few lines of condolence. Most communications of this kind are by letter."

"I will not quarrel with you again, Hilda, even for Madame de Bereny," said Frank, seating himself at her writing-table; "but when I see Pallersberg I shall not forget to tell him that should I lose my life in the next engagement a short communication by letter addressed to you will be all that is necessary, even should he or any other friend be within a day's journey of your place of residence."

He opened the paper-book while speaking, and saw the facsimile of his own last letter to Pallersberg on the blotting-paper before him.

"It is fortunate that you have preserved this memento of treachery," he said, turning towards her.

"Why so?" she asked quickly.

"Because I might have forgotten these words, which I can now make intelligible in a satisfactory manner. I had been requested while here to ascertain if the country were really so devoted to Austria as we had been led to suppose, and desired to give the information in the usual manner, that is to write of Tirol and the Emperor Franz as of lovers separated by force or adverse circumstances.* Tirol was the 'lost one,' that is the lost country, 'as passionately attached as ever.'"

"Can it indeed be so?" cried Hilda, coming towards him and fixing her eyes on the writing, though she knew every word of it well by heart.

"Does it require further explanation?" he asked, pointing to the words, 'the separation forgiven.' "You know the Tiroleans thought the Emperor ought never to have consented to that part of the treaty of Presburg."

"True, most true," said Hilda, confused.

"And," continued Frank. "the intense desire of Tirol for reunion with Austria was a fact beyond my most sanguine expectations."

"I see,—I understand it all now; but at least, Frank, you must allow that these words were quite as applicable just then to me, or——or——to that Madame de Bereny!"

"I don't know any such thing, Hilda," he replied, "for I certainly had had no reason to flatter myself that there was anything like an intense desire for reunion on your part,—rather very decidedly the contrary."

"Well, Frank, I should think you could hardly have expected it to be otherwise, all things considered?"

"I have no clear recollection what I expected until my aunt sent for me," he answered; "but I remember perfectly

* In this manner much useful information was communicated at that time.

my deep mortification at a reception for which I was so unprepared, and the vow with which I consoled myself when standing afterwards at that window."

"A vow?" repeated Hilda.

"A vow," he continued, "that the next proposal of union should come from you. I asked Doris to try and induce you to make a concession, but she declined further interference. I was, however, myself tolerably explicit after bringing you back to Innsbruck lately; but now you know without reserve the conditions on which we can live together and cease to be at odds."

"I thought this was a whim," said Hilda, in a low, constrained voice, "and am sorry to find you have been tempted by a very pardonable demonstration of womanly pride on my part to make a vow that places such an insuperable barrier between us! We must resign ourselves to live apart, Frank ; but——can we not cease to be 'at odds,' as you call it?"

"We can try," he said, starting up from the table, and beginning to walk up and down the room with long strides, while she reseated herself, and bent over her work in real or affected diligence.

"I suppose," she said, after a pause, and without looking up, "I suppose you will now consider yourself at liberty to go to Meran?"

"By no means," he answered, stopping before her; "I must keep my promise as well as my vow, and you have only given me permission to write to Madame de Bereny."

"Go to her if you prefer it, Frank," said Hilda, with forced composure; "I release you from your promise, and require henceforward no more deference from you than is due to me as your cousin."

"Why, Hilda, we shall then be more at odds than ever!"

" No," she answered ; " for I am as fully resolved as you can be not again to quarrel."

" We have but a short time to put our good resolutions into practice," he said, forcing a smile ; " for you know that a few days hence I must leave Innsbruck !"

" But we can meet again in Meran, Frank."

" I don't know whether or not it will be possible."

" You cannot, perhaps, ask for leave of absence ?"

" That depends upon circumstances over which I have no control."

" But you *will* return to us as soon as possible ?"

" I daresay I shall be fool enough to do so should an opportunity offer," was his somewhat irritated reply.

And Hilda, concealing her displeasure, observed blandly, " You will, Frank, for——Madame de Bereny will be in Meran !"

His eyes flashed, but he turned to the writing-table, saying, " Thank you for reminding me ; I had altogether forgotten her existence."

" Now, how can I believe that ?" thought Hilda, after watching him for some time seated at the table, his head resting on his clasped hands, and his quick breathing and flushed face betraying great internal emotion. " He feels his guilt, and finds it hard to write words of consolation to a woman who——"

Frank just then sat upright, drew a sheet of paper towards him, took up a pen, and began to write with a facility that might have overcome her jealous suspicions, had they not instantly turned into a new channel. " That was certainly not the first letter he had written to Madame de Bereny ! He was probably writing on other subjects— perhaps regretting that his jealous wife would not allow him to condole in person ?—perhaps even urging her to return to her relations, among whom he would soon have an opportunity of seeing her?"——

And still Frank wrote—wrote—wrote—and took another and another sheet of paper until Hilda's resentment turned into passionate anger, which was, however, not in the least perceptible, as she laid down her work, rose deliberately, and walked with dignified composure towards the door.

"Hilda," he said, snatching her hand as she passed him, "yield this time, and command me ever after."

"No, Frank; you cannot expect me to forget my sex, and ought to know that it is your part to propose, and mine to accept, or you may command—I believe you have a right to do so—and I must, of course, obey."

"I cannot propose, and will not command," said Frank, letting her hand fall, and taking up his pen again.

*　*　*　*　*　*　*　*　*
　*　*　*　*　*　*　*　*
*　*　*　*　*　*　*　*　*

"Did you not invite Frank to come here this evening, Hilda?" asked her mother some hours later.

"No, mamma, I never thought of it—I left him writing a long letter to Madame de Bereny."

"Which, I suppose, he expects you to send to the post," said her mother, pointing to the large sealed packet, lying on the writing-table.

"I don't—know,"—answered Hilda, taking it up reluctantly, but a moment afterwards starting and becoming very pale when she perceived that it was addressed to herself.

She turned from her mother and sister when she broke the seal, but had scarcely read more than a few line before she exclaimed, in a voice of anguish, "He is gone! gone without taking leave of us, and we may never see him again ! "

" You must have offended him deeply," said her mother, reproachfully ; " nothing else would have induced him to leave us in this manner."

Hilda walked quickly out of the room without attempting an answer.

Her mother turned to Doris. "What do you say now ? " she asked ; " is this also a mere lovers' quarrel ? "

" We must hope so," answered Doris, " though it is certainly a very ill-timed one."

" Ill-timed, indeed," repeated her mother ; " for, as Hilda herself says, we may never see him again ; he has left us to join an army on the eve of battle, and who can tell what may be the result of the next engagement for him ? "

" That thought may induce her to answer his letter in a conciliatory manner," suggested Doris, with tears in her eyes ; " and, should he be spared to us—a few months' correspondence will be a good preparation for their next meeting."

CHAPTER XXXVII.

FOR BETTER FOR WORSE.

" This state of suspense is dreadful," cried Hilda, a few weeks later, as she walked up and down the room, holding a torn and soiled newspaper in her hand ; " I believe—that is, I—I fear the French have gained a victory."

" Of that, unfortunately, there can be no doubt," said her mother ; " for without good information that salvo of artillery would not have been fired from the fortress of Kuffstein; but I cannot yet believe in the truce, of which people are talking so much."

"Why not?" asked Hilda; "here you can read it printed in the supplement to the Munich newspaper."

"We know it is printed," said Doris; "but the manner in which the half-dozen copies of that supplement have reached Innsbruck is not calculated to make us suppose it official."

"Now, my dear Doris," interposed Hilda, "we know from experience that if an officer with a trumpeter had been sent among your patriots, they would either have made him a target for their rifles, or, at best, taken him prisoner. You cannot deny their want of chivalry on such occasions."

"I do not deny their ignorance of military etiquette, Hilda; but you cannot expect me or my patriots to give much credence to information brought to us by a man in his shirt-sleeves, mounted on an old white horse, flourishing above his head a few copies of a newspaper, and shouting, "A truce, a truce—don't fire at me—I'm only the baker from Kochel!"*

"Well, I believe in this truce," said Hilda; "and I hope it will soon be succeeded by a peace. What would I not give for a few lines from Frank, to assure me of his safety."

"As he has promised to write to you," said Doris, "you may depend upon it he will do so as soon as he can."

She was right. The next day Hilda held a letter from Frank in her hand—a few, a very few, hurried lines, merely

---

* In this very undignified manner — perhaps for the reasons mentioned—the intelligence of the truce of Znaim was first conveyed to the Tiroleans.

intended, as he said, to let her know that he was alive. Pallersberg had promised to write more at length, and he also would do so as soon as possible.

Pallersberg's letter contained a concise account of the battle of Wagram, ending with the words, "We lost no cannon, and the enemy took no prisoners, so that but for the retrograde movement of our troops, it would have been impossible to have decided which had gained the advantage. It is said that Napoleon is much chagrined at the indecisive result, and the death of some of his best officers. Our losses are great. The Archduke Charles, and almost all our generals, are wounded, and some of my best friends are at this moment under the hands of the surgeons."

"He does not say a word about Frank," cried Hilda, impatiently.

"Why should he, when Frank himself has written?" asked her mother.

"But what a letter?" rejoined Hilda. "He generally writes so well, and this is scarcely legible. I never received such an unsatisfactory letter in all my life."

"I think it is very satisfactory to hear that he is alive and well," said her mother; "and I do not know what you could expect or desire more under the present circumstances."

"Just such a letter as you have received from Major Pallersberg," answered Hilda, "with perhaps the addition of some words about the truce, and some wishes for a peace!"

"I doubt his having heard anything about a truce when that was written," observed her mother.

"And I," said Doris, "am quite sure that Frank could not have written otherwise than hastily, and, perhaps, illegibly, if his best friends were under the hands of surgeons."

"You may be right, Doris," said Hilda; "for he spoke very feelingly of those he lost at Aspern, and, as my mother says, I ought to be satisfied that he is alive and well."

For several days there was much uncertainty concerning the truce, but at length General Buol, who commanded the Austrian troops in Tirol, having received despatches from the Archduke John, issued a proclamation announcing the conclusion of an armistice at Znaim, one of the stipulations of which was an immediate evacuation of Tirol on the part of the Austrian troops. He recommended the people to lay down their arms, and submit to what was inevitable with patience, resignation, and fortitude; finding them, however, determined not to follow his advice, and pertinaciously incredulous respecting the truce, he retired from Innsbruck, with the troops and cannon under his command, and, taking the route over the Brenner, with great reluctance left Tirol to its fate. A large army under Lefebvre soon after entered the country. Innsbruck, destitute of defenders, was compelled to submit; and, when upwards of 26,000 men marched into the town, the peacefully-disposed citizens began to hope that the war in Tirol was terminated.

"It is very provoking," observed Hilda, "that Madame d'Epplen, though restored to liberty, cannot leave Innsbruck: the state of the country is such that any attempt of the kind would probably end in another compulsory mountain excursion, so she has at last resigned herself to remain here, and return to her old lodging, where she now intends patiently to await the arrival of her husband."

"She may have to wait long," said Doris.

"Not if the present truce lead to a peace," observed Hilda; "for, notwithstanding all the reports in circulation of the proceedings of the peasants, and their wild mode of warfare in the defiles of the mountains, she cannot believe that they have any chance against Lefebvre and an army such as he has now under his command."

"And what is your opinion?" asked Doris, with some hesitation.

"I feel myself growing superstitious," answered Hilda, gravely, "and begin to believe in the prophecy that the Tiroleans are always to be successful on Mount Isel. If Lefebvre were a Bavarian, I should send to warn him; but as I hear he was, or rather pretended to be, surprised that General Deroy could not subdue the country with an army of six thousand men, I should have no very great objection to his finding out that *he* could not do so with one of six-and-twenty thousand."

"I believe he is beginning to have some fears on that subject himself," said Doris; "at least he was, by all accounts, signally defeated yesterday."

"Where? when?" cried Hilda, eagerly; "but, perhaps, you have only had your information from our rebel landlord, Mr. Hartmann?"

"Not the less true on that account," answered Doris; "and as to your Duke of Danzig——"

"He is Napoleon's duke, and not mine," interposed Hilda, in playful deprecation; "and I only feared a little, just a very little—exaggeration on the part of our furiously patriotic landlord: he looked intolerably triumphant when speaking to you just now in the corridor, and that was the reason I did not stop to hear what he was relating to you and mamma."

"There is no exaggeration necessary on this occasion," said Doris, with heightened colour; "Marshal Lefebvre, who left Innsbruck with the intention of forcing his way over the Brenner into Southern Tirol, has not only been altogether unsuccessful, but has returned to Innsbruck in as disastrous a manner as can well be imagined. His column, while winding in straggling files on the mountain road, was attacked in all directions by the armed asantry, and, after an obstinate conflict, the whole army, twenty thousand strong, were routed and driven back with immense loss. The disorder was so great that the Marshal himself escaped in the disguise of a common trooper."

"This is intelligence, indeed," said Hilda, "and what may we expect now?"

"Another battle on Mount Isel," answered Doris, "where the peasantry are already in great force, with all their best leaders."

Her words were prophetic, for the Tiroleans, animated by their success, no longer stood on the defensive, but, flocking from all quarters to the standard of Hofer, assembled in multitudes on Mount Isel, the scene of their former triumphs, and destined to be immortalized by a still more extraordinary victory. Lefebvre had collected his whole force, with thirty pieces of cannon, on the small plain which lies between Innsbruck and the foot of the mountains on the southern side of the river Inn. The Tirolean army consisted of about 18,000 men, and some Austrian soldiers who had remained in the country to share the fate of the inhabitants. Speckbacher commanded the right wing, the Capuchin monk, Haspinger, the left, and Hofer the centre. At four o'clock in the morning the energetic monk roused Hofer, and, having first united with him in fervent prayer, hurried out to communicate his orders to the outposts. The battle commenced soon afterwards, and continued without intermission until late in the evening, the troops under Lefebvre's command constantly endeavouring to drive the Tiroleans from their position on Mount Isel, and they in their turn to force the enemy back into the town. For a long time the contest was undecided, the superior discipline and admirable artillery of the enemy prevailing over the impetuous but disorderly assaults of the mountaineers; but, towards nightfall, the bridge of the Sill was carried after a dreadful struggle; the enemy gave way on all sides, and were compelled to retreat into the town with great loss.

This victory was immediately followed by the liberation of the whole Tirol. Lefebvre fell back across the Inn on the day after the battle, and evacuating Innsbruck, retreated rapidly to Salzburg. Of this event he wrote to Napoleon that it was—

"*Non une defaite, mais un movement retrograde. Oui, Sire, c'est une de ces retraites dont l'histoire parle tant, que vient de faire votre armée!*"

While Lefebvre was making this retrograde movement, which even the officers under his command scarcely hesitated to call a flight, Hofer triumphantly entered Innsbruck. He sat with Haspinger in an open carriage, drawn by Madame d'Epplen's well-known greys, and was surrounded and followed by an immense crowd of peasants, whose shouts were accompanied by the incessant pealing of the adjacent church bells. His presence in the town had become necessary, in order to check the disorders consequent on the irruption of so large a body of tumultuous victorious peasants into a town containing numerous rich citizens, whose patriotism was considered more than doubtful. He dined at the house of a friend, and while at table received a deputation from the town requesting protection of person and property. The streets had become filled with the peasant influence; an endless procession, preceded by a man carrying a large crucifix, forced its way forward, and with the feeling of importance and freedom from the thraldom of law, civil or military, came the resolution to seize and appropriate whatever they required. It was known that the arms which had been taken from the different parishes by Lefebvre had been stored in the Imperial Palace, and to this arsenal the crowd at once turned. The Castellan would not deliver up what had been intrusted to his care, and sent immediately to Hofer, who, at last out of all patience, started up, rushed to a window, and, throwing it wide open, shouted to the crowd below—

" What are you here for ? To rob and plague people ? You ought to be ashamed of yourselves ! Why don't you go after the enemy ? They are not too far off ! Go after them to the Lowlands—go, I say, for I won't have you here ! And if you don't do as I bid you—I won't be your leader any longer ! "

This speech, to the surprise of many anxious hearers, gave great satisfaction ; and the threat at the end produced instant obedience. The crowd dispersed : some, as he had ordered, went in pursuit of Lefebvre ; others returned to their homes. The commencement of this speech was prompted by the impulse of the moment ; the last words proved how perfectly he understood that his power depended altogether on the free will of his countrymen, and that by not arrogating more than they chose to give him, and making a favour of being their leader, he could prevent the outbreak of those scenes of riotous anarchy that usually accompany insurrections ; and, in fact, he managed by these means to give to the revolt of his countrymen that stamp of heroism which has made it one of the most interesting episodes of modern history. The entire command of the country was now assumed by Hofer ; proclamations were issued and coins struck in his name as Commander-in-Chief of the Tirol ; and the whole civil and military power was placed in his hands.

"Well, Doris," said Hilda, "you were very much shocked at Lefebvre's taking old Count Sarntheim and the Baroness Sternbach with him as hostages—what do you say to Hofer detaining Madame d'Epplen and Baron Voelderndorf as reprisal?"

"I heard," answered Doris, "that it was a party of peasants who took them prisoners on the Volders-road, and Hofer could not well refuse to detain them when they were brought to him. I am sure he treats them as well as possible, and I daresay will allow us to visit them if we ask his permission. Shall we try?"

"By all means," said Hilda; "but before we go into the streets we must cut off or otherwise dispose of our hair, for a proclamation of his this morning has forbidden the women here to wear curls, low dresses, and short sleeves!"

"Well," said Doris, "can we not make plats of our curls, and hide them under our hats?"

"But is it not absurd his issuing sumptuary laws?" asked Hilda.

"I don't know that," answered Doris; "for the new French fashions are enough to provoke any one in authority to forbid them."

"I confess," said Hilda, "that I like everything that is fashionable, and should persist in wearing my curls and short sleeves and low dresses whenever and wherever I pleased, if it were not for the warning at the end of the proclamation."

"What warning?"

"That the offending curls may with impunity be cut off by any peasant who chooses to prove his patriotism at my expense!"

"I wonder who put this into Hofer's head," said Doris.

"I can quite imagine the idea original," observed Hilda, laughing; "for, besides the real cares and labours of elevated situation, he contrives to give himself incessant occupation by attempting to arrange private quarrels of all kinds, but especially those between husbands and wives." *

"Then let us go to him directly," said Doris, smiling archly. "Who knows but he may be of use to us in more ways than one?"

"I have no intention of making him umpire between me and Frank, if that be what you mean," said Hilda, rising; "my reverence for Hofer has not reached that height yet; but I should like to obtain permission to see Madame d'Epplen, and find out if we can be of any use to her."

They continued so eagerly occupied in discussing these subjects, that until their progress in the streets was actually impeded, they scarcely perceived them to be unusually crowded; but a sudden rush of passengers at length induced them to send their servant to inquire the meaning of a noisy procession that began to issue from the neighbouring street.

"Some prisoners, ma'am: taken, they say, by Speckbacher at Unken."

"How can we best avoid the crowd?" asked Doris, looking round.

"By going on to the palace as fast as we can," answered Hilda, hurrying forward.

At the entrance to the building two stalwart men from Hofer's own valley were posted; the noise in the street seemed to have in some degree attracted their attention, for, though they still continued to lean indolently on their rifles, their eyes were fixed keenly on the moving multitude in the distance.

Doris and Hilda entered, mounted the broad staircase, and wandered about for some time, the servant knocking

* This remark has been made by every historian of those times.

at, and trying to open, the doors of the state apartments, which, however, were all locked, and apparently uninhabited.

"You had better," said Hilda, "go downstairs again and make inquiries ; or, if possible, find some one who will take us to Andrew Hofer."

The servant left them; and when she and Doris prolonged their walk into an adjacent corridor they saw at the end of it a couple of men, in size and costume precisely resembling the sentinels at the palace gate. These, however were seated on wooden benches, had small pipes in their mouths, and beside them stood a little girl, who, in a clear, expressive voice was reading a legend of some saint, to which they were listening with profound attention : this child was Babette d'Epplen,* who, on hearing the footsteps of Doris and Hilda, looked up, and with an exclamation of delight sprang towards them.

Admittance to Madame d'Epplen was demanded, but of course refused, and little Babette, standing on tiptoe and putting her mouth to the keyhole of the door, called out—"Mamma, Doris and Hilda are here, and want to see you, and Leppel says he dare not let any one into your room without an order, because you are a prisoner; and I want you to allow me to go away from the corridor that I may show them Andrew Hofer's room. They think he will tell Leppel and Peter to open your door whenever they come here ! "

"You may go," said her mother, "but don't forget to tell Katty."

Katty, the person who attended the prisoner's rooms, was in a not very distant room, the door of which was ajar, and she now looked out and nodded her head to signify that she required no further explanation ; where-

* Fact.

upon Babette jumped and danced along before them, showing herself already acquainted with every turning in the palace, until a couple of sitting sentinels again indicated the door of an apartment containing inmates of more importance than the others.

Fortunately at this moment a man came towards them carrying a tray on which were dishes of steaming pork and saur-kraut, and he immediately undertook to announce them, though he explained that the "commander-in-chief" did not at all like being disturbed at dinner time.

"Then say nothing about us at present," suggested Doris; "we can wait without inconvenience."

The man entered the room, but before he had time to close the door she saw Hofer and his friends seated at table with their coats off. The apartment was of the simplest description, very plainly furnished, and a strong odour of bad tobacco was wafted into the passage, already redolent of saur-kraut. Doris turned away her head in a manner that made Hilda laugh and whisper, "You must not object to a little patriotic perfume, Doris, or I shall begin to think that Andrew Hofer would suit me for a hero better than you. I like him for not requiring finer tobacco or ordering a better dinner than he could have at home, and he certainly looked as picturesque as jovial just now with that tumbler of wine in his hand!"

Before Doris could answer a number of peasants turned into the corridor, trampling along it in their clouted shoes and talking loudly and eagerly. They advanced to the door of Hofer's room and attempted to force an entrance, but the sentinels opposed their passage, pushing them back with very little ceremony while informing them that the commander-in-chief was at dinner.

"We want to see Andrew Hofer," cried one.

"We must see Andrew Hofer," shouted another.

"We have a right to see Andrew Hofer," vociferated several at once, and almost at the same moment the door opened and Hofer stood before them.

He was still without his coat, but his red waistcoat and broad leather girdle, ornamented with the embroidered initials of his name, made the incompleteness of his dress scarcely perceptible, the more so as, according to his custom, he had placed his broad-brimmed black-plumed hat on his head.

"Father," cried one of the peasants, well knowing it was the manner in which he best liked to be addressed—"Father, the prisoners taken by Speckbacher at Unken are in the court ; what are we to do with them ? "

"Treat them humanely," he answered, "and in a Christianlike manner, but don't let them make their escape."

"Some officers are among them," continued the man.

"So much the better," he answered ; "perhaps we can exchange them for Count Sarntheim and the Baroness Sternbach."

"But, Father, one of these officers was at Schwaz, and helped to burn and plunder the town ; we expect you to make an example of him and order him to be shot without delay."

The whole expression of Hofer's countenance changed in a moment—it was as sombre as it had previously been cheerful—and he strode forward towards the staircase without speaking.

The peasants followed, loudly reiterating their accusations against the unfortunate prisoner until they were out of sight and hearing.

"Let us go home," said Hilda, answering her sister's look of dismay with a shudder ; "Heaven knows what we may see or hear if we remain longer in this place ! "

" Don't you think we ought to take Babette back to her mother ? " suggested Doris, turning to the child, who had no sooner heard of prisoners in the court than she had vaulted on one of the corridor window frames, leaving her thin legs and small feet dangling downwards, while she pressed her face against a pane of glass and gazed eagerly into the space beneath. " Come, Babette—come——"

" Oh, Doris," she answered without moving from her place of observation, " there's Count Emmeran among the prisoners, and the peasants are dragging him forward, and have torn all his uniform ! "

In a moment Doris and Hilda were beside her, but only for a moment; the next they were rushing down the stairs and into the court, where, forcing their way through the crowd, they reached Hofer's side just as Emmeran, with wonderful self-possession, was giving the assurance that he had never commanded or aided in any act of incendiarism, and had not been in Schwaz at the time of the conflagration.

" He was in Innsbruck, and with us," cried Doris vehemently, " in our house, wounded, and unable to leave his bed. Numbers of people can bear witness for him ! "

" Who ? " asked Hofer, looking round—" who said they saw him in Schwaz ? "

" I saw him."

" And I."

" And I ! " cried some men who had been rather ostentatiously loading their rifles, as if to encourage Hofer's wavering severity, " I remarked his light hair and gaunt figure well, and resolved to have my revenge when I met him at Unken ; and I would have had it after it was all up with his regiment, if he had not sprung into the river and been taken prisoner by our captain himself ! "

" Is this true ? " asked Hofer, turning to Emmeran.

"Yes," he answered; "I was overpowered and taken prisoner when swimming in the Saalach, but these men mistake me for some one else, for I was here in Innsbruck when they supposed they saw me in Schwaz."

"This is true—quite true," said Doris, pushing aside the men who were holding him. "Surely," she added, appealing to Hofer, "surely you will not allow him to lose his life for the fault of another person? Oh, for Heaven's sake, take him out of the hands of these vindictive men."

"If," said Hofer, looking round appealingly, "if it can be proved that this officer was not at Schwaz, he has a right to be treated as humanely as the other prisoners. You say," he added, turning to Doris and Hilda, "you say he was at that time in your house?"

"Yes," cried Doris eagerly; "at that time and long after. He was wounded at the hospital gate in April, and our landlord and many others can prove that he was unable to leave his room for several weeks afterwards."

"Is he your brother?" asked Hofer.

"N—o."

"Or your cousin?"

"Not—exactly," answered Doris, embarrassed.

"That's the truth, at all events!" cried a man forcing his way through the crowd. "The brother or cousin was shot in April, and lies buried in our churchyard! This is quite another sort of relationship. The man's her sweetheart, and she wants to save his life by palming him off on us as the other one!"

After this explanation, the peasants again closed round Emmeran with threatening gestures, while Hilda and Doris vainly endeavoured to make them understand that one brother was killed and the other wounded. Hofer pushed aside the men who had placed themselves before him, and coming close to Doris, as she stood pale with terror and unconsciously grasping Emmeran's arm, he asked with unmistakable sympathy, "Is he indeed your sweetheart ? "

"Yes—oh, yes ! " she answered, scarcely conscious of the meaning of her words until she felt her hand strongly clasped in Emmeran's.

"Betrothed with your mother's consent ? " continued Hofer, with increasing interest.

"Yes—yes—betrothed—anything—if you will only save him from these men ! "

"Stand back ! " cried Hofer authoritatively. " There may be some mistake here, and I won't have any one shot without better proof of his guilt. Stand back, I say, and be satisfied that one of the darkest cellars in the palace will be his prison until we know all about him and his doings."

Then, without waiting for a demonstration of approval or the contrary, he gave the necessary directions to his aide-de-camp, and turned to the other prisoners. Emmeran was conducted and followed out of the court by several angry-looking but quite as many good-humoured peasants, the latter rather loudly whispering that they liked a wedding better than a funeral, and wished that Hofer would send for Peter Haspinger and let the marriage come off at once.

Still accompanied by Doris and Hilda, Emmeran descended to the vaults beneath the palace, silent until the castellan, who officiated as jailer, stopped before the oaken door of one of them. Then Emmeran bent down and whispered, " Doris, dearest, what am I to say when questioned by Hofer concerning our betrothal ? "

"Whatever you please," she answered, blushing deeply, " I cannot contradict you, for I was so terrified that I scarcely remember what I said."

" May *I* remember ? " asked Emmeran.

At that moment the door grated on its hinges, and discovered a long, damp, and perfectly dark cellar.

The faces of the angry peasants assumed an expression of satisfaction at the dreary prospect; the others as evidently exhibited their disappointment at finding the vault filled with lumber instead of the choice wine they fully expected to find there.

As the castellan politely made way for Emmeran to enter, the latter once more turned to Doris and whispered eagerly, " Give me the assurance that we are indeed betrothed, and I shall feel happier in this gloomy cellar than I have ever felt in all my life ! "

Doris unhesitatingly placed her hand in his, but turned away her head, fearing the numerous witnesses might discover that more was meant than simple leave-taking.

A moment afterwards the door of the vault was closed and doubly locked upon Emmeran, and the peasants began to ascend the stone staircase with the castellan.

" Let us follow them," said Hilda, touching her arm, " or we may chance to be imprisoned in these cold passages. Adieu, Emmeran ! " she added, in a louder tone ; " we are going back to Hofer, and hope to procure you at least a pleasanter prison."

" Thank you," he answered cheerfully; " but you need not be uneasy about me, for I am perfectly comfortable— or, rather, supremely happy just now ! "

Hofer was not in his room, but some friends of his who were there informed Doris and Hilda that he had gone to Madame d'Epplen's about an exchange of prisoners. They followed him, and had no longer any difficulty in obtaining permission to enter when it was understood they wanted to speak to him on important business.

Hofer was standing in the middle of the room, with his

26

thumbs stuck into his braces, and as perfectly at his ease as could well be imagined. Madame d'Epplen and Baron Voelderndorf, who were opposite him, were less so; for Hofer had just consented to allow the latter to go to Munich in order to effect the exchange of Madame d'Epplen and himself for the Baroness Sternbach and Count Sarntheim,* and they were thanking him for an act of courtesy and generous confidence of which they had scarcely expected to find him capable.

There is no better test of character than sudden elevation to power, and few have borne it better than Andrew Hofer. Some months previously Hilda had rather condescendingly declared her intention of making, during the autumn, an excursion from Meran to his valley—she had even proposed spending a night at his inn on the Sands, though she had heard it was but an insignificant place— and now, the life of one of her nearest relations had but half an hour previously depended on a glance or word from him, and she at that moment stood anxiously awaiting his leisure and hoping to find him favourably disposed, when she should request the removal of Emmeran to a more eligible prison.

Hofer, however, was quite unchanged by his unlimited power and great popularity ; with the same good-humoured smile and unceremonious manner that he would have received her at the door of his inn, he nodded his head, and said jocosely, "I suppose you want a better lodging for your sister's sweetheart ? Now, here's Baron Voelderndorf going to leave Innsbruck just in time to make room for him, and I know he will be as safe in one of these rooms as in a cellar, and far more snug !"

"But you," said Doris, "you, I hope, believe that he was not at Schwaz ?"

* Fact.

"Yes; Madame d'Epplen has told me all about him; but I can't consent to his leaving the cellar until nightfall—so don't ask it. Keeping him out of sight is keeping him out of danger, you know, and therefore he must promise not to look out of the window for two days at least! And you," he continued, turning to Baron Voelderndorf, "you pledge your word of honour to return here if you are not exchanged for Count Sarntheim?"

"I do."

"Well, then," said Hofer, "you shall have a passport, and may leave Innsbruck as soon as you please. I wish you all good evening," he added, stretching his hand towards his hat, which, in deference to Madame d'Epplen, he had placed on the table; and as he left the room they saw that he made a sign to the sentinels to remain seated, then placed his hand on little Babette's head, and stooped down to look into the book out of which she was reading the conclusion of the legend that had been interrupted by Doris and Hilda a couple of hours previously.

CHAPTER XXXVIII.

HEART AND HEAD NO LONGER AT VARIANCE.

EMMERAN's detention in the palace made Doris and Hilda unwilling to leave Innsbruck, and induced them to defer their journey to Meran from day to day and week to week. In the meantime, Baron Voelderndorf, unable to effect the proposed change, returned to his prison,* and not only

---

* Fact. Some years later he wrote an account of the war in Tirol.

confirmed the intelligence of the truce of Znaim, but informed Hofer that peace would certainly be concluded in the course of a few weeks, and that there was no chance whatever that Napoleon would allow Austria to retain Tirol.

"It's not true—I won't believe it!" had been Hofer's irritated answer; but the impression made was deep, and he was on the point of recalling his commanders from their posts and dismissing the peasants to their homes, when, unfortunately, all his plans were changed by the arrival of three leaders of the insurrection, who some time previously had abandoned his cause as hopeless, and left Tirol with the Austrian troops. These men had returned to Innsbruck by a very circuitous route, in order to avoid the French army; they had been long on the way, would not believe in a peace disadvantageous to Tirol, and were the bearers of three thousand ducats and a gold chain and medal sent by the Emperor Franz to Hofer, who thus at once, finding all that he had done legalized, and all that he might do authorized, no longer hesitated to continue the defence of the country.

With this chain and medal Hofer was formally invested by the Abbot of Wiltau, in the Franciscan church. High mass was celebrated, a *Te Deum* sung, and then, in the presence of an immense crowd, scarcely able to restrain their tearful enthusiasm and joyful acclamations, the prelate having blessed the chain, which was brought to him on a silver salver, Hofer advanced and received, kneeling, this much-prized token of his Emperor's favour. It was Tirol's last festival for many a day, and the climax of Hofer's glory.

The short speech which he made at the banquet that succeeded the church ceremonies has been considered sufficiently characteristic to become historical.

" Gentlemen," he said, "I thank you for having by your presence increased the honour done me. News I have none, though I have three couriers on the road— Johnny Watcher, Joey Sixten, and Franzl Memmel—they might have been here long ago; but I expect the vagabonds every minute!"

About the time that Hofer so spoke, Hilda sat in Madame d'Epplen's room, and had just concluded an account of all she had witnessed during the morning.

" Well, my dear," observed Madame d'Epplen, with a smile, " all I can say is, that you are now as great a rebel as your sister—downrightly Austrian! I always, however, thought it would be some one else, and not Hofer, who would change your political opinions."

" But are they changed," asked Hilda, "if I only say that I admire the man beyond measure? He is a hero, and perfectly sublime in his simplicity."

" At least," persisted Madame d'Epplen, "it is something like a change to say more than ever Doris said."

" Not more than I have thought," interposed Doris, "though perhaps my admiration is less personal than Hilda's. I think the whole insurrection sublime, and every Tiroler who has taken up arms a hero! Never was a revolt more purely loyal, and no one has a right to brand with the name of rebellion this effort of the Tiroleans to restore their lost province to its true owner, and insure a return to the paternal sway of their much-loved Emperor."

" In point of fact, Doris, you are right," said Hilda; " they are not rebels in the common sense of the word."

" Not in any sense of it," rejoined Doris.

Madame d'Epplen raised her hands and waved them, to signify that further discussion was unnecessary.

" It is all to no purpose," she said; "their Emperor cannot resist France backed by all Europe."

" Excuse me," said Doris, " but England, at least, is Austria's ally."

" Yes, my dear; and if ships could be sent to Vienna, it might be to some purpose just now; otherwise, a peace is certain—perhaps actually concluded by this time."

" Are you sure ?—have you heard ——? " began Doris.

" I have received a letter from Epplen, written immediately after he had had an interview with one of your peasant-heroes, Speckbacher, and tried to persuade him to induce his countrymen to lay down their arms and return to their homes, now that the war is in fact ended, and a powerful army on the march into Tirol. Epplen's letter to me was sent open under cover to Hofer,* perhaps in the hope that the arguments used in vain to Speckbacher might make some impression on him; but the untoward arrival of these men with the chain and medal has made him and his followers deaf to reason."

" Did you allow Emmeran to read Colonel d'Epplen's letter ?" asked Doris.

" Yes, and he has now so little doubt of peace and our speedy release, that he intends to urge you and your mother to go to Meran without further delay.

Hilda knocked with her parasol on the wall of the room, then opened the window and leaned out with Doris, just in time to encounter Emmeran's head protruded in the same manner from the adjacent room. A long conversation ensued, in which he strongly pointed out the advantages of a removal to Meran, and the necessity of change of air and tranquillity for his aunt.

" And you ?" asked Doris — " what is to become of you ?"

" I shall undoubtedly obtain my liberty with the other prisoners," he answered; " and a peace is so certain, Doris,

* Fact.

that I can almost promise you shall never again see me in the uniform which you once very justly observed I did not know how to wear."

"I have rather changed my mind on that subject," said Doris.

"Nevertheless," he rejoined, "I hope you still prefer seeing me in the morning or evening coat, or even the shooting-jacket, which I am likely to wear in future."

"Wear any coat you please," said Doris, smiling; "but pray forget my foolish speech about the uniform."

Her mother, who had been reading Colonel d'Epplen's letter, now joined them, and was soon persuaded by Emme-ran to decide on a removal to Meran, while the journey could be made without impediment.

"It is very unselfish of him to advise you to leave Innsbruck," observed Madame d'Epplen; "for, to judge by myself, I can imagine how much he will miss your daily visits."

"Perhaps," said Hilda, "you will follow us to Meran, as he intends to do?"

"Rather let me hope," she replied, laughingly, "that you will before long follow me to Bavaria, instead of making pilgrimages to Hofer's Valley, and visiting your hero of 'The Sands,' as I am quite sure you propose doing when at Meran."

"And why should she not?" asked Doris. "The 'Sands' will very probably become a place of pilgrimage for others as well as Hilda. But if indeed a peace be so certain as Colonel d'Epplen seems to think, I wish Hofer could be persuaded to go home at once, and not expose himself and his countrymen to unnecessary danger."

"I wish he would," said Madame d'Epplen; "but who could expect him to listen to such a proposal now?"

"No one, I suppose," answered Doris, with a sigh,

"but still you may as well send him Colonel d'Epplen's letter."

"Take it to him yourself," said Madame d'Epplen, placing the letter in her hand; "you never tried your power of persuasion in a better cause."

It was late in the afternoon when they left the palace, and, on passing the house of a friend in the neighbourhood, they were induced to accept an invitation to supper, given from an open window, and urged by youthful emissaries sent to conduct them upstairs. This caused such a delay in their return home, that when they again entered the streets they found the lamps lighted, and soon after perceived Andrew Hofer standing beneath one of them, as it hung suspended on a chain between the houses. He was endeavouring by the dim red light to read a letter, while a friend who stood near loudly and eagerly expostulated with him for having left the theatre during a performance intended to do him honour.

"Now, Doris," whispered Hilda, as she walked on with her mother, "don't lose this opportunity of giving him Colonel d'Epplen's letter."

And Doris, pushing aside her veil that he might recognize her, walked into the middle of the street just in time to hear him say, "How can I enjoy these honours when I know our cause is not prospering in other parts of the country!"*

Doris hesitated; Hofer, however, had already observed the letter, and extended his hand to take it.

"From Colonel d'Epplen," she began, but, perceiving traces of agitation in his face and tears in his eyes, instead of attempting an explanation, she turned away and hurried after her mother and sister.

---

* Hofer's words, when standing that evening beneath a lamp in one of the streets of Innsbruck.

" A short conference !" observed Hilda; "may I hope it has been to some purpose, and that I shall see my bearded hero at the Sands before long ?"

" Perhaps so," answered Doris gravely; "he has evidently just received some depressing intelligence, and therefore the letter may have some influence on his decision. I am now myself quite disheartened, and begin to fear that this insurrection, with all its enthusiasm, loyalty, and patriotism, will only have the deplorable result of bringing those concerned in it into deep affliction, if not actual ruin."

" No," said Hilda; " if they disperse and deliver up their arms, they have nothing to fear. For the leaders, indeed, there may be personal danger, and as far as Hofer is concerned, I can more than share your anxiety, because my interest is more concentrated in him than yours has ever been."

" My interest is alike for all," answered Doris; "and as it is evident they must yield in the end, we can only hope they will do so when convinced that peace is inevitable. I would rather this insurrection ended voluntarily than see it subdued by force of arms; and even you, Hilda, must desire this, if only for Hofer's sake !"

" Of course I do," said Hilda; " and if it be any consolation to you, Doris, I will also confess that I now agree with you not only about Tirol, but also in deeply regretting that this war has ended fatally for Austria. Never again will I quarrel with you or Frank about Napoleon; he had no right to bestow Spain on his brother, or Naples on his brother-in-law; and I wish to Heaven he had never burthened Bavaria with Tirol, and made us, as Emmeran says, his gamekeepers to Italy ! If such thoughts and words be rebellion, Doris, Madame d'Epplen was right when she called me as great a rebel as you are ! "

CHAPTER XXXIX.

MERAN, once the chief city and residence of the Counts of Tirol, was in the year 1809 what it is now, a small town which, though containing a considerable number of houses, had but one long regular street. This street, however, has at each side open arcades, that afford acceptable shelter in winter, agreeable shade in summer, and at all seasons an amusing if not useful walk, as it is there that the principal shops are clustered, which serve as attraction alike to loungers and purchasers. The church is large, the steeple the highest in Tirol, and, as Dr. Ludwig Steub observes, in his equally instructive and entertaining work, " Three Summers in Tirol," " In this steeple there are seven well-tuned melodious bells, rung in loud-sounding chords by sextons who are, in this respect, probably the most hard working in the world. Nowhere in Germany can we hear such artistical chimes as in Meran, when on holidays they ring the changes with pauses that strain the attention, solemn solos, gay duets, astounding unisons, and so forth. The towns most proud of their chimes in England can find a rival here; and the ' Steeple and Bell-ringing Society of Meran ' may, without hesitation, challenge the ' Lancashire Bell-ringing Club.' "

The town has a much frequented public walk, on a quay built to prevent the inundations of the river Passer, and the view from it is as charming a mixture of German and Italian scenery as can well be imagined: high mountains and vineyard-covered hills, old castles and picturesque cottages, ruined towers, and villas of southern architecture. But it is to the village of Obermais, situated on the Naif mountain, immediately beyond and above the town, that I would direct the reader's attention, for it is there that Doris, Hilda, and their mother had, with some difficulty, procured lodgings for the autumn. Not that Meran at that time was, as now, a fashionable refuge for invalids— the grape cure was then unknown—but the war had filled every tranquil place with wounded soldiers, and both the houses in the town and the old castles of Obermais were filled with them in different stages of convalescence. For this reason the Waldering family were obliged to be satisfied with a very limited number of rooms in a house belonging to the Saint George miller, close to his mill and to the church that gave it its name.

Before long they began to discover that the view from the windows was quite as beautiful as it had been in their former lodgings ; they were also within walking distance of all their favourite haunts, and had there not been so many invalid officers, not only at the mill but even in the upper rooms of the house they inhabited, they would have been perfectly satisfied. "Not," as Hilda observed, "not that these officers are at all in our way, poor men! but one cannot well use either pianoforte or harp as long as they remain here, and I never felt so musical in all my life."

"You would like to sing some of Frank's favourite songs ? " suggested her mother.

"Yes," said Hilda: "ever since I received his letter yesterday I have been longing to tune the harp and realize the picture he drew of our supposed occupations."

"Well," said her mother, "I should think that as most of these invalids are able to walk about, they are no longer likely to be disturbed by a little noise at reasonable, rational hours."

"But," began Hilda, "but those two at the mill who are said to be so frightfully mutilated ? "

" They are far too distant to hear you when the windows are closed," said her mother, " and, without flattery, we may suppose that the sound of the harp, played either by you or Doris, is more agreeable than the noises which they must hear continually when living in the mill itself."

Hilda walked straight to the harp, drew off the leather cover, and perceived to her infinite astonishment, that not one string was broken, and the instrument itself almost perfectly in tune! " Doris," she exclaimed, " is not this completely unaccountable ? "

" No," answered Doris, smiling ; " it only betrays my having had less consideration for these invalids than you; in fact, I forgot them altogether the only afternoon I chanced to be alone in this room, and not only tuned the harp but played all the Irish, Scotch, and Welsh airs I could remember by heart ; you may therefore imagine my qualms of conscience just now when you mentioned why you resisted a temptation to which I yielded without a moment's hesitation."

" I shall resist no longer," said Hilda, commencing a brilliant prelude, from which she afterwards modulated into a succession of melodies that Frank had often requested her to play because they reminded him of his boyhood and Garvagh.

At length she stopped suddenly, and seemed to speak a continuation of her thoughts when she observed, " It is odd he took no notice of my having mentioned that we had seen Madame de Bereny on the quay and at the bookseller's."

" May I ask in what manner you mentioned her ? " said Doris, with a smile full of meaning.

" You are mistaken this time," replied Hilda, more in answer to her sister's looks than words. " I did not betray my disgust at her flirting even in her widow's weeds—I merely mentioned that she seemed much admired, and was always surrounded by a swarm of men."

"In your place," said Doris, "I should have mentioned her without comment, or—not at all."

. "Of course, Doris, you would have done whatever was most judicious, but I only thought of proving to Frank that I was no longer jealous."

"I fear," said Doris, "that what you wrote will not be a convincing proof to him, and his silence on the subject is almost a demonstration of doubt."

"Then I will give him another proof," said Hilda, rising and pushing the harp aside. "I will call on Madame de Bereny—to-day—now—without delay."

"Stay, Hilda!" cried Doris, eagerly; "do not act on the impulse of the moment and commence an acquaintance with a woman to whom you feel so decided an antipathy. When your visiting her would have been a concession to Frank, I urged you to do so; but now that you are on such perfectly good terms with him, I think the effort unnecessary if he do not again make the request."

"He will never make it," said Hilda, "and I even feel certain that were he here now he would avoid her rather than quarrel with me again; but I must convince him that I am no longer jealous."

"Do you know," said Doris, gravely, "that this very effort on your part to prove you are not jealous almost makes me suspect that you are so still?"

"If I am," answered Hilda, "it is jealousy of the past, and Frank must not be allowed to suppose me capable of such folly. I shall visit Madame de Bereny, Doris, and hope you and my mother will go with me."

They made no objection to accompany her although both entertained a secret prejudice against the woman whose society and flattering regard had possibly tended to

prolong Frank's estrangement from them all. Madame de
Bereny received them with evident pleasure; and during
their short visit they had the satisfaction of discovering
that she was less young, less handsome, and infinitely less
fascinating than they had expected to find her.

" Yet she is an interesting-looking person," observed
Hilda, magnanimously, as they walked homewards and
approached the mill by the foot-path from the river;
" decidedly interesting; and her manners might be called
engaging if they were not so studied. I am sure she would
make a good actress, or *pose* herself gracefully in a *tableau*,
—and, in fact, she might have been supposed sitting for
her picture at any moment while we were with her. I
never saw a black veil so judiciously worn."

Neither her mother nor sister answered; they were
looking straight before them, and seemed to hesitate
whether or not they should proceed.

" Pray go on," said Hilda, following the direction of
their eyes towards a couple of wounded officers who were
lying beneath some trees near the mill, one of them stretched
on a mattress evidently in a dying state, the other in little
better plight, reclining on the grass beside him, and greatly
disfigured, not only by the bandages of his wounds, but also
by a thick black beard that completely covered the lower
part of his face, leaving only a thin transparent nose and
the upper part of his livid cheeks visible.

" Pray go on," she repeated; " they have already seen
us, and we must neither hesitate nor let them perceive that
we are shocked at their appearance."

The wish to seem unobservant made Hilda and Doris
look beyond the invalids, towards the windows of their
drawing-room, as if in expectation of seeing something
particularly interesting in that direction; but great was
their surprise when they actually did discover the figure of

a man standing at one of them, evidently watching for and awaiting their return.

"It is Frank!" cried Hilda, springing joyously forward; "I know him by the way he waves his hat!" And in a moment she was out of sight in the vineyard.

"If he had been a little less energetic in his movements," said Doris, "I should have mistaken him for Emmeran."

"Very naturally," said her mother; "but for many reasons we must rejoice that it is Frank."

"Of course," replied Doris, quietly; "but now that the war is at an end, I am quite sure that Emmeran will come home as soon as he can."

"Doris—you are right—it is indeed Emmeran!" said her mother, as the latter strode down the hill towards them; "but, oh! what a disappointment to poor Hilda! and just when a surprise and meeting of this kind might have set all to rights without explanation, and you, I know, would not in the least have minded waiting a week or two longer!"

Doris did not stop to acquiesce in or contradict this last supposition; she advanced rapidly to meet Emmeran, who, as he drew her towards him whispered, "I have but a very short time to stay here, Doris; may I not hope that you will return with me to Westenried?"

The wounded officers had been near enough to understand what had occurred; they raised themselves on their elbows to look after the retreating figures, and as one of them soon after sank back exhausted on his mattress, he observed with a faint smile, "I am sorry that girl who first ran past us was disappointed; she seemed so agitated and overjoyed that I suspect the shock must have been great when she discovered her mistake!"

The fact was, that Hilda no sooner perceived and knew Emmeran than, utterly unable to welcome him, she darted off under the arches of the vines, and sought a place where she could yield without restraint to her feelings and shed tears of bitter disappointment. She afterwards explained the cause of her abrupt flight to Emmeran, laughed at the chance of her having still longer mistaken him for Frank, and then appeared to think no more about the matter.

But she did think of it and of Frank incessantly during the evening, and felt so restless that on perceiving her mother reading intently, and Emmeran successfully engrossing her sister's attention, she left the drawing-room, and sauntered through the still open hall-door into the vineyard.

For more than an hour she walked beneath the rude trellis-work over which the vines were trained, until at length the moonlight tempted her to leave the shade, and seat herself on a wooden bench placed at the side of the house, whence she could look into the valley beneath and see the beautifully situated town and the dark mountains beyond it. Her contemplations were long undisturbed, and the silence around her became by degrees so profound that she actually started on hearing the sound of Doris's harp. For a while she listened, but then stood up, conscious alike that the course of her thoughts had been irretrievably interrupted, and that it was time to return to the drawing-room if she did not wish her long absence to be remarked.

Hilda entered the house, but was tempted by the open window at the end of the corridor to look once more at the moonlit landscape. She leaned out, supporting herself on the window-frame with both hands, while her eyes glanced keenly along the outline of the mountains, then over the vine-clad hills, and rested on the picturesque tower between the town and the ruin of the fortress Saint Zensburg. The intervening valley and ascent to the mill she scarcely observed; but a dark object at no great distance from the house instantly attracted her attention; it was the figure of a man leaning against the trunk of one of the standard peach trees in the orchard, and so slight was the shade it afforded him that the moon lighted every fold of the cloak thrown over his shoulders, and fell full upon a face pale as that of a corpse. Hilda's stifled exclamation of surprise, or rather alarm, may have been heard by him, for his eyes, hitherto fixed intently on the window of the drawing-room, turned slowly towards her, and she drew back horror-struck on perceiving in both figure and face an appalling resemblance to the apparition she had seen many years previously in the vault of the Chapel-island.

"Doris!—Emmeran!—" she gasped; but the tones of the harp overpowered her voice, and she precipitately retreated to the drawing-room door, and threw it wide open.

"Good heavens!—what is the matter?" cried Doris, starting up in alarm.

"Oh, come!—oh, come!—he is there—under the tree——"

"Who?"

"The bearded hussar—just as I saw him in the glass on Holy-eve—with the black bandage across his forehead, and the braided jacket—Oh, do come with me—or look out of the window here, and you will see him distinctly."

Emmeran rushed to the window, but was not very adroit in opening it, and Hilda's trembling fingers rather impeded than aided him; it therefore so happened that when they all looked eagerly into the orchard there was no trace of the mysterious hussar, and Hilda could only point to the peach tree and say, "He was there—I saw him as distinctly—no, far more distinctly than in the mirror—and I am certain, quite certain, it was the—the—very same ——" She hesitated.

" The same what ? " a'sked Emmeran.

" Person—vision—apparition—whatever you choose to call it," she answered, with ill-concealed agitation, and eyes still fixed on the trees of the orchard.

"My dear Hilda," said her mother, "the apparition of the vault was an illusion, and that of to-night merely a wounded officer from the mill! I remarked to-day that one of them had a prodigious beard, and as well as I can recollect his head was bandaged and his arm in a sling."

"You may be right," said Hilda, taking a long breath, and seating herself near the window; "but to say the least, the strong resemblance to what I saw in the mirror is very singular."

"It is more singular," said her mother, "that the likeness did not strike you when we passed him on our way home to-day."

"I did not look at him," answered Hilda; "but even if I had, perhaps I might have required the moonlight to rouse my memory. At all events, I must say that I wish either he would leave the mill or we could find apartments in another house."

"Is it possible," said Doris, "that you have any superstitious dread of the unfortunate man ?"

"Something very like it," replied Hilda; "but as we are in a manner compelled to remain here for the present, and he is not likely to leave Meran, I can do nothing but keep out of his way as much as possible, and when we chance to meet avoid looking at him."

"You need not give yourself much trouble," observed her mother, "for he has hitherto apparently avoided us, and turned away his head so obviously to-day that I think he rather shrinks from being seen by any one. He may perhaps have been a very handsome man, and has now a morbid fear of people seeing him in his present decrepit and unprepossessing state."

"I am sure," said Hilda, "if it were not for this unfortunate resemblance, his appearance would in no way be repulsive to me. You know, Emmeran," she added, smiling, "I liked you quite as well, and Doris far better than ever, when you were wounded, though certainly that straw-coloured beard that you allowed to grow for some weeks was even less becoming than my spectre's black one!"

"Suppose," said Emmeran, "I try to get acquainted with this man in order to request him to shave?"

"It would make no difference," she answered gravely; "his wounded forehead requires a bandage, his arm is in a sling, and the recollection of the tarnished gold I saw on the sleeve of his jacket to-night would still make him in my eyes the hussar of the Chapel-island, and as such an object of dread. I wish I had seen him by daylight, or not at all."

"So do I," said her mother; "but I trust when you have seen him oftener the impression will wear off."

"I do not intend to look at him again," she answered; "and hope that Emmeran will neither in jest nor earnest make any attempt to become acquainted with him."

"I have not time for anything of the kind at present," said Emmeran, laughing; "but even if it were otherwise, I should be at a loss for a pretext, now that you say his shaving off his beard would give you no satisfaction. For my part, I think we ought to rejoice that this same beard is of real tangible shaveable hair."

"What else could it be?" asked Hilda.

"The unreal beard of a spectre *selon les règles*," he answered, solemnly; "and if you did not admit the possibility of his shaving, we might be led to suppose the orchard, and perhaps the mill and its appurtenances—haunted."

A discussion of spectres, apparitions, visions, and wonderful dreams followed, as a matter of course, and continued until they retired for the night. Then Hilda, long after the others were asleep, walked up and down her room, recalling with torturing minuteness all the ghost stories she had ever heard or read, and comparing them with her own Holy-Eve experience. Why she afterwards went to the window to take another look at the haunted orchard it would be hard to say, but she did so, and was rewarded for her courage by again seeing the spectre of the vault apparently gazing upwards at the window of her room. She did not again call her sister, or draw back in alarm ; on the contrary, she not only compelled herself to look down, but even made an effort to open the window. The moment, however, he perceived the movement of the curtain, he turned away and limped slowly towards the mill.

"My mother was right," she murmured, with a sigh of relief ; "it is indeed one of these officers, though what can induce him to wander about at this hour it would be difficult to comprehend. How ill I have kept my resolution of not looking at him again. But I am glad that I have had this opportunity of convincing myself that he is—what he is ! Perhaps I can now sleep without dreaming of him."

———

CHAPTER XL.

HOW EMMERAN WAS REMINDED TO BUY WEDDING-RINGS.

MADAME DE BERENY called on the ensuing day, apparently attracted in an unusual manner towards Hilda and her family, and determined to overcome any prejudices which she may have suspected they entertained against her. When she rose to take leave, she looked alternately from Doris to Hilda, hesitated for a moment, and then said: " You resemble each other so much more than I expected, that I find it difficult to decide which is the ' cousin,' and which the ' wife,' of whom I have heard so much."

This was the first allusion that had been made to Frank, and Madame de Bereny, instantly perceiving the effect of her words, required no explanation to enable her to distinguish the smiling " cousin " from the deeply blushing " wife."

" Have you heard from Colonel O'More lately ? " she asked, turning at once to Hilda.

" Yes, the day before yesterday."

" And how is he ? "

" Quite well, thank you."

" Does he write in good spirits ? "

" Very much so."

" Then you may be sure he has got the Theresian Cross at last! I always thought he would, but feared he might lose his life in the effort to obtain it."

Hilda forced a smile, though her mortification at Frank's not having allowed her to participate in his hopes on this occasion was so intense that she answered almost resentfully, " I have no doubt that he perilled his life, but thank Goodness he has not lost it for such a bauble ! "

"Bauble!" repeated Madame de Bereny. "Do not ever let him hear you use such a word when speaking of his Theresian Cross. Surely you must be aware that it is the greatest of military honours, only to be obtained by some act of successful heroism producing results of acknowledged importance? And you may be quite sure that he will think more of this 'bauble,' as you call it, than of having received the command of his regiment. I know if any one I loved had a chance of this decoration, I should hardly be able to think or speak of anything else! May I hope that you will write or send me word as soon as you obtain any certain information on the subject?"

Hilda slightly bowed her head, and answered, "I am sure Frank would feel immensely flattered if he knew the interest you take in his affairs."

"He knows it perfectly well," said Madame de Bereny, a little piqued at her haughty manner; "it is quite unnecessary to tell Frank O'More how much I like and admire him!"

Hilda's colour mounted to her temples, but before she could answer, Doris interposed. "Every one likes and admires Frank," she said, quickly, "and nothing can give my sister greater pleasure than hearing that people do so; we only fear he knows it too well, and suspect if it were not for us he would be completely spoiled."

"He told me," said Madame de Bereny, "that 'cousin Doris' kept him in great order, but he seemed to like her all the better for it."

"Then I hope," answered Doris, gaily, "you also kept him in order, though I cannot remember that he ever said so."

"What *did* he say of me?" she asked, with evident interest.

Doris hesitated before she replied: "He spoke with

much gratitude of your and Colonel de Bereny's hospitality."

"Was that all?" said Madame de Bereny; "I hoped it was to his eulogiums and personal esteem I owed the pleasure of becoming acquainted with you."

Doris knew not what to say, and looked towards her sister for assistance.

"In fact," said Hilda, with a slightly ironical smile, "there is no doubt that he found your society singularly attractive, for he acknowledged that he was every day and all day in your house."

At this moment their mother entered the room—she had just returned from a walk in one of the neighbouring vineyards—and immediately invited Madame de Bereny to remain to "marende," a sort of afternoon luncheon usual in Tirol. But the invitation was politely declined, Madame de Bereny saying she feared the delay might oblige her to return home in a storm that had been threatening for some hours, and, the sound of distant thunder confirming her words, she drew her shawl round her and walked towards the door.

Emmeran, who had been present during the greater part of her visit, immediately proposed accompanying her to the town, and his escort was accepted with a smile that lit up her whole countenance, and gave it at once both youth and beauty.

Hilda walked to the window, looked after them, and then exclaimed, "Doris, do come here! She has taken his arm, and is leaning upon it, as if she were descending a precipitous mountain."

"Why not," said Doris, "when he proposed himself as walking-stick?"

"And now she is giving him her parasol to carry."

Doris laughed.

" Is it possible," cried Hilda, " that her coquetry amuses you? or did you really not observe her efforts to attract Emmeran's attention and draw him into conversation almost all the time she was here ?"

" I observed," answered Doris, smiling archly, " that Emmeran was very willing both to be attracted and drawn into conversation, and I was extremely glad of it, for you were so much less agreeable than usual, or rather so unlike yourself, that your presence at last became absolutely a restraint on me."

" My presence a restraint ! " repeated Hilda.

" Yes, dear ; for I should have liked to have made her talk of Frank, but the fear of irritating you, or giving you an opportunity of making sarcastic little speeches prevented me."

" And yet," said Hilda, " I really tried to like her, and partly succeeded, until her manner to Emmeran convinced me that she is one of those women who can only find pleasure in the society of men, and never relax in their efforts to captivate them."

" I confess," said Doris, " that I too liked her better before than after Emmeran joined us; nevertheless, her nearly total disregard of us afterwards, and determination to make him talk, were very amusing."

" Be candid, Doris, and say at once you perceived her effort to attract him, and disapproved of it."

" I had not arrived at disapprobation," said Doris ; " on the contrary, I could not help admiring her quickness in discovering the way to please him, and the consummate skill with which she managed to put him into perfect good humour with himself, consequently with her also, and perhaps with all the world."

" Well, Doris, as *you* don't seem to mind her finding out the way to please him, of course I can have no objection; on the contrary, if you would not think me very ill-natured, I should rather like him to be subject to her wiles, just long enough—to make you jealous for five short minutes.''

Doris shook her head. "Madame de Bereny could not make me jealous for five short seconds," she said, quietly.

"The fact is," said Hilda, a little impatiently, "you have never cared enough for any man to know even the meaning of the word."

"In the present instance," said Doris, "I am sufficiently convinced of Emmeran's affection to have no sort of objection to his finding other women as handsome or as agreeable as they really happen to be."

"Now," said Hilda, "although I perceive by my mother's face that you have spoken reasonably and rightly, you must allow me to doubt the warmth of your affection for him if you can really feel so very indifferent on this subject."

"You are unjust," replied Doris, smiling; "my affection may be of a colder description than yours, but it is strong, and not much subject to change of any kind."

"Doris," said Hilda, bending over her sister's chair until their faces touched each other, "your affection is perfect as far as your relations and friends are concerned, but surely you feel something more for Emmeran, to whom you are about to be married so very soon?"

"I feel," said Doris, "that I cannot give a more convincing proof of affection than having consented to pass the rest of my life with him, and I believe he is reasonable enough to be satisfied."

"I may as well be so too," said Hilda, laughing, "for this is one of the subjects that I know you will not discuss with any one."

Doris nodded her head, and the conversation ended.

The storm passed over, the rain ceased, and after a sunset in brilliant clouds, the moon rose so bright and clear that Doris, Hilda, and their mother were tempted into the vineyard, and were walking there when Emmeran sauntered sedately towards them.

"We don't mind your having supped with Madame de Bereny," said Hilda, glancing laughingly towards her sister.

"I have had no supper," he replied.

"Nor," she continued, in the same tone, "nor have we any objection to your finding her as handsome or as agreeable as she really happens to be."

"That is fortunate," he answered, "for she is undoubtedly both the one and the other."

"Indeed!"

"Decidedly; as well as I can judge during a short morning visit, and still shorter walk into Meran."

"Perhaps also in her own house?" suggested Hilda.

"I was not in it."

"Then where were you all this time?" she asked, with some amazement.

"Tell Doris to question me, and you shall hear my adventures," he answered, seating himself on the bench before the house.

Doris sat down beside him, but her question was, "Shall we not first desire Janet to order you some supper?"

"I have already sent a message to that effect," he answered, smiling, "and as Hilda will fancy I have fallen in love with Madame de Bereny if I do not satisfactorily account for every quarter of an hour of my absence, I must tell you that I urged your fair visitor, without any sort of ceremony, to walk more quickly than she perhaps ever did before in her life."

" We saw you carefully supporting her down the hill," observed Hilda.

" And you might afterwards have seen me almost carrying her over the bridge," he answered. " The wind there nearly took her off her feet, and blew us both about in a most disagreeable manner ; we afterwards actually ran into the town, and only recovered our breath under the arcades."

" And you call that an adventure ? " said Hilda.

" No ; that was only the beginning. We walked under the shelter of the arcades until the first violent torrents of rain were over, and then I conducted Madame de Bereny to her lodgings."

" Well, go on," she said, perceiving that he paused.

" On my way home afterwards," he continued, " I had reached the mill, and was walking quickly past it when some of the people there rushed out, and in a very incoherent manner informed me that one of the Hungarian officers lodging in their house had just died in a most sudden and unexpected manner."

" Which of them ? " asked Hilda, quickly.

" Not the one you have seen," he answered, very gravely ; " it was a very young man who has only been here a couple of weeks."

" Are you sure—quite sure—there is no mistake ? "

" Yes, for the miller and his wife requested me to visit 'their Colonel,' as they called the other. It seems he had insisted on their procuring him a horse to ride into the town, that he might find out the address of a certain Protestant clergyman who had visited him here some time ago, but had since gone to Botzen; they hoped I would undertake the commission, and not let him attempt what would be so dangerous for him, as he had already nearly bled to death twice since he came to the mill."

" Nearly bled to death !" repeated Hilda. " No wonder he looks so ghastly pale !"

" No wonder, indeed !" said Emmeran, thoughtfully ; " but his chief illness now appears to be weakness."

" Then," said Doris, " he only requires to be taken good care of, and I hope he has a servant who is attached to him."

" They told me," answered Emmeran, " that he had one when he first came to Meran, but suddenly sent him back to his regiment about the time you came here, and injudiciously supplied his place with the son of a peasant —a mere boy, who could not even tell me his master's name !"

" You inquired, of course, before you went upstairs ?"

" I asked a few questions, which were very unsatis- factorily answered ; and the only thing I discovered was, that every one at the mill was more or less charmed with this colonel, in spite of the elf locks, cadaverous appearance, and bandaged head that so horrified Hilda."

" I am sure," said Doris, " if Hilda could manage to see him by daylight, she would discover that the chief re- semblance to her apparition consisted in the pale face and black beard."

" She is not likely to see him by daylight," answered Emmeran, evasively, " as he greatly dislikes being observed by any one ; and the people at the mill say that for this reason he has latterly gone out late in the evening or at night."

" I begin to feel interested about him," said Doris, " and am curious to hear what occurred when you gained admit- tance to his room."

" I first sent up my name, and offered my services," he continued, " and, after some demur, he consented to see me."

Here Emmeran paused.

"Well," said Doris, "and then you went upstairs and saw him?"

"Not exactly; for he did not immediately enter the room to which I had been conducted, but through the partly open door into the adjoining apartment I perceived that he was standing by the bed, and closing the eyes of his dead comrade."

Emmeran paused again.

"You waited, of course?" said Doris.

"Yes—I waited—long—but at length he turned round, opened the door, and came towards me."

"And immediately accepted your offer?"

"Yes—no—that is, I forget exactly what he said or I said at first—I looked at his bandaged head, and wounded arm, and stiff leg, poor fellow—and I—I thought of Hilda and the vault—and—in short, I never was so shocked in all my life!"

"Then he does resemble the apparition?" said Hilda, starting up. "And how great must be the likeness when it struck even you so forcibly! Oh, mother, I do wish you could be induced to spend the winter elsewhere! Only think of having this man so near us for months!"

"But," said her mother, "would not a removal from the immediate neighbourhood of the mill answer our purpose just as well? It is not probable that he will follow us into the town, should we go there."

"Stay!" said Emmeran. "I have spoken very unguardedly, and did not intend to say so much. That this man resembles the description Hilda gave of the apparition I cannot deny, but I imagine that many other wounded officers would do so quite as accurately; and were this one to take off his black bandage, and shave off even part of his beard, I am convinced the annoying likeness would be destroyed at once."

"He would still be the same man," said Hilda; "and I feel an unconquerable dread of his having some mysterious influence over my destiny. Laugh at me as much as you please, Emmeran, but I cannot overcome this feeling."

Emmeran did not laugh, or even smile, and it was with a sort of forced cheerfulness that he answered, "Let us rather say no more about the matter. I have only to conclude my account of myself by telling you that I undertook to find out the address of the Protestant clergyman, and was successful; the letter now on its way to Botzen will probably bring him to Meran the day after to-morrow, and I have been thinking, Doris, we might as well take advantage of his being here, and ask him to perform the Protestant marriage ceremony for us?"

"I hope, however," said Doris, "you will defer your request to him until his services are no longer required by others."

"I hope so, too," said Hilda; "for, as it is, you bring death and marriage strangely in contrast."

"I acknowledge," said Emmeran, "that I rather expected Hilda to oppose my plan for this very reason; but," he added, turning to her, "but you really must begin to restrain this inclination to superstitious thoughts on all occasions, or you will cause yourself, and perhaps others, much unnecessary uneasiness."

"You are quite right," answered Hilda, "and I would make the effort if it were possible to forget that unlucky Holy-Eve, and all that occurred afterwards in the cathedral at Ulm to remind me of it."

"The best cure," suggested Emmeran, "would be our

finding out that some one had actually managed to conceal himself in the vault that night."

Hilda, who had latterly been walking backwards and forwards before them, now stopped, and, fixing her eyes on Emmeran, asked eagerly, " Were you there ? "

" No—but it may have been Frank ; for, as well as I can recollect, you never asked either of us the question in direct words."

"And how," asked Hilda, " how do you account for the ring that came to light so unexpectedly ? "

" I forgot the ring completely," he answered, thoughtfully ; "but I dare say it could be accounted for in an equally rational manner."

" Let us," said Hilda, a little ironically, "let us, for instance, suppose you threw it slyly on the ground that it might there be found—but still you will have no objection, I should think, to Doris's procuring one for you in a more satisfactory manner ? "

"Thank you at least for the hint," answered Emmeran, laughing. " I shall buy both my own ring and Doris's in Meran to-morrow."

CHAPTER XLI.

THE SCENE CHANGES.

Doris's marriage, or rather her marriages, took place three days later; the first in all the quiet privacy of a small drawing-room, the second in the St. George's Catholic Church near the mill. The Waldering family walked in a perfectly unostentatious manner through part of the vine-

yard and orchard to the church, and were not a little surprised to find it so crowded with peasants that they and
their friends found some difficulty in reaching the altar.

That Doris was dressed in white, with flowing veil and
chaplet of myrtle and orange blossom, was a matter of
course; that Hilda appeared in a dress of precisely the
same material, with merely a wreath of green leaves on
her head, stamped her at once as bridesmaid in the minds
of the admiring spectators.

Now, Hilda's wreath was composed of tastefully arranged willow-leaves, and instantly attracted the attention
of a man who stood outside the church, his straw hat
drawn down over his bandaged forehead, his figure concealed by a long cloak, and the deep interest he felt in the
marriage taking place made manifest by his eager glance
and quick, hard breathing.

In the Roman Catholic Church marriage is a sacrament,
and the upturned eyes and moving lips of the greater part
of the congregation soon proved that if they had come
to gaze, they remained to pray; and when the venerable
priest, with his long snow-white hair, ruddy cheeks, and
mild blue eyes, encircled Emmeran's and Doris's hands
with the stole, and pronounced the solemn words, " *Con-
jungo vos*," the assembled peasants, with a loud simul-
taneous movement, sank on their knees, unconscious of
the deep impression which their prostrate figures made on
the one sad spectator who continued to stand, or rather
lean, in rigid helplessness against the side of the doorway.

The autumn sun sent bright coloured rays through the
painted glass windows on the bridal party as they waited
for the crowd to disperse; but curiosity had again regained
its place in the minds of the peasants,—they collected
together, forming a lane, through which Emmeran instantly
perceived that he and Doris were expected to pass and

submit to be stared at, and he therefore drew her arm within his and moved forward.

It has been observed that some people have an instantaneous consciousness of eyes fixed intently on them; and either for this reason, or in consequence of some slight impediment in passing the threshold of the church, Doris suddenly looked up and saw close to her the pallid, agitated face of the officer from the mill. Doubt, consternation, and dismay were successively reflected in her expressive features,—while a hectic flush that passed across the invalid's cheeks seemed suddenly to confirm her worst apprehensions, and she grasped Emmeran's arm in a vain endeavour to make him stop, or at least retard his progress. For the first time in her life she found him inattentive to her wishes; he even drew her forward after she found voice to gasp out the words, "Wait—oh, wait a moment!" and he continued to stride on, though aware that her head was turned backwards, and nothing but his restraining hand prevented her from leaving his side.

"Emmeran," she whispered, breathlessly, "didn't you see him? Didn't you know him?"

"Yes, dearest; but you must restrain your feelings, both for his sake and for Hilda's—she must not be told that he is here."

Doris made a great effort, and regained her self-possession so completely that when they reached the house she was able to speak to her friends, and made a plausible excuse for leaving them by expressing a desire to change her dress. Her heightened colour and flurried manner when whispering a few words to Emmeran as she passed him was so natural that it excited no attention, still less that he should afterwards sit down beside his charming sister-in-law, and assist her to do the honours of the breakfast-table.

In the meantime Doris rushed up the stairs to her room, pulled the flowers and veil from her hair, threw a long grey travelling cloak over her shoulders, and, taking her bonnet in her hand, ran down the stairs and out of the house, not stopping for a moment until she found herself at the entrance of the mill. Fortunately the family were at their early dinner, and she was able to continue her journey uninterrupted to the part of the house in which the room she sought was situated.

She knocked with unhesitating impatience, and on receiving permission to enter, sprang forward with a stifled cry of anguish, and threw herself on her knees beside the couch on which her wounded cousin lay. " Oh, Frank! what a meeting!—what a parting is this!" was all she could utter before her pent-up feelings found relief in a passionate burst of tears.

Frank's lips quivered. " You know me, Doris, in spite of all disfigurement? "

She looked up for a moment, but immediately afterwards buried her head in the sofa cushion, and sobbed aloud.

" I understand you," he said gently; " I am indeed a frightful object to look at—and it is for this reason that I have kept Hilda in ignorance of my present state."

" No, Frank,—no,—it is not that—I am—and she will be—far more afflicted now than had she heard the truth at a time when her fears would have served as preparation for the shock. Your letters—your cheerful letters have deceived us completely—cruelly."

" No, Doris, darling, there was no cruelty to you, or Hilda, or my aunt, in this concealment. It was at first said that I was mortally wounded, then I nearly died of fever. Suppose Hilda had proposed coming to me."

" You need not suppose," said Doris, raising her head

and pushing back her dishevelled hair. "You may be quite sure she would have gone to you! And she will come to you now, and no longer hesitate to tell you how devotedly she loves you!"

"Not yet," said Frank, raising himself upright, while Doris seated herself on a footstool beside the sofa. "I cannot allow Hilda to be told either that I am here, or wounded, for I should doubt any demonstration of affection from her now, or at least not value it as I ought, from the suspicion that compassion alone prompted it! The thought is natural, Doris, after having so signally failed to overcome her pride at Innsbruck."

"Oh, Frank, how little you know Hilda's, or any woman's heart!"

"I know yours," he said, bending down and looking into her overflowing eyes until his own filled with tears. "I know yours so well, Doris, that were I even torn to pieces by a cannon-ball, like poor Louis d'Esterre, I could wish to see you without a moment's fear that you would love me less."

"Has Louis been so dangerously wounded?" asked Doris, with compassionate interest.

"He is dead!" answered Frank, "and I must speak of his death, as he sent you a message which I promised to deliver to you."

"You were able to be of use to him?" said Doris; "you consoled him in his last moments?"

"N—o," said Frank, reluctantly, "I—saw him during the battle of Wagram lying under a tree in a state I dare not describe to you—in short, mortally wounded—and should not even have known him had he not called to me. I dismounted, and he requested me to take from him your miniature, of which he confessed he had possessed himself without permission at Ulm, and ever since worn next his heart. You must forgive him, Doris—he loved you more than you supposed, and desired me to tell you so with almost his last breath, poor fellow ! "

" Then you saw him die ? "

" He asked me to shoot him, Doris—asked me to put him out of torture that must end in death—but I was a coward, and could not do it."

" And you were obliged to leave him in that state ? " said Doris breathlessly.

" No ; he persuaded one of our men to have compassion on him. I only heard the shot, Doris, but felt as if the bullet had struck my own heart too. It was a mental wound that will never heal, that will bleed whenever it is touched as long as I live ! "

" How horrible ! " murmured Doris, covering her face with her hands.

" I wish I had not spoken of him," said Frank, " but unfortunately he was in my thoughts when you came into the room, for I had been considering how I could manage to send you the miniature, that you might give it to Emmeran as a wedding present."

" It belongs to my mother," said Doris, " and if I give it to her now she will inevitably ask where I found it."

" Then," said Frank, " you must keep it yourself for the present, as I cannot give you permission to tell her. I wish I had resolution to leave the mill, but it is hard to resign the pleasure of sitting at this window and seeing Hilda so frequently, especially since my fears of being recognized by her have been nearly removed by Emmeran, who told me that she had resolved not to look at me again because I reminded her of the spectre she saw in the——"

At this moment a hasty step on the stairs, and immediately afterwards an unceremonious hand on the lock of the door, made Doris snatch up her bonnet from the floor ; but before she had time to put it on her head Emmeran entered the room. "Doris," he said, half apologetically, "I was obliged to propose coming for you, or else Hilda would have gone to your room, discovered your absence, and the consequences might have been fatal to Frank's secret. Have you told him that he will soon see us again? —that we return to Meran for the winter?"

"I have not had time to speak of our plans," she answered; "but am now sorry we cannot remain here altogether, as you might have visited Frank daily, and even I could have managed to see and speak to him occasionally."

"We can do so when we come back," said Emmeran, cheerfully; "and in the meantime Frank must take care of himself, and grow strong and handsome again. I quite approve of his former, and can perfectly understand his present, motives for concealment."

"I can *not*," said Doris; "and I am sure that Hilda would feel as I do, and only love him ten times better for all these wounds." While speaking she pushed aside the black bandage, raised the thick hair from his temple, and kissed repeatedly the still red scar she had exposed to view.

"Farewell, Frank!" she said, with difficulty restraining her tears. "Farewell!—but only for a few weeks. I do not think I can wait until winter to see you again."

Frank stood up, embraced her in silence, looked after her as she left the room, and then wrung Emmeran's hand without making an attempt to speak.

"Emmeran, I cannot yet go to the drawing-room," said Doris, stopping at the foot of the staircase; "it would be impossible for me to think or speak of anything but Frank at present; but my not yet having changed my dress, and Janet requiring directions about packing, will serve to excuse me a little longer."

The dress was changed, and Janet had carried off the wedding-garment, but still Doris lingered in her room, walking about uneasily for some time, until at last, throwing herself on her knees, she covered her face with her hands. It was so that Hilda found her at the end of half-an-hour, and though she stood up immediately, and forced a smile while listening to her sister's playful reproaches for having played truant so long, there was something in the expression of her face that made Hilda first hesitate, then stop suddenly, and at last, after a pause, exclaim, "Doris, what is the matter? Something dreadful has happened—"

"It might have been worse," she answered, turning away; "but even as it is I hesitate to tell you."

A horrible suspicion flashed through Hilda's mind; she put her arm round her sister, and whispered, "You are not unhappy?—you do not repent your marriage—— ? "

"No, oh, no!" said Doris, quickly. "It was not of myself that I have been thinking—it was of you and—of Frank."

"Dear Doris, how very kind of you! But indeed you must not look so disheartened about us, as I have now not the slightest doubt that our next meeting will unite us for life. Will you not come downstairs? I fear if you remain here any longer our friends may think——"

"Never mind what they think!" exclaimed Doris, with such unusual impatience, that Hilda was not only silenced, but so astonished, that she gazed at her sister in stronger interrogation than many words could have expressed. And she was understood, for Doris soon continued: "You may well be surprised, Hilda; but you must have patience for a few minutes. I have something that I wish to tell

you—that I believe I must tell you, though I know I am
not at liberty to do so. It is true," she added, rather
speaking to herself than her sister, "it is true that no
promise of secresy was exacted, and none made; but it
was understood—I know it was—and the reliance on my
silence was so great, that not even an injunction was given
me!"

"Now pray, Doris, don't excite my curiosity any further
if you have no intention of telling me your secret, whatever
it may be."

"It is not mine," said Doris; "it is the secret of another
person, and mere sophistry my trying to consider myself at
liberty to divulge it. But I feel certain of pardon hereafter—pardon from all concerned—yet nothing could
overcome my scruples of conscience but a dread of the
responsibility of leaving you here for months in ignorance
of what so nearly concerns you."

"Then tell me all about it, Doris, and I will promise
any amount of secresy and discretion that may be necessary."

"Your words are well chosen," said Doris, placing her
hand on her sister's; "I require both from you."

"Well, go on—I promise."

"Promise solemnly," continued Doris, "that nothing
—nothing will tempt you by *word* or *deed* to betray your
knowledge of what I am about to tell you. Remember I
warn you beforehand that you will be severely tried, and
that no entreaties by letter will induce me to release you
from your engagement."

For a moment Hilda hesitated—then looked intently
at her sister's grave face, thought suddenly of Madame de
Bereny, and ended by pledging herself to secresy as solemnly as was required of her.

"Hilda," began Doris, "did you see the wounded

officer from the mill standing at the door as we came out of church!"

"No," she answered, rather surprised at the question; "the effort to get through the crowd and overtake you and Emmeran prevented me from looking at any one, and I fortunately did not see him."

"But I did," said Doris, slowly; "I saw him distinctly, and was so near him that I could perceive his face flush and his eyes fill with tears as I passed. There was something in the expression of his eyes that attracted me even more than their form and colour, though both were familiar —very familiar to me."

"Some one we knew at Ulm?" suggested Hilda.

"At Ulm?—yes——" said Doris, completely perplexed by her unconsciousness.

"Not Major Pallersberg, I hope?" said Hilda. "Mamma would be so shocked."

"No," answered Doris, sadly; "but she will indeed be greatly shocked—as much as I was—but scarcely as much as you will be."

"Ha!" cried Hilda, suddenly alarmed; "but no—it is impossible! Oh, Doris," she added, with a trembling smile, "you have tortured me unpardonably!"

"No, dear Hilda, I have only prepared you for what you must hear, for what is bad enough, but might be far more——the wounded officer is——"

"Don't say it!" cried Hilda, vehemently; "this is some horrible fancy of yours——there may be a likeness —I will not deny it; but oh, Doris, you must not expect me to believe that the ghastly invalid at the mill is my noble, handsome Frank!"

Doris slowly moved her head in sad confirmation.

"It cannot be," continued Hilda, with increasing agitation; "you are—you must be mistaken. Doris, dear Doris, say that it is so; you forget that I have received letters from him with the Znaim postmark on them."

"They were written here," said Doris; "and sent to Major Pallersberg to be posted there."

"How do you know that?"

"Emmeran told me so as we walked from the mill together, about half an hour ago."

"Then you have already been there—you and Emmeran have seen him?"

"Yes."

"Spoken to him?"

"Yes."

Pale as death, Hilda sat down on the nearest chair. Her doubts were at an end, her hopes that Doris might have been mistaken extinguished; but her grief was at first too acute for utterance, and she remained motionless, pressing her clasped hands on her heart, and breathing audibly, while her sister bent over her, suggesting every consolation that could be offered. "I am sure," she said, in conclusion, "you will at least acknowledge we ought to be thankful that *his* life was spared when tens of thousands fell!"

"Yes, dear," panted Hilda, "I am indeed very thankful."

"Besides," continued Doris, "Emmeran assures me that Frank's complete recovery is now merely a question of time."

"And care, Doris," cried Hilda, suddenly rousing herself; "and care! And you will release me from my thoughtless promise, and let me take care of him—won't you, dearest?"

"I *cannot*," said Doris, firmly, "for Frank will not have it so; he said he should doubt any demonstration of affection from you now, or, at least, not value it as he ought,

from the suspicion that it was prompted alone by compassion."

" How little he knows me ! " cried Hilda, passionately.

" I told him so," continued Doris ; "but men cannot
understand us on such occasions, for even Emmeran said
he approved of Frank's former, and perfectly understood
his present, motives for concealment."

" I believe," said Hilda, " from what he once said, when
speaking of Colonel Bereny, that I can guess his motives
for silence in the first instance, but his reason for not seeing
me now is as unjust as it is ungenerous."

" It seems so," answered Doris ; " but when you take
into consideration your former quarrels and misunderstandings, there is some excuse for him. Besides, it would be
unreasonable to expect him to remain altogether unconscious of his great personal advantages, or their value in
the opinion of most people, and must therefore forgive him
if he attribute at least part of your regard to what the
world has forced him to consider one of his chief merits.
In short, Hilda, it is evident that he is unwilling you
should see him in a state that he imagines would only cause
you to pity him."

" This is a hard punishment for my pride and jealousy,"
said Hilda, "and proves that my letters have not made
him forget either. I can now only hope that he is not so
ill as he appears to be—that he does not absolutely require
the care and attention he spurns so unkindly."

" He is greatly emaciated," answered Doris, "but I
believe his wounds are nearly all healed, and the one on
his forehead will scarcely be perceived when the scar is no
longer red."

" And his arm ? "

" Is only in a sling ; perhaps he cannot yet move it, for
the sleeve of his jacket was cut open."

" But he walks with a crutch, Doris—and I fear—I fear——"

Doris remembered that Frank had raised himself on the sofa with great difficulty, and had required a crutch when he stood up; she turned away, saying, "I don't know—I hope not."

" Doris," cried Emmeran, knocking at the door, " the carriage is packed, and our guests are preparing to take leave."

" I am coming," she answered, tying on her bonnet and taking up her gloves.

" One moment!" cried Hilda. " May I tell my mother ?"

" Yes, but only on the same conditions that I have told you—a promise of secrecy, which I know she will keep. Tell her that I have betrayed Frank, not only to prevent you from leaving this house in order to avoid him, but also in the hope that, if circumstances favour you, means may be found to induce him by degrees to lay aside his incognito."

Doris spoke these last words as they descended the stairs together, and they were soon after in the midst of noisily sympathizing friends, who naturally supposed that Doris's heavy tearful eyelids and Hilda's colourless lips were caused by their approaching separation.

What occurred during the succeeding quarter of an hour appeared to Hilda like a feverish dream; she heard the murmuring of voices without distinguishing the words; she looked at her mother and wondered how she could smile so brightly and seem so happy, and then she followed the others when they descended the steps that led alike to the miller's wine-cellars and the gateway opening on the road. She felt herself embraced by Doris and Emmeran, saw the carriage drive off, forced a smile, and tried to appear interested in what was said during the procrastinated leave-taking of the assembled guests, but no sooner was the gate closed upon the last of them, than she turned round, flew up the stairs to her room, locked the door, and yielded to her painfully restrained grief without control.

Some time elapsed before her mother thought it advisable to follow her and propose a walk in the surrounding vineyards. Hilda opened the door, but turned away her head while saying that she did not feel much inclined to go out. Her mother drew her towards her, looked affectionately at her agitated face, and said, with a smile, "Your anxiety about Doris is unnecessary, dear Hilda. I wish I were as sure of your happiness as I am of hers."

"Of that," said Hilda, "there is no chance. My happiness was lost in the cathedral at Ulm; and I now know but too well that Frank not only never cared for *me*, but even doubts *my* affection for *him*."

"Have you heard from him again?" asked her mother, quickly.

"No, but I have heard *of* him; he does not want or wish to see me."

"Jealous again, Hilda!" said her mother, sitting down with a look of resignation. "Come, then tell me all about it, and as Doris is no longer here, I must take her place, and laugh at or scold you as the case may be."

"Rather say," answered Hilda, seating herself on a footstool, and placing her arm and head on her mother's knee, "rather say you will take her place and console me — if you can."

"I shall try to do so," said her mother, with a quiet smile; "and now tell me what you have heard *of* him."

But Hilda, in her turn, felt the difficulty of communicating ill-tidings to a person unprepared to hear them, and, when urged to speak, answered hesitatingly, " I ought to try to tell you, as Doris told me ——"

" Doris ? " repeated her mother, surprised.

" Yes, but first of all I must obtain a promise of secresy from you."

The promise was given without a moment's hesitation, and then Hilda suddenly raised her head, and in a few passionate sentences explained all.

CHAPTER XLII.

NONE SO BLIND AS THOSE WHO WILL NOT SEE.

HILDA's grief subsided by degrees into resignation.. She spoke constantly of Frank, and found her mother not only a patient and indulgent listener, but even inclined to join her in any feasible plan likely to induce him to betray himself. For a whole week he kept more out of sight than ever, the most sultry weather no longer tempting him to seek shade beneath the chesnut-trees, or the mildest evenings inducing him, as had been his wont, to sit at the door of the mill until the darkness permitted him to limp unseen in the sheltered walks of the vineyard. Tired, however, of the confinement, he at length resolved to undertake some short excursions in the neighbourhood, and, as few can be made otherwise than on foot or on horseback, he first used the miller's little carriage to visit Lana and the Badl, and then hired one of his horses to ride to the castle of Tirol ; it was seeing this animal undergoing very unusual ablutions that induced Hilda to make inquiries as to the cause.

" The colonel, ma'am, feels himself so much better that he is going to ride to Tirol."

" But is that horse safe ? " she asked, with an anxious glance towards the fore-feet, which seemed somewhat impaired by heavy draught.

" Lord bless you, ma'am ! the colonel's servant, as was here before you came, told us his master could ride any 'oss."

" I have no doubt of that," said Hilda, " but with a wounded arm and—and the leg——"

" You may be right there," said the man, looking up ; " that leg is less than no use to him, and he knows it too, for he told me to bring a chair and a man to help him to mount, and to be sure to choose a time when no one was likely to see him."

" Are you—or is the man you spoke of, going with him ? " asked Hilda.

" No, ma'am ; I offered, but he wouldn't hear of such a thing."

" And," said Hilda, " if the horse makes a false step on those paved roads, and he has not strength to pull him up, what will be the consequence ? "

" Bad enough, ma'am ; but when I recommended him to look sharp, especially coming down hill, he said his right arm was still fit for service, and I needn't have no fears either for him or for the 'oss, ma'am."

Hilda went immediately to her mother and informed her of Frank's intention, adding a wish to follow him to the castle of Tirol, if it could be done without exciting his suspicions.

" Let us take chance for that," answered her mother, " and send at once for horses, but, as neither they nor the roads are likely to tempt us to go out of a walk, I propose that we engage peasants to lead them. We must not set out for at least half-an-hour after Frank, and can take Hans with us in case we should return late."

"Is there no danger of his recognizing Frank?" asked Hilda.

"I think not; but what matter if he do? I could almost wish that Janet had not gone away with Doris; she went so often to the mill, that a meeting with Frank in the end would have been certain, and equally certain that she would have known him, and would neither have made a promise of secrecy nor considered herself bound to be silent under such circumstances. The question now is— can you now see Frank with the necessary composure, and if I am able to persuade him that we do not recognize him, can you speak to him as a stranger?"

"I will try," said Hilda; "I *must* try, as there is no alternative between avoiding him altogether or keeping my promise to Doris."

Before they set out on their excursion, Hilda received a letter from Frank, in which he informed her that he had at last obtained the object of his ambition—a Theresian Cross—was to be made Baron, and, if she approved, would take the name of More von Garvagh."

"These honours," observed her mother, " have probably already more than consoled him for his wounds; and I am convinced, if it were not for this eccentric concealment from you, he would be perfectly happy."

"And so should I," answered Hilda; "but you seem to oversee the unkindness of his requiring conceal-ment from me alone! Now, I should like to know," she added thoughtfully, "whether or not Madame de Bereny knew all this when she was here last week? Frank's letter bears the date of that very day, and he may have seen her—in fact he may have often seen her before we came to Meran."

"I don't think he did," interposed her mother, "for by all accounts he was too ill to go out when he first came here, and if she had ever been at the mill, the family there would have spoken of it."

"I hope you are right," said Hilda, "for without being supposed jealous, I think I may say it would have been very hard if he had consented to see her and refused to see me! Do you think I ought to comply with her request, and let her know what he has written? I fear a note or message will bring her here again."

"Let her come," replied her mother, "for if we could manage to make her meet Frank, her recognition of him would save us a great deal of painful acting."

"What a pity we did not think of this plan before," said Hilda. "It would have been so easy to have induced her to go to Tirol with us to-day."

"No, Hilda! Let us first see him alone, and put our self-possession to the proof without witnesses."

"It will be a hard trial," said Hilda, "and I can only hope that circumstances will favour us."

An hour later they were on the road to the village and castle of Tirol, mounted on horses such as guides generally place at the service of strangers—quiet animals, whose only pace seems an eager walk that is generally supposed to be warranted safe. Hilda did not think it necessary to consider herself on horseback at all—she placed the reins in the hand of her guide and, heedless or unconscious of the beautiful scenery around her, indulged in a long retrospect, beginning at the early winter morning on which she had seen her cousin Frank as he stamped his feet on the snow-covered ground of the Chapel-island and laughingly shook the water of the lake from his dripping clothes, and ending with the spectral figure of her husband standing beneath the tree in the orchard ten days previously. It was a retrospect of nine years ; but how short the time appeared ! A few important circumstances, chiefly those recorded in these volumes, had made an indelible impression on her mind, but all the rest was a mere consciousness of having lived more or less contentedly at Westenried, Ulm, and Innsbruck. The current of her thoughts was undisturbed until she reached the tunnel conducting to the castle, but it was not the deep bed of the mountain stream nor the steep high sandbank on which the remains of the castle stood that then attracted her attention,—it was the miller's horse held by a little boy, who allowed him to nibble at pleasure the herbs that grew thick and green up to the very threshold of the castle.

As Hilda and her mother dismounted, they were rather surprised to perceive a number of peasants standing in groups about the entrance; several others were in the building itself, and some followed them to the room in which they thought it probable they should find Frank. Nor were they disappointed, for on entering they instantly perceived him close to one of the windows, with his wounded leg stretched at full length on a row of chairs, and completely engaged in explaining to some sturdy-looking peasant riflemen the necessity of laying down their arms and resigning themselves to a peace that was now inevitable. He was intimating his intention of going to see Hofer as soon as he could venture on so long a ride when his eyes fell on Hilda and her mother, and it was astonishing the self-possession with which he continued to speak while carefully drawing the black bandage over the greater part of his face.

There was nothing in the room to tempt strangers to visit it, except the magnificent view from the windows, and though Hilda hesitated, her mother instantly advanced to the one of which Frank had obtained possession, and

29

availing herself of the excuse that the others were occupied, requested permission to look out of it.

Frank instantly made an effort to move the chairs.

"Pray, don't disturb yourself," she said; "I can pass quite easily. Hilda, come here. The weather is so clear that we can follow the windings of the Adige the whole length of the valley, and see distinctly the towers of the castle of Eppan. How beautiful!"

"Beautiful indeed!" murmured Frank, his eyes fixed upon Hilda, as she stood beside her mother in a sort of forced rigid composure that gave her unusually pale features a statue-like expression.

Her mother continued to speak, and was soon able to turn towards Frank and half smile at his exaggerated disguise, but Hilda's stolen glance had a different effect; her limbs trembled, her eyes grew dim, a cold moisture overspread her brow, and, after a few ineffectual efforts to conceal her increasing weakness, she put her arm within her mother's, and, leaning heavily upon it, whispered, "Let us go—I cannot—stay here—any longer."

Frank, who had watched her increasing pallor with great uneasiness, placed his hand on the back of the nearest chair, and raised himself suddenly on his feet. He could not have chosen a better means to revive her, for the movement made it evident that the pieces of wood and leather straps which she supposed to be the substitute for a lost limb were, in fact, but the supports of a wounded leg, that seemed in no way curtailed of its fair proportions. She did not trust herself to look at him, but, with eyes bent on the ground, walked slowly out of the room.

"I cannot do it!" she exclaimed, vehemently, as they sat under a tree near the castle. "All my former self-possession in Frank's presence is gone, and, in order to keep my word to Doris, I must carefully avoid meeting him again. Oh, why did she tell me? Of what use is my knowing that he is here if I must continue under such restraint?"

"Very true," answered her mother; "it was unlike Doris, betraying him in the first instance, and still more unlike her not having courage to brave his displeasure, and leave you at liberty to act as you think best on so momentous an occasion."

"I am sure she meant well," began Hilda.

"Of that there can be no doubt," said her mother; "she was evidently tempted to make this injudicious disclosure by a strong desire to promote a reconciliation between you. But there is no use in now talking of her error in judgment, or his provoking eccentricity. Let us believe in her good intentions, and leave him to choose his own time for putting aside his incognito; we can, at least, while apparently avoiding him, have the satisfaction of watching his progressive recovery."

And Frank's recovery did, in fact, from that time forward, progress rapidly; he made almost daily excursions, and though Hilda resolutely refrained from asking in what direction he was likely to ride, the miller, or some member of his family, regularly informed her of his plans for the day.

"I have just heard of Frank's intention to ride to Fragsburg," she observed, one morning, as she entered her mother's room, "and the miller proposed getting horses for us in case we wished to go there also."

"You refused, of course?"

"Yes; I said the weather was too warm, and then he told me, very significantly, that he suspected the colonel would be disappointed."

"What did he mean by that?"

"He evidently imagines that Frank is tired of being

alone, and kindly wishes to procure him some acquaintances. At all events, it seems he has asked the miller a great many questions about us, and wondered why I did not play the harp, and sing as I used to do."

"And I," said her mother, "I wonder what our friend the miller answered?"

"Very probably," suggested Hilda, "he told him I was inconsolable for the loss of my sister, for he advised me not to take on so about her, as a marriage was not a misfortune in a family, but rather the contrary, when it was agreeable to all parties, and the young man faithful for nine long years, as he had heard from Mrs. Janet."

"It seems Janet was loquacious," observed her mother.

"She always was, and always will be," answered Hilda; "and while she was here, Frank obtained information enough about us without the trouble of questioning any one."

"Then you do not think he is inclined to make an advance?" said her mother. "You do not imagine he wishes to meet us again?"

"No," replied Hilda; "I think the Fragsburg proposal was merely a sociable inspiration of 'our miller' for 'his colonel.'"

"You may be right," observed her mother, thoughtfully, "but if you could see Frank with more composure than at Tirol Castle, I think a sufficient time has intervened to admit of another advance on our part being made without its exciting a shadow of suspicion in his mind."

"Then let us go!" cried Hilda, evidently delighted at the proposal. "I shall be glad to see him again on any terms."

Not long after Frank, with very little assistance, mounted the miller's horse, and rode from the mill. "How quickly he is recovering !" observed Hilda, who had been watching him through the foliage of a trellised vine ; " all the wooden supports and leather straps have been taken from his leg, and he seems scarcely at all lame now."

" Well, my dear, did not Doris mention in her letter that he had written a very good account of himself, and hoped to throw aside his crutch in a day or two ?"

"Perhaps," said Hilda, "he has already been some time without it."

" Not at all improbable ; and if we walk down to the mill while waiting for the horses, we shall be sure to hear everything about him that can interest us."

And so it proved. They were immediately informed that the colonel had received a letter, brought by a man who was supposed to be a messenger from the Archduke John, if not from the Emperor Franz himself, and, after reading this letter, and speaking to the man that brought it, the colonel had become so impatient about his recovery, that he had first sent into Meran to consult his doctor there, and afterwards despatched an express for the famous surgeon at Botzen ; both had been with him the previous day, and, after a long consultation, had declared that his leg was so nearly well again, that he might now go wherever he pleased, provided he rested at night, and did not walk too much for the next month or six weeks. As soon as the surgeons left him he had told the miller that he intended in a day or two to undertake a longer excursion than he had yet attempted, but, as he proposed setting off early in the morning, there was nothing to prevent his returning at night, although the days were unfortunately very short just then.

"Very short, indeed," said Hilda, "and, therefore, I think the sooner we set out now the better."

CHAPTER XLIII.

NOW OR NEVER!

THE road to Fragsburg passes through the best land about Meran; on each side of it there are fields of wheat and corn, belonging to the rich peasants who reside on the mountain; and, after wandering for some weeks through endless vineyards, the change to less romantic scenery is more welcome than people generally are willing to acknowledge.

The old fortress of Fragsburg is situated on an elevated rocky projection commanding the country beneath, but having reached the summit, one is surprised to find it part of a highly-cultivated plain of considerable extent, beyond which the mountain rises again a rugged mass of wood and rocks, and among these there is a waterfall that is not only an object of interest to tourists, but the termination of every Fragsburg excursion undertaken by the inhabitants of Meran.

With the old castle itself, its square tower, and marble-pillared verandah, its wainscoted rooms, and wonderful stoves, we have no concern, for, at the entrance to the dilapidated court, Hilda saw the miller's horse, and soon ascertained that Frank had gone to the waterfall, and intended to rest there for an hour or two. Her mother urged her to follow him, proposing herself to visit the family at the castle, with whom she was slightly acquainted, and, after some hesitation, Hilda consented, declaring, however, that she could not, and would not, make any attempt to induce Frank to speak to her.

She knew the way well, and did not pause until she reached the end of the fields and commenced a descent to the ravine, into which the water fell in cascades of various heights. Then she began to feel the difficulties of her situation in full force, and to doubt her power of keeping her promise to her sister as she ought. She sat down on the trunk of a felled tree, hoping by a short delay to fortify herself for a meeting that certainly had the most satisfactory appearance of chance, and could raise no suspicions in his mind; but just as she clasped her hands round her knees, and began to conjecture what he was likely to do or think when he saw her, she discovered that he was actually at no great distance from her, standing on the edge of a small plateau of grass, whence a view of the waterfall could be obtained without much exertion.

How secure from her observation he must have thought himself as he leaned on his mountain staff, his hat on the ground, and the black bandage no longer concealing his forehead! Hilda also perceived at a glance that his hair had been cut, and the greater part of his wild beard removed, so that he now looked so like himself that an attempt to ignore him would be perfectly absurd. This was a dilemma for which she was quite unprepared, and she started from her seat with such impetuosity that some chips and stones loosely attached to the bark of the tree rolled downwards, and instantly attracted Frank's attention. When he looked up she stood for a moment still as a statue; then, as the thought flashed through her mind that flight would betray consciousness, she sprang forward, and choosing a more precipitous path than the one near which he stood, never once stopped until she reached the bottom of the ravine, and found herself close to the small pool formed by the waterfall before it found an outlet through the rocks and became a rivulet.

Breathless and agitated, she leaned against the nearest tree, and began to repent the course she had taken. "What was the use of my coming here?" she thought, looking round her; "I cannot remain beside this noisy waterfall for two hours, and must therefore make up my mind to pass him again. Perhaps, however, he will have tied on the black handkerchief, or put on his hat, or he may turn away, or—or have gone away; but no,—I hope not, as I believe I could pass him now with tolerable composure."

And while so thinking, Hilda began a deliberate ascent, pausing occasionally as if to admire the view, but in fact to reconnoitre the ground around her, and if possible see Frank without being seen by him. She forgot the advantage of his position above her, and was for some time unconscious that she was watched; but even when aware of it she continued her ascent, not even venturing on the slightest deviation from the beaten path that she knew would bring her quite close to him.

Great, however, was the relief afforded by a protruding rock, behind which she could hide herself for a short time; but no sooner did she feel the certainty of being unobserved than her courage failed, and, utterly disheartened, she pressed her burning forehead against the cold stone, raised her clasped hands above her head, and wept with the noiseless agony of forcibly restrained grief; her whole frame shook with sobs scarcely louder than sighs, and her sorrow was so absorbing that she was quite unconscious of the sound of approaching footsteps, though they were accompanied by the loud striking of a staff on the ground. Her name even was pronounced twice by Frank before she turned round and saw him standing almost beside her.

Pale as death, and scarcely less agitated than herself, he faltered, "Doris has written to me, Hilda, and I now know that further concealment would be folly."

"It would be cruel, Frank," she answered, smiling through her tears: when, forgetful of all his resolutions, he embraced her passionately. " It would be cruel, and indeed I did not deserve that you should doubt my affection so ungenerously ! "

Whatever doubts he may still have entertained were, it may be conjectured, removed in a very satisfactory manner ; it is rather to be feared that Hilda's impulsive nature induced her to make a fuller confession of her love, and greater profession of penitence, than was necessary. What actually was said no one ever ascertained ; but Frank never afterwards seemed in the least to distrust any demonstration of affection on her part, or for a moment to attribute it to compassiou,—and perhaps the greatest, and at the same time first effort on his part to prove this was, when the short afternoon began to draw to a close, he accepted her arm, and leaned upon it while ascending the steep path that took them out of the ravine.

The ride back to Meran and the miller's house was very pleasant,—the evening spent together in perfectly unreserved conversation, singularly cheerful. Frank lingered on from hour to hour, until at length his aunt, after having repeatedly fallen asleep, stood up and quietly wished him good-night.

"I understand the hint," he said, laughing ; "but it is very hard to be dismissed in this way when I know I shall not see you all day to-morrow."

" Why not ? " asked Hilda.

"Because I must go to the Valley of Passeyer to speak to Andrew Hofer,—he is surrounded by people trying to induce him to head another insurrection, and I hope to induce him to lay down his arms and secure his and their personal safety while it is yet time. You see this is an affair that will admit of no procrastination, and I intend to be on the road to the ' Sands ' at eight o'clock to-morrow morning. Hilda," he added, with difficulty suppressing a

smile, " you once said you would visit Hofer——that you
wished to see the little inn on the Sands——"

" Nothing I should like better," she answered, quickly;
" and if you will take me with you to-morrow, I promise to
be ready at any hour you please."

" You had better set off early," interposed her mother,
" or else you will not be able to return before it is dark."

" Oh, we shall have plenty of time!" cried Frank,
gaily. " It will be altogether a delightful excursion, and
I don't so much mind going to the mill now that I know I
may return to you so soon again. Nevertheless, I wish it
were morning."

  *   *   *   *   *

A few hours later they were once more assembled, and,
after a hasty breakfast, descended to the road.

" Good-bye, dear mother!" said Hilda, springing on
her horse; " we shall come back early that you may not
have time to be uneasy about us——and while you are
alone to-day you can write a long, long letter to Doris and
tell her——"

" Tell her," interposed Frank, " that her last expedient
for the promotion of our happiness has been completely
successful, and that instead of reproaching, I shall thank
her for it when we meet."

The horses moved slowly on; Hilda looked back, smiling
brightly, and her mother heard her exclaim, " What a
charming ride we shall have!—I never felt so happy in all
my life!"

" Or I either," answered Frank; and though immediately afterwards they were out of sight, the sound of
their mirthful voices, as they slowly descended the hill on
the paved road through the vineyards, was still heard by
the profoundly inquisitive and much amazed inhabitants
of the mill.

  *   *   *   *   *

As evening approached, a peasant from the valley of Passeyer was seen walking up to the miller's house; he was the bearer of a note from Hilda, containing the following lines :—

"Dear Mother,—Frank says that returning to Meran to-night would fatigue him dreadfully, so of course we must not think of attempting it; but you need not be uneasy, as the ride here appears not to have been in the least too long for him. I am sorry to say that all his efforts to persuade Hofer to accept the offered amnesty, and to refuse to command the projected continuation of the insurrection, have been fruitless. He first answered evasively, until the Archduke's name was used, and Frank urged more strongly, when he at length exclaimed, 'I would comply with your request if it were in my power; but if I moved one step from my house with such intentions, my own people would shoot me on the spot!'" *

The next day brought another letter from Hilda, containing a communication for which her mother seemed wonderfully well prepared. She smiled as she read :—

"We have eloped, dear mother, and when this reaches you we shall be riding over the Jaufen on our way to Innsbruck; there we shall remain a few days, in the hope that you will send us some clothes, so that we may be able to go on to Ulm and Westenried. I wish you could have heard dear old Hofer yesterday evening admonishing us to love one another and live in peace. Frank knows so well his great predilection for the adjustment of conjugal quarrels, that he listened with the most exemplary patience, and delighted Hofer by observing that inasmuch as Napoleon at Ulm had been indirectly the cause of our separation, so had Andrew Hofer at Innsbruck promoted our

* Hofer's own words.

reconciliation : he ended with the assurance that we were now the happiest and most attached couple in the world ; and you shall have proof that this assertion is true, dear mother, when we return to you a few weeks hence with Doris and Emmeran, for Frank's perfectly satisfactory explanations on every subject have made it impossible for us ever again to be at odds."

THE END.

Simmons & Botten, Printers, Shoe Lane, E.C.

www.ingramcontent.com/pod-product-compliance
Lightning Source LLC
Chambersburg PA
CBHW022010110726
47901CB00006B/1471